W9-AXC-262

COLLEGE BOY

The Urban Griot

SIMON AND SCHUSTER PAPERBACKS
New York London Toronto Sydney

SIMON & SCHUSTER PAPERBACKS
Rockefeller Center
1230 Avenue of the Americas
New York, NY 10020

First Simon & Schuster mass market paperback edition 2005

SIMON & SCHUSTER PAPERBACKS and colophon are registered trademarks of Simon & Schuster, Inc.

For information about special discounts for bulk purchases, please contact Simon & Schuster Special Sales at 1-800-456-6798 or business@simonandschuster.com.

Manufactured in the United States of America

10 9 8 7 6 5 4 3

ISBN-13: 978-0-7434-8273-8
ISBN-10: 0-7434-8273-5

Education is power, but only for those who use it.

The Urban Griot

PROLOGUE

It was December 1988, two weeks before finals. Troy Potter, a young Black male from inner-city Philadelphia, sat alone in his cold dorm room thinking about the future. His chemistry book was resting open at his desk. He had been stuck on page 306 for the past thirty minutes while staring at the plain white walls in front of him. He was unfocused, feeling unsure of success and afraid of failure. And he had learned a hell of a lot in only a year of study inside one of America's major institutions.

It was Troy's dream as a high school basketball star to attend a Division 1 college: national television exposure, state-of-the-art campus facilities, thousands of fans, and a top-rate education. State University, housing thirty-five thousand students, ninety percent of whom were White, afforded him the opportunity.

State U was located in the East, inside Marsh County, which held a population of some 750,000 citizens, roughly sixty percent White, thirty percent Black, and ten percent multiethnic. The large, green campus was clean and spacious, the pride of Marsh County.

Troy was impressed, and proud of its colorful basketball stadium and the football field with a nine-lane track; the recreational center and the gigantic cafeteria; the sky-rise dormitory buildings; and how the immediate campus took up six square blocks near downtown. Buses escorted students to the dental school, the medical school, the engineering building, and the White fraternity houses.

Madison Avenue, a huge, five-lane street (three lanes heading north and two lanes heading south), ran straight through the middle of campus. Henry Road, a scenic and grassy curving road, headed uptown on the far northwest side. Charleston Street, on the far southeast side, headed downtown and had most of the shops, stores, and traffic.

Black Americans had raised hell during the fifties and sixties, so that the seventies, eighties, and nineties generations could attend institutions of the caliber of State U. A government-imposed affirmative action clause to create underprivileged-minority scholarships made it possible, despite low academic testing, which is believed to be culturally biased. However, the experiment of having Blacks on predominantly White campus grounds remained an enormous task. And Troy felt its full weight.

To all African peoples
who have an undying courage
to complete their destinies.

Omar Tyree

Fiction is the lie that tells the truth.

Stephen King

DAY ONE

"Hello, students, my name is Pam Whatley, and I'm your course counselor from now until the time you graduate from State University. You all have been accepted to this university under the condition that you maintain a two-point-oh grade point average as members of C.M.P. C.M.P. stands for 'College Motivation Program.' What this means is that you all are required to take strengthening courses in math, general science, and reading and writing. You also will be required to enter an academic student course, which is a two-part class designed to help needy students in study skills and planning.

"You students have been placed in this program as a result of low S.A.T. scores, but that does not mean that you're incapable. State University has specifically installed this particular program to help strengthen your academic skills in needed areas. After the completion of your first year's courses in C.M.P., you will have no further requirements from the university and may work in subjects of your major. Now, I would like to meet you all," said the heavyset, cinnamon-skinned woman in a hot-pink skirt suit. She pointed to the tall and slim student seated in the front row. "So you are . . . ?"

"I be Troy Potter, Ms. Whatley," he answered jokingly. The other freshmen giggled. Ms. Whatley assumed that Troy was a bit overconfident, a headstrong inner-city boy with a chip on his shoulder.

"I see. So you're pretty smart, hunh?" she asked, smiling to herself at his humor. "I hope your grades after the first term will reflect that."

"Yeah, me too," he said.

"Who are *you?*" Ms. Whatley continued. Her eyes focused on the student sitting directly behind Troy.

"My name is Peter Barnes," the second student answered. Peter was cream-colored, with thick brown hair and an unblemished baby face. He stood when he introduced himself, drawing the undivided attention of his twenty-seven classmates.

"Well, aren't you a properly mannered young man," Ms. Whatley said to him. Troy turned his head with a frown and glanced out the window, unfazed. He figured that standing up was unnecessary.

"My name is Matthew Forbes," said the next, loosely dressed student. Matthew wore extra long shorts and a brightly colored Hawaiian shirt obviously too large for him. He was as brown as Troy, with short wavy hair. He brushed his small waves to the left and kept a part to the right.

A well-dressed, darker-brown-toned student giggled for no apparent reason from the back row, grabbing Ms. Whatley's attention. "Excuse me, Mr. Chuckles, you mind telling us what your name is?" she asked, challenging him.

"My name is James Clayton," he responded in a mellow tone. James spoke as if he were planning to seduce Ms. Whatley, making some of the students snicker. He then turned and faced the rather large student sitting beside him, who had continued to smile since Troy's introduction.

"Tell her your name, homes," James said to the larger student.

Skeeerrk!!

Bruce helped himself from his chair, smiling at the noise it had produced from scraping a newly waxed tile floor.

"Ah," he began, taking a peek at Troy, who portrayed a goofy look, a tilted head, and an open mouth. Bruce stopped in his tracks and cracked the hell up. Several classmates were getting rather bored with all the silliness going on. They decided not to join him. But Troy did.

"Hold up. My man Troy is makin' me laugh," Bruce said, trying to gather himself. "Yeah," he responded, finally settling down, "my name is Bruce Powell."

Witnessing the massive size of the young man, Ms. Whatley was curious about his college status. Bruce was six-two, 220, with massive arms, legs, and shoulders.

"Are you on the football team?" she asked.

Bruce shook his head before he answered. "Naw. But I plan to go out for the team."

"Well, good luck," Ms. Whatley told him, moving on.

"My name is Tanya Moore," said a bashful girl who sat in the front row next to Troy.

"Hmm, don't *you* have a Southern accent," Ms. Whatley commented.

"Yep," Tanya agreed, grinning. "I'm from Atlanta, Georgia," she said. Her reddish brown, silky hair matched her skin and eye color.

"I'm from Atlanta, too," Bruce yelled to her. Tanya turned and smiled at him. Troy looked back to Bruce and gave him an "OK" hand signal in reference to the pretty, well-shaped Southern belle.

The lagging introductions took nearly forty minutes for the twenty-eight students. Ms. Whatley then took a deep breath and clasped her meaty hands together. "Well, since we've all met each other, it's almost time for the freshman picnic on the west lawn. There will also be a dance, later on tonight, in the Student Activity Center, next to the Baxton Dormitory Hall. I've given you all a map of our large campus, and I'll see you tomorrow at nine o'clock, sharp, to orient you for your math and reading placement exams," she informed them. She gathered the leftover maps and pamphlets while the students filed out of the room.

Troy was the first to speak as several of the guys walked in the same direction toward the picnic area. "Yo, we was buggin' out in there, cuz," he said, followed by Bruce, who had already taken a liking to him. "And that counselor's a little overweight, but I'd do her," Troy added.

"Yeah, mayn, you had me crackin' the hell up," Bruce said, walking beside him.

"Yo, homes, I'll meet y'all over there," said James. "I gots to go change."

"Aw'ight, troop, we'll be over there somewhere," Matthew answered.

Bruce and Troy chuckled, watching James walk away in a shirt and tie.

"Hell he wear a suit and tie for anyway, as hot as it is out here?" Troy responded to Bruce. Everyone else wore shorts and T-shirts in the ninety-degree August weather.

The pack of freshmen drifted toward the fried chicken table in the picnic area, flooded by thousands of White students. Their small Black group was a few specks of pepper mixed in a table full of salt.

Troy shouted across the yard, seeing a friend that he knew from high school. *"Yo, Clay, what's up, man? Come over here!"*

Clay was with another small crew of Black students. "Well, if it ain't my boy Troy. What's up, man?" he asked, reaching out to shake hands. He already appeared excited about college. "You shoot game to any girls up here yet?"

Troy shook his head. "Naw, not yet. It was this tough girl in my advisory class. She looks good as hell. But let me introduce you to my boys," he offered, turning to face his companions. "This is Bruce, Mat, Pete—and damn, I don't know where the rest of the dudes went." Troy pointed to each individual, realizing that the majority of the students had gone off on their own missions. "My man Jay will be here after he finishes changing his clothes," he said, giggling. "Nigga came out here in a shirt and tie."

Clay introduced his group of new friends. Both crews then proceeded to rack up food like a platoon of hungry soldiers after a day of training.

Troy and Clay, unintentionally separated from the bunch, found themselves in a private conversation. "Ay', Troy, I had no idea that it would be this many white mugs up here," Clay hinted, shaking his head in amazement.

"Yeah, cuz, me neither," Troy responded. "I ain't never seen this many White people in my life. This shit is like a rock concert. Yo, here comes my boy Jay now! *Yo, Jay! We're over here, cuz!*" Troy shouted, while raising his hand to direct James in the right direction.

James said in a hurry, "Ay', y'all, we should go to the gym. Everybody is up there. Well, a lot of *brothers* are, anyway." He seemed to be in a rush as he bent over and retied his shoes. "I'on know about all these White boys. I hope it ain't a lot of them up there. They can't run ball anyway. It might be a bunch of 'em up there thinking they Larry Bird."

Troy nodded. The group headed off to the athletic hall, on the northeast side of campus. As James had expected, the courts were filled with Black students. A few White groups gathered their teams to challenge the winners, who were almost always the Black teams.

James drifted away from their pack as he joined several upper-class students. He seemed to know them already. After a few minutes, he came back to discuss his plans with the rest of the group, but mainly with Troy.

"Yo, Troy, you wanna run with us, homes?" James asked, confident of a positive response. He rubbed his left hand over his goatee, neatly trimmed along with his mustache.

Troy tilted his head back, presenting a frown of confusion. "With who?" he asked, looking in the direction from which James had returned.

"My boy Big Lou picked me, and they wanted another man. So I told them that you could run," James answered.

"I thought we was gon' all run ball together," Troy said.

James smiled, glancing at the confused group of classmates. He whispered back to Troy. "Yo, homes, most of them dudes don't look like they can run ball. I mean, *you* look like you can play," James explained while looking over Troy's athletic, six-foot frame.

"Naw, man, that's aw'ight," Troy told him, backing away to rejoin his new friends. He thought that everyone would remain together. However, Bruce jumped at the opportunity.

"Yo, mayn, I'll run with y'all," he announced, taking off his shirt to join James, Big Lou, and two other tall teammates.

Troy smiled, curling up his tongue. "Go ahead, then. We gon' wax y'all next game anyway," he said. He called to play the winner for the next game. He then turned to Peter and Clay, who stood nearby. "You see how people get new on you?" he asked them.

"Yeah, that was kind of raw," Clay said, realizing his own confusion. "Well, Troy, who we gon' run with now?" he asked.

"We got enough people. We can run with what we got."

Matthew, who wasn't particularly happy to be in the gym in the first place, attempted to back out.

"Yo, Troy, I ain't that good at running ball. I'll just watch."

Troy insisted that he play. "Naw, man. We came up here to run ball, and that's what we gon' do. You can't let yourself get all intimidated by them knuckleheads. Now, as soon as their game is over wit', we gon' play ball."

As they all waited, Troy glued his eyes on James to see if he was any good. James made countless turnovers and missed shots. Time and again, the rest of the team covered for his mistakes as they pulled off a last-minute, four-point win. Bruce, on the other hand, played well, connecting with four jump shots and completing two layups for twelve points. He also grabbed eight hard-fought rebounds off the backboards.

"Yo, boys, the game is over. It's our time to start balling!" Troy shouted, facing his nervous teammates.

Matthew walked and gave him a handshake. "Yo, you aw'ight, troop. And I forgot to tell you that you have a good memory. You knew all our names earlier. That was pretty good."

"Yeah," Troy responded, "it comes in handy with the women, too."

"Word, right, so you can get them digits and knock some boots."

Troy was not familiar with the term. "Yo, cuz, I ain't tryin' to knock no girl's boots," he said. Matthew started to laugh as Troy stood there and smiled, waiting for an explanation.

"You funny as hell, man," Matthew told him. "But naw, knocking boots means gettin' some ass, in New York."

Troy laughed himself, feeling relieved. "Man, I ain't know what you was talkin' about. So that's what Salt-n-Pepa meant in that 'Tramp' song, hunh?"

"Yeah," Matthew said, still chuckling to himself as the team entered the court.

Troy was one of the shortest on his team, second to Peter's five-ten. Matthew was six-four, Clay, six-two, and Reggie, whom Clay had introduced, was a skinny six-six.

"Y'all got all of y'all men?" James asked, checking Troy the ball.

"Yeah, we ready, you traitor," Troy said, smiling.

James chuckled, anxious to start the ball game. "Aw'ight, homes, let's get this shit on, then."

Troy connected on the first jump shot to get the game rolling. Capitalizing on James's mistakes, Troy made a couple of steals, followed by passes to his teammates to guarantee that everyone got a shot. Matthew proved quite effective on the backboards. He had lots of rebounds. On the whole, their team played well, except for Peter, who had a problem shooting underhanded. Players on both teams laughed at every shot he took, especially when he missed. And Peter missed a lot.

With Troy's team ahead 36–32, because of teamwork and James's turnovers, James's squad brought the basketball downcourt. Bruce was having a tantrum because his baskets refused to fall. As a result, he started to lag up the court, giving Troy's team a defensive advantage. But no matter what the odds were, it came down to James's three big men doing a job on Matthew. Their defense tightened as well, and

Troy's teammates found themselves receiving few second shots. Having collected eighteen points, Troy took charge of the game. He hit the next and last four points that his team was able to amass. James's team was again victorious. They won 44-40, just as they had beaten the last team.

"Unh-hunh, homes. You were talking all that shit and couldn't pull it out," James said, rubbing it in.

Not even a slight smile showed from Troy's face of rebellion. "Ay', Jay, you didn't do a damn thing! I had twenty-two points and, like, twelve assists. I had six steals and, like, five rebounds. Now tell me, Jay, 'cause I really want to know. What the fuck did *you* do?"

Everyone laughed a good hard one as James joined in himself. "I won, and I'm still on the court for the next game. That's what I did," he responded.

Troy turned and faced Clay for an explanation. "Now, Clay, if a person didn't do shit to win but is bragging about the victory, then he's a damn fool, to me, for not being true to himself. You know me from high school, Clay, and if I don't do shit in the game, I'll say that y'all won instead of 'we.' Now, that's an act of a man and not a mouse, and I think Jay got cheese sandwiches in his book bag."

By then, everything Troy said was awarded by a roar of laughter. "You know what, Jay? I'll play you whenever you wanna go, and then we'll see how much you've learned from riding the bandwagon," he added.

James giggled and didn't care, as long as he was on the winning team.

* * *

Troy arrived at his dorm room, a double. He noticed that it had been filled with clothing and boxes. Suspecting that his roommate had arrived, he walked into the floor's bathroom, to find a crowd of freshmen being lectured to by an older Black student who spoke proper English and wore blue high-water slacks:

"Any damages on the floor will be paid for by, if not the person who has perpetrated the particular crime of damaging campus property, then by the entire floor."

Troy searched the faces of his fellow floor mates, who all appeared to be bored. Not including the speaker or himself, he counted only three brown faces: there were two massive football players and one small student wearing glasses.

The speaker acknowledged Troy's presence. "Hello, fellow floor mate. My name is Charles Davison, and I will be your resident assistant for the year. Aah, what have you missed? Well, basically, nothing. The boys and I are just sitting in here bullshitting around and playing with ourselves," the cone-headed resident assistant said. He paused to collect the laughter before he continued.

"No, basically, we just went over the rules, I told the guys my duties, and we introduced ourselves. So what else do you want to know?" Charles asked, receiving more laughter from the students. He looked as if he wanted to pat himself on the back.

Troy watched the football players, who were smiling.

"No, seriously. Aah . . . person," Charles said, extending his hand for a shake. The students were all beside themselves with hardy laughter. "Come on now, you guys, so we can get this thing over with," Charles told them. "Well, I. We," he continued, smiling to himself, "would like to know your name and room number. R-i-i-ight guys," he said, stretching his eyelids and expecting another laugh. Charles was trying hard to be a comedian.

Troy smiled and shook his head. "Yeah, well, my name is Troy, and I live in room eighteen-ten," he told them seriously. He effectively stopped all the silliness that had been going on.

"Hey, guy, that's my room! You must be my roommate, then!" yelled a tall, green-eyed White fellow with light brown hair. He stepped toward Troy for a handshake.

"Do you see what we have here? You two buckaroos are roommates," Charles said. "Now isn't that special?"

"Yeah?" Troy responded, wishing that Charles would shut up and get on with business.

The wavy-headed roommate was still excited. "I saw you running ball at the gym, Troy. You're pretty good. By the way, my name is Simon Osenberg," he said.

After more discussion, the ordeal was finally done with. All of the students were released to their rooms.

"So you was up at the gym, hunh, Simon?" Troy asked to start things off.

"Yeah, I was there. But the guys I was playing ball with were bums, a bunch of Italians," Simon told him. "They couldn't run ball for shit, I tell ya. Your team was doing all right against those big guys, though."

"Dig, cuz. You see how big them suckas were? And we still hung in there!" They chuckled as Troy felt proud of himself.

"Maybe we can go run ball sometime, Troy," Simon offered.

"Whenever you down, man. I'll go."

"Great, but Troy, I have some more stuff in my car, if you could give me a hand."

"Aw'ight, man. Let's go get it," Troy responded. He left the room immediately and headed for the floor's elevators. Simon quickly followed him.

They jumped onto the elevator, conversing while riding down eighteen floors and stopping to pick up other students. Lots of freshmen, as well as returning students, crowded the large freshman dormitory lobby. The college hype was stirring, and classes did not begin for another two days.

Entering the refreshing night air, Simon showed Troy to a dark gray, up-to-date Cadillac Coupe de Ville parked inside the student car lot.

"Damn, cuz! This is your car?" Troy exclaimed, shocked.

"Yeah, I just got it a couple months ago," Simon said with a grin.

"Is it brand new?" Troy asked. He looked at the shiny outside coat and the clean, gray, velour-looking interior.

"Well, it's not exactly new," Simon hinted. "See, my father had gotten it from some guy who wanted to trade it in."

Troy nodded. "Y'all Jewish dudes get all kinds of deals."

Simon looked at him, surprised. *"Wow! Get out of town! How did you know I was Jewish?"* he shouted.

Troy searched the parking lot to see who had heard before answering. Simon had a loud mouth. "Because of the name, man," he explained. "All names I've ever heard of with 'Bergs' and 'Steins' in it, I just thought were Jewish."

"Yeah, I forgot all about that. You're right," Simon agreed.

They grabbed two handfuls of items to take back to the dorm. Troy quickly realized that Simon had a lot more stuff than he. He began to wonder if his roommate was rich. He thought that not only would he have a so-far-cool White roommate, but a wealthy one as well. Troy didn't plan to be a leech, he was simply interested in experiencing how wealthy Jewish people really lived.

After they returned to the room and put the items on Simon's side, they began to discuss their separate plans for the night.

"So, Troy, what are you going to do tonight?" Simon asked, as though he was interested in tagging along.

"I'm goin' to that freshman party in the student game room. They're supposed to have a reggae band over there too. Why, you wanna go?" Troy offered. He would feel guilty if he did not at least invite Simon.

"Yeah, I like reggae," Simon said. "Then again, I still have a lot of unpacking to do, and I'm the type of person that has to do something immediately, or it won't get done."

Troy looked around at all the chaos created by Simon's things inside their small, shared room. "Who you tellin'? You got shit all over the place. This place looks like a damn flea market in here," he said. "You might be unpacking until tomorrow."

They shared another laugh as Simon agreed. "Yeah, I know, right."

"Aw'ight, Sime, I'm 'bout to take a shower and go to this party, then," Troy informed him. He took off his clothing, partially, while keeping his underwear on. He rubbed plenty of thick yellowish shampoo into his hair and grabbed his slippers, soap, washcloth, and drying towel. After cleansing and grooming himself, he got dressed and returned to the freshman dormitory lobby to catch up to his friends, succeeding only in finding James Clayton.

"You going to that party?" James asked him. He spoke with the smooth voice that he had been speaking with all day. To Troy, it seemed a bit fabricated. He suspected that it might sound sexy to some women, though.

"Yeah, man, but where's everybody else?"

James hunched his shoulders. "I'on know, homes. I thought they was with you."

Troy, thinking about his new friend's voice, began to grin.

"What's so funny, homes?" James asked curiously.

"Nothin', cuz. Nothing at all," Troy insisted, still smiling.

"Did you meet your roommate yet?" James asked. He frowned as though he were expecting bad news.

"Yeah, he's cool as hell, too. He got his own car, a nineteen-inch color TV, and clothing up the ass," Troy answered.

James sucked his teeth. "Homes, I got this fat-ass White boy, man. This dude is goofy as hell. But oh, he got a computer with games and shit on it. And he got a printer hooked up to it, homes. So you know I'm gon' be right there using it," he said, cracking a smile.

"You got any sisters, Jay?" Troy asked, leaning up against a video game.

"Yeah. How you know?"

"Oh, I was just askin'."

James shrugged and looked around. "It's a whole lot of White girls up this college, homes. I know I'm gon' be gettin' me some," he said, as if he had planned it all.

Troy looked bewildered. "You had some White girls before?" he queried.

"Hell yeah, homes!" James exclaimed. "This White girl lives right next door to me at home. I used to knock her every day."

Troy smiled in amazement. "You live right next to a White girl, hunh?" he asked. "I 'on know, man. These White girls look like virgins to me."

They both looked around at the flirtatious damsels who seemed to be everywhere in packs of five.

"Naw, homes, some of these White girls are dying to talk to a brother," James assured him.

Troy stood firm. He was in need of proof.

"Watch this, homes," James said.

They gave their attention to a slender, dark-brown-haired, olive-toned girl.

"Excuse me, pretty, what's your name?" James asked her.

The olive-toned girl glared, responding as if James

had said something nasty to her. She leaned away to avoid him.

James rubbed his goatee. He seemed to treasure it, as though he had waited awhile for it to grow and was in love with it. "Oh, you ain't got to act all scared of me," he commented, smiling at the olive-toned girl.

Three other girls appeared from nowhere and rudely inserted themselves into the conversation. "Well, h-i-i-i. Who are you guys?" one asked. The first girl then decided it was safe to talk to James, since the cavalry had arrived. Her feathery white hand reached out toward his chest.

James was intrigued. "My name is James, but just call me Jay," he responded.

Troy backed away to avoid being so close to them. They were already invading his buffer space. He knew his time was coming, though. He looked away in an effort to halt the aggression of the four single White females, who all of a sudden appeared to be in sexual heat.

"So what's your friend's name?" one asked James. They all looked toward Troy.

"Oh, that's my boy Troy," James answered, grinning ear to ear and continuing with his plot.

"Well, he's cute. But is he that shy?"

Troy frowned, turning his back to them completely. He could not believe that a skinny, long-nosed White girl had called him shy.

James chuckled. "Naw, he ain't shy. So what y'all gon' get into tonight?" he asked, deciding not to bother Troy. James figured that the first girl he had spoken to was indeed the prettiest. He directed all of his questions to her.

"Well, I don't really know," she responded. "It's like whatever comes up, I guess."

Troy turned back around to view their facial expressions. He felt that James was attempting to go for the gold.

"So aah, why don't you and your girl chill with me and my boy Troy, since you don't have anything to do tonight?" James suggested to the girl who had called Troy cute.

"Well, she would like to, but I don't think her boyfriend would go for that," one of the remaining two interrupted.

James grew testy. "How come she ain't say nothing about him, then? I think y'all two should mind your own business," he said, asserting himself.

Troy started to enjoy the situation.

"Look, why don't you two just go ahead? Your girlfriends will see you later," James suggested. He was determined to convince them. And like clockwork, his plan succeeded; the two outcasts fled while the two prospects remained.

"So what we gon' do?" James asked them.

"Well, we're gonna go to the party because our friends will be waiting for us. And besides, I have to get up really early tomorrow for the reading and math tests and all. Don't you guys have the exams?" the olive-toned girl said, all in one breath.

Troy was dazzled by her quickness of tongue.

James, however, was not impressed. He attempted to hold her by the arm and sweet-talk her. "Come on, now, you gon' see your girlfriends every day up here. They ain't goin' nowhere. I mean, you ain't gon' be out all night. It's only nine o'clock," he said slowly, to let it sink in.

Breaking free of his subtle hold so as not to make him angry from rejection, the girl whined. "Well, that's really OK. We'll just get with you guys another time," she suggested, backing away in the direction of the party.

Her long-nosed friend, who had expressed her liking to Troy, stayed to take a last look at him. And he ignored her.

"Damn, homes! We almost had 'em!" James shouted to Troy. "See how you talk to White girls? You gotta be rough with them dips so they know you ain't going for no dumb shit. We ain't get 'em tonight, but they'll remember us. Watch."

Troy just smiled, thinking that James had a case of jungle fever. He then strolled in the direction of the party.

"Where you going, homes?" James asked him.

"To the party. It's probably thick as hell by now," Troy answered.

"Yup, it probably is," James agreed, following. They both wore logo T-shirts and shorts. They entered the party and had to point out fellow Black students through the overflow of Whites.

"It ain't that many brothers at all at this school, just a bunch of White people," James mentioned. "It's a whole lot of Oreos here, too."

They walked though the crowds, both searching for pretty women. Troy was searching specifically for Blacks. James was searching for them all.

"Ay', Troy, I introduced myself to this one brother, and he sounded just like a White boy, homes," James alluded. "I was like, 'Hold up' and shit, you know? 'Is homes a brother, or what?' "

James continued talking while Troy observed the sights.

"You know what else, homes? I was talking to this old-head, and he told me that most of the Blacks up here are in C.M.P."

He finally got Troy's attention. "For real?" Troy asked him.

James's smile turned into laughter. "Yup, homes. I guess we just ain't smart enough to get into *this* school, besides them Oreos. And they might as well *be* White, to me. So they don't really count and shit."

They chuckled as Troy agreed. "Yup, cuz. It was, like, thirty people in our C.M.P. advisory group today. Only two were White."

While at the party, Troy observed, time and again, James getting turned down by White girls. Troy then spotted an entire crowd of Blacks. Finally! He approached them as James followed, practically begging to go to bed with someone's phone number in his pocket.

All their conversations went smoothly, and before the night was over, Troy had left the party with three phone numbers to James's four. All of Troy's numbers were from Black students. But James got a number from a White girl to break the tie in their contest. Troy told him that the White girl's number didn't count. Returning to his room at three o'clock in the morning, he found Simon still awake and listening to his radio through a pair of earphones.

"Hey Troy, how was the party?" Simon asked, taking off his earphones.

"It was cool, man. I met, like, ten girls and got three numbers," Troy answered. "But yo, my boy Jay got flagged by, like, twenty white babes."

Simon sat up in his bed. "Did he really?"

Troy smiled. "Naw, he just got flagged by, like, seven," he responded, chuckling. "Damn, Sime, I didn't even think to buy some earphones."

"Well you're welcome to use mine when I'm not using them," Simon offered.

"Aw'ight, then, bet," Troy told him.

They talked all night, getting better acquainted as the new day set in for scheduling and testing.

Troy caught the elevator down to the dormitory lobby in the morning and spotted Matthew walking out from the staircase.

"Yo, Mat, what's up, man? You're in the same building as me?"

"Yeah, I guess so. What floor you on?" Matthew asked him.

"The eighteenth."

"Word? You way up that dip? I'm only on the third floor."

"Yeah, cuz. But where was you at last night? I ain't see you at the party," Troy quizzed.

"Oh, I knocked some boots last night, troop," Matthew said in a low tone, as if it was a secret. He was loosely dressed again, with an extra long red T-shirt that covered half his blue shorts.

Troy grinned. "You workin' kind of fast up here, Mat. Was she good-lookin'?"

"Naw. She's kind of big, too," Matthew answered.

Troy laughed. "You had a fat babe?"

Matthew giggled himself. "Yeah, but yo, don't tell nobody," he whispered.

"Aw'ight, cuz, I gotchu. I'm just jokin', man. Ain't nothin' wrong with having a fat babe every now and then. It's probably good for you."

After their second meeting with the C.M.P. counselor, everyone went their separate ways, except for Bruce, who followed Troy.

"Yo, Troy, where you goin', mayn?" Bruce asked.

"To my reading test in room three-fourteen."

"Yeah, well I gotta go to another building," Bruce informed him. Troy continued to walk as Bruce followed. "So, Troy, what y'all do last night?"

"Me and Jay was at that party," Troy answered nonchalantly. He was not up for a discussion. He was thinking about a girl he had met.

"Yeah, well I was talking to my girl back at home last night," Bruce told him.

"All night?" Troy asked, finally showing some enthusiasm.

"Yeah, mayn, she got me in love in do."

Troy frowned, turning the corner of Mason Hall, located in the middle of campus. "Yeah, well you and your girl picked a hell of a time to fall the fuck in love," he hinted.

Bruce chuckled again as Troy smiled.

"Troy, you's a funny-ass dude, mayn," Bruce said as they parted ways.

"Aw'ight, Bruce," Troy responded, still beaming about his comment. He entered room 314 and realized that he was the only Black student. He hoped that another melanin face would appear before things got started. However, the instructor wanted to set a friendly atmosphere, inquiring about the party.

"How'd you guys all like the party last night?" he asked.

One blond student, wearing black combat boots in eighty-five degree weather, spoke up first. "It was OK, I guess. But I didn't like that first group."

The rest of the White students seemed to agree. "I know, 'cause I don't really like reggae music," a platinum-haired girl added.

Troy thought the reggae band was best. The music had attracted more dancers. It had definite rhythm and tempo, and he could understand the words. The second group sounded like a bunch of noise to him. From the way the discussions were going, he expected it to be a long day.

As time neared to take the test, Troy's hope for more color faded. Seeing that he would be the only Black in the class, he felt lonely. The White students had their own conversations. He felt that maybe he wasn't trying to be friendly. So he decided to try.

"Excuse me, where did you get that bus schedule from?" he asked a neighboring brown-haired student. Not that he cared about the bus schedule. He just felt he could start a conversation through it.

"I beg your pardon?" the White lad queried.

"Never mind. Ta hell with it," Troy snapped. He had always hated the words "I beg your pardon" because they made him feel like he was illiterate. Coming from inner-city Philadelphia, he simply wasn't used to the term.

Finishing the reading test in less than two hours, Troy followed some students to the cafeteria on the southeast side of campus near the freshmen dorms. It was his first college meal. The students waited in eight long lines. Troy got a tray, some napkins, and silverware to join in. But as the lines moved, he noticed Black students jumping in front of people they knew. He then spotted Matthew and decided to do the same.

"Yo, Mat, let me get up, man," he said, smiling. He got up in front, expecting Matthew to give him the OK.

"Yeah, sure. Why not?" Matthew said, making room.

After receiving their food, they moved on to the soda machines. Troy sat his tray down to fill his glasses. White students crowded in, reaching over his plate to fill up theirs before he was quite finished. With quick reflexes, he knocked their glasses from in front of his tray, warding them off.

"Yo, cuz, you better wait till I'm finished before you plan on reaching overtop of my food again," he fretted. They stared at him as though *he* was in the wrong.

"Jeez! I'm sorry, man," the perpetrator responded, hunching his shoulders in confusion. Troy backed out with his tray, turning to spot Matthew, who had chosen a seating area. Troy took note of how all of the Black students sat in one corner section in the back of the cafeteria.

"Why is everybody sitting way back here?" he asked.

"I'on know, man," Matthew answered. "I just figured I'd sit where Black people were. Maybe everybody else did the same thing." They chuckled and began to eat, checking out the sisters sitting nearby.

"It's some good-looking babes up here, cuz," Troy commented.

Matthew grinned. "I know."

"I'm gon' have to charm a few of 'em," Troy said with a devilish smile. "But these White people are impolite as hell, cuz, leaning over my plate and all," he added.

"Everybody does that here," Matthew assumed.

"Do you do it?"

"No." They giggled as Matthew continued. "But you can't get all worried about little stuff like that, man."

"Yeah, yeah," Troy said, brushing off Matthew's advice.

They soon finished lunch, traveling back to Mason Hall for the results of the placement exams, only to bump into James, who appeared to be coming from that direction already.

"Did y'all hear, homes?" James asked them.

"Hear what?" Matthew piped up.

Troy stuffed his hands inside his pockets and leaned up against a tree.

"Us three busted the placement tests. We can take other hard classes with the White people," James answered.

Troy still was uninterested.

Matthew got excited. "Yeah, so only us three passed, hunh?"

"Yup. The rest of them are still in them C.M.P. classes," James informed them, snickering. Matthew smiled, but Troy frowned, standing upright.

"So how do you know this?" Matthew asked James.

James grimaced. "Damn, you ask a lot of questions, homes," he said, jokingly. "I asked our counselor. What's her name again?"

"Ms. Whatley," Troy said, finally joining in.

"Yeah, that's it. Ms. Whatley," James repeated.

Troy turned to surveyed his surroundings. Swarms of students were passing by. "Well, since we all exempt, let's go register for our classes," he said.

Matthew and James agreed, following Troy across Madison Avenue to the campus's west side. Inside the registration building they cut in the lines again.

"It's nice meeting you here, Clay," Troy said. They all laughed, softly, to avoid the extra attention from the already angry students who waited patiently in line.

"Yeah, aw'ight, Troy, just don't make this a habit," Clay said, smiling back.

Troy, Jay, and Matthew got in front of him. As the line moved, Troy spotted the executive-looking White woman and got nervous.

"Next," she ordered from behind a computer desk. Troy stepped forward and took a seat. "Fill out your name, social security number, and complete your courses over at the desk," the administrator said, pointing to a section of the registration room. It was packed with Whites. Seeing that, Troy decided, instead, to fill out his form near his friends. Taking about ten minutes to finish, he returned to the registrar to submit his course form.

"Check over your classes to see if everything is correct," she told him. Troy did so, skipping information to quickly return the form to the woman. "Did you check all of your alpha codes?" she asked doubtfully.

"Yeah," he told her with an attitude. She gave him a disapproving look. He captured it, and gave it back to her.

"OK. Thank you very much," she responded, calling for the next student.

The four Black males all finished in a short time and walked out.

"Well, fellas, tomorrow starts a new day," Clay announced with a glow. "Doesn't it, Troy?"

"Yup, man. It feels like starting over again, with a million White people and shit."

They all laughed.

"I know what you mean," Matthew said.

James shrugged. "At least we're here," he commented. "This school is the shit."

FITTING IN

THE FIRST DAY OF CLASSES PRESENTED THE MOST HECTIC crowds that Troy had ever witnessed in his life. Thousands of students traveled in a hundred different directions as he swiftly dodged and weaved through them. White students were extra clumsy, though. They kind of moved like trucks with no steering wheels, causing him to accidentally collide with several of them.

"Gosh, that guy just bumped all into me!" said a White girl dressed in an all-white nursing uniform. "Why doesn't he slow down or something?"

Troy, already late for his first class, decided not to waste more time with a rebuttal, even though he wanted to give her one.

Entering an auditorium that held five hundred students, he noticed Peter, the well-mannered, underhand-shooting, baby-faced, cream-colored boy. Wanting to join Peter in the front row but not wanting to ruin the class lecture, Troy ruled against it. He knew he would draw too much attention walking down thirty rows of seats in the middle of their first meeting. So he sat in the back, counting brown faces. Four, eight, thirteen, nineteen; twenty-two Black students out of an estimated total of 450. The small number of Blacks represented merely five percent of the student population.

Troy threw a friendly hand on Peter's shoulder after the lecture. "What's up, Pete? I ain't know you was in this class."

"Oh, my man, Troy," Peter responded, extending his hand for a shake. He was surprised to see him. "I heard that you, Jay, and Mat were exempt from taking the C.M.P. classes," he mentioned.

"Who told you that?"

"Jay told me."

Troy frowned as soon as he heard the name. "Yeah, that figures. But we still have to take that study skills class."

They headed for the cafeteria, still dodging floods of White students, as it started to drizzle. Neither of them had carried an umbrella to class, so they hurried before it started to rain harder.

Inside the cafeteria, Black students continued to jump in line, angering White students, who dared not to speak on it. Troy and Peter followed the lead.

"Yo, what's up, boys?" Troy said, speaking to some new associates. He had met a lot of students over the past few days. "Oh yeah, Pete, if you need a haircut, I can hook you up, man," he added, turning back and facing Peter. They moved to the Black section of the cafeteria in the back corner.

"I didn't know you cut hair," Peter said. He patted how much his hair had grown since his last cut. "So you got a license?" he asked.

Troy shook his head and hastily swallowed his bite

of turkey sandwich. "Naw, man. I just did it as a hustle around the way," he answered. "I charge six dollars a head. I give some fresh-ass cuts, too."

Peter suddenly raised his head to look over Troy's. "Ay', Troy, here comes Jay now," he said.

James excitedly sat his tray down next to Troy. "Yo, homes, I got some sex last night from that sophomore girl," he bragged.

Troy joined in with his own excitement. "Yeah, me too, cuz. I ended up bein' late for class this morning."

Peter shook his head. "I don't believe you two are disrespecting our beautiful Black women like that," he interjected.

James looked at Peter and laughed. "Where you grow up at, homes?" he asked, planning to make fun of him.

"Oh, I grew up in a nice home in a mixed neighborhood," Peter answered reluctantly. He could sense a setup coming on.

"You mean you grew up wit' the White peoples," James said, giggling.

Troy smiled, trying not to.

"Yeah, but it was a lot of Black people there, too," Peter explained.

"Naw, homes, my family didn't move to the suburbs until I was sixteen, so I already had my Black identity," James said. "Then my pop had gotten this big government job."

"I'm still a Black man," Peter snapped. "I know myself. I don't talk like no Oreo and I don't live in no suburbs. I just live in a nice area," he responded to redeem himself.

"So did you get some sex up here yet, homes?" James requested. He smiled at Peter, preparing himself to laugh again.

"No. I met a few nice girls, but I wouldn't try to take them to bed so soon. I feel I would lose respect for them like that."

James cracked up. "Yo, homes, I'm tellin' you now, this is college, and it ain't like they gon' wait around for you to get ready. You gotta act like you want some."

"Dig, Pete, you can't come up here thinkin' these girls are all little princesses. You gon' get hurt like that," Troy suggested. "So what you do is, you always try a girl first, then you see what happens and how she acts."

Peter nodded as if he was planning to heed the advice.

"Yeah, 'cause a lot of these babes have boyfriends back home that they cheatin' on anyway. Don't they, Troy?" James asked, assuming.

Troy nodded and smiled. "Yup."

James checked his watch and saw that he was running late for his next class. "Damn, I gotta get up out of here!" he wailed, grabbing his jacket and books. He left his tray on the table.

Peter and Troy finished their lunch soon after. They left the cafeteria after tossing their trays onto the dirty dish rack and walked through the freshman lobby.

Peter promptly recognized a friend he wanted Troy to meet.

"Hey Troy, I want you to meet my boy Doc. He's from here," he said, leading Troy to him.

Doc was leaning against a soda machine, lighter-toned than Peter, with curly black hair. He was what some women would call a pretty boy.

"Doc, this is my boy Troy. And Troy, this is my boy Doc," Peter said as Doc and Troy shook hands.

"I seen you up at the gym last night. You got a nice game," Doc said.

Troy smiled at Doc's squeaky voice as he humbly agreed. "Yeah, man, practicing makes you talented. And the more you work, the better your results," he commented. "But look, I got some work to do, so I'll catch y'all later," he said, leaving Peter and Doc standing next to the soda machine.

"Ay', Pete, that's a strong-minded brother, man," Doc said, watching Troy head for his dorm building.

Peter grinned. "I heard he's from a tough area. I figure he has to have a strong mind."

Doc nodded. "So what building are you in, Pete?" he asked.

"I'm in Forrest Hall right now, but I'm trying to get transferred to a single room, over at Clayton."

"You got a roommate?"

Peter laughed before answering. "Yo, man, your voice takes me out," he said. "But I got three roommates. We're all pretty cool, though."

"Yeah," Doc responded blandly. He motioned toward a girl he knew. "Well, I'll get with you later, Pete," he said, heading toward her.

Peter smiled. "Aw'ight, then, Doc." He walked in the opposite direction, still beaming as he began to think about the classes, the responsibilities, and the freedom he had acquired in college. No more Mom and Dad telling him what to do. No more household chores or errands to run. No more curfews and third-degree questions. No more feeling mistreated. No more missing out on wild adventures. No more external discipline. Peter could finally do what *he* wanted to do.

He could finally have sex. He no longer had to wait for permission to go out. And he had no older brothers or sister to get on his nerves. He hated being the youngest and the most obedient anyway. His siblings had gotten away with murder.

"I used to steal dad's car late at night, but don't *you* do that," his oldest brother told him.

"I remember Mom and Dad told me not to go to Bermuda, and I did anyway. I had the greatest time of my life there," his sister had said. "Mom and Dad felt that girls shouldn't travel without an escort. But *you* should listen to them, 'cause they know best."

"Yeah, Pete, I used to sneak this girl in the house all the time, but you really should wait to get married before you have sex," his other brother suggested.

Each story made Peter feel like an idiot for obeying. But in college he was on his own and ready for the world.

Entering his crowded room, shared with three White roommates, on the northwest side of campus near Henry Road, Peter was shocked to see three tipsy White girls straddled across his neatly made bed. His roommates were listening to extra loud rock music, eating popcorn, munching chips, and drinking sodas.

"How the hell are you, Petey? Join our fuckin' party, man!" one roommate loudly offered.

Peter could barely hear him over the blasting rock music. "Naw, that's quite all right," he said, suppressing his anger with a tolerant smile. He stood over the party girls, who remained on his bed. He expected them to depart from his new college property. Yet they eyeballed him as if he was an intruder, and didn't budge.

"Oh, you guys, this is Petey," another roommate said to the girls.

Peter glanced toward the gang of White guys and girls wildly dancing on the other side of the room. Arms, legs, hair, and shoulders were flailing about with no specific rhythm.

"You don't mind us sitting on your bed, do ya?" one of the party girls asked, staring with large gray eyes.

Peter couldn't believe his eyes and ears. He found himself exerting more energy to remain calm as he looked around at the mess they had made. "I'd rather you sat on one of their beds," he said to her.

"Yeah, OK then," she responded sourly. "I mean, we're not harming your bed, but if you feel that way about it, we'll move. OK?"

The rest of the group paid Peter no mind. He then decided to call Troy on their dorm phone.

Brrrloop . . . brrrloop . . . brrrloop.

"Answer the damn phone, Simon!" Troy shouted from his desk. He was reading over some homework.

"All right already. You don't have to scream," Simon said, taking off his earphones. He got up to answer the phone as they smiled at each other. "Hello," he answered. A siren of rock music served as Peter's noisy background. "Jesus Christ! Is there a party over there or something?" Simon hollered through the phone. Troy looked on, waiting to be given the word.

"It's for you, Troy," Simon said.

"Yo, it's Troy," he answered.

"Yo, man, can you sign me in?" Peter yelled.

"Aw'ight. But what's all that noise over there?" Troy asked, straining to hear him.

"I'll tell you about it when I get over there."

After waiting thirty minutes, Troy went down into the lobby area to find Peter calling his room again from the lobby phone.

"Yo, Pete, I'm right here, cuz," Troy said, walking over to the desk to sign him in. "So what's going on in your room?"

"Oh, ah, my roommates are having a party," Peter answered nonchalantly. He didn't want to talk about it.

They took the elevator, not saying a word as Troy thought the worst of Peter's situation. He got three White roommates, Troy thought to himself. He introduced Peter to Simon as soon as they entered his room. "Simon, this is my boy Peter."

"How are ya?" Simon said as the two shook hands. "So what's all that racket in your room?"

"My roommates are having a party, that's all."

"Well kick them the hell out, man! Ta hell with that!" Simon shouted.

Troy and Simon chuckled.

Peter smiled and straightened. "Naw, you know, sometimes you gotta let things slide to avoid a lot of dumb stuff," he said.

Simon frowned and shook his head. "Hell no, man,

you can't let shit slide. They'll walk all over ya. You gotta make your stand right away. Then people won't even try you."

Troy was proud to hear his roommate express such a statement.

Simon continued: "Look, Peter, I have this friend back home who let his girl get away with all kinds of stuff. She sold the charm he bought her on her birthday. She stole his jacket one time 'cause he wouldn't let her hold it. She slept around on him. Then, to top it off, she got pregnant by another guy and tried to get my boy to pay for the abortion. That's when he finally let her go. But I told him he should have gotten rid of that tramp a long time ago."

Peter nodded again once Simon had completed his story. Peter nodded his head frequently, yet he seldom agreed with anyone. He felt it was time to make his *own* decisions.

Friday night, Troy, James, and Peter were all hyped and ready for a party. They had all gotten fresh haircuts and were neatly dressed, eagerly anticipating the first Black event of their freshman year.

"Yo, Troy, you ain't no joke, homes! You really do give a bumpin'-ass haircut," James said, looking into the mirror. He was rubbing his goatee again. It had just been trimmed.

"Yeah, it is a nice job," Peter commented.

"Nice job. Is that what you said, homes?" James asked him.

Peter smiled as he glanced into the mirror at his own haircut. He planned on ignoring all of James's downgrading. James, however, didn't plan to bother him. He gave his attention back to Troy.

"I still can't believe you cut your own hair that good."

"Practice makes perfect, cuz. Nobody goes to the barbershop around my way; they all come to me. So I stayed paid."

"You gon' get a lot of customers up here, too, homes."

"Yeah, I know. I'm like my own private businessman already."

James pulled a beer out of his bag. He had snuck a six-pack into the dorms, since restrictions were placed on minors and reinforced as school policy. "You want one, Troy?" he asked, pulling another from his book bag before Troy could answer.

"Yeah, throw me two," Troy answered.

James grinned as Peter got nervous. "You tryin' to get drunk, homes?" James asked Troy while glancing at Peter.

Troy smiled. "Yeah. You got the best game for women when you're drunk," he said.

Peter looked away. He wanted to avoid even the sight of beer.

"Yo, Pete, you want one, man?" James finally asked him. It was the moment Peter had feared.

"Well . . . ," he said.

James interrupted him before he could finish. "Come on, homes, this is college. You can't be acting like a mommy's boy up here."

"Yeah, aw'ight, then. But I only want one," Peter whined.

James grinned. "Shit, homes, that's all you was gon' get. I'm keepin' the rest for my damn self."

Troy laughed and started on his second. And after they all got buzzed, they merrily traveled to the Student Activity Center, near Charleston Street. Black students had waited impatiently all week long for the occasion.

Arriving at the entrance, the three new friends spotted students getting their hands stamped as they went in.

"Yo, hold up, y'all," Troy said. "Let's see what the mark is and do our own hands." He pulled out a pocket full of colored markers. Peter and James chuckled.

"Yo, what's up, Troy?" Bruce hollered, running over to join them.

Troy copied the mark that a sister had showed him on each of his companions' right hand and on his own. They then started toward the doors. Troy led the pack, feeling confident as the others hurried behind, feeling unsure. They slipped into the party without suspicion as Troy had expected. Peter felt the most relieved. He thought getting caught at the doors would be a most embarrassing situation.

While wandering around the room, Peter stared at many of the sisters. Some stared back, believing he was attractive. He danced with as many women as the beer in his blood allowed him to successfully ask. Since he had not been to that many parties, he did not know any up-to-date dances. He looked rather uncoordinated. Yet, he had never drunk a beer before either. Alcohol had given him a feeling of total looseness.

Searching through the party while still dancing,

Peter spotted Troy and James speaking to a pleasing pair of browns. He watched Troy's hand smoothly gliding across the one sister's backside. He suspected that his two friends were planning on taking care of their macho needs. Peter then decided that it was his night to get lucky, too. Or was it the beer that had decided for him?

Later that evening, Peter actually found himself inside his room accompanied by a curvaceous brown in a blue satin dress, not really knowing how she got there. The alcohol content in his blood had decreased. Whatever he had said or done was recent history. After he returned from the bathroom for about the sixth time in the past two hours, it was like baking a cake from scratch.

"So ahhh . . . ," Peter began, trying to recall her name.

She was tall and vivacious, with a beautiful pair of dimples. "Marsha," she said, not appearing to be offended that he had forgotten.

"Oh, you didn't have to tell me. I was just about to say it," he lied, smiling at her. She smiled back, and her dimples widened, making her appear even more attractive. It didn't matter, though. Peter didn't know what to say to her.

"You didn't tell me you had roommates," she mentioned as she peered at the sleeping White students.

Peter stared out the window, trying to remember what-all he did tell her. He was mad at himself for not being able to get lucky. He figured he could try again another night.

"Well, make sure you leave your phone number so

I can call you," he said confidently. He didn't realize how declarative he sounded. Obviously a trace of the beer was still in his bloodstream.

Next morning at brunch, the entire freshman group of friends joined together to eat. They had all awakened at about the same time. All were restless, hungry, and filled with stories.

"What y'all do last night, troops?" Matthew asked, starting off the conversation. He was the only one who hadn't been at the party.

"Me and Troy got some ass together," James answered with a grin. "Clay went to this babe's crib, and even Peter took a girl home. But what happened to you, Bruce? You, like, disappeared on us."

Bruce grimaced. "That party was boring to me, mayn. I went back to the crib and chilled. But what do you mean, you and Troy 'got some ass together'? Y'all had the same babe or something?" he asked.

"Naw, homes. Troy's roommate went home for the weekend, and me and the girl I was wit' went to Troy's room. So we was side by side and shit," James responded, beaming.

Peter and Matthew remained quiet, since neither of them had any sexual stories to tell.

"So, Pete, did you jump in some flesh last night, homes?" James asked.

Peter knew it was coming. "I'd rather not comment on that," he said, annoyed.

James started to laugh. "I'on know, homes. The way you talk about nice girls and all, you might never get no ass in college."

Troy planned to put a stop to it all. "Leave him alone, cuz."

"Aw, come on now, Troy. This brother is weak, man. I mean, he grew up in the damn woods, homes."

Even Troy laughed before Peter could speak up and defend himself.

"You know what, Jay, it doesn't make you a better man than me just because you have sex a lot, 'cause when it comes down to the final chapter in the book, we'll see who's on top to get the last laugh," Peter exclaimed. He gathered his tray and left for another table.

"You gon' start jerking off soon!" James shouted.

Troy made another attempt to spare Peter for the future. "Ay', Jay, you gots to stop messin' with him, man. That shit ain't cool no more."

Time passed on. Peter continuously struck out sexually, as James made fun of him. Peter had nights of studying, only to not remember what he had read for two and three hours. He thought constantly about proving his manhood to James and to himself. Yet party after party he received the same excuses. "You're nice and all, but . . . and besides, I just met you." He began to ask himself, Is getting drunk and acting vulgar and disrespectful the only way to get a woman? At the same time, he had turned down less attractive sisters who would have loved to establish a long-term relationship.

Several more weeks passed without Peter being able to pay full attention to his work schedule. Troy and James had slept with at least four girls apiece, while Peter could not score with one.

The first month of college was not at all what he had expected. It was troubling. And it had superficially caused him to fail his first exams.

Nevertheless, Peter refused to believe so. He'd rather believe that he was not dedicated enough to his studies. He did, however, have something to be pleased about after his first month and a half at State University; he had finally moved into his own, private room.

WORKING HARD

"IN THE PAINT, POTTER. NOW POP IT! THAT'S THE WAY. NOW do it again and make sure you make it count every time.

"Bring it down and give it up. In the paint, Potter. *Quick! Pop It!*

"Jesus Christ! That's the way you do it, young man! Now go ahead over and talk to Coach Smith."

Troy walked over to the bleachers, after another hard day of practicing, to speak to one of the assistant coaches.

"Young man, I don't know how we missed you, but I think you have most definite talent. What high school are you from, kid?"

Troy stared into his pink face and his bald and shiny forehead. "Booker T. Washington," he said. "Our basketball team wasn't all that good. We had a terrible record, so scouts didn't really look at us."

"Yeah, yeah, well you have a hell of a chance to show your ability now, son. We get a lot of sorry walk-ons who think they're gonna be college stars, but it's very seldom that we get a guy with your potential, Potter. You've given one hundred and ten percent at each practice so far, son, and if you keep up that type of enthusiasm, you'll be a part of this ball club. Jesus Christ, you're a player! Hey, Mike, get me a team jersey for Potter," Coach Smith said, signaling to an equipment manager.

Finally, after two weeks of practicing, Troy received a jersey. He was halfway through. He only wondered how long he would have to prove his abilities.

"Ay', Potts, is it hard playing ball on the East Coast?" a teammate asked, from the bench.

Troy nodded. "Yeah, man. Every brother in a pair of Jordans think they can run ball. Where you from, though, man?" he asked, sitting down next to his tall, dark teammate.

"I'm from California."

"California? They got you from all the way out there?"

"Well, naw, really, I wanted to come here just to be on the East coast, since I live all the way west."

"Yeah, you damn sure do," Troy agreed with a laugh. "I've only been to North Carolina for a four-day family reunion. Other than that, I haven't been a damn place. But I could count Marsh now, since I don't live here."

"Yeah, but the Black people in this place are kind of weird, man. They be wearing wet, drippy curls and calling soda 'pop' and shit. I was up here in the summer, and they don't seem to be down with nothin' here," the teammate said. The coaches called him Hecker. Troy didn't know his first name, nor did Hecker know his. They all were calling Troy "Potts," his new basketball team nickname.

Troy grinned. "I'on know, man. I thought y'all wore curls out there in California too."

He stopped and contemplated for a minute as Troy continued to listen. "Not my area," Hecker said. "But yeah, a lot of people do relax their hair out in California. You know, a lot of people think that California is filled with nothin' but rich people. Man, them White people rich out there, 'cause we still got Blacks livin' in slums. Some of them get out, but you know how it is with niggas turning their backs and all.

"Anyway, at first, I was gon' go to this college out in Colorado," Hecker alluded. "Brothers out there was like, 'We don't listen to that rap music stuff.' I said, 'Y'all never heard of Run-D.M.C.' They said 'Run-D.M. who?' Maann, I said I gots to get the hell outta dis place. So I came here, 'cause I know y'all down with the program on the East Coast." They shared a laugh again while Mike, the team manager, gave Troy his jersey.

"You on the team now, hunh, Potts?" Mike asked.

"Not yet, but I'm working on it," Troy told him. He sounded as though he doubted himself. He was only being humble.

Hecker frowned at him. "Yo, Potts, I've been watching you. The only thing they got on you is height. You on the team, man, just keep comin' to practice. We need an extra point guard anyway."

Troy smiled with confidence. "Yeah, I know. But I'll check y'all out later. I got work to do," he said, slapping hands and gathering his things.

"Hey, Potter, keep working hard, you hear!" the coach yelled, noticing Troy leaving.

Back at his room, Troy walked in on Simon listening to his earphones. The room was a total mess, with Simon's clothing and books all over the floor, the dresser, and the closet.

"Damn, Simon, this room is trashed, man! Why don't you clean it up sometimes?"

"Why don't you?" Simon asked, taking off his earphones with a grin.

"Because all of this ain't my shit," Troy snapped.

"All right, maybe I'll clean it up tomorrow."

"No, you gon' clean this shit up *tonight*!" Troy boldly exclaimed before grinning. "You's a crazy dude, cuz. I thought Jewish people were supposed to be smart. But you don't study for shit, Simon. You keep a sloppy room *and* you get all C's."

"Yeah, I guess I didn't get it. My older brother got it, though," Simon said seriously. "Troy, my older brother has this company that's paying his way through college. Then he has an automatic job when he gets out. Aw man, that makes me mad as hell."

Simon shook his head, disgusted. "I mean, Troy, it's not like I didn't try, you know. I used to bust my ass in high school, but all I got was C's and B's, so now I'm like, 'Ta hell with it.' "

Simon then remembered a message he took for Troy. "You got a few phone calls," he said. "A girl named Tanya Moore and Lisa called." He had written the names down in his notebook. "Oh yeah, Troy, some kid named Mat called for you, too. I told him you were at basketball practice."

Troy grimaced. "You told him I was goin' out for the basketball team? You stupid, man!" he hollered.

Simon smiled in confusion. "What, you don't want people to know?"

"Fuck no, man!" Troy shouted, shaking his head. "Simon, cuz, let me tell you something about my people, man. I hate to say it, but it's the truth. We have very limited minds, man. If I tell a black dude I'm gon' try to make a Division 1 basketball team, unless they know I'm a star, they'll laugh at me. We don't believe that we can do a damn thing, Simon. My friends didn't think I could make it to college. Period. But I'm here. And all I've gotten on my first three tests is A's. And if I tell them that, they still gon' doubt me.

"And see, you White boys, if y'all say, 'I wanna be the fuckin' president,' it's cool," Troy added. "But me, being Black, I can't even say I'm gon' make it through college without gettin' those skeptics and shit. That don't make no sense, but that's how a lot of us think."

"Well, just don't listen to 'em," Simon suggested.

Troy smiled and left for Matthew's room.

Bloomp bloomp bloomp.

"Yo, come in," Matthew said through the door.

"What's up, Mat?" Troy asked, entering his neat room.

"Yo, troop, your roommate said you was on the hoop team."

"Naw, I ain't on there yet, I'm just trying out," Troy responded. "That's why I didn't tell anybody about it. I hate failing. And I hate losing."

"Everybody hates to lose, man," Matthew commented. He turned from his work and got up to brush his hair and look over his waves in the mirror.

"Yeah, but not like me, cuz. So what you been up to, Mat?" Troy asked again, attempting to change the subject.

Matthew shrugged. "I've just been in here studying."

"Yeah, I know what you mean. I study all the time myself. I don't have time to bullshit around like all them hip-hop dudes hangin' out in the lobby."

"Word, right. 'Cause, like, them dudes act like college is a big party. You can't hang in the lobby every day and expect to get your work done," Matthew agreed. "Them dudes get all drugged up and party like it's going out of style. Them White boys can do that and still pass the tests. But if one of us tries that—yo, man, you know what's gon' happen," he said. He shook his head and pointed his thumb toward the floor.

"Like Peter, man," he continued. "He claims he studies all the time, right. But I got him in two classes and he's flunked both his tests already. Now, Troy, if you know from high school, man, you can't scuff the first test up and hope to get a good grade. You gotta ace the first one to get a good start."

"Yeah, I know. As a matter of fact, me and Pete got a psychology test tomorrow," Troy remembered. "I gotta study for that after dinner."

Brrrloop brrrloop.

"You want me to get it?" Troy asked, already walking toward the telephone.

"Yeah," Matthew said, realizing that Troy was closer.

"Hello . . . Yo, what's up, Pete? We was just talkin' about you."

"Speak of the devil," said Matthew as he neared the phone. "Yo, what's up?" he asked Peter. "Aw'ight, troop, I'll be down."

"He wants you to sign him in?" Troy asked.

"Yeah, I'll be back."

Matthew returned with Peter in five minutes.

"So, Pete, did you start studying for that test tomorrow?" Troy probed anxiously.

"I'm gon' try to bust it out tonight."

"What? You just gon' start studying tonight?"

"Well, I basically know it a little bit. You wanna quiz me?" Peter suggested, smiling.

"OK, then, what is cognition?" Troy asked, starting up the quiz.

"Oh, that's when you, aah, make a guess at what an answer will be."

Troy started to laugh, falling on Matthew's bed and grabbing a pillow over his mouth. "Hold up," he said, regaining his composure. Matthew continued to chuckle.

"Naw, man, cognition is the basic concept of thinking, not guessing what something is. See, you have to get this college stuff in detail, or the test questions will kill you," Troy explained. "We all should know by now that they don't put no easy questions on the tests. Most of them damn questions are just to fool you. But anyway, what is the bystander effect?" he asked.

"That's when you stand by and watch something," Peter answered.

Troy tried not to laugh. Matthew held in his laughter as well.

"You almost have it," Troy told Peter. "The bystander effect is the tendency of a person to help someone in need less, if someone else is present that doesn't help. What's an attitude?" he asked, continuing.

"Oh, I know this one. That's an easy one. It's when you make certain assumptions about something," Peter answered.

Troy no longer found it amusing. "No, that's when you have a personal like or dislike reasoning for a certain stimulus. What is a conditioned response?"

"That's when you do something without knowing."

"No, it's a trained response to a given stimulus."

Matthew began to chuckle again as it neared time for dinner. "Ay', Peter, it doesn't sound like you know anything, man," he said.

"It's not that I don't know it. I just have to get it in detail."

Troy frowned. "Ay', look, Pete, after dinner I'm gon' come to your crib so we can study together, 'cause you need help, cuz. Now it's getting late, so let's roll out to dinner."

Peter hesitated. "Aah, I'm gon' get with you later, Troy. I still gotta read three chapters."

Matthew cracked up, but Troy was angered.

"You haven't read the chapters yet?" Troy shouted. "Man, this test is on nine chapters. You gon' tell me the night before the test that you still gotta read three? What the fuck you been doin', man? What you think college is, a joke or some shit?"

Matthew stopped laughing. "Yo, Troy, you act like you're the one in trouble," he said with a smile, trying to lighten things up.

"Yeah, well, you call me up as soon as you finish those chapters," Troy said to Peter, almost ignoring Matthew's comment.

"Yeah, OK, then. I only have three more chapters to go."

After dinner, Troy eyed Doc standing next to the the soda machine in the lobby again. He noticed that Doc was an expensive dresser—brand-name clothing. He wore a red Polo jacket, a Gucci hat, Timberland shoes, and blue Calvin Klein jeans.

"Yo, Troy. Come here, man," Doc called, motioning with his hand.

Troy walked over to him. "What's up with that voice? That shit gives me the chills every time I hear it," he said. "But what's going on with you, cuz?"

They sat on a nearby bench. Doc smiled and stared into Troy's smooth, brown face. "Remember that girl in the party with the blue leather jacket that I was talking to?" he asked.

"Yeah."

"She said she likes you. She wants to go to the theater with you this weekend."

"The what?" Troy responded.

"The the—," Doc repeated, stopping himself before he finished. "The movies, man."

"Well, why didn't you say so in the first place?" Troy teased. " 'The theater'. Ha ha ha. What's wrong with y'all in this city?"

"So what's up, man?" Doc asked, pressing the issue. "You want me to hook it up, or what?"

"Yeah, hook it up, cuz. That babe was a freak."

Doc was confused. "She's not nasty, man. She's a nice girl," he said.

"What?" Troy asked, smiling. "I meant that she looks good, not that she's nasty."

"Oh, OK. I'll hook it up, then," Doc assured him. "Her girlfriend gon' be down here for me, too."

"Cool, Doc. But we gots to separate when they get here, though, 'cause I'm not into that double-date shit."

"Oh, I know, man. Me neither."

They separated after shaking hands. Troy was obligated to study with Peter. While riding the elevator back to his room, he thought about hanging out with Doc, a native of Penn City, who knew a lot of pretty girls. The possibilities were endless. Doc wanted to hang out with Troy, too. Nevertheless, it was time to get back to studying.

Troy entered his room and found Simon finally doing some homework. He decided not to say anything. Simon was too easily provoked and was very talkative.

Troy sat and looked over his chapters. He knew what information was more important and stressed by the instructor. He scanned page after page, reciting the material. He covered every course the same way; outline, read, recite, review, and quiz. Hard work and planning was a virtue. He studied for two long hours before Peter finally decided to call.

Brrrloop brrrloop.

"Ay', Simon, get the phone. It's probably Peter."

Simon was stretched out on his bed right next to the telephone. He had quit studying an hour and a half earlier to listen to his music. "Well, hell, man, if you know it's for you, then you get it," he said.

"Aw man, you're a jerk-off. Do you know that, you geek?" Troy joked. They chuckled as Troy leaped to the telephone from his desk. He snatched it up before it could ring again. "Peter," he answered, anticipating who it was. "Hello . . . Hello."

Peter laughed. "What are you doin' answering the phone like that? It could have been one of your lady friends."

Troy was in no mood for games. "Aw'ight, let's cut out the bullshit," he snapped.

Simon snickered in the background.

"So are you ready to be quizzed?" Troy asked Peter.

"Yeah, I'm ready."

Troy pounced on his bed to begin the quiz. Once again, Peter knew almost nothing. It was eleven o'clock at night and they had the exam at 9 A.M. sharp. The quiz looked more like a private lesson. Troy remained patient, however, determined to help a friend in need.

"Damn it, Pete, you don't know anything! All I've been doing for the first hour is tellin' you shit that you should know already," Troy shouted over the phone. He stopped to think for a minute. "What's your major, anyway?"

Peter stammered. "Oh, well, umm, I was interested in being a math instructor. Now I'm thinking about majoring in this."

Troy frowned, assuming that Peter's change in majors probably had something to do with the first test in algebra that he had failed. "How you gon' major in psychology when you don't even read the damn book? You gotta be good, or at least interested in what you do," Troy told him. He held the phone away from his face and smiled. I don't believe this guy, he thought.

"Yeah, you're right," Peter said. "I'm starting to get the hang of it as you're telling me."

"Hey, Troy, I'm tired. It's almost twelve o'clock and I wanna go to sleep. So go in the hallway," said a droopy-eyed Simon.

Troy immediately took the phone out into the hallway, where he was approached by two shoeless White girls.

"Excuse me," one asked while the other giggled, "would you happen to know where John Hughes lives?" John Hughes and his roommate were the two Black football players that lived right next door.

"Yeah, they live right here," Troy said, pointing.

"Who is that, Troy?" Peter asked over the phone.

Troy could hear the excitement in Peter's voice. "Aw man, calm down. It's just two silly White girls," he said. They returned to studying, and Peter finally gave some correct answers, to Troy's applause.

"Good, man, it's about time. I thought I would have to be up all night with you," Troy commented excitedly. "It's already a quarter after one."

"It's ten after one," Peter corrected, looking over at his desk clock.

"Shut up, man, it's about the same thing," Troy snapped.

John Hughes's roommate walked the two girls back to the elevator. "OK, then, I'll see you," he said before the elevator doors closed. He stormed back to his room, angry for some reason.

Troy continued to listen.

"Shit, John! What the hell I tell you 'bout dem White girls! All they wanna do is be friendly with us and shit! I told you to leave them ugly ones alone anyway! Every night you got some new monsters coming down here to act stupid and leave!"

"Yo, is someone arguing or something?" Peter asked, hearing the disturbance.

"One of them football players is mad about them White girls I was telling you about," Troy answered. He chuckled to himself as the clamor decreased. He and Peter returned to the quizzing.

"OK, Pete, what is a control?"

"That's an experiment where the observer can manipulate the stimulus, to see the changes in the effects."

"Bet! Now you doing aw'ight," Troy told him.

"OK, you think you're ready by now, Peter?" Troy asked, entering the auditorium. They had remained on the phone until two o'clock in the morning.

"Yeah, I think I can kick it out. But damn, where did all these people come from?" Peter asked, observing an enormous increase in the class population.

Troy smiled. "These are the people who'll only come to class on test day. It's, like, five hundred of us. Who gon' recognize Joe Blow?"

After six minutes of explanations and the passing out of tests, it began. Troy found few difficulties with the sixty-question test, although he guessed four answers. He finished the test in precisely thirty-eight minutes out of an allotted fifty. Seeing that Peter, who sat near him, was not yet finished, Troy held on to his test answers to help him out. He watched for the instructor's assistants as he did so.

"Ay', Pete, number seven is *b*," he whispered while Peter changed the answer. "Number thirty-four is *e*."

Troy stooped down to fake picking up a pencil whenever he spotted an assistant nearing. They cheated until time was consumed, changing ten of Peter's original answers.

"Thanks, Troy. I hope I did well on that exam," Peter said after dismissal.

"Oh, sorry," a White student apologized. Peter had accidentally bumped into him, but he paid no attention as he listened to Troy.

"Don't even worry about it, man. I'll always help a friend, no matter what it takes," Troy assured him.

Back inside the cafeteria, a rush of Black students was jumping in line as usual. Troy and Peter saw Doc and jumped up in front of him.

"Hey, you guys just can't be jumping in front of people. I've been waiting here," a muscular White girl protested.

Doc responded before Troy could. "Why don't you just shut up and mind your business?"

"Yeah, well what are you gonna do to me?" she asked, challenging him.

Doc stared at her. "I'll punch you in the face. That's what I'll do to ya," he answered. The rambunctious girl sulked and romped away to another line.

Troy spotted someone he knew, deciding to sit with her instead of with Peter and Doc, who sat nearby.

"What's up, girl?" he asked, placing his tray in front of hers. "Why are you sitting by yourself?"

"My friends all have different schedules from mine," she said. Lisa had light brown eyes, hair, and skin, but with a smaller head than Vanessa Williams. "Yup, Troy, I'm working real hard, but I think I'm getting tired of gymnastic practice," she mentioned.

"Yeah, that's right. I forgot you was into that," he lied, straight-faced.

Lisa frowned, knowing better. "Now, Troy, I told you that at least three times before. You forget everything, boy. What do you be into?" she asked him jokingly.

Troy didn't forget, he just didn't want her to know that he remembered. He laughed it off, avoiding her question. "With the body you got, you can teach me some of that gymnastics stuff whenever you want to," he said to produce a smile. "You got, like, one-hundred-and-eighty-degree curves all over," he added for a chuckle. "Yeah, but, umm, Lisa, what are you doin' later on tonight?"

"Studying."

"Well, dig this, I gotta study too. So let's do it together," Troy suggested.

"OK," Lisa agreed. "But I hope we get some real homework done *this time.*"

"Get in the paint, Walton. In the paint, I said. Quick!

"Damn it, Walton! Potter, get in here and show him how it's done! OK, watch him bring it down. Now give it up, Potter. In the paint. Back out. Take the shot. *Boom!* Do you see that, Walton? Now why can't you do that? Good work, Potter," the coach said, smacking Troy on the butt. "*Jesus Christ!* This is going to be a long season! We got starting guards slopping the plays up every day. Potter's the only one who looks good, and he's a walk-on."

Troy was pleased that his coach had mentioned his name, but he felt eerie about being called a walk-on. The word "walk-on" started to haunt him.

"Potter, come on over here, I wanna talk to you," said the head coach. He was moving over to the side of the court, wearing tight green shorts, with a potbelly hanging over the elastic waistband. "Now, son, I can't promise you any quality time because we got boys on scholarship up here, but you've proven to me and the staff that you're an excellent ballplayer deserving a spot on the team. Congratulations, son," he said, shaking Troy's hand. "Now go on over there and talk to Coach Grady."

Troy gladly walked over to the assistant coach, who was standing near the bleachers.

"Young man, you're a hell of a ballplayer," Coach

Grady said, shaking Troy's hand. Troy struggled to hold in all of the joy he felt inside. "Let me tell you something, Potter. If you show in the games what you show in practice, you'll be in a good position to get some money, you hear?" Coach Grady informed him while patting him on his shoulder. Troy could not help cracking a gigantic smile when he heard about the money, since he was luckily in college with financial aid, university grants, and his mother's winning lottery payoff of $5,000. He told no one about that.

"What classes are you in, anyway, Potter?" the coach asked.

"I got chemistry, psychology, general writing, trigonometry, and a studying class," Troy answered excitedly.

"Well, how are you doing so far? 'Cause I want you to know, as soon as we start the season, you won't have time to catch up on things you left behind. We would hate to lose you for grades."

"Oh no, I've gotten straight A's so far. I'm having no problems," Troy retorted. He was extremely proud of his grades.

"Well, your Thanksgiving vacation is next week. So go home and rest, 'cause when we all get back, it's no bullshitting around, you hear?"

Troy nodded.

"Here's your number," coach Grady said, handing Troy another practice jersey. Troy opened up the jersey to number three. He didn't really want number three, yet he was too excited to complain.

"I told you I could make it with hard work, Mom! I studied hard, I practiced hard, I got a bunch of girls on me! Aw, Mom, college is it! I'm almost there, I can feel it! I'm gon' make it out, Mom. *Yes!*" Troy shouted, parading around his family living room. He was back home for vacation, elated about his achievements. His uncles, aunts, and cousins all stared and waited to ask him a bunch of questions.

"Hey, Troy, is it a bunch of people from Philly up there? My girlfriend is thinking about going to State U," his youngest aunt asked. Kim was only five years older than he.

"Yeah, I think we have the most people up there, besides the Blacks who commute from Marsh County," Troy answered.

"Yeah, I remember that real smart guy, Dutch, that I went to high school with was up there. And that boy ended up on drugs and went crazy years ago," Troy's oldest uncle mentioned. "He had bought some crazy stuff from some White boys up there, and he went out his damn mind," he informed them. Mark had lived a long, hard life. He had been in and out of jails and detention centers since he was fourteen years old. He was lucky to reach thirty-four.

"That's right. I remember that boy, real strange kid he was. Gon' go right up there and get fooled by them White boys," Troy's grandmother added, coming out of the kitchen. "You watch yourself, Troy, and make sure you stay in a group, 'cause that's one thing them White people hate is for a colored boy to make it out the ghetto," she said. Bessie Potter was a good-natured elderly woman with youthful energy. She was golden brown and had only a few gray hairs.

Troy's mother then decided to grab her son upstairs

to her room, where she could talk to him in private. She led him up the noisy wooden stairs. No one could sneak up those stairs. They entered her room, where Troy saw a small mouse slip into a hole next to the dresser. No big deal.

"How you feeling?" his mother asked him. She promptly prepared a spot for him to sit on the bed.

Charlotte had the same smooth, brown skin and pointed eyebrows that Troy had inherited. She had never married his father. She loved him dearly, but their relationship had never worked out.

"I'm feeling OK. College is aw'ight and all, I just hope I can keep it up," Troy answered, staring into his mother's calm face.

"Well, you keep up the good work, but watch out for those girls," she warned. "I remember when I was sixteen and a lot of my girlfriends used to try and get pregnant by college boys. Some of them did, too. But the only one that got one to marry her was this girl name Cindy.

"Cindy was a crazy, caramel-skinned girl with curly hair and green eyes. Guys were just dying to get her pregnant," Charlotte said, stopping to chuckle to herself.

Troy began to think about Lisa. He had rolled in the hay with her several times already.

"She had this real fine Indian-looking dude with thick black hair," his mother continued. "He was real well-dressed, too. I think his family had some money. But anyway, that man ended up losing his mind, beating her up and all.

"She had four daughters by him. Four *beautiful*

daughters. Two are around your age. They're all drugged up and pregnant now, just like their mother. So, I don't know how them girls are up there, but you watch out. And make sure you wear protection, 'cause you know all these diseases and whatnot are floating around." Charlotte smiled and patted her son on his left shoulder. "OK, that's all I wanted to talk to you about. And I love you."

Troy left the house to join his neighborhood partners after answering about twenty questions from his relatives. He was so excited that he stumbled up the steps and accidentally knocked the already-broken screen door off the hinges.

"Yo, Scooter!" he hollered, walking right in.

"Yo, Cool, I'm downstairs, man!" Scooter yelled from the basement. Troy went down the stairs to see Scooter, Raheem, and Blue, all smoking marijuana on the couch. They were watching a brand-new television set. It was a twenty-seven-inch console. Juice, the youngest, was knocked out and sitting by himself in an old, brown La-Z-Boy chair.

Scooter shook Troy's hand, happy to see him. "So what's up, Cool? You gettin' a bunch of drawers in college?" he asked.

Raheem and Blue continued to smoke, waiting for an answer themselves.

"Where that TV come from?" Troy asked, disregarding Scooter's question.

"That's Raheem's TV. He don't want his mom gettin' hyped about him sellin' drugs, so he got it and brought it over here," Scooter said. He was slightly shorter than Troy. He could almost pass for Peter's brother. However, only their appearances were similar. Scooter was no Peter, and Peter was no Scooter.

Troy looked at Raheem and smiled.

"So what's up, man? You get some sex, or what?" Raheem demanded as he smiled back. He was tan-skinned and slightly taller than Troy, with a clean-shaven face.

"Now, why you gon' ask me a stupid question like that? Y'all know damn well that wherever I go, I'm gon' get me some drawers," Troy snapped.

"You should have brought some pictures back, nigga," Raheem suggested. He took another puff of a joint and squinted his eyes.

"You trippin' now, 'cause you the only guy I know that's into pictures and shit. I ain't thinkin' 'bout no damn pictures."

"Did you stick any White girls up there? That's what I wanna know," Blue said. Blue was an extremely dark, handsome brown. He had deep-set eyes and a strong-boned nose. Blue sat next to Raheem, who commented before Troy could answer.

"Blue, you always worried about some White girls. What, you wanna marry one, man?" he quizzed. "You the blackest nigga in this basement and worried about White girls all the time. I know what you want, you tryin' to get some lightness out your black ass."

They all burst into rib-hurting laughter as Troy settled down to answer. "Naw, man. I ain't pop no White girls," he said.

"What, cuz, you can't get no White whores?" Scooter queried.

"Man, them White girls don't know what black

beauty is. They think we all ugly, I guess," Troy told him. "The fat and gruesome White girls be the ones trying to get with Black guys, not the pretty ones. I'm tellin' y'all now, it's hard as hell to get a good-looking White babe if you're Black. I think a lot of White girls would masturbate before sleeping with one of us."

"Naw, man, I think you just ain't tryin' enough," Blue insisted.

"I'm telling you, man, some Black dudes can get White girls, but it's usually them Black dudes that can act White and speak their fake-ass language. Man, we hard-core niggas from back here. What do we know about actin' White?" Troy paused to view their facial expressions. They all looked on as if they were learning something that would save their lives. Juice was still asleep.

"They fake as hell anyway, man. You know what dem White people are?" Troy asked rhetorically. "They're emotional liars and shit; smilin' and actin' all happy all the time. I got a cool roommate, though. But really, he's a funny, stupid-actin' Jewish dude."

"You got a Jewish roommate?" Scooter asked excitedly. "Shit, cuz, I'd rob his ass if I was you."

"Dig, cuz. Jews got money up the ass," Raheem agreed.

"Aw man, here we go. That's exactly why White people are scared of us now," Troy said.

"Man, look, fuck dat! Them White motherfuckers took everything from us. So why the hell shouldn't we rob them?" Raheem rebutted.

" 'Cause they gon' throw your ass in jail, that's

why," Scooter interjected. "I mean, I was just jokin' when I said that shit."

Raheem snickered at him. "Yeah, 'cause you's a coward anyway."

"Look, fellas, I got some good news," Troy interrupted. He went silent for a few minutes to make sure he had their full attention.

"Aw'ight, what, nigga?" Raheem asked, tired of waiting.

"Yo, I'm on the hoop team. I told y'all I would make it!" Troy said, expecting a burst of excitement. Yet they all just sat there, not budging.

"So you got a scholarship?" Blue asked.

"Not yet, but the coach said if I play well in the games, he'll hook it up."

Raheem frowned, disappointed. "You ain't gon' get no time without a hookup. You gon' be ridin' the pine," he predicted with a grin.

"We all gon' be watchin' the game down here and shit, and gon' see Troy, like, 'Yo, there go Troy on the bench, three seats from the coach. Yup, it's him, right there on the bench.' "

Troy felt stupid for opening his mouth. He wanted to punch his friend in the mouth, but he wasn't sure if he could beat Raheem. "Yeah, aw'ight, cuz, but I made the team. You didn't think I'd do that either," he responded to him.

"Yo, Troy, come get somethin' to drink, man," Scooter said. He walked up the stairs as Troy followed him to the kitchen.

"We got the crib all night. My peoples went to my aunt's house to fix it up for tomorrow's Thanksgiving

Day dinner," Scooter said, fetching Troy a glass to drink from. "Yeah, cuz, don't worry about dem niggas, man, dey nuts anyway. They ain't goin' nowhere. But you on the team, hunh? I knew you would make it. You the strongest-minded nigga here.

"I remember we told you to jump off that damn roof as a dare. You remember?" Troy nodded as Scooter continued. "Yeah, you damn near broke your fuckin' legs. You did it, though."

They laughed before calming down.

"Yup, Crazy-Ass Troy we used to call you. 'Don't ask Troy to do shit, 'cause he'll do it,' " Scooter added, giggling. " 'You can't keep that crazy nigga down.'

"I mean, you always did your own thing. That's why you made it out. You didn't get trapped into that group shit, like I did."

"Naw, Scoot, I ain't out yet. But when I do get out, I'm gon' get y'all, too, even if y'all do laugh at me now," Troy told him. "But what's been goin' on back here, man? What's the news?" he asked, looking positive again. He drank the juice Scooter had given him with one big swallow.

"Man, ain't shit going on back here. You the news, I guess," Scooter told him. "You wanna hear the news? Well, here's the news. Tommy got shot tryin' to steal a car up Nicetown. Malika, that freak babe, was on drugs and tried to sell her baby. That nice old lady that used to live around the street from us got mugged and had a heart attack.

"That ain't no fuckin' kind of news, man! You the news, Cool. You the only thing we got to talk about. And don't worry about Raheem and them, man, they just jealous. 'Cause as soon as the first games come on, the whole damn neighborhood gon' be watchin' you, man, and you know dat."

Scooter took a second to calm himself as he set Troy's glass in the sink. "Yeah, Troy, man, you keep workin' hard up there in college and make it out for all us. I want you to show dem White people that we can make it, man, even from the fuckin' ghetto."

CHANGING VIEWS

TROY COULD VISUALIZE THE EDGE OF A STEEP CLIFF, PROMPTing him to form a new outlook. The university had become his safeguard against the poverty and despair of home. His only concerns inside the university walls were studying, hanging out, romancing. and playing basketball. He started to think about never returning home, to the g-h-e-t-t-o.

Simon entered the room, throwing his luggage on the floor. "Hey, Troy, how are ya'? How was your holiday?"

Troy was stretched out on his bed, daydreaming. "It was aw'ight. Nothin' special. How was yours?"

Simon opened his suitcase across his bed to unpack. "Man, it was great! I didn't want to come back to college. I seriously felt like dropping out. You just don't know how close I was, Troy," he answered. "My friend back home, he's gonna travel to, like, Europe, Mexico, Jamaica, and Brazil.

"You should hear this guy. He's got it all mapped out already. I was really ready to go with him, but I had already paid to come here. So I said, 'Naw, ta hell with that.' "

"Yeah, well, I wish me and you could trade places, 'cause I would say, 'Ta hell with college,' and go."

"Oh yeah, Troy, you wanna?" Simon asked with a smile.

"Are you crazy, man? I don't have the money to do that."

"Yeah, well that's too bad, 'cause I wasn't going to go either. My dad paid too much money for me to go to college, to just throw it away."

"Look, man, since your mom and pops own their own shit, you could just work for them and you won't have to go to college," Troy suggested.

Simon continued to put his things away. "I don't wanna do that. Plus, I don't really like computers and I would die in law school. I'm thinking about owning my own consulting business, you know?"

"Naw, man, I don't know," Troy told him.

"Aw, quit pouting. You got better grades than me, *and* you're on the basketball team. You're in a much better position than I am," Simon said.

"You really are crazy," Troy commented. "I could never be in a better position than you. You're rich and fruitful compared to me. If I fail in college, I return to nothin'. But if you fail, you got your folks. And you're a White Jew anyway."

Simon hunched his shoulders and frowned. "What does that have to do with anything? If you work hard, you succeed. It's just as simple as that."

"Yeah, well, we gon' see, Simon. I'll always remember that you said that. It doesn't matter that I'm Black. If I work hard, I will succeed."

* * *

Next day, Troy had a group meeting with all C.M.P. students to discuss college integrity. Ninety percent of the C.M.P. students were Black. The event was monitored by the five C.M.P. counselors. Four of them were Black and one counselor was Latino. Three counselors were men and two were women, including Troy's counselor, Ms. Whatley.

"Today we want to have a group session to talk about your thoughts on college life so far. But before we start, I would like someone to answer something for me. Why did you come to college?" the short and stocky counselor named Paul asked.

A large, talkative girl was the first to answer. "I came to college to get a better job, which would put me in a higher economic position than what I am in now. I live in a nice home and all, but I want more."

The rest of the freshman class agreed as Troy looked around, spotting Doc, Bruce, Clay, James, Peter, Reggie, Tanya, Lisa, and Matthew, along with several other freshmen he had met through C.M.P.

A smaller sister picked up where the first left off. "Well, specifically, I wanted to come to a White college because I wanted to learn how to deal with White people, for when you go out into the real world. I grew up in an all-Black neighborhood, and I could have gone to a lot of Black schools, but I don't feel that that's a realistic situation. 'Cause when they step out of college, it's Whites who are hiring."

Her statement triggered Max, one of the other counselors, to comment. "Hey, wait a minute here," Max interjected, with a rumbling beer belly. "I graduated from an all-Black university. I still know how to deal with people. None of the people I know speak as if they're from another planet or dress funny. So why would that affect you in getting a job?"

The students roared with rebuttals to defend their young thoughts.

"It's a White world, so you have to learn how to deal with White people. It doesn't even make sense to go to a Black school," one student commented.

"Yup, 'cause I have a cousin in an all-Black school, and all she talks about is Black Power. I keep tellin' her she gon' have to deal with White people as soon as she gets out," another sister added.

"Well, I came to this White college 'cause I wanted to play football. The Black schools don't get no respect," Bruce added.

James had a rebuttal. "That's only because all the good Black players go to White colleges. They got the money and publicity. But if all Blacks decided to go to Black schools, they would have to get respect. Black players run ball better than Whites."

"You know, we all talking that 'I got to learn how to be with White people' stuff, but I don't see where we spend all this time being with them. I mean, although we're up here together, they do their thing, and we do ours," said a strong-spoken sister from the back row.

"Yup, that's true, 'cause I got *three* White roommates, and none of them hang out with me. I've even tried to hang out with one of them. She gave me the cold shoulder, so I said, 'Ta hell with you too, honey,' " another sister tacked on.

"Unh-hunh, 'cause my roommate tried to tell me that she was about to have company, like I was supposed to leave or something. I stayed right in my room and met all of her little girlfriends. She had the nerve to be mad, too, 'cause she damn sure don't speak to me no more.

"Excuse my mouth, but that just really pissed me off, you know?"

The Black women were taking over the discussion. The few White students didn't say anything. The discussion was quickly being transformed into one on college racism.

"Them White girls are a trip. They want you to help them with stuff, and then they don't want to help you when you're confused. This girl asks me all the time, 'How do you do this?' and, 'How do you do that?' And when I ask her something, she never knows anything, right. And I know she does, 'cause she gets straight A's on all her tests," the first talkative girl added.

"Look, all White people are not like that, OK? I mean, that's just that girl's problem. You can't say that every White person is like that," a defensive White student said, finally.

"Well excuuuse me, but ain't nobody say that all White people do it."

"Can I say something, here?" a well-spoken Black student asked, dressed in a vest, tie, slacks, and penny loafers. "OK, I grew up in the suburbs around predominantly White people, and I feel that a lot of times, Blacks have negative attitudes toward Whites. I've also noticed that I get more back talk from my own than I do from them."

His comments were snickered at because of his tone of voice.

"Well, we can see why. I mean, to tell you the truth, I'm real tired of people trying to say that if you don't speak like this guy here, that you're illiterate. I don't use slang, but I still sound like a Black person, and I *do* speak with the properness that I need to be comprehended by anyone. So that's bull. And I'll make sure that my children will never speak like him. I mean, if he called me up on the phone to talk to me, I would think he had the wrong number and hang up or something," a sister dressed in a black silk suit snapped.

The freshmen class scoffed in a frenzy.

"See, this is exactly what I'm speaking about. It's not my fault that I speak as I do, OK? I guess that my parents did not want me to grow up in some ghetto neighborhood."

"You know what, I ain't grow up in no ghetto, and I damn sure don't see where you came out any better than us. You can't even get along with your own people."

"I know. Who he think he is?"

"Word, right? How come this kid in C.M.P., then, if he's so much better off than us?"

After the discussion had ended, James drove Troy to one of his aunts on the west side of campus. State University was close to downtown, near the center-city shopping area.

"Yo, Troy, that discussion got wild as shit today, didn't it, homes?" James asked. They were going to watch the school's last regular season football game on cable television.

"Yeah, that one dude set it off," Troy mentioned.

James chuckled. "I know. Homes was stupid, though. I'm glad I wasn't raised in no suburb."

Troy nodded. "Dig. It's rough when you can't get along with your own people. As far as I'm concerned, his parents fucked his life up. All he can be with is White people now. He's like a sideshow for them. I mean, it's cool to want better housing and all, but you gotta let your kids know who they are, or they'll turn out like him every time."

James kept his eyes glued to the road. "Yup, homes." He then reflected for a moment. "I grew up right here, Troy, in Marsh County. This city has the most bridges in the world," he commented.

"How do you know that?" Troy asked. He observed the pleasant surrounding of trees and grass as they continued to travel. It was relaxing compared to Philadelphia's miles of urban row houses and concrete. Nevertheless, Marsh County was too quiet and kind of boring to him.

"I read about it in the encyclopedia," James said. "I used to be into stuff like that. This was rated the number-one city in the country."

"Who said that?" Troy quizzed, not believing it.

James laughed. "The national census," he responded. "Yup, they said it's the most livable."

"How can this city be the most livable when y'all got all these hills and shit here?"

"I'on know, homes, but it is. And your city got the longest street in the world."

"Yeah, Broad Street is kind of long."

"My man Troy knew exactly what I was talking about," James said.

"Hell, yeah. Broad Street runs through the whole city."

Realizing what words he used, Troy began to smile. "Man, Bruce got me sayin' that 'hell, yeah' shit. Now I forgot what I used to say. You know what I mean, cuz?"

James chuckled. "Your city got me sayin', 'You know what I mean,' all the time, homes," he said. "Yup, Troy, New York got the highest population of Black people, followed by Chicago and then, I think, Detroit, Philly, and Washington, D.C. They only got two Black areas here."

Troy sat quietly, enjoying the ride as James continued to express himself. "Homes, this city is racist as shit, though," he commented. "People that live here think it's all interracial and shit, but the truth is ugly.

"Check this out, homes. The White politicians separate the two major Black areas and break their voting power by making them vote with White people. That's their integration shit. That's why Marsh County can forget about having a Black mayor. Matter of fact, they only have one Black politician in the whole town. Now, you know that's fucked up.

"I grew up hating White people, homes, 'cause they would make you go to the White schools, where you'd be a minority. And them White boys be talking shit. I used to kick dere ass every day."

James paused, debating if he should tell Troy what he was about to say. He decided that he would. "I remember when I was five years old, and me and my mom went shopping at this White mall. My mom went to try on some clothes, while I waited for her outside the dressing room. This White boy tried to say she was stealing some dress. My mom told him that she didn't have the dress and that it was someone else's. He called my mom a 'lying nigger bitch,' and they started harassing her. They was pulling on her, and I was like, *'Get off my mom!'*—crying and shit, homes. But when we got home, my mom told my pop and uncles and shit, and they went and fucked dem White people up, homes, with bats."

James fell deep into his story as his eyes watered. "I started hating White people ever since. And I'm glad I got outta here, 'cause they be actin' like damn fools. These backward-ass niggas try hard as hell to be like brothers from New York, and yet they be hangin' out with White people."

They finally reached his aunt's house, just in time for dinner. It was a five-room brick home with a large lawn and a green picket fence. After his aunt answered the door, James introduced Troy and turned the game on immediately. The first quarter had just started.

"Look at all dem White fuckers on that team, homes," James said, stopping to set his plate on the floor. "Talk about being outnumbered; if their football team don't even have that many Blacks, then that school is really White," he added, referring to Brigham Young, who State University was playing in the Thursday night football game.

"It takes me out how all the Black athletes get used

in these White, racist-ass schools, homes. It seems like them big, dumb football players don't care about nothin'. They're too stupid, I guess, to understand their situation. 'Cause if you don't make the pros, it's all over wit'."

James stopped, only to swallow down some macaroni and ham before continuing. "We could of had this bad-ass Black quarterback at State U, but since he was Black, they asked him to play cornerback, and he left and shit. Troy, don't you know that boy is doing work now at West Virginia. He's only a sophomore now, ranked way higher than that garbage-ass White quarterback we got." And Troy listened as James talked all night long about "those damn White people" this and "those damn White people" that.

That Friday after basketball practice, Troy went to hang out with Matthew. Each time he would go to Matthew's room, he found Matthew studying at his desk. He would always take a break to chat.

"You study more than I do," Troy said to him, walking in.

"No I don't. We study about the same, 'cause I go jogging to release stress during the time that you're practicing. But yo, how come you don't hang out with them dudes on the basketball team, Troy?" Matthew asked, turning from his desk as usual.

" 'Cause, man, all dey do is talk about girls and ball. I'm a much deeper person than that."

"I know what you mean. After a while, it all gets kind of redundant. But did you speak to Peter since you've been back from Thanksgiving?" Matthew asked, as if something was wrong.

"Naw. Why?" Troy asked. He hoped that nothing had happened to Peter.

Matthew cracked a large smile, observing Troy's panic. " 'Cause, man," he said, shaking his head with a grin, "he came back after Thanksgiving talkin' about he was saved."

"Saved? Like, religiously?" Troy asked, breaking into his own grin.

Matthew began to laugh. "Yeah. So, like, I asked him what that shit meant, and he told me that he will serve his life for the Lord."

Troy frowned. "Aw man, what the hell is going on with him, cuz? First he's chasing around after all the girls in school. Now he wants to be religious."

"Ay', yo, he's serious, too, man. But you know what? I never was into that kind of stuff. I always thought that religion was for weak-minded people," Matthew commented.

"Yeah, that's the same way I think of it," Troy agreed.

Brrrloop brrrloop.

"Hello," Troy said, answering the phone. "Ay', yo, Mat, it's Pete. He wants you to sign him in."

"Word, now we can both ask him what's going on," Matthew responded, slipping on his shoes. He returned to the room shortly after with a happy-faced Peter. Troy wasted no time finding out what had changed his friend into a follower of Christ.

"Ay', Peter, man, what's going on with you, cuz?" he asked as soon as Peter entered the room.

"Well, I was home thinking, and something just gripped me and took control of me, restricting me from moving," he answered. "I felt real weird and started crying and all, and I began to pray. The Lord told me to follow his lead. I felt a great joy inside like I had been uplifted in happiness. I felt joy that you wouldn't feel in a hundred years. It was a great relief. Then I told my folks. They sat down and spoke to me about it. And I suddenly felt the strength to conquer whatever I had in my path. I decided then to do God's work."

Troy and Matthew just stood there in a daze.

Matthew spoke up first. "What do you need strength for, man? And what does that mean, you're going 'to do God's work'? You're only eighteen. I mean, exactly how much can you do?"

"First of all, there will be no adultery, no cheating on tests, and no parties. I will have total discipline and self-evaluation to get my work done," Peter answered happily. He appeared to be pleased to answer their questions.

"Come on now, Peter. Me and Troy do our work every day. Neither one of us is religious. It seems like you're taking more away than you're gaining, to me. I mean, is this to get you better grades, or what?" Matthew asked.

Troy sat and listened, trying to make sense out of it all. He still couldn't believe it. How is this nigga gon' just go home for a couple of days and come back saved? Troy wrangled to himself.

"Well, basically, it should help me to concentrate on what it is that I want to accomplish. At the same time, it should make me a better person in accordance to the Lord's teachings," Peter said to Matthew.

Troy finally decided to speak on it. "Peter, you were already the nicest, friendliest dude that anybody could know. You speak to everybody. Everyone likes you and can get along with you. I mean, to be truthful, man, I don't see why you're into this stuff."

"Troy, my brother, it's not just for me; the Lord wants all of his people to join him. You and Matthew should listen to me and hear my words."

Matthew laughed and blew his nose. Peter's lost his mind, he thought. "Look, fellas, I would love to finish this discussion, but I have a lot of work to do. So if y'all don't mind," Matthew said, still smiling. He stood up from his bed to show them out the door.

Peter and Troy left to continue their conversation in Troy's room after riding the elevator. Simon sat studying at his desk. He spoke as soon as they entered. *"Hey, Peter, how the hell are ya?"* he shouted. Usually, Troy found entertainment in Simon's vulgar tongue. In the present circumstance, however, he felt embarrassed. "Hey, Troy, man, some kid fuckin' stole my ball up at the gym today, so I took someone else's. Ta hell with that, man. I'm not leaving with nothin'. But this rotten-ass ball is a piece of shit compared to mine. I'll steal a better one tomorrow."

Troy laughed, forgetting how embarrassed he felt at first. "I didn't know White boys stole shit."

"Hell yeah! Nobody steals my ball and gets away with it. Somebody's gotta pay the piper," Simon said.

Troy thought, This White boy really is from Brooklyn.

Simon soon settled down, giving Peter a chance to speak. He looked at Simon with pity. "Well, like I was saying, my brother, I was weak to the trickery of the devil. Now I have the strength I need to fight him off and not fall into temptation," Peter said to Troy.

Simon eavesdropped with a keen ear as Peter continued:

"The devil has a lot of trickery in this world. You have to see through that before you can know the light of the Lord."

"How come the so-called Lord hasn't called on me?" Troy asked seriously.

Peter smiled. "The devil has ways of blocking a person's hearing while keeping you from the Lord, who is the truth of all mankind," he answered.

Simon smiled to himself at his desk.

Peter said, "Well look, Troy, I have just begun, but as I learn more about the Lord and his words, I can be better equipped to help my confused brothers." He left and went back to Matthew's room to be signed out, leaving Troy alone with Simon.

"Ay', Troy, Peter's religious or something now?" Simon asked, as soon as Peter had left.

"Yeah, cuz, ain't you?"

"Hell no! There ain't no God. If there's a God, tell him to come down here and speak to me then," Simon said humorously.

Troy laughed hard. "Man, I thought all Jews were into that."

"Yeah, everybody thinks that dumb shit. There are

three kinds of Jews. There are Orthodox, who *are* really into that shit, and Conservatives, who are a little bit. But I'm a Reformed Jew; that means I don't really give a fuck. I'm more into money.

"Shit, I'm just like any other American! I just have Jewish heritage, that's all." Simon then dug into some of his books, searching desperately for some literature he wanted Troy to see. "Aw fuck, I can't find it."

"You can't find what?" Troy asked him.

"A passage I had read about religious people," Simon responded, still looking. "You know, Troy, I learned in philosophy that only weak people follow that shit," he said, flipping through pages in his philosophy book. "Here it is. It says, 'Individuals who do not believe strongly in themselves believe more in outside forces.' "

"Damn, cuz, that's the same thing that me and Matthew said," Troy told him. He grabbed Simon's book to read the passage himself, before realizing something. "Yeah, but this is what some White person said. That would mean that most of my race is weak. I mean, what if there really is a God?" he wondered.

Simon tried to assure him. "Aw man, don't start worrying yourself about what Peter said. He was always weak anyway. You remember when we would let him use our room, and he could never get any girls, when he lived with them three guys? And yeah, he was scared to tell them to stop having fuckin' parties every night. He can't play basketball for shit, 'cause I've seen him. I mean, Troy, let's face it, he's weak. He fits right in with that religious shit."

* * *

Troy twisted and turned in his bed that night. The religious issue was getting to him. He felt that he was strong enough to lift his own cross. And what of his grandmother, the kindest woman in the neighborhood? Bessie Potter had always said, "I ain't no religious woman, but I do a lot more for *humankind* than most of them who are. 'Cause some of them *followers* can be as stingy and evil as they wanna be."

Why couldn't God judge humans on their merit?

Curiosity pulled hard on Troy's conscience. He could not seem to fall asleep. He wanted to find out, once and for all, what the truth was. If God wanted him to follow, why didn't he receive any signs? "Give me a clue that could change me," he asked the heavens.

It became an ultimate showdown between Troy and God. Troy could not sleep without knowing. His prayer was the first since he was seven years old and praying for a new bike on Christmas.

"Dear Lord, I don't know if I'm right in not believing in you, but I really want to follow. And if there is any way that you can help me, please do."

When he had prayed for the new bike, his dream had come true. But was that because his mother had already bought the bike?

There were no clues or signs that next morning when Troy awoke. The streets were still black, with yellow and white lines. His book bag was still green. He didn't feel particularly special as he walked to class in the cool breeze. White students still found difficulty in allowing him a pathway to walk as he weaved through and around them. He still felt alienated in his classrooms. And he began to feel a spiritual emptiness as well. God had not answered his call.

There was no light after praying. Nothing had changed. Nothing was different today than it was yesterday. So he began to think that maybe God had rejected him. Therefore, there was no God.

"Ay', yo, Mat, I prayed last night, man," Troy said quietly. He and Matthew sat eating inside the cafeteria.

"You did?" Matthew asked, setting down his sandwich to listen.

Troy noticed, all of a sudden, that a majority of Black students sat down and prayed before eating. Was it his sign? He didn't feel that it was big enough. Or maybe the sign was right in front of him all of the time and he had always ignored it. White students never prayed inside the cafeteria, though. And his Jewish roommate expressed a strong disbelief in God.

"You daydreaming or something, man?" Matthew asked, snapping Troy out of it.

"Oh, yeah, I was just thinkin' about somethin'."

"So you prayed last night, hunh?" Matthew repeated. "Well, what happened?"

"I couldn't go to sleep. So I asked to let the truth be known, and nothin' happened. But if you notice, a lot of Blacks are prayin' before they eat here. And White people don't, besides some of these Southerners."

"Yeah, I know. They get that from their families. And maybe you just don't see when White people pray," Matthew said.

"Yeah, maybe so. But do you notice how religious

people are all strict, and beat their kids' asses all the time? Like Peter. You can tell his family used to whip his ass, giving him low self-esteem, which would make him weak and cause him to run to the 'Holy Ghost' to give him strength," Troy said, philosophizing to validate his nonreligious position.

Matthew grinned. "Yeah, it does kind of seem like he came from one of those strict families that wouldn't let him do shit," he said. "I used to tell my mom that I was going out, and just leave. So I kind of had to build my own strength out in the streets."

"I know, man. Me too. I used to fight every day, cuz. My mom never let me get too far out of hand, though," Troy mentioned.

"Oh, naw, I'm not saying that I did everything, 'cause my mom used to catch me and warm my ass, too. She gave me a lot of freedom, though," Matthew retorted.

They chuckled as Matthew got up to leave. "I'll see you later, man. I gotta go to my next class, all the way across campus."

"Aw'ight, then, Mat, I'll catch you later."

When later had finally come, Troy had barber business to attend to. His floor's R.A., Charles Davison, needed a haircut badly.

"So how do you want your hair cut?" Troy asked him. He had already cut both James's and Doc's heads as they watched inside his room.

"Just give me a regular cut. Even it up all the way around, and shape it up," Charles said.

James began to laugh as he looked at his high-rounded, tapered haircut in the mirror. He felt it was comical for a person to want a plain, low haircut. Charles was funny-looking to him anyway.

"Ay', yo, homes, you don't get no tapers, hunh?" James asked with a smirk. Homes is a dickhead, he thought.

"No, I don't get those hoodlum-type haircuts," Charles answered.

James got hyper. "What, homes? Who said these were hoodlum haircuts? Man, I've been wearing my hair with a nice height since I was, like, seven years old. I don't know what you're talkin' 'bout," he snapped, peeking again at his hair. "Gon' call this a hoodlum haircut?"

James looked at Doc, who was smiling. Doc also had a high haircut, displaying his curly black hair.

"Ay', little brother, I'm tellin' you now. When you go to Whitey for a job interview, they ain't gon' hire you looking like that, unless you got curly hair like my man here. 'Cause he can wear his hair high without them sayin' shit," Charles said, referring to Doc.

"*What?* Homes, you must be crazy out your mind, talkin' 'bout what I gotta do for White people!" James shouted. "Why you gotta have curly hair to wear it high? You ain't my brother, homes. I don't wanna be a part of nobody who's ashamed of being Black!"

James would go on and on about race matters. He never dropped the issue. He continued even after Charles Davison had left. "You hear that shit homes said, Troy, talkin' 'bout I can't wear my haircut because of these White motherfuckers? That makes me mad to hear a brother say some shit like that. He's already given up the fight against White people."

Troy nodded. "Yeah, that's the same dude who was makin' a damn fool out of himself when I first got here. You know how White boys laugh at stupid shit. Well, he was in the bathroom at this floor meeting, actin' like a clown for them."

James shook his head in disgust. "Troy, man, I'm tired as hell of hearing about how we got to do all this extra shit for White people. They don't have to change for us. That's why I hate White people, homes! We got our own fuckin' cultures, and they ain't important because White people say so!" James shouted with tears in his eyes.

"The real world is like that, though. White people own everything. They don't have to change for us. They're the ones doin' the hiring," Doc said, as though it was an old and boring argument.

"Naw, fuck that, man! That's why, when I get paid, I'm gon' buy up some land and let money fall in my lap," James said, irritated. "See, it's too many Black people up here thinkin' about gettin' a regular job. If you really want to get ahead, you gots to own things."

James stopped only when he realized it was time for his night class. "Yo, homes, sign me out. I got a class to go to."

Troy signed Doc out as well and returned to his room to set up for two more customers. He first signed in John, a Black student from the suburbs. Later he signed in Peter.

"Hey, John, what's up, man? I didn't know you knew my brother Troy," Peter said, as soon as he spotted John in the chair.

"You two are brothers?" John asked. "I had no idea of that."

"Yeah, we're all brothers," Peter responded.

"Yeah, OK," John said, not knowing what he was talking about.

Troy frowned, finishing up his haircut.

"Are you a follower of the Lord, brother John?" Peter asked.

"No, but if there is a God, I hope he likes me."

Troy laughed, in no mood for religious lessons. He hoped Peter didn't have any.

"Ignorance is the route to all evil," Peter commented.

John started to feel annoyed.

"Ay', look, man, don't come down here messin' with my customers with that religious shit," Troy stated in John's defense.

The situation was useless. Peter kept talking about the Lord. It only got worse with argument. So Troy finished up John's haircut and began on Peter's after signing John out.

"Ay', Peter?"

"Yes, my brother."

Troy shook his head, sickened every time Peter uttered "my brother." It was starting to get on his last nerve. "Anyway, man. This dude was in here today, and he said that Jay shouldn't get a high haircut because the White employers will think he's a street hood."

"What brother said this?" Peter asked, grimacing.

"This Black R.A. named Charles Davison. He's a senior."

"Yeah, well the way I see it, a haircut is trivial. You mean to tell me that just because I wear a high haircut, I won't be hired for a job? What, my résumés and grades are no good? What if you're a straight-A student and you happen to have a high haircut? You don't get the job? Naw, my brother, that's crazy. It doesn't make any sense." Peter laughed softly for the first time in days. "Yo, man, this brother needs help, 'cause I wear a high haircut too, not to be a hoodlum, but because it's my preference."

Troy wore a high haircut as well. He was proud of being Black and having brown features. He was also happy that Peter didn't seem to change his views on his blackness. For some reason, Troy had previously felt that being religious had no room for being Black. The jubilation made him reveal his prayer.

"You know what, Pete? I prayed last night, but nothin' happened," he said, sneezing.

"God bless you," Peter said. "So you prayed last night, hunh, my brother?" he queried with a grin. "Well, what did you expect to happen?"

"I thought I would feel this big impulse like you claim you did."

"It doesn't work like that. God gives everyone a choice to live for him or to perish in hell with the devil."

"Why can't I just live for me, my family, and my people? Why is God gonna make us live for him or die?" Troy asked. He was starting to feel frustration.

"That's just it, my brother. God doesn't make you do anything. You have a choice."

"Well, what kind of a choice is that? It sounds like

we have a choice to be a puppet for God or for the devil, to me. If I don't follow God, I'm going to the devil. So every time I do something wrong, it was the devil, Pete. Is that what you want me to believe?"

"My brother, the devil can only influence you to do things. You determine if you want to do them or not."

"Aw man, fuck it then! God is real selfish if he expects us to just live life like that. Why didn't he just make us into mindless robots? It ain't no God. Black people just don't believe in themselves, so they run to all this religious shit and catch the 'Holy Ghost,' " Troy said, giggling away his tension.

Simon walked in as he continued: "It ain't no damn God, man. I don't believe that stupid shit. It's all dumb."

When Troy finished cutting Peter's hair, Peter got up angrily and put his coat on, leaving $6 on Troy's bed. "You know what, Troy, I hate to see you be lost to the dark roads that lie ahead, so I'm gon' pray for you. And by the way, I'll sign myself out."

Peter left disappointed in Troy. He thought that Troy, of all people, would be able to see the light. Troy had helped him more than anyone else on campus. Peter thought that Troy cared a lot about people. As he closed the door, he shut it softly enough to give his friend a conscious message.

Simon looked at Troy as soon as Peter disappeared. He was ready for a chat about it. "Hey Troy, Peter's really serious about that religious stuff, isn't he?"

"I guess so, man. He ain't backin' down at all."

Simon shook his head. "There ain't no God, Troy. And Jesus Christ was a regular man with a crazy dream that he was a messenger. OK, if there is a God, why don't *he* cut Peter's fuckin' hair?" Simon said humorously. "Now stop looking all sad and shit, wouldja."

Troy thought about it. "I'on know, man. I hate being wrong, especially about something as deep as religion."

"Yeah, yeah, you're Black, too, so you're weak-minded, just like the rest of 'em," Simon responded. He laughed and put his earphones on, stretching out on his bed.

"Yeah, well ta hell with you too, Simon. You damn Jew."

MISERY

THE COACH HAD SAID THAT PRACTICE WOULD GET ROUGH when the season neared. He said he would run ten pounds of sweat off of each fat-ass. Water bottles were minimal, breaks were cut in half, and mistakes were not tolerated. It was time for the true men of the game to show their colors.

"Come on, Potter, push it up. This is not the time to get tired! Do you want to take someone's job on this team, or what, young man? Show me right now what you want out of this ball club! This isn't high school, son!"

The coach shouted up and down the court, trying to inflame the fire in each player's blood.

"Damn it, Morris! Get in there quicker and box the man out! 'Cause let me tell you, son, when you're up against Georgetown, they're not gonna wait for your sorry ass to decide when you want to work in the middle for a rebound! And Hecker, the next shot you miss like that, you'll be watching all year, son! Those are not the kind of shots that guys at your level should be missing!"

Finally, Troy received a short break while the next group of guards practiced.

"Yo, Potts, I'm getting tired of this dumb shit, man. We should be practicing more plays and perfecting 'em. All he tryin' to do is make us sweat," Morris said. "I'm tellin' you, man, I'm 'bout to say, 'Ta hell with this team,' and go play ball for Florida State. They was gon' give me more money anyway, and it's closer to home. But naw, I wanted to come to State 'cause they had national rep."

Troy listened, barely. The bulk of his attention was on a light-brown-haired White girl who watched them practice.

"Yeah, man, I know. It gets on my nerves, too. But, cuz', who's that bad-ass White girl in the bleachers?"

Morris looked and smiled. He was taller than Troy, with long, lanky arms and legs. "That's this white hoe that Dave is pimpin'. She be around his crib all the time. These white hoes will be dying to give up the panties when the season starts."

Troy smiled, as his teammate continued: "Man, I never had a White girl in my life before I started runnin' ball up here. But now, I know, like, hundreds of 'em," Morris commented. They started to laugh and the coach caught them.

"You two, what the hell are you laughing at? You give me twenty laps around the court after practice, on the clock, since you both got something to laugh about! You think this is a damn joke out here, do ya? We'll see how hard you two laugh after the season starts!" the coach screamed.

By the time Troy got back to his dorm, he was exhausted, falling out across his small, twin-sized bed.

"Practice is gettin' hard as hell, Simon, just like the coach said it was. And it's Friday, too."

Simon was at his desk doing much needed homework. "Yeah, well, you don't get to be a star for nothing," he responded. "I still can't believe that my roommate is actually on the basketball team. It's unreal. I mean, what if you go to the pros and I see you on TV and all? I'll say, 'Hey, that guy there was my roommate in college,' and probably nobody would believe me. Hell, I could even be your agent, Troy!"

Simon faced him wearing a huge smile.

Troy shook his head. "You know what, man, you White people take me out. Y'all don't care a damn thing about Black people unless they're a star or something. Then y'all run around like assholes just 'cause you know somebody on the basketball or football team."

"So the hell what?" Simon asked, laughing. "Race doesn't have anything to do with it. Anyone who is a star will be wanted."

"Yeah, that's true, but I can't help noticing how you White people act, since I've been up here damn near four months now. I just can't help reactin'. And I'm the most liberal of all my boys. So I know they can't make it up here with you fuckers."

"Aw man, shut up. I'm studying," Simon said jokingly. "Oh yeah, Troy, your boy Doc called and said he'll be here around nine, to pick you up for the party."

Troy nodded and picked out an outfit for the night.

"Ay', Troy, come on, man. Why you always gotta be late?" Doc asked. He was growing impatient. He had already waited longer than an hour for Troy. "The party started at nine. It's ten minutes till eleven," he pouted.

"Look, Doc, when you walk in real late, you draw the attention of all the people who wanna see who's comin' in next," Troy told him.

Doc sucked his teeth. "Yeah, right. By then all the dudes in the party will have the best girls already."

Troy pulled his Polo shoes from underneath his bed.

"Those are some nice tennis shoes," Doc mentioned.

"What? Man, these ain't no tennis shoes. These are casual sneakers, the kind you see in *GQ* magazine. And if you see anyone playing tennis in these, they crazy. Niggas don't play tennis anyway."

Doc chuckled.

"Oh yeah, Doc, is that girl with the green eyes gon' be there?" Troy asked him.

"Yeah, man, I told her about you. She's probably in the party now," Doc said, looking out the window. There was a crowd of students, eighteen stories down and strolling on the sidewalk. "See, man, come on, you wastin' time. You already look as pretty as you gon' get," Doc persisted. He then turned and watched Troy in the mirror, admiring himself. His thin mustache was starting to grow in fuller.

"Ay', Doc, man, it's funny, 'cause my mother was telling me about some girl with green eyes, back in the day. And she went on a college campus to get knocked up by some college dude."

Doc laughed before he responded. "This girl don't go to college either. She might try to do the same shit to you."

Troy grinned. "Naw, man, I use rubbers, *all* the time. Ain't no girl gettin' knocked up by me until *I'm* ready," he declared. He tugged on his long, brown leather coat to head to the party. As usual, they sneaked in by creating fake stamps on their hands.

"Hey, what you say, Troy? Where you been all week?" Bruce asked. He was always the first to greet Troy upon entry, as though he was waiting for him. He smiled and patted Troy on the shoulder.

"I've been studying for finals and practicing up at the gym," Troy answered. He observed the crowds while they walked around to see how many good lookers they could entice for a future date. Troy was pleased that it was packed, although his cool demeanor didn't show it.

Several sisters had their eyes on him. Troy felt lightheaded, shaking the hands of the many guys who respected him. It seemed that every brother at State U knew at least his name. He had become quite popular from taking cuties home with him on the weekends. He also had a reputation for not calling them back.

Troy felt that he was too smooth, freshly dressed, and too smart to be turned down. He could imagine himself in movies with screaming fans and constant women. Yet it was no longer exciting. He no longer felt those irresistible urges of first-sight lust. Women were no big deal to him now.

He spotted Ms. Green Eyes, well dressed and with a pack of her girlfriends. She wore a yellow turtleneck and a yellow sweater. Her sweater had four equally spaced black diamond-shaped designs on the front, matching her black leather minskirt. She wore black leather boots and Troy noticed that one of her girlfriends held her long rabbit-fur coat. In a word, she was fabulous!

Troy began to wonder how he could lure her away from her girlfriends. He knew he would have to impress them. Yet he had a new fear. He had earlier decided that he would try and go for the gusto on the first night. He had met Tamara before, briefly, through hanging out with Doc. And he suspected that she wanted him.

"Ay', Bruce, you see that girl with the yellow sweater and the black leather skirt?" Troy pointed his right index finger to the left, across his body, in an attempt to camouflage.

"Naw, man, what girl?" Bruce asked, looking in the wrong direction.

"Not that way, man. Look at where my finger is pointing."

"Oh, my fault," Bruce said, chuckling. He peeped in the right direction and spotted her. "Oh, cuz, she bad as hell," he responded.

"I'm tryin' to decide how to get her away from all her girlfriends," Troy told him. "It must be about six of 'em. I ain't tryin' to have all those girls up in my face."

"Word, cuz. I know what you mean. I'on like that shit either," Bruce agreed.

Either it was luck or just meant to be, but Green Eyes happened to look in their direction. Troy gave her a fast finger motion for her to come to him. He thought that she would wait until her new dance was over. Yet she stopped, whispered something to her partner, then to her girlfriends, and began to walk toward him. Instead of feeling overjoyed, Troy began to feel more vainglorious and engineering. He felt like he could do anything. He headed away from where he stood, slow enough to allow her to follow, into an unattended corner where he could lay his game.

"Sit down right here," he directed. He looked her over from head to toe, as if she were a platter at a restaurant. Her seductive smile made him believe, definitely, that he could score on the first night. "What time do you have to be home tonight?" he asked her.

"I don't have to go home, if I don't want to."

"Oh yeah? Well make sure you get with me after the party if you wanna stay over." Troy felt the game would end or continue after her response. If she declined, he would feel the shock of a challenge that he longed to have. If she agreed, he would feel, although happy that he had succeeded, a lack of respect and a touch of pity.

"I'll see you after the party, then," she answered with a smile.

After signing Tamara out, Troy returned to his room, finding Simon wide awake and waiting for him.

"Hey, Troy, man, this is it. I'm tired of you keeping girls over here all night." Then he smiled. "She was one pretty girl, though, I'll tell ya that."

Troy chuckled to himself, modestly. "Yeah, man, that girl told me she has a baby, and she's only seventeen. Everybody told me she was down. I really don't understand her, though, man, as pretty as she is. But fuck it, I'm goin' down to eat breakfast."

"Yeah, well bring me up a bagel," Simon said.

"That's another thing I've noticed; you White people love bagels," Troy commented, leaving.

Inside the cafeteria there were no other Black students up yet. Troy was the only one who had made it up after the party so early. He realized that it had been the same every week. He would be the only Black up early and eating breakfast, until he was almost finished. A bunch of other colored faces would float around later.

Out of boredom, Troy began to watch the half-dressed White girls. He felt a strong and sudden craving to have one. Nevertheless, they still seemed like virgins. They seemed somehow untouchable to him.

Yet and still, White girls conveyed a certain looseness. They appeared positive and gay. Troy's curiosity for their flesh increased by the second. He felt a challenge. I wonder if I can get a White babe, he mused. And of course, he would want top choices.

"Here's your stupid bagels, man," Troy said, returning to his room.

Simon was watching an early college football game with big, bright green eyes. "Hey, great, Troy! Thanks a lot, man."

"Yeah, yeah," Troy responded, thinking of the news he had to tell. "You know what, Sime, I think I wanna pop a White girl. I mean, they been walkin' around here every day, and I haven't even tried one yet. It's thousands of 'em up here. And it's not that I'm really interested in your girls, I just wanna see if they feel different or something."

"Go for it, man. They'll probably be with it. You're kind of cute, and you're on the basketball team. Oh yeah, you can score. Easily!" Simon assured.

"Oh, since I'm on the basketball team, hunh?" Troy responded.

That Monday morning, Troy began to observe the race of which he was not a member to see if there were any instances of inner discrimination among Caucasians. He had already taken a liking to an olive-complexioned, black-haired student in his chemistry lecture.

Late as usual, she stomped into class making extra noise and turning heads. The classmates would turn, only to see who it was, before paying attention to the lecture and taking notes.

She was beautiful to Troy. He had always noticed her, even without the noise she regularly made. Maybe she was angry at the world for having darker hair and darker skin than her peers.

Her eyes always seemed to follow a sandy-haired guy who was a cheerleader for the football team. He sat next to his blond-haired girlfriend.

Blonds had more fun because no one White paid any attention to the dark-haired girls, although Troy felt they were prettier. They had fuller, more contrasting features. And over the next few days, he continued to watch his Caucasian classmates in their social behavior.

"Ay', what's up, Joe?" Troy asked, setting his tray of food down inside the cafeteria.

"Nothing much, Troy. What's up with you?" Joe

said, already seated and eating lunch. Joe was tan-skinned, with slick wavy hair that he combed to the back, the Duke Ellington look.

"Ain't nothin' goin' on, man," Troy told him. "Ay', man, I noticed that you get along with White people pretty good," he mentioned, expecting a response to start a discussion on the topic.

"Yeah, I went to a high school where the population was, like, half and half," Joe said.

Troy nodded. "I went to an all-Black school. I can't talk to them White people too much. It seems like they're actors to me." He took a sip of soup. "Their personalities don't seem real. My roommate is cool, though."

Joe nodded back to him, chomping on his tuna sandwich and wiping the sides of his mouth with his napkin. "It was the same way with me. But I've learned how to bullshit around with them."

"Tell me somethin', though," Troy asked. "Do you, umm . . . find White girls attractive?" He lowered his voice. He didn't want anyone to hear him talking about finding Whites girls attractive.

"Some of 'em," Joe responded aloud. "Like, before I went to high school, I couldn't judge a White girl. I grew up in an all-Black neighborhood. But after I was around them and all, the ones I liked, the White boys called them fat."

Troy laughed. "I know. They like real skinny women."

"And another thing," Joe went on, "I like the White girls that have tone, like Italian and Spanish women. But White boys said that they're boring. Blond hair and blue eyes are beauty, to them. I don't understand it," he commented. "Like, a lot of White guys I know can't tell when a Black girl looks good. And I was like, 'What?' They all seem to like Whitney Houston, though."

Later that night, Troy spotted Clay studying inside the library. He began on the same topic, about White girls.

"Yo, what's up, Clay? You studying hard, hunh?" he asked. He scanned the area to see who was sitting near them.

"Yeah, man, I'm studying this algebra for the final comin' up," Clay told him. "You, Mat, and Jay are lucky, man, 'cause this C.M.P. stuff is just gettin' in my way." Clay wore the typical high Philadelphia haircut, and his mustache and beard were starting to thicken since enrolling in college.

"Yeah," Troy said, still looking around. He spotted an Asian woman with jet black hair, all the way down her back. "Ay', Clay, you see that girl over there?" he asked, pointing to the nearby desk.

"That Chinese girl?" Clay said, making sure.

"Yeah. Do you like that hair she has?"

Clay's eyes lit up. "Aw, man, I wish I could find a Black girl like that, 'cause we'd get married. But you know what, though, Troy? White guys don't like that. It's this black-haired babe in my economics class, and White boys don't pay her no mind. They act like she got a disease," Clay told him. "And don't let a brother try to talk to her. Her type don't seem to like us at all up here. It's like, when they come to college, everybody's looking for White boys," he added.

"It's like, if you're Black, you can't get nothin' but your own."

Clay smiled and tossed a hand on Troy's shoulder. "But you're on the hoop team, Troy. You should be in good shape when the season starts. *You* can get whoever you want then."

Troy smiled as James walked up to join them. He was passing out membership cards.

"What are these?" Troy asked after receiving one.

"They're for BAR, a Black activist group that fights racism on campuses across the country. I'm trying to get enough brothers to join so we can set up a chapter at State. It stands for 'Brothers Against Racism,' and all we need is, like, twenty brothers to set up a chapter."

Troy handed the membership application back to him. "Naw, man, I'm already playin' basketball and studyin'. I ain't got no time for that. Besides, what can that do for me?"

Clay wanted to hear an answer for that too.

James cleared his throat. "Look, homes, this college only has one group for Blacks, so we're trying to set up an alternative for students to have more functions on campus," he answered. He was slightly angered by Troy's question. "Now look, all we have to do is give five dollars each for us to start a chapter. Then we'll have trips to other campuses, and we can start contacting more Black speakers through networking functions."

Troy and Clay sat speechless, contemplating as James continued.

"Matter of fact, Troy, other than the parties, I haven't seen you at any Black functions. I've seen Clay, but not you."

"Aw man, 'cause I've been runnin' ball and studying."

James faced Clay and began to laugh. "That's just what we were talkin' about in a meeting last Thursday. It's too many Black athletes talkin' about they too busy to get involved. Y'all gotta understand that you are being used, like everybody else," he said to Troy. "Intelligent brothers like you are sellin' out the race by not wanting to back anything or participate, homes."

"I'm down," Clay said, pulling a five-dollar bill out of his pocket.

Troy shook his head defiantly. "Y'all can have that shit, man. I never did like the NAACP and shit like that. They always looked like a bunch of rich niggas to me, fightin' against stupid shit like flags."

"I don't think you see the importance of it yet," James pressed. "A lot of Blacks need to be informed about these organizations, especially the youth."

"OK then, Jay. How many other people joined this thing?" Troy quizzed. He challenged James to tell him something other than what he was thinking.

"Well, a lot of people are involved in other things and—"

Troy cut him off. "See, man, ain't nobody down to join that shit. We already have too much to worry about, just gettin' grades and finances."

In defeat, James left Troy and Clay to finish their discussion. He couldn't understand why Troy would turn him down on joining a Black campus organization. He didn't know that Troy had gotten to college by deviating from groups. His individualism had allowed him to become strong-minded. James also didn't know that Troy feared groups. He had learned to survive as an individual.

The following weeks of school were filled with finals. Again, Troy missed the importance of togetherness. He studied hard and long for his test while other students studied in groups, having an easier time at scoring good grades. Troy didn't care. As long as I got mine, he insisted.

"All right guys, it's the first game of the season. You guys have worked your tails off, now we start the fun part. I want quick, good shots and boxing out under the boards. Their guys are quick, but small, so I want to use our height advantage. And remember, the key to winning the game is to have few turnovers and to execute. Now let's get out there and do the job. Talk is cheap," the coach said.

"HOORAY! YEAH! WHISSWEEERRR! COME ON! YEAH!"

The students, alumni, and local fans yelled and whistled as the band played in the stands. Troy felt a surge of pride, practicing in the team warm-up. His shots were crisp and accurate, missing only three out of twelve. He felt that, surely, he would get some time in the game.

The tip-off was swiped by Georgia Tech. They scored immediately. Troy had a bad feeling about the game already. Things never looked up. The guards were nervous, appearing unprepared. Troy eyed the coach several times, dying to get his chance. Yet the coach never looked his way. He continued to watch the incompetent guards, who supposedly represented the best of the team. Troy realized that they were not as skilled as he was, but *they* had scholarships.

At halftime, State U was down 47-38. The head coach was furious.

"*God damn it!* No one's doing anything that was planned for this game! No one's boxing out, so there's no rebounds! You're not getting back on defense, so we're getting killed on fast breaks! And how the hell do you guys think you're gonna win a ball game if you're missing open shots? We're lucky that we're only down by nine, I'm telling ya. The way you guys are playing is truly pitiful, like we haven't even practiced."

He continued his reprimand throughout halftime, only to return and lose the first game of the season by twenty-one points. The first home game, lost, without Troy seeing a second of playing time.

"I'on know now about this basketball team. Did you see how the guards were messin' up? And the coach *still* wouldn't put me in the game. It don't make no sense, Simon." Troy sulked while pacing in his room. "I'm the better man, but I can't get a chance 'cause they all got scholarships."

Simon frowned. "I mean, Troy, come on, this was only the first game," he told his moping roommate.

Troy let out a deep breath. "Yeah, you're right. I gotta learn to hang in there. But I can't stand waiting to show what I already have. That don't make no sense. I'm qualified now, so why the hell do I have to wait while those scholarship dudes make us look bad?"

"Look, Troy, a lot of guys would kill just to be on the team. You made the team, so now you just have to stick it out and see what happens."

"Yeah, aw'ight, Sime. I'on know if I can take too much of this, though. I feel like I'm being cheated out of my time."

Basketball practice was harder and longer than before. Stress began to rise as Troy found his dream to play in the NBA fading. The next couple of games were replays of the first. He and the coach began to have arguments when Troy pressed to be utilized. Sitting on the bench and losing every game didn't settle well with his friends back at home either. They watched the first televised game, only to see their neighborhood partner being sold out to a team of sloppy scholarship players who were not getting the job done.

"I told you they was gon' jerk Troy around. Walk-ons never get no time. And this team has *a bunch* of scrubs," Raheem said disappointedly. "I'm tellin' you, man. Walk-ons go out for the team, make it with talent, and get jerked. It happens all the time."

"It looks like the team is the only Black people in the college," Blue said. "All you see is White people in the stands and shit. I wonder if Troy screwed a White girl yet," he pondered, watching the all-White cheerleaders at halftime.

Scooter shook his head in disgust. "Man, you know Troy's mad as hell right now, cuz. He don't like riding nobody's bench. Even if it's a championship team, he wants to at least get in. Some walk-ons do get time, though. Troy just has to hang in there."

After the fifth game, however, Troy's confidence was sinking. Hard work had gotten him on the team, but economics and politics kept the others playing.

Troy felt like quitting. The coach had misled him. A scholarship was far-fetched, at best. How could he show his prowess and be awarded a scholarship if he didn't even receive a chance to play?

The first school term had ended. Troy called home only on Christmas and New Year's. The team had had games and practices during the vacation, only to start a season of misery. Troy did happen to make the acquaintance of a handful of White girls. But it was simply from being on the team, as everyone had foretold.

"So you met a few white chicks, hunh, Troy?" Simon asked, smiling.

Troy sat in a usual studying position at his desk. "I met some goofy ones, but I'm not really worried about that now. I'm thinking about quitting the team and concentrating on my studies."

Simon shrugged. "If that's what will make you happy, then do it. But don't start crying when you realize that you blew your chance."

"What chance, Simon? Most Black athletes come out to these big White colleges to be used, and then end up being a street cleaner or something," Troy argued. "Shit! My boy Jay was right. I have a good head on my shoulders, so I should put it to work. But, ummm . . . I'on know, man. I'on care about nothin' no more. I like playin' ball, but *everything* seems like it's falling apart now because the basketball team was a flop. I wonder what they wanted me there for," he pondered, tapping a pencil against his book cover.

"Damn, Simon. Life is a hard thing to get through," Troy commented. "All kinds of little stuff can get to you. Especially when you want it all." He stood up, kicked off his shoes, and stretched out on his unmade bed to stare up at the ceiling.

"Well, stop wanting so much," Simon suggested.

"That's easier said than done. I don't think there would be half as much depression in the world today if people didn't want stuff. Like, if you could cut off that portion of your brain, then everyone would fall into a long span of happiness. And there would be nothin' to make you sad.

"Like us, Simon. We sittin' in here every night, bustin' our brains out for the future, because we don't have any choice, if we wanna live good. Then again, *you* have a choice. It's easier for White people, you always got something to fall back on. And sometimes, man, I just feel like throwing up my hands and quittin', like, 'Fuck it all!' "

"Yeah, well I got news for you, Troy. You may not believe it, but even us 'rich' White people feel like that sometimes. And what about poor White people? They don't have anything to fall back on," Simon said.

Troy sucked his teeth. "Man, the only thing poor White people need is money. Now shut up and listen to your music."

Troy's desperation for happiness was not in a vacuum. It seemed everyone around him was having tough times. In fact, most of his peers figured he was doing well.

"Troy, you got a three-point-seven G.P.A., you're on the basketball team, *and* you get all the girls you want. I wish I was in your shoes, homes," James mentioned while getting his hair cut. "My grades were terrible, man. I feel like I might as well start over. I wanted to cry when I saw my grades, homes. They were the worst grades I've ever gotten in my life."

James tried to will away his sorrow but couldn't. "I was thinking about becoming a lawyer. But after my grades, I don't know what I'm gonna do. It just makes you feel like dropping out of school."

All week long, Troy heard more of the same sob stories. Even when he went to shoot the breeze with the counselors at Pratt Hall, he walked into more bad breaks.

"I'm telling you, Paul, I can't take it no more. I've been in this system for twelve years, and ain't got a promotion the first," Max was saying when Troy eased into his office. "I could work for the public school system and make more than I could *ever* get here. Unless this university starts paying us what we're worth, I'm out of this C.M.P. shit."

"Max, you always saying that same stuff, day in and day out. You ain't never gon' leave this place, man. I mean, yeah, you probably could make more money working for the public school system, but you can't be sure that you gonna get the position you're asking for. Besides, Max, you love this place," Paul said. They then recognized Troy, who sat quietly in a chair near the door.

Max and Paul were both short and stocky. They could pass for athletes or gym instructors. Yet they were approaching forty and growing gray hair.

"Ay', Troy, I hear you got a three-point-seven, man. That's kicking it out," Paul commented.

Max turned and shook Troy's hand. "Troy, we need Blacks like you here. You can show these White people that we can excel in something other than sports."

After chatting briefly with them, Troy went to speak with Ms. Whatley, who was also having a downing discussion in her office.

"Dawn, I told the girl that I had originally graduated with a degree in administration, and that I wasn't trained to be a counselor, but I took the job anyway. Well then the girl tried to let me down easy. You know how the White people are: 'Well, I'm extremely sorry, but we have only one position, which you don't really qualify for.' I mean, it doesn't seem to matter what you do, you *never* qualify," Ms. Whatley was saying. She shook her head, disappointed. "Now see, that Black girl who got the other position down there knew somebody. But if you don't know anyone, there's nothing you can do about it."

"Pam, they don't think any Blacks are qualified, for real. It just goes to show that you have to know somebody," the counselor named Dawn said before leaving. "And thank God for affirmative action, because without that, none of us would have a job. I'll be in my office if you need me."

Ms. Whatley gave her attention to Troy, who had been waiting patiently. "Well, Mr. Potter, you made honor roll while on the basketball team. No one, I think, has done that," she said. "No one who was Black, anyway.

"You and Mat had the highest averages on the dean's list from all the C.M.P. students," she added.

"What was Mat's G.P.A.?" Troy asked.

"Aah, Mat got a three . . . point-eight-two," she said, trying to remember. Troy remained silent, figuring that she would tell him some other information. He was not usually interested in other people's business, but he would listen to *anything* that wasn't negative in his state of woe.

"So are you going to the banquet, Troy?" she asked him.

He nodded. "I didn't wanna go, but I called my mom, and she said it might help me in the future to let my face be known."

Ms. Whatley nodded back to him. "She's right. It's highly important that you get in with people. Trying to do it alone is the hardest thing you'll ever want to do."

Troy left the C.M.P. offices and found Clay, sweeping up floors on the bottom level of Platt Hall. He wore a green campus uniform with an identification card on his shirt pocket.

"Ay', Clay, you got a job here, hunh?" Troy asked, smiling.

Clay stopped to take a break. "Yeah, man, everybody can't be a self-employed barber like you. Some of us have to work in the system. I heard that you and Matthew on honor roll up here, though," he mentioned.

"Yeah, I worked hard for it, but I'm still not happy," Troy glumly said.

"Aw man, shut up. You sound like the White people. I don't believe you actually gon' stand here and tell me that you're not happy after getting a three-point-something."

They started to laugh as Clay continued: "You sound just *like* them White people. Them mugs be talkin' that mess all the time: 'Oh my God, Clay, I didn't study for this test at all. I'm gonna get an F, I just know it.' Then after the test, they get, like, an A-minus, talkin' 'bout they got lucky. And they're always downgrading the teachers: 'Aw man, he's such an asshole. I don't understand anything he says.' But they sure do bust the tests out, though. I tell you, man, it's a trip being up here with them."

Troy smiled, said, "Later," and walked slowly back to the dorms. The weather was beginning to feel colder with each step. He thought about how easily White students adapted to college. He had always heard them complain, but as Clay had said, they all seemed to have good grades and good times. Even Simon had a 3.0, which Troy figured wasn't all that bad for someone who admitted he wasn't all that bright.

"So how do you want it cut, Doc?" Troy asked as Doc sat in his chair with a towel wrapped around his neck.

"Oh, just do the regular. Tape the sides and round up the top. Blend the sides in, though," Doc squeaked.

"Blend it in? I didn't know that. I thought you wanted a sraight-up Mohawk," Troy quipped.

Doc grinned. "So Troy, Jay told me you got a three-point-seven-three, man. That's good as hell. I wish I had that, 'cause my grades were finished," he commented. "I gotta go to summer school now. And I hate school, man. I mean, I like being on campus and all, but I hate the testing part."

Doc paused to think for a moment. "We gotta go through all this shit just to get a job. I be feelin' like leavin' civilization and goin' to a deserted island sometimes, man. Then I wouldn't have to worry about all this dumb stuff we go through in America. I'd eat fish while livin' in a hut with a woman and kids, wearing a pair drawers strapped around my waist and shit. And I'd take a shit in the woods, get some ass out on the beach; and *fuck* paying you six dollars! I wouldn't even need a haircut. Who the fuck cares about a haircut when you live on an island?"

Troy cracked up, having to stop himself before he messed up the hair cut. *"Awww, shit, cuz!"* he yelled, still laughing. He bawled for three minutes after putting his clippers down. It was a great stress relief. Everything felt beautiful for a moment.

Troy returned to work with watery eyes. Doc had explored total freedom. Troy welcomed and needed the relief. He had been knocked off his high horse and forced to realize that some sweet dreams turn sour.

LEARNING THE GAME

PROUD OF THEIR ACADEMIC ACCOMPLISHMENTS, TROY AND Matthew wore suits and ties to attend a banquet being held for freshmen honor roll students inside the campus ballroom. There were 137 honorees packed inside the large, elegant room. Waiters and waitresses served, donning formal black-and-white uniforms. Troy, Matthew, and two other students were the only Blacks. There were a few Asians and Latinos, and the rest were White.

The banquet organizers had arranged the seats in a random order. In the mix, the four Black students would have been the farthest apart. But they all chose to sit where they pleased. Troy and Matthew sat together.

Speeches were made, buttons were received, and dessert was served after dinner. Most of the White students and parents did not finish theirs. Matthew and Troy had two servings. They felt uncomfortable, yet not alone. They had pleasant rapport, joking about the proceedings.

Troy's mother had to work that Sunday night and Matthew's mother couldn't make the trip either. Their mothers were both proud of their successful boys. They had worked hard. Banquet night was one to be cherished and remembered for years to come. They had succeeded as academic hopefuls at a White university.

Troy's new courses, however, were much more difficult than during the first term. He had the next section of chemistry and the lab, as well as calculus, economics, physics, and anthropology. He feared the chemistry lab the most. He would have to work side by side with White students, and laboratory classes were three hours long.

During the first chemistry lab, the instructor handed out the syllabus for the experiments. Troy figured he would snatch a partner who was less dominant so that he could contribute without arguments. He never thought of himself as inferior, but he realized after the first semester that Whites still felt they were smarter.

Unfortunately, for the semester opener, there were groups of five students working together instead of two. Troy planned to be assertive.

A tall, brown-haired student took first crack at group leadership while Troy plotted, jockeying for a position. "Well, you guys, we have to get all of the items on this list. I'll get the ether and the methyl chloride. You get . . . ," the White chieftain directed. Troy noticed that he was immediately exempt. The three White students moved right in close to the group leader, using conversation.

Troy felt like a bee trying to find his way into an

unfamiliar hive. He didn't belong; it was not his type. Nevertheless, This is America, he thought, moving his way in and speaking up. "All right, since you guys are getting that, I'll mix the chemicals together for the next part," he suggested.

"Hey, great, guy! Then we'll filter it and do the next part. Great!" the tall leader said enthusiastically. The others brought the chemicals as Troy continued to mix the solution. The White students backed off, involving themselves in another conversation.

Troy began to feel like an idiot. He stood there, mixing chemicals, while they laughed and giggled behind him, doing nothing.

"Are you finished yet, guy?" the tall one asked after a while.

"Yeah. Almost. But my name is Troy."

"Oh, OK, then, Troy." They gathered around him, making Troy feel like a part of the group. After he had finished, the group proceeded with the next set of chemicals for the experiment. Again, Troy mixed the solution as they laughed and joked in the background.

At the completion of the experiment, the group was assigned a series of questions to answer. Troy knew the answers, yet he was ousted from the conversation. The group had allowed him to do all the actual work, but decided they would answer the questions without him. Troy knew they would have to ask him for information eventually, so he sat and waited.

"It can't be that, because it turned yellow after

the bromide was added. So it would have to be this equation," a short and chubby student in glasses argued.

"No it isn't. He said that that would only be from the first product," the towering leader insisted.

Troy still waited, knowing that he held the answers. After waiting five more meaningless minutes, no one consulted him. He concluded he would have to force his way inside their discussion with corrections. It was time to intervene.

"It's the fourth equation because we filtered twice, which would turn out a more purified product," he said.

"Yeah, that's right," the chubby guy agreed. "The solution was smaller in quantity than before, so I guess it is the last equation."

The chieftain was disappointed. He wanted to play hero. "Well, I don't see how we could get a more purified solution from that, but OK. If that's the answer, we'll keep it," he said.

Troy left his first lab feeling like a champion. He had shown that he was a quality player. And he had already picked a lab partner who would not get in his way.

"Ay', what's up, Mat? Man, I feel good today, cuz. I was the savior in our chemistry lab experiment, with four White boys," Troy said. He sat down to join Matthew inside the freshman lobby area.

"Yeah, I had chemistry lab yesterday," Matthew said.

"I didn't know you had chemistry labs," Troy responded. "Your major requires that?"

"Yeah, man, I'm gon' be a chemistry major. I like that shit," Matthew told him.

"Yeah," Troy said, thinking to himself. "Ay', Mat, you remember last term when that White guy was talkin' to us, and he gave that long story about his friend, who ended up being a chemistry major?"

"Yeah, that bugged me out. 'Cause, yo, he started off like his friend had failed or something. He was like, 'My best friend from home, he studied that chemistry every night. And aw man, he got an A in it. He's majoring in it now,' " Matthew reflected as they both laughed.

"I know, cuz, 'cause I thought he was going to say, 'And he still failed that shit,' " Troy said.

"And you notice how when the White students say they messed up on a test, they get, like, a B?" Matthew commented. "Man, if a Black dude say that, it's an F. Them White students ain't so smart, though. 'Cause when the teachers ask questions, they don't be knowing much. Matter of fact, I answered all the questions in my lab group yesterday. Then they all crowded around me for answers," Matthew said.

"Yeah, well let's study tonight, man, 'cause I get tired of studying now. I need someone else there to stimulate me," Troy responded, packing up his books to leave.

"Yeah, aw'ight. But yo, I heard you quit the basketball team. What's up with that, troop?" Matthew asked before Troy could leave.

Troy sat back down. "Well, I wasn't gettin' no time, so I quit. I felt like they had allowed me to get just so far, then they just kept me there, like they wanted to control me and make me beg to get in. Fuck them coaches, though, man. They don't know what the hell they're doing. I ain't no benchwarmer, cuz."

Troy stood back up and thought for a minute. "I don't even like number three, man. I took it 'cause they said I was on the team. I didn't even want to make a fuss; I was so happy. But ta hell wit' that team, man. Dem White coaches just using everybody anyway."

"Yo, you should have hung in there, troop," Matthew insisted. "I'm not as good as you in basketball, but I'll hang in there till the last whistle." Matthew extended his hand. "Aw'ight, then, Troy, I'll see you tonight," he said, seeing that Troy was eager to leave. Troy left the lobby for his next class, feeling that Matthew was right.

That evening, Simon sat inside their shared room with two of his friends, talking about a basketball game on television. Troy knew both of Simon's friends but he didn't talk to them much. They seemed sincere; Troy just never allowed them to get too close.

"Hey, what's up, Troy?" one of Simon's friends asked as Troy walked in. They would always beat him with politeness before Troy could get a chance to speak. "I heard about you quitting the team, Troy. But don't worry about it, because they're no good anyway."

"Yeah, Troy, as long as you're getting the grades you got, you don't need that team," the other added.

Troy was stunned. "How y'all know what kind of grades I got?" he asked, feeling deprived of privacy.

"Simon told us."

Troy wanted to say something about Simon spreading his business. At the same time, he felt kind of proud that these two White students knew that he was an achiever.

"So you went to the banquet, hunh, Troy?" the other asked.

"Yeah, I went," Troy said, feeling proud again.

The four sat and watched the ball game until nine o'clock, before Simon's two friends departed. Troy had forgotten about studying with Matthew. He didn't feel up to it anyway. He and Simon decided, instead, to go play table tennis in the Student Activity Center. Troy needed a stress release. Simon, on the other hand, was going just to have a good time. They talked and warmed up prior to beginning the actual games.

"So what kind of grades did your boys get, Simon?" Troy thought he'd ask.

"They got three-sevens, too. They just didn't go to the banquet, because they felt it was kind of corny. Matter of fact, I know a lot of kids that got real good grades and didn't go," Simon revealed.

"I knew it. I thought that crowd was kind of weak, 'cause too many White people in my classes were getting good grades for it to be so few on honor roll. But why didn't your friends tell me their grades?" Troy queried.

Simon hunched his shoulders. "Aw man, because it ain't such a big deal. Besides, you didn't ask them."

Troy used all his best serves in the practice games. The ball continued to spin off Simon's side of the table before he got a chance to hit it. Simon was actually impressed with Troy's performance, yet the real games had yet to begin.

"Ay', Simon, check out this slam," Troy said, putting a spin on the ball that Simon couldn't handle.

"Wow! That's a great spin you have. I'll have to watch out for that," Simon told him, taking the practice games lightly. He only returned the ball as Troy worked himself up to show how good he was.

"Getting back to your friends, Simon. If they wanted me to know about their grades, they would have told me. That's how I feel about it," Troy commented, pressed to get his views off his chest. Simon hunched his shoulders as they started playing the real games. Simon won the first five out of seven. Troy was disgusted, wanting to play more games until he won back all that he had lost in the beginning.

"Ay', Troy, I gotta go study now, man," Simon said, grinning.

"Naw cuz, ta hell with that. We don't leave until we finish at least four more games!" Troy shouted in anger.

Simon remained calm, with a smirk on his face. "Hey, come on now, Troy. It's my ball anyway, so I'll just take it and leave. Then what are you going to do?" Simon asked. "See, if you didn't show me all your best shots, you probably would have beaten me a few games. But you had to show off; that's why I won. Now let's go back to the room and study." When they finally did get back to the room, Troy had lost three more games.

"You lost, Troy, and I won. It was fair and square,"

Simon said, opening his books at his desk at eleven-thirty. Troy, worn out and defeated, hit the sack instead of studying.

He attended his anthropology class, across Madison Avenue, the next morning. He answered several questions from previous readings. The students were all supposed to have read the first two chapters, yet Troy was the only one who answered anything. White students were not as bright as they had everyone fooled into believing. Troy even provided humorous quotes and statements from the book that his classmates found entertaining.

A White girl, who Troy considered attractive, sat beside him, impressed. She had the dark hair, thick eyebrows, and the olive skin that Troy felt he liked. She read another book while sitting through what she considered a boring lecture, except when Troy had made comments. It was a long Tuesday class that lasted an hour and twenty minutes. After a while, she decided to befriend him.

"You're pretty smart, and you make me laugh," she said. She smiled and ran her hand through her dark, shiny hair. "This class would be boring without you," she added. Troy would have turned down an opportunity to make friends with a White girl during the first term. Now he had experience with them. Or so he thought.

"Yeah, I read these chapters two days ago," he said softly.

She laid her hand across his arm, snickering. "You know, I didn't even buy the book yet," she said. "By the time I get the money, I probably will have failed the first test already." She still held on to his arm gently as she continued. "So what's your name?"

"Troy Potter."

"Oh, well my name is Mary."

They spoke with each other after class about nothing in particular while heading to the dorms.

"That teacher is really good. She explains everything in detail. Last term, I had some real jerk-offs, who I really couldn't understand, you know," Mary said, walking fast to keep up with him. The wind threw her hair back and forth and in front of her face as they marched along.

"Yeah," Troy responded, feeling nervous. He didn't like being seen with White girls out in public. Although he had broken the ice and had sex with several of them, he still felt uncomfortable. To top it off, they were crossing Madison Avenue, the busiest street on State University's campus.

"I had calculus last term, and this guy we had was from China. I never knew what he was talking about. I got a B-plus in the class. So I did all right," Mary said, tacking on information about her studies.

"Yeah," Troy said again, still walking like he was in a hurry. He wanted to ask for her phone number but found no opportunity to do so. Whenever he said something more than "Yeah," Mary spoke like there were no periods in her sentences.

"My biology class last term just killed me because I hated having to read it. It was, like, severely boring to read, like, all these long massive chapters of information, you know? So I had gotten these quizzes from the teacher, and they came in handy."

"Yeah," Troy repeated. But I wish she'd shut the hell up, he wrangled to himself. Her constant jabbering was getting on his nerves.

"Oh well, I'll see you, Troy, 'cause I have a test to study for tomorrow and I have to meet my girlfriend at the library at seven. So I'm going to take a nap, then I'll probably eat before I go to meet her, OK. I'll see you."

"All right, then," Troy said as they broke off. He then realized that he knew very little about her. Mary had spoken strictly about her schoolwork. Troy had not received a chance to talk at all. If someone had asked him where Mary was from, what year she was in, or what her major was, he would have had nothing to say.

"Yo, what's going on, Pete?" Troy asked, entering the freshman lobby, spotting Peter sitting by himself on the aluminum benches.

"Grades. I don't know what I wanna do now. I heard that psychologists have to search real hard for jobs, and they don't get high wages unless they're extremely good, like a top-notch professor or something," Peter moaned. He looked depressed. He sat with his book open across his lap. "The Lord shall give me strength to overcome. And with his strength, he will lead the path that I will follow." Peter perked with glowing confidence.

"Yeah, well I'm gettin' tired as hell of studying. I hope the Lord can give me some strength, too," Troy said.

Peter kept a straight face. "The Lord can and will strengthen all who follow him, my brother."

Troy grinned deceivingly. "Well, Matthew has his own strength. He still studies every night. I think I need the power of the Lord, though, 'cause I'm weaker than Matthew."

"You don't need to be weak to need the Lord's strength. His strength is for every man, for protection against the influence of evil," Peter insisted.

"Yeah, man, there you go with that devil shit again," Troy said, shaking his head. However, before he could start on the religion issue, Peter got up and left to avoid it, passing by Matthew, who had just returned from class with some White students. Troy got up and left without bothering to speak. For some reason he felt a sense of betrayal while heading back to his room. When he arrived at his door, Bruce and John were waiting for haircuts.

"Troy, mayn, I've been over here for twenty minutes, cuz. Where have you been?" Bruce asked him.

"I'm sorry, boys, I ran a little late," Troy explained. He opened the door to a messy room. It looked as though no one had cleaned it for weeks. No one seemed to comment on it.

"Yup, Troy, mayn, I'm goin' out for the football team this spring. Training camp is in four more weeks," Bruce said, sitting in the chair before John could. "Oh, I'm sorry, mayn. I beat you to a haircut, didn't I?" he asked, teasing. "So yo, cuz, how you get in that White fraternity?" Bruce asked John. They were having a conversation before Troy had arrived.

"I'on know, I just pledged," John answered. "I just hung out with a lot of the kids in that fraternity. It's another Black guy in there, too. We went over at the same time," John said. Troy noticed that John was as dark as his friend Blue, but John kept a low haircut. Blue had never had his hair cut low, as far as Troy could remember.

"Ay', man, did you get any good-lookin' White girls yet?" Troy asked John. He felt that if John could get into a White fraternity, then he would be an expert on the subject.

"Nope. It's like too many White guys up here to get any. And I'm not gonna go for an ugly one," John said. "A lot of fat and ugly White girls keep looking at me. My friend dates one. I just won't get laid for all that," he hinted. They all laughed as Troy started on Bruce's cut.

"How come it seems that it's harder to get a dark-haired girl?" Troy asked.

"I'on know. Some dark-haired girls are more down than the light-haired ones. But I think it has something to do with that blond-haired, blue-eyed stuff," John answered. "See, since they have dark hair and dark eyes, sometimes they may feel like an outcast. And if they mess with you, they're kicked out completely. So they try to stick with the light-haired White people."

"Yeah, that's the same thing that I figured," Troy told him. "That's kind of deep, though, to see that they discriminate in their own race. Just like us and shit."

"Hell yeah, especially against poor Whites," John said.

"Yeah, but I don't know about them poor Whites

who talk that 'I'm not racist' shit. I always wonder what they'd do if they had some money," Troy pondered. Bruce had no comment as Troy finished their haircuts after about an hour.

Troy emptied the hair into the hallway before going to get a vacuum cleaner from the downstairs office. It was his usual procedure. He would empty the hair on the hallway rug, then get it up after he got the vacuum cleaner to keep it from accumulating inside his room. A White student who lived two doors down the hall said, "Hey, buddy, I'm a little tired of you putting all this hair all over the rug. People have to walk out here after taking a shower."

Troy looked down to see that he was barefoot. "Well, learn to put some shoes or something on, *buddy,*" Troy responded in mockery. "I was going to get the vacuum to clean it up anyway. So don't worry about it," he added with an attitude. The White floor mate looked at him and left, and when Troy returned to his room, he found shaving cream all over the door, with Simon trying to clean it up.

"What the hell happened?" Troy asked Simon.

"I don't know. I was going to ask you the same thing. I thought maybe one of your homeys was playing some kind of joke on ya."

"One of my homeys, hunh, Simon?" Troy asked, chuckling.

"Yeah, man, one of your boyz," Simon said. He crossed his arms over his chest and leaned his head to the side, trying to look tough.

Troy shook his head and smiled. "I know who it was, Sime. It was that punk-ass White boy that did this shit. He was complaining about the hair in the hallway. And I had already told him that I'd clean it up," Troy said seriously. He felt like breaking something. He walked right over to the student's room to speak his mind.

"Ay', yo, cuz, you think that shit is a joke or something? I'm telling you right now, if you do some dumb shit like that again, I'ma kick ya ass," he declared.

Simon remained inside their room, waiting for Troy's return.

"What are you talking about?" the student responded to Troy.

"You sprayed my damn door with shaving cream. Don't play that dumb shit with me."

The White floor mate remained calm, keeping his cool throughout the ordeal. "Look, I didn't do it. I don't know what you're talking about. I swear to God. Look, my name is Jim. What's yours?" he asked, extending his hand to Troy. He stared Troy straight in the eyes. Like in a trance, Troy shook his hand and told him his name, feeling like a fool. He couldn't believe he didn't punch the White boy in the mouth. He had been beaten in the game of persuasion.

"*God damn it, Simon!* Do you know that White boy just suaved the hell out of me? Like I was a girl and shit. Damn! I don't believe I went for that," Troy screamed, returning to his room.

"Well, what did he say to you?"

"That lying punk said he didn't do it. And I shook his hand, like a nut! Now who the hell else had a better motive than that White boy? He did that shit. I know it! He's probably over there laughing at me now. *Damn, Simon!"*

Troy twisted and turned, trying to do his work, and was not succeeding. He could not seem to concentrate. The White students were starting to get to him. The competition did not seem equal. He felt that they always had an advantage. He could feel himself winding down, losing the strength to get back up. So he decided to study with Matthew, jumping on the elevator to the third floor.

"Ay', Mat, it's me, Troy," he yelled through the door, trying to open it.

"Yo, come on in," Matthew yelled back.

"I would have, if the door wasn't locked."

"Oh, word. It's locked?" Matthew asked, getting up to open it.

"Since when you start lockin' your door?" Troy asked, grinning. "What, you trying to hide from some ugly girl or something?"

Matthew smiled. "Naw, man, I'm just trying to get some work done. And yo, y'all niggas keep comin' in, distracting me," he commented, chuckling to himself.

"Yeah, well look, man, I need someone to study with, 'cause I can't concentrate no more," Troy explained.

"Aw'ight, troop. I'm always willing to study with someone. You get kind of lonely when everyone else is out partying and whatnot," Matthew said.

They studied chemistry for an upcoming test. Hour after hour they underlined concepts that would most likely be covered. What Matthew didn't know, Troy would help with. And what Troy didn't know,

Matthew would help with. The teamwork set a winning combination. The material was comprehended in more detail and in less time than either could have ever expected to achieve alone. It reminded Troy of the quizzing sessions he and Peter had. And it reminded him of the teamwork he maintained in basketball practice, although he received minimum time in the games.

Back inside the chemistry lab before the first test, Troy found that he was tricked by his previous four partners on the first week's experiment. The instructor handed the assignment papers back several weeks later. Troy was shocked to see that his partners had changed the answer that he had provided them. His answer turned out to be correct, yet they had entered the wrong one. They denied his research because they felt they knew more than he. They felt that he was incapable. Still, Troy led the class discussion as they sat back, seeming to know nothing.

The test results, however, proved that they did know. The average grade was high. Troy hit only the median score. It made no sense to him. Or maybe he had showed too much in class and slacked up on the test, thinking that he knew everything.

In anthropology class, Mary had talked him out of his homework one day. Troy didn't even have her phone number. He had later spotted her with a blond-'n'-blue White boy. No one had to tell him that he had been duped. Mary was as good a liar as Jim, who Troy was sure had sprayed his door with the shaving cream. Mary had succeeded in using Troy for his homework.

Troy had given ninety percent of the correct answers in anthropology class discussions, only to score a B on the test. To top it off, Mary got an A, after not even having a book for the first two weeks. Or so she had said. Troy found out that her roommate had had the book and the same class on a different day. He began to wonder if any Whites ever told the full truth.

Troy, again, had to release stress. He had not been to the gym since quitting the basketball team in early January. And it was nearing March.

"Ay', Simon, you down to go run some ball tonight?" he offered after dinner.

"Yeah, all right," Simon said, taking off his earphones. "Let's go."

They ran north to the gym, playfully wrestling each other on the sidewalks with the basketball. When they arrived, the court at the far end of the gym was empty. They had an entire court to themselves.

Troy had talked of embarrassing Simon on the court since the first night they had met in late August. Troy took the floor and worked himself up before they got a chance to play. He was out of shape since quitting the team, but it was only Simon. He felt he could beat him easily.

For fifteen minutes, Troy ran up and down the court, practicing his moves before they began. They were ready to face off. Simon wanted to change the rules.

"OK, Troy, let's play. But we don't have to check the ball after making a basket. We'll just take it back to the foul line and go up again, 'cause checking the ball just wastes time. And take it easy, 'cause my ankle is sore," Simon said. Troy was so ready to whip him that he agreed without thinking about what was said.

Simon hit his first three shots right from the foul line. He then slammed twice off of rebounds. The score was suddenly 10-0 before Troy had even touched the ball. He felt as though he was cheated but did not know how. His Jewish roommate was beating him.

Simon pocketed two more baskets, increasing the score to 14-0. He was four inches taller and thirty pounds heavier than Troy, able to force his way under the basket for easy hoops.

"Hold up, man, let's start the game over," Troy demanded, grabbing the ball and shaking his head. "Your ankle ain't hurtin', you ain't takin' the ball to the foul line without me checking it, and I was tired as hell before the game started anyway," he blurted out.

Simon cracked up before responding. "You're the dummy that was running around getting all tired. And who told you to believe me when I said that my ankle was sore? You fell for the oldest trick in the book, boy. Always know what the rules are before you start the game. I don't even think you listened, since you felt you could whip me so bad," Simon said with a smirk.

"Yeah, well like I said, let's start the game over," Troy repeated, still holding the ball.

"Hell no, I'm up by fourteen and you didn't score yet. If you think I'm giving up that kind of advantage, you're crazy."

Troy grumbled on their way home. He was frustrated. Simon had even won ten out of the twelve bets that they had had on college and pro basketball. Simon had a subscription to *Sports Illustrated,* which Troy did not think contributed to the winning of bets. Simon used his body weight when playing basketball, which Troy did not figure helped. Simon also had different spins he would use each time they played table tennis, where Troy had only one good serve he felt would suffice.

"Damn, you play Ping-Pong good as hell, and basketball," Troy said. He took off his sneakers and clothes to take a shower once they had returned to their room.

"Yeah, well I have a table at home in my basement. My brother and I used to play all the time," Simon revealed.

"What? You didn't tell me you had a table at home."

"Yeah, well it never came up."

"Yeah, aw'ight, you probably not tellin' me about some basketball team you were on, too," Troy said to him.

Simon began to snicker as Troy waited for another surprising comment. "Yeah, I played small forward in high school," Simon told him.

Troy listened while thinking how stupid he had been. He was fooled without a clue as to the information abruptly being presented. Simon was from Brooklyn, New York. He had played against New York's finest high school basketball teams. His school was ranked twenty-third in the nation. He had been used to boxing out quick Black players. He had perfected his jump shot. Simon also used to bet with a bookkeeper in his hometown. And he was an announcer who had called the games in a Brooklyn summer league. He kept up-to-date with all the athletic news. He knew if one team was unhealthy or missing players. He also knew how many games each team played, to predict if they were tired. And Simon checked the history of each team rivalry to get a historical edge.

Troy was astonished. There was no way to compete with an opponent who knew things that he had not known. For six months he had talked up a game that he thought would be equal. Simon didn't look like an authentic athlete. As it turned out, Simon had received a scholarship to play basketball at a small college. He turned it down. He said that he would rather watch the game with an education ahead of him, instead of jumping in and possibly reinjuring an ankle he had problems with during his senior year in high school.

Later that night, one of Simon's friends came over to borrow a calculator. Troy and Simon were both busy doing homework.

Bloomp bloomp bloomp.

"Go the hell away," Simon said jokingly. His friend, hearing Simon's voice, decided to come in on his own. Kevin was from West Virginia, of German descent.

"Hey, pal, I need to borrow your calculator. I messed around and lost mine when I was running from the premed library," he said.

"Well, go get it. It's right on my desk, stupid," Simon told him.

Kevin went to get it, only to be tackled onto the bed. The two, playing, reminded Troy of playful puppies. They were just like the White couples who would cuddle up, kissing and hugging, all over campus. They were free-flowing, positive-attitude-having, joyful White people.

"Come on, Simon. Cut it out, man. You're getting my shirt all wrinkled," Kevin said, trying to free himself from Simon's wrestling hold. Simon let him up, only to be wrestled down himself.

"Oh, OK. I let you up so you can sneak me," he said.

"Well, no one said I wasn't gonna jump on you, just because you let me go. That's why you never let your enemy back up, Simon. I could keep you down here forever if I had to. Now, do you give?" he asked. Simon was bigger than Kevin but he was helpless because of the position he was in. His hands were tied behind his back, with his face pressed into his pillow.

Troy finally stopped from studying to watch them.

"Well, do you give, Simon?" Kevin repeated.

Simon continued to struggle to free himself. "Yeah, damn it. You win. Now get the hell off me!" he shouted, scuffling to his feet with a pink face. He was too out of breath to counterattack. Kevin then gave his attention to Troy.

"Hey, Troy. How's it going, pal?" he asked.

"I'm aw'ight, man. But did you say you were coming from the premed library?"

"Yeah, I was in the premed library. Why, are you thinking about going into medicine, too?"

"Yeah, man, 'cause doctors make a whole lot of money."

"Oh yeah, well that's great. You'll be there with me. There aren't that many Blacks in medical school, though. Have you had biology and calculus yet?" Kevin asked him.

"Not biology, but I'm taking calculus," Troy answered. He hoped that Kevin would not ask him any more questions about medical school requirements. Troy was informed that most students going into medical school carried about eighteen credits a semester. He had only fifteen and was already behind.

"Yeah, well I had that stuff in high school. So it was like a review for me. I got A's in both," Kevin said. "And Troy, if you need any help, I got some old exams that you could get, too."

Troy nodded his head, starting to feel a little pressured. He began to feel like maybe he should have kept his mouth shut.

"But Troy, you really shouldn't get into something just for the money. I really want to help people," Kevin added.

Troy felt a jolt of suspicion. Another White lie. Money was the key. It was part of the reason Troy wanted to play basketball, and why he wanted to become a doctor. He thought that money was the reason why *everyone* was in college.

Nevertheless the field of medicine was limited for Blacks. The counselors had said it, the students knew it, the records showed it, and the chemistry class represented the fact that Blacks were not going into the science fields en masse. It would be hard to go it alone. Then again, there was Matthew, and possibly Clay, who had also expressed some interest in the sciences. They would all have to be pioneers. And Troy conceived that the only way to stay on top of Whites was by playing their game of acting dumb. He speculated that "they," the White power structure based upon limited opportunities, would never allow a Black student to become the class leader. So young Mr. Potter decided that he would play the dummy role, hoping to gain successful leadership right under their noses.

HOW THEY WIN

IT BECAME MORE DIFFICULT FOR TROY TO CONCENTRATE without listening to the radio on a study break. He found himself doing what Simon had done the first term. Books became irrelevant. Classes were a constant aggravation. And homework had become the hassle that Doc said it was for him.

Troy began to wonder what actually happened to Black college graduates. He had only seen one Black doctor in his life. He asked himself, Do Blacks really come out of school and go to work? Is it really that hard for Blacks and that easy for Whites? He still believed that America was the place for an equal opportunity, but was it a place for an equal start? Maybe Blacks would have to spend too much time catching up, and not enough time getting ahead.

Troy was always the first to help, the first to ask for help and the first to participate. Yet the White students were the first to get helped, the first to finish the test, and the first to receive high grades. No matter how well he did academically, Troy still felt he was somehow behind.

He had finally stopped daydreaming and rode the elevator down to Matthew's room. Troy had lain in his bed for two hours, not even touching a book.

He dove onto Matthew's unmade bed. "Ay', Mat, how do you study all the time without getting tired, man? I'm sick of studying."

Matthew was sitting at his desk, studying as usual. "I just do it, man. I don't know," Matthew said. "Maybe I do well studying because I like to do good on the tests. I mean, a lot of Black people want to settle for regular grades, but you got to want more than that. A lot of Blacks want success fast and easy, but it won't come like that."

"Why not, cuz? Why can't it come fast and easy? It does to them. White people don't seem to be busting their asses," Troy argued.

"I'on know, man. It's kind of like, they got a head start or something. Maybe they worked harder before college, so they don't have to struggle as much in college," Matthew commented. "A lot of 'em do bust their ass, we just don't see when they're doing it."

Troy became further intrigued by his thoughts about race and society. He decided to diagnose his surroundings. He went to lunch in the cafeteria, noticing things. All of the workers were Black, except for an immigrant and one mentally slow woman. It had never dawned on him before. The White students acted friendly, always greeting the Black lunch women kindly. Troy thought, Maybe that's where White people want us to be, serving them.

He noticed that all the dormitory janitors were Black. White students would talk with them for hours at a time. Maybe that's what they want all Blacks to do, clean up after them.

The cooks were all Black, working in hot, stuffy kitchens, fixing meals for a predominantly White campus. Maybe that's where they want all of us to be, cooking their food in their kitchens. Troy's thoughts of misery had opened his eyes to racial disharmony.

He walked around campus and up and down Charleston Street, noticing that the store owners were always White. Every store seemed to have Black employees, though. Maybe that's what they want us for, doing their dirty work. Most of the maintenance supervisors, engineers, and construction workers were White. Maybe that's where they want themselves to be, in the higher-paid, skilled positions.

Except for C.M.P.'s, whenever Troy entered an office inside Platt Hall, none of the administrators were Black. He began to question why he had never realized it before.

The television news paraded Blacks involved in violence and in sports, never showcasing businessmen and businesswomen; they were found only in Black magazines. Blacks were treated as though they did not exist. But they existed, cleaning bathrooms. They existed, sweeping and mopping floors. They existed, changing bedspreads. McDonald's, Burger King, and Roy Rogers, surrounding the campus area, were filled with them. Nevertheless, Whites only flooded the stadiums to watch the 260-pound football players and the seven-foot basketball players, who they seemed to love. Troy believed that the White administrators did not care about the average Black student (not even those who had a 3.7 average). They just want us to fill their quotas.

Troy's life had taken a sharp twist. He began to pay more attention in his anthropology class, learning more about the rest of the world and how Whites got such a running jump on success. He had reasoned through his basketball experience: They only let you get as high as they want you to get before they jerk you.

In anthropology, he learned cultural principles that only made him calculate even more. He deciphered the games of history, how it all began. He learned how Africa and other Third World countries had played the game before the Europeans changed the rules. He learned how people of color were systematically devastated by White destruction. He studied the deaths of cultures, animals, souls, and the uprooting of entire civilizations. He studied the capture and rape of millions of colored women. He studied the European hunt for natural resources, stripping the land in all of the Third World. And he studied how the stolen resources left these nations poor.

Troy learned that Africans were the first to practice domestication of plants and animals, methods that were later adopted by Southwest Asians and Native Americans. Domestication brought about a change in social structure. As the levels of society progressed, marked inequalities developed as work became stratified. People became ranked according to the kind of work they did or the family they were born into. Social institutions ceased to operate on simple levels of kin. They became more formal, political.

The specialization of more advanced societies separated the rich from the poor and the skilled from the unskilled. The inequalities produced waves of crime. And in the status evolution, the more ancient peoples were depicted at the lowest levels of social importance.

The anthropology professor, Dr. Polinski, an archaeologist from Germany, compared European male mentality to Robin Hood, who was a thief, stealing from the rich to give to the poor. "The European motto," she called it.

She said that European males believed in aggression, sexism, and competitive societies. They attempted and succeeded to limit the competition by "underdeveloping the undesirables." To keep their edge on the world, European males regulated the population sizes and maintained systems of family and hierarchal rule. "They then spread throughout the Third World with the use of imperialism and Christianity to fulfill their greed," Dr. Polinski informed her class. The White woman instructor led Troy to understand and to believe that no man created was more devious and tricky than the White man.

Troy went on to learn for himself that in some cultures, the Europeans attempted and succeeded in killing entire nations and tribes of colored people. As the weeks passed on, Troy absorbed more and more information. He learned about the many things that he had previously failed to realize conceptually. He wondered how many other Blacks knew and felt powerless. Or how many of us don't know or don't care? An entire world had been captured by a single race of people with white skin, a minority. A world of peoples of color, the majority, were killed, enslaved, traded, hunted, ignored, starved, and set up to live in slums.

Crime and hatred increased among all those who had been beaten by the White race. Pigmented children were born into poverty and into environments of social despair. Their families were broken from the lack of economic efficiency while being trapped within capitalism. So they became "slaves to the system."

An entire planet of colored people was trying, unsuccessfully, to live up to one people's philosophy. The Third World could learn and advance, but they were not taught correctly and not allowed to progress without the fear of death, the punishment for defiance to White rule.

The Europeans had tricked the world as he had been tricked. Troy gave up his answers in class, showed off his basketball skills on the court, and gave away his homework assignments after class. The White students would copy and not teach. They had deceived the colored nations into feeling inferior, while Whites were deemed gifted and most able.

Troy felt that Whites oppressed colored nations through the power that they allowed them to have. The Third World had submitted their minds to the material, conceptual, historical, academic, philosophical, and spiritual confusion of European mentality.

Colored people had already possessed the knowledge of truth within themselves. And as Troy continued to think critically, he realized that college played a vital role in the game. It would weed out the "undesirable" and the "underprivileged." Even those who had strength enough to succeed would effortlessly be swallowed up by the White establishment—the disappearance of successful Blacks.

Matthew had already begun to hide out, as he seemed to stop discussing his grades and test scores. "Once you succeed yourself, then you can help your people more because you know more and have more to offer," he would say. Troy listened but he never believed it. He had already helped many fellow Black students to study as well as cheat for tests. And it had worked. Troy was confident that he would succeed as well. Yet suddenly, all the Whites around him seemed to drain him of his energy and of his confidence.

He continued to sink into his anthropology book for nights of reading information. He began to wish he had taken a Black studies course to learn all he possibly could about the struggles of his people to figure out a way to win the war of integrity between the races.

Blacks had lost their power of authority. Without the power of authority, they could not control their culture, their environments, or their education. Having the power of authority would allow them to deal sufficiently with their economic, social, and political problems. Yet they lacked a real revolution, and they lacked the economic resources and the knowledgeable skills to train and to hire. Without economics and skills, they were left with spirit, purpose, hope, and a dream.

"Yo, y'all wanna run a game of ball before the intramural games?" Troy shouted. It was Friday, a week from finals in April, and he decided to play basketball to release stress. Stress began to take a grip on his mind each night.

The intramural basketball championships would be held the following week. Troy was too late to get on the roster of an intramural team after quitting varsity basketball in early February.

He picked a short squad, preparing to play a team that had won four straight games. Troy's team was not confident or diversified. They were unskilled in offense, and the defense alone could not win the game. Every team needs points to win, Troy thought. So he scored twenty out of the thirty points that his team accumulated. They lost by fourteen. Afterward, he had a lot to say about it.

"Y'all some weak niggas, man! I don't know why I picked y'all. Y'all ain't help me a damn bit! Y'all act like y'all didn't even want to play!" he shouted. He was loud enough for the entire gymnasium to hear.

"Ay', Troy, man, just because you can score all those points don't mean that we can. You act like everybody on the team is as good as you," one member said. Troy didn't bother to respond as the scheduled teams took the court for the intramural contests.

Most of the intramural teams were all-Black or all-White. One Black team, called the Brothers, was well organized. Their players, who were skilled at their positions, all wore their name on the back of their black-and-gold jerseys. The other team was predominantly White with two average-skilled Black players. The two Black players did not have outstanding ball-handling talent, so they chose to run with the Whites, who were very appreciative.

The game started in a fast tempo, just as the Brothers wanted. They scored the first four baskets, for an 8–0 lead. Their execution on the court crushed the predominantly White team. It was a quick game. The final score was a killing 74-36.

"Jesus Christ, man! The only way those guys will lose is if the other Black team beats 'em," a White student said to a friend. They watched from the bleachers, sitting next to Troy.

"Yeah, but if they play each other before the finals, they may run each other so hard that we may have a shot at beating the winner," his friend responded.

Troy left with Bruce and Doc after watching a few more games.

"Ay', Troy, cuz," Bruce said, chuckling before he could finish. "Dag, mayn, you got me saying that cuz shit all the time now. Anyway, mayn, you been comin' up to the gym, shouting and hollering at people for the past month, cuz. What, you having girlfriend problems or somethin'?" Bruce asked him.

"Yeah, man, but not girl problems. I'm having world problems," Troy responded. "I use the courts to forget about the shit."

They entered the freshman dorm lobby to hang out and talk while sitting on the benches. As they sat and watched, floods of White students crowded the lobby, going to and coming from parties.

"Damn, man! We up here with nothing to do on a Friday night while White people got a million and three parties and shit," Troy said. "They got all the bars on the avenue. They have frat houses. And they got all the women they could want."

"I know. Imagine if this was an all-Black school, and all these people were Black. We'd probably go crazy," Doc joked. "We'd be running around trying to talk to all the girls. And the dudes that been there already would be like, 'Yo, what's up with y'all niggas?' "

"I wonder what it's like at an all-Black school," Bruce pondered.

Troy was quiet. He decided to just sit and listen.

"I bet it's parties every week," Bruce said. "And we wouldn't have to sit around, doin' nothin' when there ain't none, 'cause it would be so many black babes to chill wit'. You know what I mean, cuz?"

"I hear there's a lot of light-skin/dark-skin conflicts at Black colleges, though. That's what everybody says, anyway," Doc interjected. Troy remained calm, still listening.

"Yeah, but it's still thousands of girls up that dip. The ratio is like four girls to one," Bruce said.

"But you don't learn how to deal with White people up there, man. You just gon' come out and be a minority again. So you might as well get used to it," Doc argued.

"Aw man, we always talkin' that 'deal with White people' shit The fact is, we're being separated up here, too," Troy said, finally. "It ain't like we really involved with them. And when we get out of here, it's still gon' be up for grabs. So you might as well go where you'll feel the most comfortable, which is at a Black college."

Troy shook his head with a thought. "Damn! Now I wish I would have gon' to a Black college myself." They all sat quiet for a moment before Troy continued. "Could y'all imagine, at a Black college, that we could see thousands of Blacks graduate? That would be somethin' else," he imagined. "But up here, we gon' have to search through a thousand White people and say, 'Yo, there's a black dude, fifth over in the back.' "

They all laughed as Bruce agreed. "Hell yeah, cuz," he said, still giggling. "You's a funny mug, Troy. I told my girl some of the stuff you told me, and she cracked the hell up in do. You should have heard her, man. I said, yup, that's my boy Troy," Bruce said. "I told her about the time you and your boys went to another Black neighborhood and got chased back home and shit."

"Dig, man. I can't even go to other Black neighborhoods in Philly, 'cause they'll try to kick my ass just for being there. And we're all Black," Troy commented. "But you know what? White people made us like that. 'Cause to tell you the truth, it's easier for a brother to release his anger on another brother instead of a White boy. Matter of fact, a perfect example is when a kid gets a beating from the father, and then gets an attitude with the mother and takes the anger out on her. 'Cause you know your pop'll kick your ass."

"Hell yeah, cuz. I remember when my pop used to beat my ass, and my mother would sit in her room and watch television. I used to get mad as hell, like, 'Mooomm, get this nigga off of me!' " Bruce reminisced.

Doc got up to buy a soft drink from the machines in the lobby.

"Oh, sorry," a White student said to him. Doc had bumped into her on purpose. She didn't seem to know if it was her fault or not.

White people always say "Sorry," Troy thought to himself, watching.

"Man, I'm tired of moving out their way. I ain't movin' no more. This shit ain't slave days, man," Doc said, returning with his drink.

"Ay', yo, Doc, you call that 'pop,' don't you?" Bruce asked, grinning.

"Ay', man, I'm tired of y'all making fun of me," Doc answered. His high-pitched voice was squeamish, but everyone was used to it.

"Yeah, well y'all stupid down here, man. I mean, something is wrong with y'all in this city," Bruce said.

They sat and talked for several hours, having nothing to do, nowhere to go. Troy and James had once tried to go to a White fraternity party on Henry Road and were denied admission (even though John, who was a member, had invited them). They had also heard of a Black girl who had gone to a White party. She was told to leave while she was still urinating in a bathroom, displaying her privates to the White students, who laughed. There also had been several arrests of Black students for petty reasons around campus. There was only one Black security officer out of twenty to twenty-five. The Black students called him an Oreo.

James had even gotten arrested for arguing with a clerk at a grocery store, who falsely accused him of stealing. The Asian clerk had never suspected the three White students, who had actually stolen the sodas. James shared his opinion of the store and its owner, which free speech gave him a right to do, only to be taken to the neighborhood precinct for a night.

The situation on campus for Blacks was helpless. And after Troy, Doc, and Bruce broke off, Troy went to hang out with Matthew again. It was a typical weekend. Matthew's roommate was always gone on the weekends, providing the opportunity for the two friends to talk each other to sleep.

"Yo, Mat, I was up at the gym and I got mad as hell when my team lost, cuz. You should have seen me shouting," Troy said with a smirk.

"I know, man. You get too damn emotional about stuff like that. I mean, when I play, I just play for the game. I don't really care if I win," Matthew said. "Sometimes you ain't gonna win, man. So there's no sense in gettin' all hype about it. That's just goin' to mess your health up."

Matthew stopped to take a study break, just as he did on every other night when Troy came to hang out.

"Ay', Mat, how come you didn't go anywhere tonight, man?" Troy quizzed. "You don't do shit but study."

"Because I ain't got no babes, man. They don't

really like smart dudes. It's like I'm a big goofball or something," Matthew answered. They shared a laugh before he continued. "Yeah, it's like I can't really relate to people anymore. It's stupid to feel this way, but I think I'm becoming a loner."

"Yeah, well as long as you don't fall into hangin' out with the White people, that shit is cool. 'Cause you get a lot done that way," Troy told him.

Matthew nodded. "You know, umm, Troy . . . a lot of them White students are racist because they were brought up that way. Like, this other dude was supposed to be my roommate, but his parents got him to look up my number before school started to see if I was Black. And yo, after he heard my voice, his parents got his room assignment changed," Matthew informed him. "I found out about it. He told me his parents made him do it. 'Cause he's pretty cool, man."

"Damn, cuz, that's some deep shit right there. His parents put him up to it?" Troy asked in amazement.

"Yeah, and this girl Lucille, her roommate was missing some money, and she called her parents down here to get the cops to lock Lucille up. Then the White babe ended up finding the money in her other jacket," Matthew said.

"What? How come she called her parents?"

"She was scared that Lucille would beat her up or something. You know how some White people are with us, man, actin' all scared all the time."

Troy looked into Matthew's face of budding pimples. "Damn, Mat, you starting to get acne. That means that you're stressed out, man."

Matthew squeezed a pimple and laughed. His

waves were starting to fade, too, as if he hadn't brushed them in a while. "Yeah, man, they do say acne comes from being stressed out."

"The boys around my way say it's from not getting any ass. My boys call 'em 'want-some bumps.' That means you want sex or something else that you're not getting," Troy said, snickering.

They went on talking for hours. Troy ended up spending the night again. The brief discussion they had had about acne carried Troy over into another observation while eating breakfast the next morning.

He noticed that, on the average, Black students had more acne than Whites. Many Asians and other ethnic students seemed to have more acne as well. The only Whites who seemed to have it were goofy-looking nerd types. It was an amazing analysis. He felt he was onto something else. Blacks were more stressed out than Whites. He also thought about his friends at home. None of the most popular people had acne, just the ones who were not doing too well on the streets.

It was finals week. Troy locked himself into his books for the last exams of his freshman year. He could not study in his room any longer, so he studied at the library. Whenever he attempted to study in his room, he would end up crashing into his bed and daydreaming. Still, his mind would wander while in the library. He took frequent breaks to relieve himself of the frustration. And for five hours he studied his chemistry.

Troy was worried most about chemistry because he

had a D. He needed at least a high B on the final to get a C out of the class. In the rest of his courses, he had straight B's. He was not as concerned about them. Chemistry, however, was in a position to make or break him. He had already done poorly compared to his first term. Nevertheless, Troy was certain that he would not allow chemistry to kill his high G.P.A.

The chemistry test came after two more days of tough, dedicated studying. Troy felt prepared, planning to do extremely well on the final. Actually, he felt as if he could get an A.

The students crowded inside the auditorium. Everyone sat at least a seat apart as instructed. Troy had one pencil, feeling secure. There was no way in hell that he would mess up the chemistry final. The test did not begin on time, so he focused his attention on the White students around him.

"Hey, Tom, are you ready, man?" one student asked his friend.

"Yeah, I'm ready. I even got my lucky shirt on. Every time I wore this shirt, I got at least a B on the exam," the other said.

"Yeah, well I have my lucky pencil. I made sure I brought it with me, 'cause I need serious help on this damn test," the other said.

Troy also listened to a couple of females who walked by.

"Oh gosh, Susan. I hope I don't fail. I even called my father last night. And every time I call him before a test, I seem to do all right," the first girl said.

"Yeah, well my boyfriend and I always have sex right before our exams, to release stress. And it works, too," the second said as they walked down the aisle. Troy giggled to himself. He thought of how Peter used the Lord's strength the same way the White students seemed to use lucky gimmicks.

The test finally started as Troy's heart rate increased. The exam was five pages, with thirty chemistry questions, half of which were calculations. Troy found few difficulties. Only five questions confused him. He sat in an area enclosed by five White guys who knew one another. They all began to trade answers, making Troy look to change some of his own.

"Hey, Ralph, what's number seventeen?" one whispered.

"It's *d*," the other said. Back and forth they gave one another answers as Troy captured the four questions that had confused him. He also changed some others answers according to the White students' responses. He left the test feeling happy that he sat where he did.

Returning to his room, he felt relieved and finished; a huge burden had been lifted. He had received the answer sheet to check his score. He answered twenty-six out of thirty correctly. The median score of seventeen out of thirty would be a C, so his score on the test would be an A, enough to squeeze a possible B out of the course. He was so happy that he called up Clay, who had had the same test. Troy had already told Matthew and Simon. Simon sat, listening to his radio.

"Ay', Clay, it's me, Troy . . . Yeah, man, I busted that chemistry final today. Man, you should have seen these White boys, cheatin' their asses off, cuz. What they do is wait for the most important test, *then* they cheat."

Simon had listened to Troy's comments about White people for the past month, and he was getting fed up with it.

"White boys were cheating in your class, too?" Troy asked, listening to Clay's comments over the telephone. He listened again while Clay told him a long story. Simon waited patiently for Troy to hang up the phone. Once he did, Simon was free to speak his mind.

"You know what, Troy, you're becoming more racist than some White people. All you did for the past couple of months is talk about what White people did and how they act."

Simon was serious for the first time since he and Troy had been acquainted. However, he spoke up on the wrong subject at the wrong time.

"Ay', man, let me tell you somethin'. You and I have been excellent roommates with very few problems, but I have a reason to be racist, if you wanna call it that," Troy told him. "White people don't have no reason to be racist. We didn't do shit to them! They kicked our asses for hundreds of years, man! And here you are, a Jew. Your people were killed by the millions. But y'all don't need to be racist! Do you know why, Simon? 'Cause Jews are rich as hell, that's why! So when you go to get a fuckin' job, they'll hire you on the spot, because you're expected to be smart. Yeah, so what, Simon! So what White people talk about the Jews! I've seen all the markings on the bathroom doors about niggers and Jews. The difference is, most of them same White people that talk shit about Jews are doing business with them. But when you're Black, and you come from a ghetto, even your college degree won't save you from their racism. And they don't have a fuckin' reason not to like us! That's the shit I still can't understand, Simon. We bust our asses to get a degree, and White people still see us as Black dummies. *So I gota fuckin' right to be racist!"*

"Yeah, but what's it gonna change? You think you're gonna get a job, being a Black racist? You think they're gonna hire you over a guy who's not? *Hell no*! You'll be just giving them an extra incentive not to hire you," Simon expressed, with tears in his eyes. "Look, Troy, word to the wise, man, just get your education, get out of college, and then help your people. Being racist will only stop your progress."

"Yeah, maybe you're right," Troy said, calming down. "And maybe I'll start my own business. I can't help feeling the way I do around White people. I don't feel comfortable around y'all," he admitted.

"Where do you plan to get a loan for your business?" Simon asked, as if money came only from Whites.

"I don't know yet. But it'll probably be from from some Black people. I'm not into being bought out. So, I guess I'll just have to wait and see."

TROY'S HOME

THE STREETS OF WEST PHILADELPHIA WERE NO LONGER THE same when Troy returned home for the summer break. He used to feel comfortable there. It used to be a beautiful neighborhood years ago. A lack of capital for sanitation and repair caused its ruin.

A few houses were actually kept up, like Troy's. The Potter home seemed to shine like a palace compared to the rest of the row houses. Several other buildings appeared to have not seen paint since they were built, maybe fifty years ago.

Troy remained numb for the first few days of his return. He was awakened by his younger cousins, breaking stuff at six o'clock in the morning. The arguing and screaming inside the house had reacquainted itself with Troy's consciousness. The competition for food, the constant street fights, and the all-out chaos had reawakened.

Troy remembered when he and his friends used to run through old houses, playing tag. He remembered when they would jump off roofs onto a set of old mattresses. His West Philly crew traveled and fought other neighborhood kids in street gangs while they were as young as nine. They engaged in sex in old houses at twelve. They would steal and fight the authority of their elders. It used to be entertaining, just something to do. Now Troy knew better. The chaos of ghetto life was mapped out, planned.

For as long as Troy could remember, there had always been violence. Even within his own home, uncles and aunts battled each other using fists, chairs, brooms, knives. Troy was always afraid, yet he had adapted by numbing his emotions to violence.

The day that Troy was born, his father was beaten by his uncles, denying him permission to see his newborn son. Charlotte loved Steven Williams, Troy's father. However, he cheated on her constantly. They called him Slick. He felt incompetent because of job insecurity, stress, and despair. He would take it out on her with promiscuity. A man's gotta do what a man's gotta do to *feel* like a man, he believed. Charlotte had finally found the strength to leave their relationship, returning to her mother's house. Slick pursued her with his ever-so-frequent pleas for forgiveness.

He was a handsome man, loved by many women. Steve had had several children from his various relationships. Troy's mother, though, was the prettiest of the lot. Slick loved Charlotte so much that he constantly rejected the others, except when he wanted sex. Charlotte would tell him, "I'm not a sex toy, so go fetch your other women for that." Since Steve was addicted to sex, he did fetch other women, leading to eight children.

Troy had received more love, care, and attention,

as compared to his half brothers and half sisters. He was his mother's only child. Because he was such a curious and active son, the attention that he received had him spoiled. Troy was always on top. He had learned to reject compromises.

Scooter had bet him that he would never go to college. Troy decided that he would go to college even if he had to steal the money. No one told him what he could never do.

Troy sat in the living room, watching an old black-and-white television. His two tomboyish cousins ran about, playing with three neighbors and making lots of unnecessary noise. Troy's natural response would have been to tell them to leave, but in his state of numbness, it didn't matter.

It had been almost a week since he had left school. He was not up for his friends' depressing news, so he decided to hide out in the house. He had quit the basketball team, and he was sure that he would hear it for that.

Charlotte came down the stairs to find her son sitting by himself. She was delighted to have an opportunity for conversation with him without any interruptions. "Well, Troy, your grades will be here soon," she commented.

"Yeah, Mom, I know."

"Aren't you happy with yourself?"

"I guess so."

"You guess so! What's wrong with you? Is something bothering you?" She sat down beside him on the couch.

Troy exhaled deeply. "Mom, I didn't know that we were all oppressed like this, that's all."

"What are you talking about now, boy? Black people?"

"Yeah, Mom. I mean, I just grew up. I didn't have any idea of the lopsidedness between Blacks and Whites."

His mother smiled and patted his shoulder. "Well, if you work hard, you can take us away from here," she said.

"What about everyone else who's Black and poor?"

"The world ain't fair, Troy. You just have to deal with the cards you're dealt. You'd be surprised how many of these Whites have all kinds of money and are still miserable. Some of them live the most lonely lives, despite their wealth.

"I had read in the paper, three days before you came home, that a young princess killed herself in England when she found that the guy she loved didn't love her. Hell, I was in love with your father, but the hell if I woulda killed myself over him. So you count all the good things that you got goin' for yourself, and just live."

An elderly women entered their open front door and stared into Troy's face. "Now I know that ain't Troy," she said with a cracked voice. "I'll be damned! That boy has grown tall and handsome, like his father."

"Yup, that's my son. He just got back home from college last week," Charlotte said to her.

"Child, I remember when that boy used to steal everything you left unattended. And he would lie like a politician if you accused him," the elder woman said, giggling.

"Unh-hunh, well he's up in college now and getting real good grades, too."

"Yeah, well as long as he ain't stealing nothin'."

"Naw, he ain't into that no more. He stopped that when he started cutting hair," Charlotte said. She was starting to get irritated.

"My boy in jail for robbing some liquor store. My other son got arrested last night in a stolen car up in Wynnefield, some damn place," the elder woman added.

"Well, Troy ain't into that no more," Charlotte responded with an attitude. "Look, Ms. Helen, my mother ain't here, and we ain't got no more sugar. So if you'll excuse me, I would like to talk to my son in peace." Charlotte stood up to show her back to the door. Troy found it humorous, cracking a smile.

Once they received word that he was back home, Raheem and Scooter dragged Troy outside and headed with him downtown. After seeing his friends, all of Troy's bad feelings seemed to gradually disappear.

"Yo, I thought y'all was gon' get on my nerves about me quitting the team," he said, smiling.

"Naw, man, 'cause we all knew you would quit after that third game. Y'all was losing by, like, thirty points. The coach might as well had put you in then, 'cause it was no way y'all was gon' come back to win that shit. Especially in the last three minutes," Scooter said.

"Yeah, man, but you made the team, though," Raheem added.

"Fuck that team if I can't even get in. Where's Blue and Juice?" Troy asked.

"Oh, we forgot to tell you, cuz. Juice got sent up the Mills," Scooter answered.

"For what?"

"Well, you know he had a long-ass record already. Then he smacked this dude in the head with a pipe. That was it, then," Raheem said.

"What the hell he do that for?"

Raheem smiled after viewing Troy's contorted mug. "Oh, I forgot you was in college, where it ain't no violence and shit," he said with a smirk. "But, umm, Juice was after dude for some money that dude owed him. He had gave the dude three-hundred dollars to get some cocaine, so he could start up his own thing. And cuz suckered 'im and kept his money."

Raheem waited for Troy to settle down before continuing. No one bothered to turn their heads to listen to their conversation on the bus. It was all the same news to the Black passengers.

"Troy, man, I told the boy like five times that he could work with me, but he didn't wanna listen. Then I said that I would get a package for 'im. But naw, he had to get in with these big-time dudes. So he got his shit taken. And he's lucky that the cops picked 'im up, too, 'cause dem niggas would have been after 'im. I wasn't about to have no shoot-out when he didn't listen to me in the first place. He is lucky he younger than us, 'cause he would have been more than sent up to the Mills. That nigga would have been in jail."

"Yeah, well what about Blue?" Troy asked, changing the subject. He had enough with the negative news already.

"Aw man, Blue is in love and shit, with this bad-ass Puerto Rican freak," Scooter said.

Raheem smiled. "Yeah, but I'on know what she see in him."

"She got jet black hair?" Troy asked.

"Naw, man. She got like, orange-colored hair. You know how dem Puerto Ricans is. She got, like, light eyes and shit, and a tough-ass body," Scooter told him.

"He done messed around and got her pregnant, though," Raheem added. "Matter of fact, dey talking 'bout getting married, Troy, 'cause her parents like that nigga."

They all laughed as other passengers joined in, listening.

"You know what I mean, cuz?" Raheem asked, continuing. "Blue ain't ugly, he's just darker than the average dark." They all cracked up again as they neared the last stop, inside Philadelphia's downtown area.

Nothing had changed physically, Troy was simply changing mentally. Everything had transformed into an uncommon element. He no longer saw the shoppers as plain people in places. He saw them as symbols of a dominant White America.

Blacks were carrying shopping bags full of clothing and consumer goods. White men carried briefcases. Blacks wore loud, bright clothing, blue jeans, and sneakers. White people wore suits and dress shoes.

Blacks flowed in and out of malls. Whites flowed in and out of banks and company buildings. Blacks rode the buses. Whites took taxis home or parked in high-priced parking lots. Troy had a pocketful of money and he was ready to buy. Yet suddenly he had lost his purchasing appetite.

He and his friends walked in and out of stores, owned by Asians, Jews, and Italians. They owned shoe stores, jewelry stores, clothing stores, and radio shops. Troy thought it was amazing; all of the items that Blacks purchased the most were being sold by non-Black opportunists.

Raheem and Scooter put money down on gold chains in a Korean jewelry store. They then bought a couple of rap tapes from an Italian-owned record shop. Both the Asians and the Italians had Blacks and Puerto Ricans working for them inside the larger clothing stores. They always find a Black person to do their dirty work, Troy thought.

"Ay', Troy, what's up with you, man? You haven't bought anything or said shit all day," Scooter mentioned.

"Yeah, man, I know. I'm just lookin' at all these Italian, Jewish, and Asian businesses. I mean, their stores may as well be called Nigga Shops, 'cause we look like the only ones who buy shit from 'em."

Raheem laughed. "Nigga Shops, hunh? Yup, when you think about it, we are the only ones that buy all kinds of shit from these dagos, chinks, and Jews."

"Yup, cuz. They got every fuckin' thing," Scooter added.

Raheem hunched his shoulders. "Yeah, but fuck it,

though. Where else we gon' buy the shit from? They got the cheapest prices."

"Dig, 'cause I done talked these Italian motherfuckers down plenty of times," Scooter added.

"I know, cuz. They sell their shit like it didn't cost them nothin'," Raheem interjected. "I mean, Troy, that shit is true. But they own all the stores. So what the fuck you want niggas to do?" he asked.

"We gotta own our own stores and shop in 'em," Troy plainly responded. Raheem looked as though he would respond to him. He decided not to.

They roamed to the Gallery Shopping Mall to eat, passing several Asian street vendors selling cheap watches, bags, hats, and shirts. Troy stopped and picked up a shirt to read aloud.

"Yo, hold up. Check this out," he said. He lifted the black T-shirt into eye view as the cautious vendor woman watched him. " 'Black, and popular by demand,' " he read before smiling. His friends joined him in laughter, not really knowing what was so special about the event.

"Imagine that, Orientals selling us shirts expressing Black pride, while they take our money," Troy said. "I see why we 'popular by demand,' " he added. Again Raheem looked to speak, deciding not to. He wanted to tell Troy some things that he had learned, yet he didn't feel it was time yet.

Inside the Gallery, Troy noticed all of the food stands, racially. The Chinese stands had all Chinese employees working for them. The Italians had all Italians working for their pizza shops. Even the Greeks had other Greeks working with them. Blacks, on the otherhand, worked for corporate-owned chain stores, doughnut shops, and hot dog businesses. The janitors and general-duty workers were always Black. Just like in college, Troy thought. He imagined the head of operations, a White man wearing a suit and a tie. He would sit in an office, spinning left and right in a plush leather swivel chair, a large wooden desk in front of him, displaying his name and position.

Troy, Raheem, and Scooter entered another Italian-owned clothing store and were surrounded by attractive Puerto Rican and Black saleswomen.

"Hey, man, can I help chew wit' sometin'?" a dark-haired Puerto Rican asked. Troy watched her approach Scooter. She looked as though she was going to hug him. A Black girl approached to help him and Raheem.

"Ay', what's up? Y'all brothers lookin' for anything in particular? We got some new stuff in the back. The new stuff is out and sellin' fast," she hinted. Raheem was out of money and Troy didn't even want to look at clothing.

"Naw, cutey, I already spent my paycheck, unless you got some free shit for me," Raheem said to her. He smiled while checking out her body.

"What about you, handsome?" she asked, staring at Troy. She seemed to ignore Raheem. He had obviously made the wrong comment.

"Well, I'm just looking today," Troy said, passing her by.

"OK then, sweetheart."

"Ay', Troy, she was on you like a champ, cuz. You

better jump on that, man," Raheem said in a low tone.

"She got a fat-ass nose," Troy told him.

Raheem frowned. "What? Since when you start worrying about noses? That babe is pretty as hell, cuz. I'd talk to her, if she was on me."

They walked toward the back to join Scooter with the Puerto Rican. Troy watched her lean up in Scooter's face every time he would turn to see a new item. She stayed glued to him, waiting on his every move to see what he wanted to purchase. Scooter tried on several pairs of pants and jackets as she tailored to his every move.

"Yo, Carmen, dem jeans look pretty good on you. I wouldn't mind buying them, and the package," Troy said, trying to entice her. He figured she would most likely try to correct the name. By using the wrong one, he would spur an automatic conversation piece.

"Oh, you do, do you?" she asked, turning to face him. Troy was stunned, for a second, at how fast she responded. "By the way, my name ain't Carmen. It's Joyce."

He chuckled. "I was just jokin'. I got that shit off that movie, *Beat Street.* So, what time do you get off work, so I can call you tonight?" Troy was going for the kill, trying to slip one past her.

"I don't think my boyfriend would like that," she responded, smiling.

Shit! I'm even losing my touch with the women, Troy thought to himself. "Yeah, well, what would your boyfriend say about you being all over my boy while he tries jeans on?" he snapped at her. Joyce simply walked away from him, unfazed.

Troy walked out ahead, after Scooter got his bags together. "I'm tired of girls fuckin' around with people, man. If they don't want to talk, they should act like it."

Raheem laughed softly. Scooter was busy counting money. All the Italian owner did was guard the cash register, while the girls worked hard to sell his inventory.

They rode the bus back up to Lancaster Avenue once they had finally left the downtown area. They peeked inside more shops, wondering about better deals. Once again, the Asian-owned stores were everywhere.

The Italians had at least one pizza or jewelry shop on each block. Most of the larger stores were owned by an established White Christian or Jew, who Troy believed hired friendly Black managers as their front men.

Blacks owned barbershops, hair salons, and a few old, small candy stores. They also had a few bookstores on the avenue. But Troy had always told himself, *Ain't no niggas interested in buying books.*

He could not manage a wink of sleep that night. Troy tossed and turned for hours, thinking about the predicament in the Black community. His people owned about as much as a baby in diapers. In their own neighborhood, Blacks bought three chicken wings with fries from the Asians. Fried potatoes and chicken wings were supposedly soul food, yet the Asians sold it.

Nearly every Friday, Troy and his crew would buy cheese steaks and sodas from the Italians without even thinking about it. They would spend, on the average, $20 to $30 a week in Gino's Steak House. Only a few dollars, every once in a blue moon, would be spent inside a Black-owned store.

The night had brought bitter dreams and a harsh awakening. Nevertheless, the new day brought hope. Troy's grades had finally arrived. His mother was the first to congratulate him.

"Troy, I got it," she said.

"Got what, Mom?" he asked, from the living room couch. He had slept there for the past couple of nights.

"Your grades. And you got a B in that chemistry class you were struggling with," she told him.

Troy leaped from his prone position to take a look at it himself. "*Aw, bet, Mom!* I'm in a good position for some money now. That means that I got somewhere around a three-point-four G.P.A. for the year. That's aw'ight," he said, parading around the house again, bragging about how hard he had studied. The excitement made him courageous enough to get dressed, and run to the playground.

It would be his first trip to the playground since he had been home. It looked as though there was a party on the courts, it was so crowded. He watched the many talented players, who all looked like NBA stars to Troy. As he neared the courts and was soon spotted, he began to fear the attention that he would receive. They may have all watched the game in which he had sat on the bench. He felt like he had let the neighborhood down for the first time in his life. His pride began to shrink, step by step, as he approached the courts.

"Yo, dere goes Troy!" a tall young man shouted, catching everyone's attention. "Yo, what's up, boah? Come here, man. It's about time you got home," he said. Troy walked over, heart filled with anxiety and fear. He knew what was coming. "Yo, man, why you quit?"

He took a deep breath. "Aw, Nate, man, that team is a trip. I was good enough to start, or at least to get in the game. So I said, 'Ta hell with it, then,' " he responded, still feeling unsure of himself.

His friend looked at him quizzically. "You should have hung in there, though, cuz," he said. "You only a freshman, right? So you still had more seasons. You act like you was about to graduate or something. You never know what could have happened." Nate was tall, massive, and a lover of the sport called basketball.

"Naw, man, whenever a person makes you wait for something you should have already had, then most likely they're using you, or they don't want you to have it," Troy said, philosophizing again.

Nate smiled, knowingly. "You never did have any patience. I wish I could have talked to you while you was up there. I damn sure would have told you to hang in there."

"Troy is a sellout. He sat the bench. Aah," a T-shirt-wearing kid said, running by and pulling no punches.

Nate shook his head with a grin. "Don't even worry about it, man, just get your grades together. But you know what? The way people get jerked around in college, it ain't worth trying sometimes anyway," Nate explained.

"My cousin had a scholarship to college to play ball, but he hurt his ankle in the second season. They never really gave him another chance after that. So now, he's back home, working at this recreational center down South Philly. It's fun and all, 'cause he always liked working with kids, but it don't pay nothin'. So you make sure you get that education first, man, 'cause too many Black people go away to college and forget what they're there for."

After Nate had finished talking to him, one on one, it was open season for questions, answers, and comments. Troy had spoken to people he hadn't seen since he was a kid, ten years ago. He talked to them about college life. He bragged about the women he had scored with, and then proceeded to talk about the standouts on the basketball and football teams. He got many word-of-mouth invitations to parties, but he remembered that he was back home. He could expect violence afterward. College life had softened him up. He was beginning to fear the dwellers of his neighborhood.

"Yo, Troy, you should go to this party with me on Thirty-sixth Street," a well-dressed teen said. Hank sported a gold ring with a dollar sign on his left hand. He wore a pair of expensive Alpina sun shades and was known for selling drugs

"Thirty-sixth Street? Next to the projects?" Troy asked him rhetorically. He felt as if he had become an outsider, and he needed to come back to his people. He knew that Thirty-sixth Street was in a bad area.

Yet and still, he wanted to convince himself that he was not afraid of anything.

"Yeah, aw'ight then, Hank. I'm down. I can probably get some sex up there tonight, too. The girls haven't seen me for a while. I know dey gon' be on me," he commented, trying to pump himself up.

It was ten o'clock at night. Troy and Hank drove to the party in Hank's black Jimmy jeep. Troy continued to talk up his confidence by referring to the "good old days." Yet when they arrived at the door he began to panic. He remembered beating up one of the project's tenants, and they always hung in groups.

Troy entered the cluttered, smoke-filled party apprehensively. It was nothing like the clear, spacious settings for college parties. He was back home at a common thug jam.

He searched around the basement before walking down all of the stairs. After not seeing the project crew, he decided it was safe. He was not at all interested in dancing. He only wanted to romance a cutey and leave. Troy spotted, and quickly approached, who he thought was the prettiest girl there.

"Ay', Brenda, long time no see."

Brenda was light-skinned with straight black hair, smooth and cut short on the sides, long on top. She was short and slender, with keen facial features.

"Hey, Troy, what's up, honey? I ain't seen you for the longest time." Brenda's big gold earrings shined in Troy's eyes as he pushed closer to talk through the loud music.

"You still go with Dean?" he asked her.

"Why, does it matter?" she said, smiling. He was back home, realizing there was no longer a need to beat around the bush.

"You down to go chill somewhere, then?" he asked her, feeling that he was in already.

"Yeah, that's cool. We can go to my girlfriend's house," Brenda said, leaning into him. "You gon' get on with us, Troy? We got some blow," she told him. Again he was reminded too bluntly that he was back home.

Troy responded in shock. "What, you snort blow, Brenda, as pretty as you are?"

"Damn! I mean, what chew, my guardian now? Shit. I can do what the fuck I wanna do! It's my fuckin' life, right! I'm tired of people talkin' that shit about me," she countered radically, sparking unnecessary attention.

"Ay', yo, Brenda, what's up?" Troy didn't recognize him, as the glaring youth stepped up, surrounded by four others.

"Nothin'. Don't worry about it," Brenda told them.

Troy took a deep breath, thanking her, mentally, for letting him off the hook. However, the party had quicky lost its interest. He didn't seem to be a part of the people he thought he knew. Nevertheless, before he got a chance to leave, another tough youth approached from the smoky crowds.

"Ay', yo, cuz, did you say something to my girl?" He had a hostile expression, alerting Troy for an attack.

"Naw, man. I don't even know who your girl is," Troy responded. He was desperately trying to work his way out of the situation. He began clutching his fist behind his back. Troy had long ago felt that Hank had left him in the party alone.

"Yo, what's up, man?" his friend Hank asked, seeing that Troy was stationed for a rumble.

"Oh, Hank, I ain't know this was your boy. I was ready to fuck cuz up. He don't be comin' off at my girl and shit," Troy's challenger said. Hank looked at Troy, knowing exactly what he was thinking. Troy had long ago learned the survival game. He knew that the only way to resolve the problem was to fight or be disrespected. Disrespect would only lead to more fights.

"Cuz, you ain't talkin' 'bout me like that," Troy told him. "We just gon' have to get that shit on."

"So what's up, then? What chew sayin', nigga?" Troy's challenger asked while throwing his hands up.

They went outside, followed by a crowd of instigators. It was nothing new to the neighborhood. Fighting was a way of life.

The air was dry and chilly. Troy was already tired, but alert. His challenger began taking off his jacket. Troy rushed him into a car with a flurry of hard, solid punches to the face and head. He had hurt his hand, punching his challenger in the mouth, his hand catching a broken tooth. The challenger buckled and fell. He got up, bruised, and ready to continue.

Troy was much too sharp and pumped with energy to be hit. He punched the youth in the head, body, and face, spurting blood as the hushed crowd watched.

No one bothered to break it up or to phone the police. After knocking his opponent down three times with lefts and rights, Troy went on to kick his victim when he was down, stomping him in the head, hoping that he would not get up again.

Finally, they broke up the violent bloodbath. Troy, charged on destruction, spun toward Brenda for causing the commotion. He had never hit a girl before, but he socked Brenda with a punishing left hand to the jaw, knocking her off her feet before anyone could stop him.

"Ay', Troy, come on, man! What the fuck you doin'?" Hank shouted, grabbing him back.

Hank hauled Troy away as Brenda recuperated, crying and yelling. "You pussy. You gon' get your ass kicked, nigga. Watch," she hollered, staggering into the opposite direction, followed by her girlfriends.

"Aw'ight, then, cuz gon' get his!" someone else shouted.

"Yeah, well which one of y'all niggas want somethin'?" Hank snapped, pulling a gun out of his beige Fendi handbag. He hustled Troy inside his jeep, purchased from drug money, and hauled him away.

"Ay', Troy, what's up with you, man? You didn't have to punch her. I mean, you beat the shit out of the dude already," Hank said, laughing.

Troy had nothing to say to him, staring out the window, feeling nerve vibrations pulsing throughout his body. As soon as they arrived at his house, he jumped out and ran inside to his empty, secluded basement. He sat on the steps and thought. He had never felt such tension. All of his limbs wanted to form their own bodies. His thoughts were hectic. He knew that he had been in a fight, which he had won, yet for some reason, he was ashamed.

"Ay', Troy, what's up, man?" Scooter ran in the basement to ask. "I heard you was fightin', cuz." No words entered Troy's mouth as he got up and listened, pacing back and forth across the cold basement floor. "We can get everybody and go back down there, if you want," Scooter suggested.

Troy shook his head, still trembling. "Naw, cuz. I'm gon' go to my aunt's crib tomorrow and settle down."

Scooter nodded. "Yeah, aw'ight, then, cuz. If you feel that way, then it's cool. 'Cause you don't need to be back out here fighting anyway." Scooter sat on the basement stairs himself, above his troubled friend, and shook his head. "Damn, cuz! Niggas don't know how to act!

"You come home from college and can't even go to a party. That's fucked up! All they wanna do is start fights and sell drugs. You the only one that got a chance at making it out, and look how they treat you when you come back home. Niggas just don't care about shit. They try to bring everybody down. We don't deserve shit any damn way, 'cause all we gon' do is tear it up, no matter what it is. You know?"

Scooter continued to talk for as long as they could stay awake in the basement. His views seemed to shine with new truth. Blacks terrorized one another constantly. Never was there a concert where there wasn't a robbery. Never was there a social function in the neighborhood without a fight.

Troy knew little about slavery, but he could see the effects of it. Blacks were the lowest, nonhaving humans in the United States. He walked around his aunt's neighborhood for the next couple of days, finding the same results. The Black residents made up ninety percent of the geographical population. However, they owned only twenty-five percent of the commercial businesses.

Troy sat outside on the patio each day, thinking about and watching his roughneck cousins play with their friends. He wondered about their future, the next generation.

"Troy, can you go to the store for me?" his aunt asked him, opening the silver screen door.

"Aw'ight. What do you want me to get?"

"A box of cereal and milk for tomorrow."

Troy ran to the store, happy he had something to do. When he arrived, the Korean owner went to his stockroom while his young son tended to the cash register. In a dash, three Black kids grabbed a bunch of candy and ran out the door. The Korean boy hollered to his father, who returned much too late to do anything. They had gotten away free.

Troy looked embarrassed. Maybe he and his young son could work side by side in business one day.

"I don't know who they were that stole the candy bars, but I'm willing to pay for it," Troy offered. His nerves were shot as he reached out an extra $2.

"No, no, dat's all right," the owner responded. He smiled, shaking his hands in front of his face.

Troy smiled and shook his own head. "You know, us Blacks live such a hard life that sometimes it's hard to care about anyone else."

"No, dat's fine," the owner repeated, still smiling.

Troy was pleased with the wide smiles he had gotten from the Korean father and son. He felt that he had given them something to remember. A young Black man was willing to make amends for a crime he did not commit.

For the next couple of days, Troy continued to survey his aunt's area. It was cleaner and had nicer homes, but violence still plagued the neighborhood hot spots. His aunt had already told his two young cousins to defend themselves if attacked. Most likely, it would be against another Black child. The chain of violence would continue. But who could stop it? Every other parent on the block would say the same thing to their kids. It was a never-ending story.

Troy pondered reasons as to why Blacks could not own business enterprises in their own communities. As long as the Italians had the stores, it was OK. As long as the Jews owned the stores, it was OK. If Asians owned the stores, it was OK. Yet when another Black owned a store, jealousy seemed inevitable.

"Troy, are you gonna get a job this summer?" his aunt asked after he fixed himself a ham and cheese sandwich to watch a martial arts movie on television. "Oh, I see you like that karate stuff too, hunh?" she asked. Aunt Judy didn't bother him much. Still, Troy didn't hear her; he was trapped in the plot of the movie. "Troy!" she shouted, walking closer.

"Hunh, what did you say?" he asked, facing her from the sofa.

"Are you gon' to be looking for a job this summer, 'cause it's a whole lot of money you'll be missing out on?" his aunt asked again, standing over him.

Troy nodded and took a bite of his sandwich.

"Yeah, you're right. As a matter of fact, I might as well go looking for one today."

He left at the end of the movie and caught a bus to the nearby mall. Blacks worked in every store there. He felt confident he could get a job after finishing a year of college, although he had never had a job before. He had always thought that jobs restricted your freedom. He laughed at his friends, working on Friday and Saturday nights while the crew was out enjoying life. He had learned different now. He was back home, from a hard year at college study, looking for a job like everyone else.

Troy desired to work in a large department store where he could feel low-key, as opposed to employment at a no-class place like McDonald's.

He entered a John Wanamaker's department store. It had large, elaborate clothing displays. He imagined the weekly gross of the seven floors of accessories from clothing to furniture. All of the designer names represented private entrepreneurs who went out on a limb to perfect a product. Their only bosses were those of public taste and demand. For the self-made man and the self-made woman, the sky was the limit.

Entrepreneurship was the American way, not working for people. In the future, Troy planned to have his own business. It was a must!

"Yes, could you possibly direct me to the employment office?" Troy asked the White woman sitting in the information booth.

"It's on the third floor," she informed him.

He didn't bother to say, "Thank you." He was rude. He figured it was her job to provide the information.

He squeezed onto an elevator holding nothing but White suit-and-tie wearers. They spoke of politics and governmental plans. Troy never thought such issues applied to Black people. What reason would there be for them to vote?

At the employment office, on the third floor, Troy was pleased to see a brown face for a change. "How are you?" he asked, trying to be polite. He was simply happy to deal with one of his own, where he could speak freely.

"I'm fine. And how are you?" the freckled-faced woman responded.

"I'm OK, but I was wondering if you were hiring."

She grimaced. "Well, not at the moment. But we do have openings for a temporary position, if you're interested."

"Yeah, OK, then," Troy said.

She grabbed a piece of paper. Troy filled out his name, phone number, address, and social security number.

"Ok, Mr. Troy Potter, if you could get here Saturday morning at ten o'clock, we can set you up with the first interview group," she said. Troy wasn't really interested in a temporary position, so he continued to shop around.

He went on to JC Penney, Sears, and Bamberger's, determined to get hired. It was only Tuesday. He had plenty of time before Saturday, so over the next couple of days, he traveled to large department stores all over the city. He wished he could just talk his way into a position. Nevertheless, all of the offices he had visited had only representatives with no authority in hiring. All he could do was fill out applications. By the time he was tired of job hunting, Troy had filled out at least thirteen applications. He waited all that week, expecting to receive a call, and got nothing. Since he had never had a job before, Troy didn't realize that sometimes it took longer than a week to get a call-back. All he had secured was an interview with John Wanamaker's, for a temporary position.

Friday afternoon, Troy received a call from his friend Blue. They went to a suburban mall, just to look around. Troy had not talked to any of his friends for a week. He no longer felt an urge to be near those whom he grew up with. After his college experiences, he felt torn from his previous social group. He wasn't lonely, just confused, needing space to think things through.

"Can I have a hamburger and some fries with an orange soda?" Blue asked at a Burger King inside the mall. Troy wasn't hungry. He watched as a high-school-aged girl got Blue's food and put it inside a bag. "Umm, I would like to eat it here," Blue told her, expecting a tray and some napkins.

"Oh, sure. You can eat it here," she responded, sneering as if Blue had made a stupid comment.

"Well, I would like to have a tray. That's why I said that. I wasn't asking you if I could eat here or not," Blue snapped.

She got the tray and mumbled, "Sorry."

Troy took a seat with Blue, who could not help commenting on the tray incident. "You see that shit,

Troy?" he asked. Troy nodded his head, smiling. "White people think they slick. She gon' sit there and deliberately try to embarrass me and shit, like I really was asking her if I could eat here. See, man, I figured 'em out. They wanna change things around to what they wanna hear. And they don't really listen."

Blue ate a few fries and took a bite of his sandwich before continuing. "Troy, man, I was messing around with this dumb White girl from Frankford while you was up in college. This chick asked me to repeat myself all the time, like she couldn't understand me or some shit. Then she always did stupid shit, trying to tell me she's sorry.

"Like, one time she called me up and said she was pregnant, as if it was a joke. I was scared as hell, cuz. Then she gon' tell me she was just kidding. Man, I damn near took her neck off."

Troy raised his brow, intrigued. "You hit her?"

"Yeah, I hit her, man. I ain't like that shit she did at all, cuz. See, White people think they can do anything and get away with it. That's why they say 'Sorry' all the damn time, 'cause they got a guilty conscience," Blue said, philosophizing. " 'Sorry' means to forgive, to me, man. It don't really mean that you acknowledge that you did shit wrong. Sayin' 'Sorry' is that cute shit that people say to calm you down."

Blue paused to eat his food. Troy sat and listened without interrupting.

"Like us, Troy. Most Black people we hang out with say, 'My fault,' which means that you did something wrong. Saying 'Sorry' don't mean shit! It don't change a damn thing. I mean, look what they done to our race. Do you think that sayin' 'Sorry' would change that shit? Fuck no! And why did I mess with a White girl in the first place? I guess I just wanted to see if the shit was different. But never again, cuz. Never again."

After leaving Blue, Troy realized that he was not alone. He began to think strongly about his college friend James. James had long ago witnessed the harassment, racism, and trickery. Troy began to wonder if all Blacks knew. Maybe they just didn't discuss it, never taking part in a solution.

Troy realized that he, too, had contributed to the self-destruction of his race by not feeling obligated or interested in change. He had never gone to any Black events at school, yet he possessed newfound nerve to be concerned with others who were disinterested.

The National Association for the Advancement of Colored People had held events on his Marsh County campus, along with the National Urban League, the National Council of Negro Women, and even Minister Louis Farrakhan from the Nation of Islam had spoken on campus, to much protest from White students, particularly from the Jews. Troy attended none of the events.

Troy got dressed that Saturday morning for the interview at John Wanamaker's. He wore blue jeans, his brown docksider shoes, a striped button-up shirt, and a thin, tan jacket. After riding an empty bus to the subway station, he waited ten minutes before the train arrived. He rode the train downtown to find that he was early. The doors at Wanamaker's were still closed.

Troy walked around, window-shopping. He doubled back to Wanamaker's after a half hour or so. The doors were opening. He walked inside thinking about the temporary job.

Troy suspected that he was heading to the same room as the other young Black teenagers who were entering the department store with him. They all headed to room 407 at a side door. The staff members were gathering themselves for the presentation to the future temporary employees.

A group of Black hopefuls sat outside of the conference room. The staff informed Troy to sit with the others inside the room of twenty-five desks. A small blackboard faced them like the inside of a classroom.

All of the desks were quickly filled. Troy ended up sitting in a chair, away from the rest, where he could easily observe everyone.

A young White woman walked in from the conference room wearing a charcoal gray suit with a pinstriped white blouse. She positioned herself in front of the blackboard and moved her hands nervously in front of her body. "Hi, my name is Carol Hanson, and I'm from Columbia University, home for the summer," she said, getting everyone's attention. "I would like to describe the temporary position to you," she added. Troy could not believe his eyes and ears. He attended State University and was home for the summer as well. What makes her any better than me? How did she get a supervisor position? he asked himself.

"The temporary position is fifteen days," Carol went on. "You will be be paid three seventy-five an hour to help clean up stock." She spoke with excitement, as if it were a privilege to receive the temporary positions. "You will work every day from nine to five until those fifteen days are up."

Troy was appalled. He thought that temporary meant at least a month or two. He figured he might as well wait for another offer and give Wanamaker's up. Yet the rest of the prospects watched as though they were paralyzed.

Troy started to twitch as he stared at the Black hopefuls sitting patiently in school desks, listening to a young White college student. She was younger than many of them. He couldn't stand it any longer.

"Well, if anyone does not desire the position, you are free to go," she ended. Troy looked around and saw that no one even budged. After Carol Hanson started up again, seeing that no one else would leave, he got up in the middle of her speech.

"That's aw'ight. I don't want to be hired for such a short time," he said, interrupting.

"Oh, OK, then," Carol responded.

Troy looked back into the eyes of the future temporary employees as he turned to leave. He took note of their helpless yet incensed stares. They seemed to look as though he had offended them. As if he had smacked them in the face. They hated him because he wanted more. He hated them because they would settle for anything.

Troy entered a dry, drafty wind, feeling powerless and alone. He returned to his aunt's house that afternoon, waiting for calls that he would never receive.

SELF-HATRED

"HI YOU DOIN', TROY?" ASKED LANCE, JUDY'S HUSBAND. "You haven't found a summer job yet, hunh?"

"Nope. I sure haven't," Troy answered him. It was the middle of July, and after being at his aunt's house for a month, nothing had been accomplished. There was nothing to do, no one to see, and laziness had set in above all other things. It seemed perfectly sane for Troy to sit around and watch television and movies all day at his aunt Judy's house. He'd stretch out on the pullout bed in the basement, hands behind his head and feet plopped up on a cushion, his eyes glued to the tube. Thirteen applications filled with no responses, except for the one temporary position at Wanamaker's.

"Yeah, it's rough out there," Lance said, tugging on his dark brown work boots. "You gotta' keep huntin', though," he added. Lance worked nights, down in South Philly, at a shipping port, unloading inventory imported from overseas. He was built for the job, over six feet tall and broad-shouldered, with a full-grown beard.

"These jobs ain't payin' nothin' no way," Troy pouted.

Lance pulled on his work hat and stood upright. "Yeah, well the man ain't gon' give us what he owes us, so we gotta secure what we do have."

Troy nodded. "Yup. That's why we gotta get our own thing."

"God bless the child that's got his own," Lance said, grinning. "Ain't no man on the moon gon' argue with you about that, Troy. But you got a lot of livin' and learnin' to do, young blood. I ain't met that many of *us* that understands shit about this thing called capitalism, yet. Maybe you young bloods can understand it better."

Troy smiled. "Them drug dealers understand it."

Lance hunched his brow concertedly. "Yeah, well you name me a black drug dealer who's been in the business for ten years or more without bein' arrested, killed, or strung out on the shit himself, and I'll shake the nigga's hand and ask him for a job." Troy started to chuckle. Lance, however, remained serious. "Let me tell you something, Troy. This life is much longer than a few strings of gold, a fast car, and a cute young girl driving you crazy."

Lance finally smiled again as he shook Troy's hand. He had said his piece and was up the stairs and off to work.

Troy had enjoyed the brief, frank chat. He realized that Lance had children to feed, bills to pay, and hours to work. Nevertheless, Troy figured if Lance had his own business, then he could give his nephew-in-law a job.

Troy then thought about his uncles. Mark, Tim, and Ronald Potter were all out trying to make ends meet. Troy never thought about having man-to-man talks with them before. What advice could they give him?

They don't own shit either, he contemplated. His conclusions all seemed to point fingers at the Black race for every downfall. As Simon had told Troy before, on one of their nights of debating, "There is no kingdom without the peasants to keep it going."

"Troy, you been layin' around here on that couch every day. Aren't you bored? Don't you have something to do?" Aunt Judy asked.

"Naw. I'm aw'ight. All I need is some food, and I'm cool," Troy answered, grinning.

"Well, Jamey and Chucky are going to New York this Saturday on a camp trip. And I need you to cut their heads."

Troy raised to attention. "They're going to New York? Dag, I never even been to New York. And they're only nine and six. Man, that ain't even fair."

"Well, if Lance doesn't want to go, you can take his place. I haven't been to New York before myself. I've been working since I was eighteen," his aunt commented.

Troy cut his cousins' heads for the trip, giving them two different hairstyles. Chucky had curly, fluffy hair like Doc, up at school. Jamey, the youngest, had woolly hair. Troy gave Chucky a high haircut, capturing the full essence of the curls with fancy parts. He cut Jamey's hair down low, with one part.

"Aw, Mom, he didn't cut my hair like Chucky's. I wanted a block, too," Jamey whined.

Judy smoothed over her son's head and frowned. "Yeah, Troy, why did you cut his hair so low? He usually gets a high cut, too. Didn't you see how thick it was?"

Troy was embarrassed by the mishap. "Yeah, well, it was easier to cut Chucky's head like that, since his hair is so much higher," he responded eerily. He began to sense that maybe the issues hit upon in college had affected him more than he had thought. Fortunately, his aunt said nothing more of the incident. Jamey stopped whining and returned outside to play.

Lance was too tired after working overtime to travel to New York Saturday morning. Troy happily filled in. Children waited joyfully for the buses outside their summer camp building. For most of the kids, it would be their first trip out of the city. The Philadelphia city government afforded the West Philadelphia Community Center the opportunity. It would be a cultural trip to the Statue of Liberty. The youths and their participating parents were scheduled to go south to the Baltimore harbor in the next two weeks. Troy hoped he could tag along on that trip as well.

Two buses finally arrived to greet fifty happy kids and parents. Troy, his aunt, and his cousins decided to board the second bus, which was nearest them. And as they sat and waited for the buses to depart, Troy read the *Philadelphia Tribune*, a Black-owned newspaper.

As he flipped through the pages, he glanced at several commentaries discussing the Dukakis and Bush presidential campaigns. Looking up momentarily, he was happy to see a Black bus driver and a Black coordinator for the trip. He then dropped his head to finish reading, only to be rudely interrupted. A gray-haired White woman, wearing the same blue T-shirt as the Black coordinator, was handed the microphone.

"Hello, boys and girls and parents. My name is Martha Simpson, and I will be your tour guide for the day. I have organized this trip to fit in as many sights as possible out of the little time that we will have. It is now ten after eight. We will be arriving in New York no later than eleven. On arrival, I will get the tickets and distribute them to you and your kids. We will remain in a group, and all kids must be taken care of, because I am much too-old to keep after them," she announced humorously. Parents laughed at her too-old joke. Troy frowned and thought that she was arrogant. She was White, the only White person on the trip. And she ran the show.

"What do you think about Dukakis?" Troy asked his aunt, who was seated to his right. The bus had begun its three-hour journey to Staten Island, New York.

"Well, Dukakis supports more jobs and everything," she responded.

"I'm talkin' 'bout what he did to Jesse Jackson," Troy alluded.

"Well, Jesse had lost, so it wasn't much he could do."

"Dukakis still could have chosen Jesse for vice president. Jesse Jackson was the best candidate," Troy commented. "Matter of fact, if Jesse was White, he would have won everything. Easily!"

His aunt Judy smiled and nodded. "Yeah, well you know how this country is. People didn't think Jesse could get as far as he did. But I've voted for and supported Jesse ever since he started. And I'll always vote for him."

Troy nodded back to her. "Dukakis thinks we got no choice but to vote for him, even after he dissed Jesse. He's taking us for granted because we always vote Democratic. So we need to show him that we can no longer be tricked by that kind of wheelin' and dealin'. I would vote for Bush."

Troy waited to see if his aunt would respond. When she didn't, he continued. "All these Blacks talkin' about what Dukakis will give us is only gon' make people more lazy and dependent. What we need is to start working hard to get our own, 'cause White people own everything already. Look at this trip today, Aunt Judy. There's only one White person here, and she's in charge. That's exactly what I'm talking about."

Judy remained silent, nodding, as if Troy's views were veritable.

The buses had arrived late. Parents and children were rushed to save time. The older White woman yelled at the top of her lungs for everyone to get a move on and to stay together. Their orange "West Philly Community Center" T-shirts made it all manageable. They could be easily identified as a group.

As the tour guide continued to shout for them to move faster, Troy felt that she was overplaying her hand of cards. And he didn't like it.

"Aunt Judy, I'm getting tired of this White lady screaming and whatnot. She act like we can't hear," he mentioned. They stood in a long line, waiting to take the ferry to Liberty Island.

"Yeah, well, that's just her job. She knows what she's doing," Judy told him.

"*Parents!* Hold on to your children and move to the right to get your tickets!" the White woman shouted. Troy felt ashamed, like a twentieth-century slave boy. He was glad he wasn't wearing an orange shirt like the rest of them.

While the line moved, he watched numerous Puerto Ricans flooding the park, waiting as well to aboard the ferry. Outside the long line, a group of Jamaican acrobats entertained the crowds.

"Gather around, folks. We 'bout to do an amazing show for you here, today! My mon Victor here and the rest of de boys are ready to entertain you. Japanese, get out your cameras! White ladies, hold your pocketbooks tightly! Nah, I'm just jokin', madam," said a short, brown Jamaican wearing biker shorts. The many tourists laughed and eyed him as his taller Jamaican brothers performed their tumbling stunts. They received loud applause while their short ringreader collected a red, green, and black hat full of money, steadily cracking his ethnic jokes.

On Liberty Island, Troy noticed Latinos behind the refreshment line cash registers. Others cleaned the small island grounds, emptying trash and collecting ferry tickets, while their visible White managers served as the overseers. Latinos were being used in

New York the same as Blacks were used in Philadelphia and in Marsh County. This reflected the annual economic reports that Troy had observed. Blacks and Latinos remained at the bottom of the totem poll of American society.

The tour guide began another shouting spree. Time was up on the island and she was ready to go. Troy tried his best to ignore her.

"Gather your kids and line up next to the wall so I can take a count!" she shouted. It was more than Troy could stand! She spoke with a harshness that equated the parents and kids as one and the same, as if they were all unruly juveniles.

Troy decided that her military-style demands would fall on deaf ears, as far as *he* was concerned. She's not going to count me next to a wall like some damn slave, he thought declaratively. He sensed an increasing urge, in fact, to tell her off. Who in the hell does she think she's talking to?

"Hey, young man, aren't you with our group? Now get over here so I can take count!" she shouted in Troy's direction.

Adrenalin-filled blood raced through his veins with the speed of a missile. His heart seemed to turn into a fireball within his chest. He had never experienced such humiliation in his life.

"I don't know you, lady, and I'm not with that group," he said calmly. But his piercing-eyed look could kill. He was determined that the old White woman would not make a fool out of him. He was appalled, filled with incensed anger toward the White woman who shouted and the Black parents who listened and obeyed. The tour guide realized, of course, that he was with the group, yet she decided not to bother him (a good decision).

After returning to the bus, the group of West Philadelphia kids and their parents headed through Manhattan for the next spot on their tour list. The east side of Manhattan, New York, seemed to be filled with Latin graffiti artwork. The parks, recreation centers, and residential walls all exposed the zesty, colorful Latin culture and its inhabitants. Latinos flooded the New York streets as their peppy Latin music flowed inside the visiting buses from their towering project buildings. The buses moved slowly through the usual midtown traffic, trapped inside a Latin carnival of cultivation.

The buses then rumbled through Chinatown, stretching for nearly twenty blocks of commercial business. Asian shops, markets, centers, and banks stamped with Asian inscriptions blinded their Philadelphian eyes. Plowing through heavy traffic, it seemed as though they would never leave Chinatown, as they headed toward Forty-second Street for a New York dinner reservation, the old White woman's choice.

When they had arrived at the small, dark restaurant, Troy failed to regard its elegance. Anyone could own something so . . . so . . . ordinary. Yet it was owned by dark-complexioned Greeks.

The tour guide slipped inside first, to inform the management of their group's size before they all entered. Immediately, some of the children had dirtied up the bathrooms before they got a chance to eat, making Troy feel worse (especially after noticing a Black janitor going in to straighten things).

"Troy, what was your problem today?" his aunt Judy asked him.

He became defensive. "Naw, Aunt Judy, I didn't like how that lady was talking to us, like we was retarded or something."

"Yeah, boy, you never did like being told what to do," she commented with a grin. "I remember you used to spend the night when I lived in Southwest Philly. And you would run back to your mother when I told you you couldn't stay out all day. I used to be scared to death, thinking that your mother would kill me. But you always found your way home."

Scooter called and asked Troy to go to the movies. Troy had gotten back from New York around seven o'clock. He, Scooter, Raheem, and Blue all went to a distant theater in the suburbs. All the inner-city theaters were too crowded and hectic. They would have gone to Center City, but the suburban theater in Yeadon didn't cost as much.

The theater employees were mostly White, except for a few Black ushers. The White employees collected the cash for the tickets as well as for the refreshments. Troy reasoned that Blacks were seldom allowed near the money since they wore the stereotype badge of thief. Yet and still, he and Scooter decided to sneak in using tickets stubs from a previous showing.

"These White people should never get any money from us. They owe us the world, cuz," Troy said to Scooter, as they snickered about the get-over.

Scooter looked over his shoulder to make sure they were clear. "Dig, cuz. Fuck payin'."

They took a seat in the back to wait for Raheem and Blue.

"Them ushers are stupid anyway," Troy added. "And you notice how it's always Black ushers at the movies?" he asked Scooter.

Scooter smiled. "Yeah, you right. 'Cause even when we was kids, it was always Black ushers that threw us out. All the White people do is stay at the counters and count the money. See. That's why I don't like Black people. We do stupid shit. We care more about protecting their shit than they do."

Raheem and Blue finally joined them inside the theater.

"Y'all niggas a trip, man. I got too much money to be sneaking in the movies," Raheem said.

"Yeah, yeah. Give all your drug money back to the White man," Troy told him.

Raheem grinned with self-assurance. "Yup, and I'll keep doing it, too. As long as I'm happy, I'on give a fuck."

"Well maybe you need to stop being so damn happy, then," Troy snapped. Raheem looked at him, smiled, and shook his head.

Floods of viewers entered just before the movie began. All throughout the film, Troy flinched at the raw portrayals of Los Angeles Blacks and Mexicans who lived and died for gang love. Nevertheless, all four of the Philly friends agreed that the depictions were indeed close to factual. But watching White heroes in the end made their stomachs turn.

When it was all said and done, Scooter tagged along and went back to Troy's aunt's house. Blue split to his girlfriend's in North Philly. And Raheem went back to selling drugs in West Philly.

"Man, that was a dumb-ass movie, cuz. They always giving us some stupid-ass parts," Scooter said to Troy inside the basement that Troy began to call his shop. "They never show the reason why we sell drugs."

Troy threw his feet up on his aunt's basement coffee table. "Dig, man. But why do we sell drugs, Scooter?"

"Man, them White people made life hard as shit for us. Niggas are tryin' be to somebody. It's real messed up, but sellin' drugs gives us that status. You all of a sudden have all the girls; you can spend all kinds of money; plus you're popular as hell when you sell drugs. Raheem got plenty of honeys now," Scooter answered.

Troy shook his head with a grin. "A person gets popular for beating somebody, up, shooting somebody and selling drugs. We don't make an inch of sense, man. People shouldn't have been praising me when I was doing all my crazy shit. We sit up here and reinforce it. Like when teenage girls call their children 'bad,' all they doin' is mappin' out a criminal lifestyle for 'em."

"I know, cuz. But you can't even get a girlfriend now without having big-time dough. And the only way you can do that at our age is from selling drugs," Scooter said.

Troy clicked on the television with the remote control. Then he laughed to himself. "Look at this. I've been watching all these White shows about a White world, and every once in a while they'll throw a Black person in there to act stupid."

Scooter joined in with him. "Dig, cuz. We always get dem roles where we a crook, or we get killed or somethin'. I mean, we just plain nuts, man," Scooter declared. "White people got all the money and we got nothin.' Like Raheem, wearing that African piece around his neck with the green, red, and black shit on it. And he out here selling drugs. He probably don't even know what that green, black, and red shit means."

"Yeah, and then we always wanna brag about what kingdoms and shit we had," Troy added. "We ain't got shit now, so why talk about ten thousand fuckin' years ago, you know? The Egyptians never looked like us any damn way."

"I know, cuz. The encyclopedia says that the Egyptians were brown Caucasians," Scooter said. "But you look like one of 'em, Troy. All you need is that wavy-type hair. 'Cause you already got dem sharp eyebrows and the skinny nose. You even brown like some of 'em." Scooter then looked at his bare hands. "Man, I'm so light I can't fit nowhere in Africa. They would send me back and shit."

They chuckled as Scooter continued. "Damn, we dumb, Troy! I'm yellow, but the White people got me calling myself Black. And it's people lighter than me, calling themselves Black. See, we just plain stupid, man."

"Yeah, well anyway, getting back to Egypt," Troy said, redirecting the subject, "I don't see why Blacks brag about that shit. Egyptians had slaves. And the pharaohs had all the power. And that's just what we don't need. We in that kind of system now, talkin' 'bout kingdoms and shit. The Egyptians had peasants and serfs and all that dumb shit that makes people miserable, but yet we brag about them 'cause they were scientific. What does science do for you if you have to pay for it and you're poor? I mean, what if we would have been peasants in Egypt? I guess that would of made us happy, hunh?"

Troy's intensity increased as he began to present information that had outdone Scooter's input. Scooter decided then to just sit and listen.

"See, man, that's the same kind of shit that White people lived under in Europe. Feudalism. And they never broke away from it," Troy said. "They had White people havin' all these kids, dirty, stinking peasants that worked in the fields all day for the king, who didn't do shit! Now who the hell is to say that a person shall be born into royalty? That shit is crazy! Then they had the lords who got their shit from fightin' in land wars. Peasants were at the bottom with slaves, poor as hell. But yet we brag about Egypt. I mean, we had it good when we were just hunters and gatherers, sharing everything. That's when people were really equal. But see, the White man got us running around looking for systems that are close to theirs. So we end up being hypocrites.

"The Native Americans were sharing people, too," Troy went on to say. "That's why the White people started up that dumb shit, calling people 'Indian givers.' The Native Americans would give the White people tools or land to use, right. Then they would come back to reclaim it when they needed it. But White people wasn't trying to learn how to share shit. All they had ever known is what is theirs and how to take it."

Troy stopped, momentarily, to use the bathroom. Scooter sat, numbed by the great span of information Troy had learned from his anthropology course. Troy then returned to continue from where he left off.

"And see, Scooter, Mexicans do the same stupid shit that we do. They brag about the Aztecs, who were the craziest of all the tribes. I mean, they were thorough in science and war. But you know what, man? I've figured it out. The more so-called advanced that a people are, the more violent they will be.

"Aztecs gave human sacrifices, killed off other tribes, and they even got a sculpture in Mexico using the skulls of the people they warred against. Now is that somethin' to be proud of? That shit is plain crazy, man. Them Aztecs cut people's hearts the fuck out! And they had serfs and slaves and peasants, too. Nobody wants to be a slave or a peasant. That shit ain't right. So why would the Mexicans brag about that? 'Cause the White people tricked us all into their psychology. That's why!" Troy shouted.

Scooter began to laugh as Troy went on.

"We all complain about this shit we live in now, but we gon' brag about when our people did the same thing. So check this out, Scooter. In this capitalistic system, Blacks, Puerto Ricans, and Mexicans are the peasants. Chinese, Koreans, and Japanese are the serfs. Then we add in all of that religious shit. And White people own everything, so they're the high chiefs and the pharaohs. So, if we so happy about the Egyptians and the Aztecs, how come we complaining about how we live now?"

Scooter chuckled again, noticing that it was getting a bit late.

"Yo, cuz, I hate to end your lesson and all, but I got to get home before I get robbed or something, out here this late. I heard about these Summerville niggas," Scooter said, walking up the steps.

Troy smiled and said something else. "Damn, man, we can't even travel among our own people without fearing what would happen to us. And we're all Black. Now try and tell some dude in the street that shit, and they'll laugh at you, right before they kick your ass."

After he had let his friend out, Troy thought about all of the information that he had expressed. Yet one thing Scooter had said had bothered him, "The encyclopedia says that the Egyptians were 'brown Caucasians,' " Troy repeated. Brown Caucasians?

Troy was appreciative that Judy and Lance were allowing him to stay with them until school would resume. He eventually watched less television and started dedicating more of his free time to reading. And he had become more interested in his family background.

Back home, the following week, Troy opened the familiar Potter front door. Ronald, his youngest uncle, and his aunt Cookie were there, sitting on the couch and smoking cigarettes. Troy had not seen his aunt Cookie in two years. He was pleasantly surprised.

"Is that my favorite nephew?" she asked (only because he was the oldest and the first nephew).

"You see me, don't you?" Troy answered with a snide grin.

Ronald smiled, shook his nephew's hand, and headed for the door. Troy wanted to stop him so they could talk, man to man, one to one. However, his aunt had leaped up and graciously hugged him before he could react to his quickly departing uncle.

Cookie led him to the couch. "Come on over here and sit down so I can talk to you, boy." She looked him over as he strolled. "My, you've grown! And got real handsome, too. You don't look nothing like your father, though."

Cookie loved to talk. Troy was in for it. But he had some questions of his own, so he wouldn't mind her babbling.

"Yeah, Aunt Cookie, was it hard dealing with White people when you went to college?" Cookie, the second eldest behind Troy's mother, was the only Potter child that had received an opportunity to go to school. Charlotte could have gone, yet she remained at home to help her mother take care of her kin after their father had died.

"Hell yes!" Cookie answered Troy emphatically. "I came back home ashamed. I didn't like my hair anymore. I wanted to be lighter. 'Cause you know I'm the darkest of all nine of us." (She was the tallest, too, standing at six-one, a family hybrid.) "And I was even ashamed of where I came from," she told him.

Grandmom Bessie had had six girls and three boys. Judy was the fourth child and Kim was last. Troy's two other aunts had relocated down south, "to get away from the crime-infested cities," they claimed.

"Aw, hell, Troy, I hated coming back here!" Cookie continued. "It was terrible. It was an all-girls private school. There was a college full of White boys right down the street from us. And ta hell if I was goin' to mess with them. So I didn't have no kind of love life. Then I had this White roommate who used to sneak her boyfriend inside our dorm all the time. And he tried to come on to me once when she went to take a shower.

"Boy, it was terrible! All I did was study, 'cause it wasn't anything else for Black people to do. But I stuck it through, though."

Troy couldn't believe it! College life had challenged his aunt just as it was challenging him. He was ashamed to realize that he was becoming attracted to females with skinny noses and small lips. He had played a favor game to his curly-headed cousin. He gave more credence to mixed girls with long hair. In fact, he and Blue, darker than Raheem and Scooter, had always dated redbones. Troy had to think *hard* to remember the last dark-skinned girl he had been with. He had been subconsciously seduced into hating Black features.

After finishing the discussion with his aunt, Troy crept up the stairs to talk to his grandmother. She stood in the middle of her ancient master bedroom, ironing her clothes for a family get-together later that evening. Bessie was a youthful and healthy woman. Blacks damn sure have that over Whites, Troy thought. We still look young with age.

He walked in and took a seat on the chair next to the dresser.

Bessie turned and looked him over with a proud smile. "How are ya', grandson? Come give Grandma a hug." Troy did as we was told.

She then looked down and gently swung her right foot. "Get away from here, you cat!" The multicolored, white, brown, and gray kitten was rubbing up against Troy's leg, begging for food. His grandmother smiled. "These darn cats get to me sometimes. But we need them to kill these mice. 'Cause those darn traps are too much a hassle."

Troy nodded and cut straight to the beef of his visit. "Hey, Grandmom, can you tell me a little somethin' about our family history?"

Bessie got excited immediately. "Well, sure, what do you want to know?" Troy then realized that his grandmother actually wasn't that old. Charlotte was born when Bessie was sixteen. Troy was born when Charlotte was eighteen. He was nearly nineteen, to date, making his grandmother somewhere around fifty-three years young. Some of his friends' parents looked older than she did.

"Well, I wanted to know what kind of mixed blood we had in us," he asked.

She nodded, thinking. "Well, *my* grandfather was a half-Spanish man from Costa Rica. He fell in love with my ugly grandmother, who was on a slave plantation in North Carolina. And he stole her from the plantation and ran north to Philadelphia," she began. Troy chuckled instantaneously at his grandmother's blunt style of storytelling.

"Troy, my grandmother was *crusty* black! I don't know what he saw in her. I had never seen her in person. She had died before I was born. But they showed me pictures of her, and she was dark, dark. But anyway, my mother turned out real, real light. I don't know how that happened, from how black my grandmother was. You remember seeing my mother, don't you? You were around seven then."

Troy thought back to his childhood years, slowly shaking his head. "Naw. I just remember that old White lady who used to come here on the weekends," he said.

Bessie bowed over in laughter. "Boy, that wasn't no old White lady, that was your great-grandmother!" she hollered. "But she lived in Jersey, and still does. You never got the chance to get close to her. You were always off, running around in the streets. She stopped visiting, though, a long while ago. Every once in a while I go to see her."

Troy smiled. "Dag, I thought she was your teacher or something from when you were young. 'Cause she sure looked White to me."

"Yeah, well she had married my father, who was part French from down New Orleans. He was traveling in one of those blues bands and ended up meeting and falling in love with my mother. And they had me. But he left her, though. She had to raise me by herself. And as soon as I got married, she moved off to New Jersey with the fella she lives with now."

"So that's French *and* Spanish blood?" Troy asked, keeping count.

"More than that," she told him. "Your grandfather—my late husband, Calvin—was part Dutch and Scottish." She shook her head and grinned. "Them White folks always talkin' 'bout how they got a melting pot in America, but we Blacks are the most melted things in this country.

"Back when me and your grandfather got married, black was the worst thing you could be. If you were real dark, you tried to get anything light that you could find. People ran out after Puerto Ricans, Chinese, Japanese, anything that was light-colored. It was terrible being black in the nineteen forties. But now, I hear people running around talkin' 'bout they 'proud to be Black.' I couldn't believe my ears after all of the things we had done to stay light. Folks used bleachin' creams and whatnot. It was terrible."

Bessie stopped and giggled before continuing. Troy said nothing. He listened and smiled to himself, enjoying it.

"Your father had a whole lot of Indian blood in his family," she said. "His mother had real long, wavy hair and was just a beautiful woman. His father looked like an Indian, too. He had these tiny black eyes, the same type that the Mexicans be having. He looked like he was either drunk or high."

Troy laughed again and continued listening. He wouldn't dare to correct his grandmother about using the term "Indian" (although it was on his mind). It was just a respect-for-your-elders thing.

* * *

Troy received lots of new information after a few hours of conversing with his grandmother,. He had gained more knowledge than he expected. He questioned the validity of the American rule that said you were Black if you had any drop of African blood, and he began to despise it.

The American rule was too limited. Black families ranged in all colors from light to dark. Many had even passed for White. However, Troy's thoughts on racial identity were quickly disregarded. Black he was. He accepted it.

He stayed and watched more television in his mother's room, awaiting her return from paying the utility bills. On the five o'clock news, it was reported that the Japanese ambassador had commented that the Blacks and Hispanics brought down the United States' educational system; they spent too much money on credit cards and general consumerism.

Troy agreed. He knew many Blacks who struggled eagerly to live beyond their means. He had come to the same conclusion weeks ago. Nevertheless, the politically astute Blacks of the United States demanded an apology. Troy suspected that the demand had come, most likely, from those upper-middle-class Blacks who politely ignored the American dilemma of race. They chose to view issues through their own economic and integrationist fantasies. They'd rather protect their claims of minority success stories than address the multifaceted problems that plagued the Black community.

Troy also found distaste in the continuous television ads for aid to starving Ethiopian and South American children. Black American kids would then create harmful slurs based upon what they saw but failed to understand.

Tired of waiting for his mother to return, Troy decided to visit Scooter's. It was fast approaching six o'clock.

Troy dashed across the street, let himself in, said "Hi" to Scooter's silent, gray-haired grandmother, and headed straight for the basement.

"Yo, Scoot, it's me," Troy hollered down the basement stairs.

"Ay', what's up, man? You had me laughing hard as hell that night I was at your aunt's crib, cuz. And yo, my grandmother don't like Black people either. She said they're loud and disrespectful. But you don't like Blacks for real, though, cuz?" Scooter quizzed, vividly remembering their discussion.

Troy fell into the three-person couch to the right. "I don't know who or what I like anymore. I wish I had never gone to that college. I mean, I didn't give a fuck before I went up there. But now, all I think about is racial shit."

"I know, 'cause I thought I was the only one that hated Blacks. But since you've been back, you helped me to get out a lot of my anger. Matter of fact, all we ever talk about is race when I'm with you," Scooter mentioned. "I mean, Black people ain't shit, though, for real. They cool to hang out with and all, but when it comes to gettin' money, I'm gon' get with a Jewish dude. They know how to get paid, cuz. Straight up!"

They sat and watched TV before either said anything.

"Man, I even hate watching some of these movies now. I leave the theater embarrassed as hell when White people put us in their movies."

Scooter laughed before he responded. "I don't like when Blacks are on TV. They don't even know how to talk, most of the time."

They started to giggle at their pronouncements.

" 'Black is beautiful,' " Scooter said. "That shit is crazy. I don't know who thought of some shit as wild as that. You know?"

Troy nodded. "Yup. Girls out here be wearin' contact lenses and getting their hair dyed blond, but yet, 'Black is beautiful.' "

Scooter laughed. "White people made contacts for us. They knew niggas wanted to be like them. So they said, 'Yeah, we can make lots of money off the niggers,' "

"And that messed it up for the Blacks who have natural light eyes," Troy added.

Scooter shook his head. "Man, White people get paid off of all the shit we do. Like, if they just make any stupid movie about us, we'll go see that shit."

"Yeah, cuz, remember that movie, *Planet of the Apes*? That could have been about us. 'Cause they had the light-colored apes, who were supposedly closest to humans, like you light-skinned Blacks are closest to Whites. And they were smart and nonviolent, just like White people think you are," Troy said.

"Oh, my God!" Scooter yelled. "And then they had them black apes that couldn't even talk right. And they was always ready to kill somebody.

"I knew it was some reason why I didn't like that movie. And Black people watched it like fools. Oh my God, cuz! *We nuts!*" Scooter shouted. He got excited and took over from Troy.

"In one of them movies they came over in cages. And the White people were laughing at 'em, just like they did us. Damn, Troy, you right, cuz! Then they had them in-between monkeys always trying to make peace, like a Martin Luther King type."

Troy laughed as Scooter's imagination went wild.

"Yup, Troy. Some ingenious White man was sitting around one day and said to his boy, 'Hey, Joe, what if we made a movie about the niggers taking over the world? Jesus, Joe! This could be the hit of the century. But we can't put real niggers in it. They'll fuck up the movie with their protests and all. So let's make them into apes. 'Cause that's all they really are, a bunch of stupid apes. We could get rich off this movie and they would never know.'

"Oh my God, cuz! I don't believe how stupid we are!" Scooter hollered as Troy giggled.

"And *King Kong* could be about us, too," Troy added with a grin. "You know how they think we crazy about their women. So they set it up where the giant ape symbolizes our biggest, strongest Black man. And you notice that they went to some African jungle to find him, right. Then he goes crazy and chases this White bitch all over New York."

"*Oh my God, cuz! I hate black people!* We stupid as shit, Troy. Aaaahhhh we dumb, and we watched all that shit, too!" Scooter shouted.

"Why you keep hollering about some God?" Troy

asked. "It ain't no God, cuz. Only poor and stupid people believe in that. White people tricked us on that, too. They made that shit up to calm people down, then they could take over the world without a fight.

"The first thing White people do is send their religious missionaries in to soften up the people. Then the armies come in to take over. I mean, us Blacks are the holiest people in the fuckin' world, thinking we gon' go to heaven and shit. That's the White man's greatest magic trick. And that's why we won't ever get nowhere.

"All Blacks do is get on TV and thank the Lord, whenever they accomplish something great. And that's tellin' White people we don't have any confidence in ourselves. We tellin' them that we need this supernatural shit to achieve something. What, we can't do shit with our own hard work? Is that what we believe? And people always run to that religious shit when they're weak, scared, or in some kind of jam. There ain't no God, Scooter. We've all been fooled."

Scooter changed his tune. "Yo, cuz, is you crazy? You better stop talkin' like that. I think you lost it in this racial stuff to talk about God like that, man. You better take that shit back."

"Aw see, they got you too. And I ain't never seen you go to church. So how you gon' believe in God?"

Scooter hunched his shoulders. "Cuz, I'on know, but there is a God. I think I'm gon' ask him to help you, 'cause you goin' crazy," he responded, chuckling to himself.

"So I guess I'm goin' to hell to burn up in the eternal fires, right? Where it's dark and black with smoke," Troy said, grinning himself. "Tell me something then, Scooter. How come heaven is white? How come everything white is good? How come Jesus is white? How come you get married in white and die in black? How come this country is ruled by the White House instead of the House of Liberty, or the House of America, or, the fuckin' House of *Freedom?* 'Cause White people made up that shit, Scooter. So it ain't no God, and if it is, the Jews are his people. *So what the fuck does he have to do with Black niggas?*" Troy shouted.

"Look, cuz, God created everything on earth! You can't count on that bullshit that the White man say. *They don't know everything!*" Scooter shouted back.

"Man, Troy. I'm gon' pray for you, cuz. You've lost it completely. I mean, you turnin' crazy. And I don't know what that college is doin' to you, but you better stop talkin' 'bout it ain't no God. Going to hell ain't no joke!"

Troy shook his head, disappointed. "Yeah, man, whatever. Pray for your damn self."

Next morning, Troy felt he had no friends left in the world. Scooter had let him down. He believed in religion. Weak. Scooter was unaware that White priests had pressed their religious philosophies down the choking throats of the world, smothering them with talk of sin and forgiveness. Troy cared nothing of heaven or hell, he was no longer afraid of death.

Black is beautiful, he thought again. He wondered what they had to be proud of. They had lost their birthplace, their beliefs, their racial purity, and their culture. Maybe a more historical approach was needed. So Troy continued to read, and to question.

"You been reading all day, hunh?" his aunt Judy asked Troy. He had returned to her cozy basement couch after an unsuccessful visit with his mother. She called and said that she had plenty of errands to run the night before.

"I just can't believe that you couldn't find a job this summer," his aunt mentioned. "You don't even *look* like you wanna get up."

"Yeah, well, I don't know how to sell myself to get one," he responded. "Them interviews are stupid anyway. All people work for is the money. So why should you have to tell a lie? That's just how White people like it. They're a bunch of liars."

Judy frowned. "Look, Troy, don't be goin' around blaming White people for you not being able to get a job, 'cause if you really want one, you can get one."

"You mean if I *beg* for one, I can get one," Troy insisted. "See, White people want you to get hungry to the point where you'll do anything for a job. Then they throw you some sorry, low-paying gig. Or better yet, a temporary job," he said sarcastically. He stopped himself short. He didn't want to slip and tell his aunt about the job he had walked out on. He knew that money was money. Judy would have been upset to hear that he turned down anything. But not his mother. Charlotte had always taught Troy to reach for the sky. And he always did.

Judy asked, reading his mind, "Did you see your mother last night?"

"Naw. But I know she wants to see me."

"Yeah, well it's already nine o'clock, and this neighborhood ain't no good at night. So you watch yourself if you decide to leave," Judy warned him.

Troy called home to his mother. He waited for a bus while holding a bag of clothing and accessories. The bus was running late. He grew nervous when he spotted six rowdy youths crossing the street in his direction. Never in his life did he shake and watch his back so much.

He arrived at the downtown subway, however, unharmed. He waited for a train inside the Broad Street station, watching three homeless Black men cuddling up in separate corners to find shelter for the night.

People watched and ignored.

"Ay', yo, homey. You got a dollar on you, man?" a dingy-looking teenager asked him. Troy had an extra dollar but he wanted it for himself.

"Naw, man," he answered.

The dingy teen grimaced. "What chew think I'm stupid or something, man? I know you got some money on you." He stepped closer. Troy prepared himself for action. He clutched his fist and stood sideways to get off a good solid punch. But the taller teen walked away. He wasn't after a fight.

Safety was the key to getting to his mother that night. Security was better than trust. What if the dude was really planning to rob me when I pulled out my wallet? Troy thought. Then again, maybe he just needed a dollar to get home. Nevertheless, safety was safety.

"Hey, Mom, are you home?" Troy yelled, barging inside of the Potter family home. He ran up the stairs to find his mother in bed.

"Yeah, boy, I'm here. But I'm tired. I'll talk to you in the morning," she said, drowsily. She barely peeked her head over the lightweight quilt. It was close to midnight. Charlotte had been busy working at AT&T's downtown office. She had been employed as a telephone operator for twelve years.

"Aw'ight, I'll see you in the morning," Troy said, leaving her room. He sprinted to Scooter's house. Blue and Raheem were there, watching a movie on cable.

"Yo, the whole crew is here, hunh?" Troy said inside Scooter's basement.

Scooter's eyes lit up. "Ay', man, we was just talkin' about you. I told them that you don't believe in God."

"I don't."

Blue stared Troy down from his usual seat on the couch. "Yo, man, there is a God. You better stop that shit, cuz."

"I told him, man," Scooter said, grinning.

"Everybody got their own opinions," Raheem injected.

"Yeah, well his shit is wrong. There has to be a God. White people don't really know where we came from," Scooter argued. "Troy been up in college listening to that scientific stuff too long. But you're right about Black people, though. 'Cause we are nuts."

Raheem looked at Troy quizzically. "You said that Black people are nuts?"

Scooter filled him in. "Yeah, we was talkin' about all the stupid shit we do. Like, how black-ass Blue hates himself, chasing after light-skinned girls all the time," Scooter said through laughter.

"Yeah, aw'ight, cuz. That's why I got a girl. You be in here jerking off every night," Blue responded.

"I mean, she only, like, fifteen years old. You twenty now. That don't make no sense," Scooter refuted. "And you got that girl pregnant, talkin' 'bout y'all gon' get married. Where the hell y'all gon' live at, in your Mom's crib? I mean, face it, we nuts," Scooter insisted.

"She's only fifteen?" Troy asked Blue.

"Naw, she's sixteen," Blue said before giggling.

Scooter burst out laughing. "He gon' say she sixteen, like it's a big difference. He still robbed the cradle, just to try and get something close to a White girl."

"Hold up, cuz, she ain't no White girl. She'll get mad as hell if she hear you say that shit about her," Blue said defensively.

"What race is she, then? She looks White to me. The only thing that ain't White about her is her body and them pointy eyes. Otherwise, she's White with a tan," Scooter argued. "And if you wanna get technical about it, us and Puerto Ricans don't have a race, for real. What should we call ourselves and shit? The White man fucked all of us."

"Man, I got a race. I'm Black. Your light-ass ain't got no race, you half-breed motherfucker," Blue snapped. "I ain't got *no* white blood in me."

Scooter sucked his teeth while Raheem and Troy listened on for entertainment. "Man, shut the hell up. 'Cause you know you hate yourself," Scooter said to Blue. "I remember when Blue used to tell me every day that he wished he could be as light as me."

Blue stood up, shaking his head violently. *"Get the fuck outta here!* I ain't never said no shit like that!"

Raheem frowned, right after he had stopped laughing. "You know what, y'all all nuts, for real," he declared. "Them White people got y'all messed up in the head. And Troy, man, I've never known you to say anything bad about your race. You was proud as hell to be Black. I remember you used to stay out in the sun all day, just to see how dark you could get. Now you up here listening to Scooter.

"Scooter always been ashamed to be Black, cuz. That's why he stay in the house all the time, to avoid the sun," Raheem said with a smirk.

Troy looked depressed as Scooter responded. "Who is you to talk? You don't even know what that shit around your neck means. You a nut, too, running around wearin' African symbols on you neck without knowing what it means!" Scooter shouted.

Raheem smiled, unprovoked. "Troy, don't listen to him, man. Scooter really wants to be White."

"What? Aw man, if you so smart, Raheem, then tell us what that shit around your neck means!" Scooter challenged.

Raheem let out a tired sigh. "Scooter, if I'm correct, the green is for the hope and the land, the red is for the blood we shed, and black is for the pride of the people," he calmly said. "See, y'all don't understand why White people really took us from Africa. Black people were like gold, man. We were the strongest. That's why we made the best slaves.

"Everybody wanted some of that *black gold, from Africa*. That's why they could sell us all around the world, 'cause *we* were the most valuable thing on earth. Y'all don't understand that White people want to trick y'all into believing that everything which is white is beautiful, good and pure. But *black is the beauty of all colors*. Matter of fact, White people came from us, and they don't want us to know that. So they keep us down and *miseducated*.

"Y'all been fooled into thinking that *black is ugly and evil*. But White people knew that *black was supreme, all along*. Blacks had something powerful, so White people took it. And that's why they will *never let us go back*, to reclaim *Africa*."

The basement got quiet as Raheem took center stage. He emphasized various points like a Black Muslim.

"*We* are a rich people, and *White people* are jealous of *us*. That's why they *hate us* so much. We never did anything to them. They kicked our ass for *four hundred years*. It gots to be 'cause they're jealous. But y'all don't even see it 'cause y'all too busy *hating yourselves*. It's *diamonds* in *Africa*. We're like diamonds. And no matter what they do to us, *we will never die*."

Troy fell asleep that night amazed at what Raheem had said. He felt proud that he even knew Raheem. That's why White people give us scholarships, to capture that *black gold* to keep for themselves. They take us right away from our race. And that's why White people are on top, Troy pondered. Whites have been taking the best-trained Blacks for all these years and leaving the rest of the Black race helpless, to rip one another apart.

He realized that the inner-city Blacks were becoming the gold of the White universities. They used them to further White people. Blacks were the golden entertainers of the world, outclassing everyone. Blacks won the basketball championships and the football championships, bringing money and prestige to White schools all across the country. It was the Blacks that won the gold medals for the United States in the Olympic competitions. It was the black gold that kept America shining. The black gold had built America. And that black gold shined the greatest in Africa.

"Troy, Troy, Troy, come here! Quick!" Charlotte shouted from the front door that morning. "They finally sent your financial aid report," she said, ruffling through his university mail. "And they said that your grades qualify you for a full academic scholarship.

"Oh, baby! I'm so happy for you! They're going to pay your way to college! *You're on a scholarship now!*"

BACK TO SCHOOL

EVEN WITH THE STRENUOUS SCHEDULE OF PREMED REQUISITES, Troy had set a goal to trace his people's accomplishments and history. The summer back home had proven to be more than just another hot, sunny vacation. It had expanded his curiosity.

However, he had forgotten that he attended a White university, which would teach him practically nothing about the attributes of Black people. As far as the history books were concerned, Blacks contributed very little to the building of America or to civilization itself. There was research to be done.

Troy moved into his single-room dormitory on the campus's southwest side, the fourth floor of Walton Hall. He gave it a good, hard look. The door was missing its lock piece. He went to get that fixed. The mirror was broken. He had that repaired. Next to his door was broken wall plaster. It would break even more every time he went in or out. The water in his sink didn't work right either. The former resident had placed rubber bands on the water valve to keep it from sprinkling all over the room. Troy took the rubber bands off, only to be splashed with a chestful of water. He later discovered that his aged window was jammed. He would have to get that fixed the following morning.

"Excuse me. Last night I found that my window wouldn't open, and I wanted to fill out a report to get it fixed," Troy explained to the gray-haired Black woman working at the front desk of his dormitory.

She turned to the gray-haired White woman standing right behind her. "Ah, Margaret. He wants to file for a room repair."

"What kind of damage is it?" Margaret asked her.

"His window is stuck."

Margaret nodded. "We can have that fixed right away." She gave him a blank three-by-five card. "Fill out your name and room number and the maintenance man will get to you as soon as he can."

Troy nodded back. He wondered what the Black woman's job was. Other students came and asked her questions that she got her White coworker to answer for them, too. Maybe she's newly hired, Troy thought.

Lunch was being served, and Troy was fortunate to be in a dorm that had its own cafeteria. Everyone else had to travel back to the freshman dorms to eat (four blocks away and on the east side of Madison Avenue).

Troy sat alone with his plate and was immediately joined by his big college friend from Atlanta, Georgia.

"Hey, Troy, what's up, cuz?" Bruce asked, excited. He leaned over and hugged Troy's shoulders. "I missed you, mayn. What chew do all summer?"

Troy smiled. "Nothing at all, man. I sat in front of

the TV and changed the channels all summer. Then I turned into a bookworm."

Bruce laughed louder than was necessary. "You still funny as hell," he said. "But I worked for my uncle as a gas monitor this summer. My uncle is, like, the manager. All I had to do was say his name and I had the job."

Troy nodded and looked around, noticing the joyous attitudes that White students were returning to school with. He averted his eyes as he ate, not wanting to see them hugging and squeezing one another. It was a heartwarming sight for them, maybe, but it was making him sick to his stomach. He always thought they went overboard with their affection. They were just too happy to be real. But so was Bruce.

"What chew thinking about?" Bruce asked him.

"Nothin', cuz. Nothin' at all," Troy lied.

Two sisters sitting at the next table drew their attention to them. "How y'all doin'?" the bolder sister asked. Bruce answered and got up to sit with them before Troy could open his mouth.

"Well, how are you two?" Bruce said, taking a seat in an extra chair. Troy no longer bothered to speak, since Bruce had obviously taken control of the situation. "Did you two have a nice summer vacation?" Bruce asked.

Troy began to snicker.

"What chew laughin' at, Troy?" Bruce challenged.

Troy shook his head with a mouthful of grilled cheese. "Nothin', man. You just sound funny," he mumbled through a smile.

Bruce cracked a grin himself. "Yeah, I always talk like this to the honeys. It makes 'em feel good to hear that sweet, baby voice. You know?"

"Yeah, well it ain't workin'," the bold sister said jokingly.

Peter appeared from nowhere to take a seat next to Troy. He was beaming like a spoiled child on Christmas morning.

"What are you smilin' about?" Troy asked him.

"Oh, it's just good to be back, my brother. Everybody seems to have made it back in one piece. And it's just a bright and sunny day."

"So what did you do all summer?"

"I worked at my church's day care center."

"You got paid for that?"

"Yeah," Peter answered. "It was a job, and I worked in the church with the kids. Troy, it's amazing how happy kids can be, that is, until they get out into the real world and find all of these problems that grown-ups go through."

"Hey, what's goin' on, religious boy?" Bruce said, returning to the guys' table.

"Religious *man,*" Peter corrected with a smile.

"Naw, I'm just joking, cuz. But what did you do all summer?" Bruce asked him seriously.

"I was just telling my brother Troy that I had a job at my church," Peter repeated. He had changed his major again after not doing so well in his previous courses. Bruce was finally a member of the football team after coming back to school in late August to begin team workouts. Their friend Doc had gotten a job painting with his cousins. Clay had no problems ever with getting jobs either, since his cousin was a councilman.

Everyone looked the same, except for Peter's low haircut and Bruce's high one. All five of them lived in Walton for their sophomore year. Troy had not spoken to James or Matthew yet. They were the only guys in their freshman group that lived outside their dorm.

Troy had not yet bought any posters for his room. He didn't want to spend any money. He had managed to save only a few dollars from cutting hair all summer.

His first class was a biology lecture to the north of his dorm. It quickly became evident that he was back at the predominantly White university. He was nearly overrun by more broken Mack trucks of White students while on his way to the auditorium. But his sophomore year he was ready to stand his ground instead of moving.

Entering his first biology lecture, Troy decided to sit next to a Black woman. She had braided hair and was wearing a green neon T-shirt.

"Hi, how are you?" she asked.

Troy immediately recognized her Caribbean accent. "Are you Jamaican?" he quizzed.

She smiled, then nodded. "My father is, but my mother is American," she answered. "Are you going into the science field?"

"Yeah. Premed."

She nodded again. "That's good. Most of us Blacks are going into business. The real money is in the science fields. You'll always have work."

"I know," Troy agreed with a grin. "What's your major, though?"

"Well, I'm leaning toward physical therapy. But I haven't made up my mind yet."

Clay walked into the class unexpectedly.

"Yo Clay, what's up, man!" Troy shouted from his seat, surprised to see him. Clay smiled and went straight to the back of the auditorium. Troy thought he was going to sit with him, three rows from the front. But Clay suspected that Troy was trying to collect the sister's phone number. He didn't want to intervene.

Troy realized it might be rude to just leave. But after a few minutes, one of the Jamaican's girlfriends came to sit beside them, giving him an opportunity to join Clay in the back without feeling guilty about leaving her alone in a room full of White students. He had experienced what that felt like during his freshman year, and it wasn't good.

Their first lecture was shorter than expected. Troy ended up alone after Clay rushed to his Marsh County job. He then hung out right across the street from the biology building on the northwest side of campus, where his two o'clock Black literature class would be held inside the cultural studies building.

Black studies was an essential. However, Troy wanted to be involved in the literary section of Black studies as opposed to the historical section. He wanted to hear about Black people from the words of Black men and Black women. He had become skeptical of books written by Whites. They'll have you saying things like "Brown Caucasian," he thought.

When it was near two o'clock, Troy walked into his Black literature class and was shocked to see as many White students as Blacks. He thought maybe he was in the wrong room, yet the young blond male next to him confirmed it.

A balding White man about fifty entered the class and began to pass out the course syllabus. It was impossible! A White man was going to teach a literary course on Black authors!

"Well, hello, class. My name is John Jameson, and I know some of you are wondering why I elected to teach this course," he assumed, hitting on a question that most of the Black students were definitely wondering.

Professor Jameson cleared his throat and smiled. "Well, to begin with, I was an English teacher many years ago. At that time I realized that the only Black work which I had come across was Richard Wright's *Native Son*.

"The book intrigued me to the point where I started to fish for other powerful Black authors. Well, as it turned out, I ended up reading hundreds of Black works and began to include them in my American literature courses, which covered mostly White male authors.

"I began to include writers like Zora Neale Hurston, some of James Baldwin's works, Toni Morrison, Ralph Ellison, Frederick Douglass, and Jean Toomer."

He began to rub his hands together in excitement while pacing in front of the blackboard. "Eventually, it got to the point where I said there were too many good Black authors being missed. So in nineteen eighty-two, I proposed that we set up a course dedicated to Black authors. I also proposed the women's literature course now at the university," Professor Jameson added. Troy was impressed and feeling more at ease.

"When I taught the first course, I only had a few students. But if you just look around the room, you can all see how much interest has grown."

The students all clapped (Black, White, and Asian) after he finished his opening remarks. He had taken great initiative.

"Well, obviously, we can't include all of the works, but I have selected a few major ones," he continued. "Now before we begin, I would like to know exactly how much you all know about slavery."

After a hushed silence, Troy became the first to speak. "Well, all I know is what I've seen in the movie *Roots*. 'Cause it's not like our parents are going to teach us about slavery. Many of them don't know," he said, garnering immediate attention in the class. Of course, Troy knew a lot more than Alex Haley's *Roots*; he was simply curious to see where his comment would lead.

"Yeah, that's the same way with me," a spirited, smooth-faced woman added. "My parents didn't say anything to me about it. So I figured it was over, and that you might as well forget about it." She sat to the right of Troy, wearing an African kente cloth wrapped around her head.

"That's because most textbooks don't seem to want us to remember. Blacks only cover about two paragraphs in the present history books. It's like we were brought here, enslaved, and then Lincoln freed us," a bearded, light-skinned guy interjected from the back of the class. He possessed a strong, deep voice that demanded respected.

Professor Jameson nodded. "It is narrow-minded to suggest that Blacks contributed so little to the shaping of this country. In fact, we are going to find that a lot of history is only told in Black-authored books. We are also going to discuss the religious aspects of the Black experience.

"Does anyone know why the Black churches were so important during slavery?" he challenged.

Troy was alert and ready to learn. He had read a few things.

"The church became the stronghold of the Black community because Whites didn't let them enter their churches," Troy commented. "They told slaves and freedmen that the Lord is the way to a good life. The church was also the only thing that Blacks owned, along with barbershops and funeral homes. No White person wanted to cut their hair or bury their dead. But as the Black preachers began to get more power through the church, White priests began to fear them."

"He's right," Professor Jameson eagerly agreed. "The White congregations also used a piece of white wood and a fine comb; only Blacks who had pale skin and straight hair could enter. Therefore, it separated the Black race as far as complexions were concerned. Of course, when the Black preachers began to talk about slavery, many White preachers told them to stick to the scripture of sin and the devil. In fact, in many instances, White preachers took over Black congregations specifically for that purpose."

"Religion was used as a pacifier for Black people. It subdued them into a nonviolent lifestyle, which in turn would keep them delusioned and stop revolt," the deep-voiced brother in the back responded. He called himself Mike X, and was a writer of nationalistic poetry.

"That's the same way I thought of it," the kente-wearing sister added. Her name was Nia Imani, and she was a history major. "Religion was used to trap Black people into believing that everything would be all right, and that you would go to heaven when you die. I don't see that as a way out for Black people's problems. We have to understand that we must solve things while we're living."

Troy had no further comments. He felt the tension stirring. He had realized that religion was not something to discredit among Blacks, who seemed to be dedicated followers of faith.

An older Black woman shook her head with a grimace of concern. "I think that that is entirely false. Through the churches, Blacks were able to teach and have power in their community. The church kept Blacks together as a people during a time when they needed it, and it is still the Black stronghold today. Whatever motive Whites initially had does not matter at this point, because the church has brought us this far and it will continue to strengthen us," she stated with authority. Her name was Rose Perry and she was in her forties. She had come back to school specifically for African-American culture courses.

Professor Jameson added to her comment. "The Black church also held the community together through spirituals and work songs to keep them going in times of despair," he said. "Later on in the course, I will bring in some of the gospel songs that I have collected."

The White students sat with nothing to say as Troy raised his hand and headed the discussion in a new direction.

"What I still can't understand is how millions of Africans were enslaved by a few White men. It couldn't have been nearly as many White men as there were slaves. So I don't see why they didn't just bum rush 'em."

Troy's classmates began to chuckle.

Professor Jameson smiled and nodded. "Many of the slaves were sold into bondage by African chiefs who had no idea of what kind of slavery it was going to be," he answered. "The African tribes had slaves from tribal wars. But these slaves were treated as regular workers and could even marry into the tribe. They thought American slavery would be similar."

"Also, the White man brought material goods and made deals with Africans to capture other Blacks and sell them off as slaves," Mike X added. "You're also forgetting that they had guns and cannons that the Africans couldn't fight against. So there were many things that contributed to the slave trade. It wasn't like the White people just went to Africa and rounded up a bunch of people. That could never have happened."

Troy could sense that Mike X was very knowledgeable. His voice seemed to shake the class whenever he spoke; he was only twenty-one. Dude is a young soldier, Troy thought.

He left that first class feeling overjoyed. It was soothing and educational just to talk about the Black experience. Troy was also pleased with the amount of enthusiasm with which he had led the class discussions. He hustled straight to the the bookstore to buy his books for class. Black literature was the only subject on his mind. He began to read the *Narrative of the Life of Frederick Douglass* on his first night back.

Next morning, Troy rose at six-thirty for his first lab class of the new school year. He imagined the lab, filled with White students, as he rode the elevator down to his dorm's cafeteria level for breakfast. Three tall and thin White students stood in front of him getting their food trays.

"Ah, yes. I'll have the, ah, scrambled eggs and bacon, please, and just a wee bit of potatoes. Thank you very much, madam," the first student said, moving along.

"Hello. How are you doing today? I would love to have the exact same thing as my partner, please," the second friend said.

"Yes, and I'll just have the, ah, bacon and French toast, please," said the third friend. They seemed to take all day to order.

Troy moved behind them, disgusted by their sluggishness. "Three French toast with eggs," he ordered bluntly. He then proceeded to fill his cups at the juice machine, where one of the White friends turned, unexpectedly, and knocked his food out of his hands.

"Damn, you's a stupid White boy!" Troy yelled at him. "How come y'all never watch where y'all goin'?"

"I didn't see you."

"Why not? I was right the hell in front of you!"

"Well, you don't have to get like that about it."

Troy shook his head, feeling an increasing sense of agitation. "White boy, I swear to God, if you say something else, I'm 'bout to punch the hell out of you!" he exclaimed.

The one Black security guard strolled in from outside of the cafeteria. "What the problem here?" he asked.

"He's making such a big fuss because I accidentally knocked his plate over," the White lad informed him, beating Troy to it.

"Yeah, well if you watched where you was goin', it wouldn't have happened. And I feel like punchin' you in your mouth."

The heavyset guard stood in front of Troy and warned him with a stern face. "You're not going to punch anybody. If you want to take it to that, you'll end up making a run downtown."

Troy realized he was struggling in a losing battle. He decided to let it slide.

Troy felt relieved, seeing two other Black students in his organic chemistry lab. He immediately sat next to one of the Black students and started a conversation with him.

"Ay', what's up, man? I'm glad to see a brother in the class," he said, extending his hand for a shake.

"What was that?" the student responded.

Troy hesitated. His friend wore no socks with his docksider shoes. His pants were ripped and ragged-looking. His hair was uncombed and mangled, not a typically Black fashion statement. "Oh, never mind," Troy said, continuing to observe. Maybe he ain't down with being Black, he thought.

A red-haired White student walked in. Troy's friend responded to him instantly. "Hey, Bob, did you guys go to that happenin' party on Henry Road last night, guy?" he asked.

"No, but was it really hot?" Redhead queried. He went and sat on the other side of the room. Troy's friend gathered his things and followed him. But before Troy received a chance to ponder the incident, the lab instructor decided to begin the class with a little joke.

"Did anyone see that guy on the news last night who overdosed on cocaine? Now, how stupid can you get?" the young macho instructor asked, filled with mockery. "They showed a desk full of the stuff. I guess the guy had watched too many *Scarface* movies, hunh, guys? I thought everyone would have learned their lesson after Richard Pryor fried himself. I mean, what kind of stupid people buy and sell drugs? I guess all I would have to do is sell some lab chemicals on a corner and I'd get rich in no time."

The White students laughed along with him, finding his comments amusing.

"I can't understand why people take drugs," a

blond-haired girl added. "They're getting locked up every day for selling 'em. I mean, it's really stupid."

Troy hated the class already. The man they spoke about on the news was Black, Richard Pryor was Black, and most of the drug dealers that the newscasters featured were Black. Troy had several friends who sold drugs, including Raheem, and he knew many Blacks who were on drugs.

When the students separated for the lab experiments, Troy was once again the only Black. However, his group had an Asian instructor, whom the White students continuously questioned. They were not the best of listeners, quick to ask the Asian instructor to repeat himself again and again, until finally they decided he was inept. They then ventured down the hall to ask the White instructor with the cocaine jokes to further explain the lab procedures for the day.

Troy shook his head and remained inside the lab room with the Asian instructor. He felt sorry for the man. He was also beginning to despise the White students. They were getting on every nerve in his body.

During his first week of classes, Troy felt an increasing sense of of isolation. He was starting to realize that maybe he didn't belong at State University.

It was Friday night, and Doc was in Troy's room getting his hair trimmed.

"Ay', Troy, hurry up with this part, man! I'm trying to go meet this girl on the ave. before the party," Doc explained.

"You should let me give you a whole haircut," Troy suggested.

"Naw, man, that's aw'ight. I got a professional cutting my hair now."

"What, I messed you up before, or something?" Troy quizzed.

"No, but I don't wanna take any more chances with you. You may have lost your touch when you went back home," Doc said jokingly.

Troy frowned while working his clippers around the front and sides of Doc's head "It's like that now?"

Doc smiled, feeling a touch of guilt. "I mean, Troy, you my boy and all, but I'm not tryin' to take chances. I got so many honeys on me this year. We sophomores now."

"Oh, so you gon' get new since you got all of the ladies, hunh? Aw'ight, that's cool. You gonna sell me out."

Doc left, and Troy later joined up with Bruce to attend the first Black party of the new school year. They were hanging out more often together for the first three days since returning to school. Troy had still not seen James or Matthew. He was almost certain that they would show up at the party. He felt guilty about cheating the Black-fraternity-and-sorority-sponsored parties out of their entrance fees, so he and Bruce planned to pay their $3 for a change.

When they arrived at the Student Activity Center, three White men checked their identification cards prior to entry. The money collector was White, the security guards and the stage crew were White.

Freshman year, Troy had gone to at least fifteen

parties, but only as a sophomore did he recognize all of the White faces. The Black fraternities and sororities had to pay the campus to use their facilities for five hours at a time. White students had free parties and beer at their campus-surrounding clubs, and frat houses on Henry Road. Their parties would last all night. Blacks averaged two parties a month, where they danced inside a small hall for a mere three hours. No one ever came on time, so the first couple of hours were always wasted.

Troy daydreamed. He had lost his interest in partying. He began to remember how, at the football games, Blacks chose to sit at the side of the end zone. He had always dragged Bruce with him to watch from the fifty-yard line with all the White fraternities. At the basketball games, Blacks chose to sit behind the end line instead of at midcourt, where the White students had the best view of the game. Whites students always had something to do and somewhere to go. Most of the campus events were created by and geared to them. Yet and still, White students managed to integrate all of the Black functions.

Troy looked around and eyed the White girls who had joined Black sororities. They were having a better time at the party than he was. One was in her last year of nursing school, the second had finished her first year of medical school, and a third was a computer science major. Many of the sisters who headed the sororities struggled to make up their minds as to what it was they all wanted to do.

The party was no longer entertaining. Troy didn't feel like dancing, picking up dates, or even walking around. He just sat on a chair, situated in a corner, and watched everyone. He had become inactive, observing everyone else's life as the focus on his own faded.

"Yo, homes, I ain't seen you since I've been up here," his friend James announced. He had walked up and taken a seat next to Troy in his daze.

"What's up, Jay?" Troy said excitedly, snapping out of it. "I was just thinking 'bout you, man. It was a long summer for me, cuz." He spoke loud to make sure James could hear him over the music.

James moved his chair closer, to listen without straining. "So what did you do this summer?" he asked.

Troy shook his head. "Man, I think I'm messed up in the head, cuz. All I see is White and Black. Nothing is like it used to be. And it's killin' me!"

James nodded. "Yup, homes, I told you them White people are deep. But I joined the army reserves this summer," Troy heard him say.

He was startled. "You did what?"

"I needed the money to pay my tuition," James quickly explained. "I bought a car, too. It's a nice little ride."

Troy was still shocked. "Man, I thought your pop had this big government job."

James smiled. "Yeah, he do. But I wanted my own dough to finish college instead of having to count on them. I wanted to teach myself responsibility."

"By joining the fuckin' army?"

"You gotta do what you gotta do," James answered. He had cut off his goatee. Troy figured that the army made him do it. James would never have cut off his treasured goatee on his own.

Troy shook his head again. "I don't believe you joined the army, cuz. I thought you knew better than that," he muttered in disdain. "This country damn sure ain't gon' own me. So *fuck* the army! You must of lost your mind."

Troy left the party, bored with it by midnight. He went to the hallway bathroom on his dormitory floor. He read the graffiti inside the stalls while sitting on the toilet. "I'm proud to be Black, and I could never be a slave," he read. Several responses followed: "Yeah, but your grandfather was." "Whoever wrote this comment is obviously a fool. We could make you all slaves again if we wanted to." The last one read, "Tell me one thing you have to be proud of, and I'll agree that you should be. But truthfully, there isn't any. So just be proud that you're free and living."

Troy cradled his head in disgust. Things were falling apart. So-called minority students were dropping out of school like flies, despite all the affirmative action and scholarship programs. Many students from the previous year were no-shows. Only one Puerto Rican remained at State University out of the six that Troy had known his freshman year.

He, Matthew, and seven other students were the only Blacks to maintain 3.25 G.P.A.'s, or above, out of all 167 C.M.P. students. Some sophomore students were still finishing reinforcement courses. It would take them forever to complete what they needed in their majors. The lack of progress in so many Black collegians was scary. Yet it was real.

Troy rushed to the cafeteria for breakfast that Monday morning before another early class. The same three White friends were there, talking loudly as they ate. Troy could not help but overhear their conversation.

"The Japanese are now the world's number-one supplier of technological goods," the first was saying. He was the culprit who had knocked over Troy's plate.

"I don't know how they did it. You figure after we blew them up, we should have kept them down," the second friend added.

"That's why they're more advanced than us now," the third suggested. "You know that after the war, we invested millions of dollars to rebuild Japan. I mean, imagine that. We bomb a country to pieces and then fix it up to surpass us. I think we should have let them all die after the war," he said with hearty laughter.

"No, because we had to keep the image that we were the good guys," the first friend refuted.

"Aw, ta hell with that good guy stuff. We should have dropped a few more bombs on 'em," the second argued.

"Yeah! No one messes with the U.S.!"

Troy left for class before they did. He walked past the bus stop on Madison Avenue and began to focus on some of the Marsh County citizens: a Black teenager with a greasy Jheri curl; another with a slicked-back wet-set, as if she had recently jumped out of the shower, stirred his embarrassment.

Inside class, Troy sat in the first seat available, next to a White girl. She moved to join one of her friends and was replaced by a much larger football player, who wanted to sit next to a girl one seat away from Troy. The big, brown-haired bruiser squeezed by and was too large for comfort. He stood six-three and 240. Troy then decided to find himself another seat.

As he searched for another empty space, a girl walked in and caught his eye. One shade darker than yellow, she strutted up the aisle with much self-assurance.

Troy watched her sit by herself, half expecting it. After class, he approached her.

Troy's heart beat wildly, fearing rejection. But he was no coward, especially not when approaching the opposite sex.

"Hi, how you doin'?" he asked her.

"I'm fine," she said, pacing ahead to her next destination.

He walked beside her. "Are you from another country?" he asked, assuming from her obvious ethnic appearance.

"Yes," she answered flatly.

Troy sensed that she was unwilling to talk, yet he pressed on. "Well, what country are you from?"

"Kenya," she responded, finally looking at him.

Troy smiled, feeling a sudden connection to her. "You from Africa, hunh?" he repeated, intrigued. She didn't resemble a Kenyan or an African person to him. But nevertheless, she was *from* Africa!

"What's your name?" he continued.

Kenya sighed with bother. "You know, you're asking a lot of questions."

Troy's ego was slammed as they continued to walk. He wasn't planning to let her get away with it. "You know what, you're extremely rude to say some shit to me like that! I bet if I was White I could ask you a thousand fuckin' questions!" He was about to call her a bitch, but refrained.

"You don't have to get all angry about it," she told him. She then crossed Madison Avenue's five-lane street toward the freshmen dorms. Troy felt more discontent. He was losing his cool. Race politics controlled his mind, making him too defensive to be charming.

Matthew was already sitting inside the main cafeteria as Troy walked over with his tray to join him. "What's goin' on, Mat?" he asked. "What did you do all summer?"

"Yo, what's up, troop?" Matthew responded, shaking Troy's hand. A week and a half had gone by before they had caught up with each other. "Yo, I had a job at the movies," he answered.

Troy grinned. "At the movies, hunh? What position did you have?"

"I was an usher."

Troy nodded and started to chuckle. "Yup, I knew it. They always make us Blacks the ushers."

"Naw, man, there's Blacks in every position," Matthew said.

"Yeah, but you live in Harlem. Your movie is in an

all-Black neighborhood, so of course. But I'm talkin' 'bout a movie where you're with White employees, too. Then it would be different," Troy assumed.

Matthew frowned, unconvinced. "You figure, how many different jobs can a guy do at the movies? The girls are all behind the counters," he mentioned.

"Damn! You're right. Aw'ight, then, forget that," Troy said, taking a bite of his sandwich. "Ay', man, I was in New York this summer," he added through a mouthful.

"Word. What part?" Matthew asked him.

"We went to see the Statue of Liberty."

His New York boy grinned. "That ain't really New York."

"But we went to Forty-second Street, too," Troy added.

"Man, it be a lot of White people down there, with money. Don't no niggas live down there," Matthew told him with a smirk.

"Well, I saw many Puerto Ricans when we were there."

Matthew nodded. "You must have been on the east side. That's where the Puerto Ricans live in Manhattan, in them broken-down buildings."

"Oh yeah. Well, it was this White lady who was forcing everybody around on that trip, Mat. She acted like she owned slaves or somethin'," Troy alluded.

Matthew smiled lightheartedly. "Yo, man, that was just her job."

Troy insisted. "Naw, cuz, I think she was old and racist."

"I wouldn't say she's racist. Maybe she's just like

that. Maybe she just shouts and yells a lot," his friend calmly suggested.

Troy gazed around the cafeteria, watching the Black lunch women cleaning up tables. "You ever notice that all the workers in here are Black, besides that one retarded lady and that mean-ass immigrant?" he asked.

Matthew fell out of his seat in laughter. He laughed for two minutes before he responded. "Maybe they like their jobs. Money is money," he said, once he calmed down and took his seat back.

Troy snapped. "What, are you crazy, cuz? Who the hell is gon' like a job cleaning up and serving college students every day?" Troy said harshly.

Matthew didn't answer.

Troy noticed his sensitivity and decided to change the subject. "Did you hear about Jay joining the army?"

"Naw. He joined the army?" Matthew was as surprised as Troy.

Troy nodded. "Yup, cuz. He just sold himself to the White people."

"Hey, Mat, buddy! Are you gonna study with us again tonight?" a tall and husky White guy asked. He was surrounded by a group of three others.

Matthew was startled momentarily. "Oh, I don't know, man. I have to see what I have to do tonight," he answered, feeling the immediate tension from his Philly friend. "Yeah, Troy, you have organic chemistry, right?"

"Yeah, and the lab, too," Troy answered. He didn't care to comment on the White students Matthew was supposed to study with. Nevertheless, he was beginning to suspect that Matthew was crossing over. He had always seemed to defend White people. No matter what they did, Matthew seemed to have an explanation for them.

Later, Troy found himself inside the C.M.P. offices shooting the breeze with the counselors. He had finished all of his classes for the day.

Paul was grinning and holding Troy's hand for a firm shake. "So, what's been going on?"

Troy frowned. "Nothin' at all," he responded glumly. "Did Max really leave?"

"Yup, he left aw'ight. He got a job as a substitute teacher with the city," Paul answered. He released his handshake and sat behind his cluttered desk. "How come you ain't left yet?" Troy asked curiously.

"Well, once you get used to something, it's kind of hard to go away. Max had been talking about leaving for three years. Now he finally did it. But did you hear about your boy Mat getting a four-point-oh?" Paul asked cheerfully.

Troy raised his brow, confused. "Naw. Mat got a four-point-oh? I was just with him. He didn't tell me."

Paul nodded. "He probably don't want people thinking he's a nerd. He's a real tenderhearted guy, you know."

Troy sat in the student chair opposite Paul's desk to think.

Paul looked over his student roster. "Yup, Troy, we didn't get as many freshmen as we got last year with you guys," he alluded.

"Why not?" Troy asked, barely interested. He was still wondering why Matthew didn't tell him about the 4.0.

"Well, for one, the college isn't kickin' out the money to get Blacks anymore. The cost to go to school keeps rising," Paul informed him.

Troy chuckled and shook his head. "Dag, that's terrible. So that means it's going to be more drug dealers in Black neighborhoods," he joked, still really thinking about Matthew.

Paul smiled. "The White man ain't makin' it no easier for Black students. Not at all," he said.

Troy left C.M.P. with Matthew's secrecy remaining on his mind. He thought they were good friends. But suddenly he felt excluded. So far, his sophomore year was filling him with despair.

Peter walked into Troy's room with two new friends. "Ay', Troy, I got some freshmen who need haircuts." Troy looked them over. He had noticed them before, and they both had been hanging out with White students. He suspected that they were Oreos, and he was planning to give them the third degree.

"Hey, you guys live out in the suburbs, do ya?" Troy asked mockingly.

The freshman giggled as the shorter, stocky one, wearing glasses, answered. "Yeah, I live in the burbs of New Jersey. But there are other Blacks who live there. So it's not like my family is the only one."

"Oh, what, it's, like, three other Black families?" Troy jibed.

"Yeah, around that."

Troy nodded and grinned. "Unh-hunh. I thought so."

The freshman took a seat in Troy's empty desk chair to get his haircut. "So what are you trying to say?"

"Oh, I ain't sayin' nothin'. What's your name?"

"Roy," the stocky freshman answered proudly. He reminded Troy of a young Paul or a young Max.

"Yeah, like Roy Rogers, hunh?" Troy responded, giggling again. "So what is your major, Roy?"

"Well, I'm thinking about becoming a technical engineer."

"Are you in C.M.P.?"

"C.M.P.? What is that?"

"Yeah, I am," the second freshman interjected. He sat in the sofa next to Troy's desk. He appeared to be the same size as Troy.

Peter leaned on the wall next to the door, smiling. He was enjoying the stir of social chemistry.

"I'm on a scholarship in the honors program," Roy informed him.

"You're smart as hell, then," Troy quipped.

"Well, I wouldn't say that. I just work real hard."

The second freshman, Scott, was from a neighborhood called Logan in Philadelphia. He was undecided about a career. He mentioned that he had tagged along with his White roommate the first couple days of school until he made some Black friends.

In the course of the next few days, Troy spoke with the two freshmen on several occasions. He found that Scott knew a lot about world history, yet his schoolwork was lacking. He reasoned that the undecided freshman should go into teaching. Scott, however, said he was after big money. He was looking into business, like so many other Black students on campus.

In biology, just the second week of the new semester, the White professor used the term "slave master" to describe his teaching technique to the class. He was a Southerner, wearing large brown-rimmed glasses. He wore his brown hair long, and he spoke loudly.

Clay was late for class, therefore Troy had no one to share his tension with. They then found a nice comfortable spot in the back of the class once Clay had arrived.

The long haired Southerner went on to use the contrast between black and white to make a point about the human immunity system. "We don't know which things are good for the body and which things are bad. But we do know that the bad guys wear the black hats, and the good guys wear the white hats. So we must get rid of the bad guys," he explained.

As the story went on, the loud instructor began to slip up. "So we get rid of the bad black guys, and keep the good white guys," he said, forgetting about the hats. Clay's and Troy's hearts jumped, beating faster by the minute. They were both in shock.

"Did you hear that, Troy?" Clay asked. "I mean, why does 'Black' always have to be bad?" He sighed and shook his head, offended. "Man, I feel like running down to the front and socking the dude."

"I don't even want to talk about it," Troy responded. His legs were wobbling underneath his chair and his hands were shaking against the armrests. The shock of an open gesture of racism was overwhelming. But the White students laughed at it. They thought that it was humorous. They were the "good white guys."

SUBMISSION

THREE TIMES A WEEK, THE THREE WHITE FRIENDS CONTINUED to haunt Troy in the cafeteria before his early-morning classes.

"Down South still has some of the most racist people in the world," the first friend was saying.

"I still think that their problem is not as bad as they say it is," the second friend suggested.

"I know. They're always complaining. But I don't see where they're trying to better themselves by violence," the third friend added.

The first friend nodded. "Yeah. That will only make the situation worse."

Once they spotted Troy seated two tables away and listening to them, they quieted down to a whisper. Every other day, they spoke as if they were at a concert. Obviously, a race-discussion audience of a fiery native son was not something that they desired.

During the biology lecture that morning, Clay went storming through the doors as if he owned the place. He marched up the auditorium stairs and headed straight to the back, where Troy waited for him. Clay seemed to always make a scene.

Troy grinned at his arrival. "What's wrong with you, man?"

Clay hunched his shoulders and smiled. "I'on know. I think I just want some attention. But these mugs don't even notice me." He looked around the class at all the White students as he adjusted himself in the seat next to Troy. "Man, I wonder if they ever think about us. I mean, they don't even act like we exist."

Troy frowned and shook his head. "They don't care shit about us. They don't have to see one of us in life, but we can't live without dealin' with them. I hate these White people, man," he said aloud.

Clay looked around to see if any White students would react. Once no one did, he turned back to Troy, smiling. "You don't care nothin' 'bout these mugs, hunh?"

Troy thought for a moment. "Man, I just wish they had left us alone in Africa." Then he got excited. "Oh, Clay, I forgot to ask you. Why the hell do you sit all the way back here?"

"Because I feel comfortable back here."

They continued to copy notes from the huge mile-away blackboard as they talked.

"You feel comfortable back here?" Troy repeated. "Man, me and Peter used to sit up front every day in psychology class last year. Matter of fact, I sit up front in all of my classes."

"Well, that's you. I only sit up front when it's a small class," Clay said.

"Why? Because then you feel comfortable in a smaller crowd of people?"

"Yup, you got it. That's when I participate."

"So you're sayin' that every time you're in a crowded place, you're going to sit in the back. What if you have a job with a lot of people? Are you gon' go to the back there too, and get the least amount of pay, talkin' 'bout you feel comfortable back there?" Troy quizzed sarcastically. He thought Clay's explanation was humorous. *Clay must be crazy out his mind!* he mused.

Clay chuckled. "Naw, man. I ain't sayin' that. But that's just how I feel right now."

Troy went to his Black literature class, where they discussed the status of Black Americans.

"Blacks own nothing in their own communities, and they got Japanese starting to build their own schools in New York because they don't think the public schools are good enough. The Italians own everything in their communities, as well as the Jews and Koreans do. But we own nothing. That don't make any sense," Mike X was saying.

"I know, and every time that one Black steps out, the White people point their fingers and say, 'There goes your progress.' But only individuals are making it, not the masses of Black people," Nia added.

"The way I see it, the White media doesn't want any strong-minded Blacks to have the spotlight. They would rather give people like Michael Jackson, whom I like musically but not as a representation of my people, the spotlight for all of us.

"Every time someone says something about Malcolm X, who was a strong Black man that I loved with all of my heart and soul, it's like a curse word. But yet everyone wants to treasure Martin Luther King," Rose Perry said.

"I think that's because not enough people know much about Malcolm X. I only heard his name onetime when I was younger, and the teachers said that he had gotten shot. So I thought he was in a gang or something," Troy commented. He, Mike X, Nia Imani, and Rose Perry headed their discussions every class period. They were the outspoken students.

"That's because Black people were scared to follow a Black man of heart and soul. You can get a bunch of people to march to the White House and sing church songs, but it's totally different when you ask them to support a Black economic movement. Blacks are too dependent upon Whites when it comes down to what really makes the world go round, and it's not sitting in White-owned coffee shops," Mike X said.

Professor Jameson nodded. "I agree. Malcolm X was a strong political figure in the history of African-Americans. I would also agree that his cry for economic parity would scare the establishment a lot more than King's talk of integration."

After dinner, Bruce and Troy rode the elevator. It was crowded with a horde of White students who spoke loudly, as usual.

"How are you, Carol? How were your classes today?"

"Fine. Everything is peachy. What did you do this weekend?"

"I went to this party, and it was really nice because they had everything set up beautifully and everyone showed up on time and it was just grand. I mean, the total occasion was gorgeous."

Troy got off at the sixth floor on his way to Bruce's room. "Do you hear how they talk, man? They make me sick with that shit. It don't even seem like they listen to each other," he said disgustedly to Bruce. "You know what? I'm gon' call 'em plastic people."

They entered Bruce's room, which was crowded with accessories. "You gon' call 'em plastic people?" Bruce asked with raised brows.

"Yeah, man, 'cause they're not real. I can't stand White people now. I don't see how they took over the world in the first place. They're stupid as hell.

"*Damn, cuz!* I feel like just beating some White people up!" Troy shouted. Bruce laughed as his friend continued raving. "Imagine slave days, Bruce, when big dudes like you were owned by a White master who was, like, five-foot-three. And you be talkin' like a big pussy. 'Oh, sure. Yes, massa. Right away, sir. Anything for you, massa.' "

"*Damn!*" Troy raged again.

Bruce fell out with laughter. "You funny as hell, man. But I hate them old movies like that," he said. "I used to hate when *Roots* came on. I used to go in my room and put my head under my pillow when that show came on."

Troy contorted his face as if reacting to a pungent smell. "Damn, Bruce, man! I should have never come to this White-ass school! I should have gone to a Black university like my Mom told me. But naw, I wanted to play Division 1 basketball. Most of the athletes don't know what the hell they goin' to do if they don't make the pros!" he shouted.

"Dig, mayn, 'cause I'm in that boat right now. I ain't seen no time yet," Bruce said glumly.

Brrrloop brrrloop.

"Hello . . . Yeah, what's up, girl?" Bruce asked, answering his telephone.

"Who's that?" Troy asked.

Bruce covered the phone with his massive right hand. "She's bad as *hell.*

"Yeah, well, I didn't get that assignment," he said to her.

"Does she live here, Bruce?" Troy asked.

Bruce nodded, and Troy headed for the door.

"Yo, where you goin', mayn?" Bruce asked him.

"To my room."

"Aw'ight, then. I'll catch you later on."

Troy went to his room and began to study, only to be interrupted by Scott, one of the freshman students he had met. His door was unlocked, so Scott walked right in after knocking softly.

"Hey, historian," Troy called him.

"You always studying, hunh, Troy?" Scott asked.

"Yeah, that's why I always get good grades."

"That's good, man. I wish that I could do that," Scott said before dropping his head.

"What, you're not doing too well?"

"Nope. I'm failing these C.M.P. classess. They're supposed to be easy."

"Ay', man, a lot of y'all gotta learn to discipline yourselves to study."

"I know," Scott responded.

"But to tell you the truth, every day I think about quittin' and just droppin' out of school," Troy revealed.

Scott was stunned. Why would *you* want to drop out of school? he asked himself about Troy. "Aw, man, you can't be serious. You're on the honor roll, and you got a scholarship," he said.

"It all doesn't matter, man. It's what makes you happy that matters. I'm unhappy here. I just want to be a part of the world again," Troy explained. "It feels like we in a different place while we're in college, like, we don't fit in anymore, especially in this White school. It just seems like the entire world is made for them White students."

Scott nodded, understanding Troy perfectly. The feeling was not at all alien to him. "I know, man, that's the same way I feel about it. It seems like we're going to be educated slaves for the White people. And they're damn sure going to be the ones doing the hiring when the money time comes."

"Yeah, man, and that's the kind of shit that makes me wanna say, *'Fuck college!'* It means nothing in the end. You're just another nigga with a job," Troy snapped. "Most niggas don't even get a chance to travel."

"My father did," Scott interjected. "He traveled a lot. He served in the Vietnam War, too. He said that it was many Blacks in the war, getting killed, and now only a few get any benefits for it. But he's been to many places around the world. He told me that the women were tryin' to marry Americans to come back here to live."

The freshman suddenly stopped and began to giggle. "My pop told me that he got some drawers everyplace he went. Women in other countries just throw themselves at U.S. military men."

Troy shook his head with a grin. "See, man, that's the kind of shit the White people started. They've prostituted the world. Them women are tired of being poor, just like the rest of us."

"But you know what, Troy? I've been to L.A. myself, man, and Blacks are living a lot better than us over there. They still have slums and all, but they're nice slums compared to ours. And over there, the Mexicans are treated worse than Blacks.

"It was pitiful when I was over there and saw that Mexicans were going through what we have already been through. They're just living any way that they can. And Orientals don't live as well on the West Coast as they do on the East Coast, either," Scott mentioned. He amazed Troy with the things he knew as a freshman. Troy remembered that he knew a little bit, but not a lot until the past summer, when he had become race conscious.

"Damn, it's that bad for Mexicans?" he asked.

"Well, not for all of 'em," Scott answered. "Those one-hundred-percent Spanish are the ones that own Mexican restaurants and stuff like that. And my pop told me that in Brazil, where people are all mixed up and stuff, that if you're White you can get a job easier. They're tryin' to keep that European look in public places down there. And if you're Black in Brazil, or mixed up, like, with Indian blood, you can only get those physical, behind-the-scene jobs."

"Yeah," Troy responded, still listening.

"Yup, man. But the people down there think it's OK. The Portuguese tricked them into believing that all people are equal regardless of color.

"That's bullshit, basically, but you have to be an outsider to see it. But you know, the United States is the most racist country in the world, besides Great Britain and South Africa. My father said that when he went to Germany and France, the women didn't care that he was Black, he was just another person."

Troy had no comment.

Scott went on. "Take a place like Haiti; it's the Blackest country on this side of the world, and it's also the poorest. My grandmother is from Haiti."

Troy began to examine Scott's darker complexion.

"And my pop told me that Jamaica is basically run by the White people with money, and light-skinned Blacks. That's why all the darker ones come here. They're the ones who have more to gain. Most Jamaicans won't tell you that, though. They try to argue about it."

Troy looked at his clock, to see that it was getting late. "Ay', man, I better get back to studying," he said.

"All right then, scholar," Scott called him.

Troy smiled. "Aw'ight, professor," he said in response. "Ay', are you going to the discussion tomorrow?" he asked Scott before he left.

"About light-skinned and dark-skinned Blacks?"

"Yeah."

"Naw, man. I saw the poster, but I got a lot of work to do," Scott answered. He closed Troy's door as he left.

* * *

Troy had been to every Black function so far his sophomore year. He was becoming quite knowledgeable, bringing up good points at each meeting he attended. All of the events were positive, but he felt that none developed any plans to solve Black people's problems.

The rooms, again, were rented from campus administration. White staff members would set up microphones and the stage set. Sometimes they would go as far as providing food and refreshments.

The discussion on light-and-dark conflicts was being held by the Delta Sorority. Troy had noticed that the Deltas sponsored a lot of progressive functions.

All of the Black sororities and fraternities had to alternate dates for their events and parties. There were simply not enough Black college students to go around. And none of them owned or even rented houses. The Alphas *had* a house near Charleston Street. It was closed years ago when a student was shot and killed during a party.

More Black students showed up for the discussion on light-dark conflicts as compared to the weak turnouts at a lot of the other functions. Everyone had something to say.

"I never really thought that we still had a problem as far as light and dark skin is concerned. From what my mother told me, we have come a long way," a tall, dark brown sister commented.

"I never thought that I was better than anybody else, but I had always gotten more attention from the guys. And I guess dark-skinned girls were jealous. So they started callin' me vanilla ice cream, banana girl, and stuff like that, which only made me call them smokeys and tar-babies, you know," a cream-colored sister said.

"I think we have to talk about Blacks who don't have their identity intact, because I feel that's also tearing us apart. It's not like they are really accepted by White people; they're just taking more resources and strength from the Black race," an onyx-skinned brother added.

"That is counterproductive. I know this girl who had a baby with a White guy, and the kid is going to school now in a White neighborhood. Now she's having problems acceptin' herself as Black, because she's real light," a sister sitting next to Troy brought up.

"I'm always hearing how Blacks from the suburbs don't have their identity, but Blacks from the inner city seem to have more problems than we do," a petite suburban sister challenged.

"Yeah, but y'all gotta know where you stand in the world, and you ain't gonna get it out in the suburbs," a reddish brown brother answered.

"OK, maybe that's true. But it's a White world, so you might as well learn to deal with White people. And I feel that I'm better suited to do so than most of you, since I grew up with 'em," the suburbanite rebutted.

"She does have a point, because you do have to speak and act a different way for White people. If you expect to be hired for a job, you do have to dress presentably and wear a civilized hairstyle, too," a light brown sister responded.

The room began to stir with energy.

A light-skinned sister with light brown hair and matching eyes spoke up from the front. "Wait a minute, now, what do you mean by a 'civilized hair-style'?" She wore her hair in a short bush, neatly trimmed on the sides.

"Oh, I mean, your hair is OK, but when girls are walkin' around with statues and whatnot on their heads, the White people are not going to hire them."

"Well, why is it that we gotta change everything about ourselves to please them? That's a trip, 'cause they don't have to change a damn thing for us. If you Black, then you should be allowed to look Black," a sister in braids responded.

Troy noticed a cute brown sister sitting right next to the speaker in the front row. She had a beautiful smile and small eyes. Her hair was cut short and curly. He made a quick decision that he would try and talk to her after the function.

"You know, I'm sick and tired of us calling ourselves Black Americans anyway," a light brown brother stood up to say. He was wearing a blue-and-gold kente outfit. "We have the Italian-Americans, the Polish-Americans, and the Irish-Americans. And everyone takes themselves back to a place. Now what are we going to say, we come from 'Blacka'? No. We come from Africa, so we should start to call ourselves African-Americans. That's where a lot of this stuff starts. 'Cause none of us is *black* any damn way."

Troy had drifted off, staring at the sister he was attracted to. He paid little attention to the rest of the comments. He felt he had nothing to add. He had come only to see how others were being affected. The cute brown sister had distracted him anyway. So he waited patiently for a chance to talk to her. Fortunately, she walked in his direction after the last comment.

"Hey, what's your name?" he asked bluntly, snatching her attention.

She looked at him and recognized his face. "Karen Lopez."

He smiled and held her hand. "I wanna talk to you."

"Ay', Karen, come on, girl," her friend called.

Troy pressed, losing a grip on himself and on her small, warm hand. "Well, can I talk to you?"

"Hold up, let me see what she wants first," Karen responded.

Troy snapped, disappointed. "Oh, you gotta follow her around. Aw'ight, then." He thought that he had been turned down again. He had lost all of his touch with women.

"No, I don't need to follow her," Karen responded, to his surprise. She smiled, looking straight into his eyes.

"Well, are you gonna talk to me?" Troy persisted. He still felt shaky about his confidence.

Karen's friend began to exit as she gave him her full attention. "Yeah, I guess so," she said, smiling a beautiful smile. She wore a kente outfit herself, green and gold. Troy wore his usual jeans-and-shirt combination, with Nikes.

"What do you mean, you 'guess so'?" he quizzed. He started to grin, back in control of himself. "Either we gonna talk or we not," he told her, beaming like a five-year-old.

"Where you from?" she asked, still smiling herself.

"Why?" he answered with a smirk.

" 'Cause I know you're not from here. You have an accent. Are you from New York?"

"Naw. I'm from Philly."

"Yup, I knew it was one of 'em. Y'all got them rough voices. Y'all sound like you about to beat somebody up."

Troy shook his head. "Naw. Do you go here?" he asked in a more pleasant manner. He was beginning to feel secure with Karen.

"No, I was just visiting my girlfriend."

"You would have been a freshman this year?"

"Yup."

"Are you gonna come here next year?" he hinted.

"Nope, I'm going to a Black college. I wouldn't be able to stand being around all these White people. What's your name, anyway?" she finally asked him.

"Troy Potter," he said.

Karen got out a piece of paper to write his name down. "What's your phone number?" she asked. After giving her his number, Troy said he would get hers when she called him, happy to know her already. Karen had a pleasant personality, and he just loved the fact that she didn't seem the least bit shy.

Bloomp bloomp bloomp.

"Yo, come in!" Troy shouted through his door.

"Ay', what's up, my brother?" Peter said, entering.

"OK, here's Holy Man," Troy responded, chuckling. He was in a good mood after meeting Karen.

"Well, how was the thing?" Peter asked, ignoring Troy's crack.

"It was the same old shit, man. All they really talked about was how we have to dress for the White man, how we have to talk for the White man, how we supposed to act; you know, stuff like that."

Peter nodded. "Yeah, I remember when my mother used to get phone calls from the White lady on her job. I'd answer the phone and say it was a White lady, and she'd get mad at me for saying it," he commented. "I didn't really understand why she would act and talk all different. But me? I don't think I'm going to go too far to please a person for a job."

"Yeah, yeah. You were scared to tell them White punks to stop having parties at your crib last year. So how you gonna keep yourself from doing what they want you to do on a job?" Troy challenged.

"Look, Troy, there is a certain line that I draw when it comes to what I'm going to accept. Now, what happened last year was solved when I left for my own room. So there was no need for a bunch of hassles."

"Yeah, OK, Holy Man. What chew gonna do when it's nobody to let you off the hook? Are you gonna call on the Lord for strength?"

Peter headed for the door. "I can see that you in one of those moods where you want to talk crazy."

"Yo, hold up, man. Let me tell you 'bout this girl I met."

"You met a girl? So what? That ain't nothing new."

"Man, look, this girl is different. She's cute as hell. She's my complexion, too."

Peter looked intrigued. "What? Troy didn't talk to another light-skinned sister?"

Troy smiled sheepishly. "Yup, man, 'cause when I went home I realized that shit. So now I'm changed about what I consider pretty. But shut up and let me finish, though."

Peter took a seat on Troy's dresser.

"She got a skinny nose and naturally curly hair," Troy began.

Peter burst out laughing. "I thought you said you changed, my brother. Why are you still worried about her nose and hair?"

"Shut up, man. I'm just describing how she looks."

"So, the White man has got to you, then," Peter said, chuckling. He ignored his friend's explanation.

"What, I can't have a preference? Everybody has a preference. We just supposed to grow up and marry anybody, just 'cause we Black? They have different codes of beauty all around the world." Troy stopped and shook his head before continuing. Peter never failed to destroy the flow of his stories.

"Yeah, well anyway, she's bad as hell, cuz. I think I might make her my girl. Her name is Karen Lopez."

"Lopez? That sounds like a Spanish name," Peter mentioned.

Troy nodded to him. "Yeah, Lopez is a Spanish name. But hell, Black people all over Latin America got Spanish names."

"Maybe she got some Indian blood, hunh?" Peter assumed.

"That's Native American blood, and I got some, too.

I got it from my father." Troy then snuck a quick look in his dresser mirror.

"Yeah, I got Indian blood, too," Peter added sarcastically. He was annoying his friend as usual. "OK, Mr. Politically Correct. My grandfather was a full-blooded Native American. As a matter of fact, I'm the only one who didn't get the good hair. My brothers and sister got it."

Troy frowned. "That's another thing. We gotta stop sayin' that good hair/bad hair shit. That's more White brainwashing. And that 'politically correct' term is White stuff too. It should be the moral thing to call a person by their correct name, not just a political thing. But that's White people for you, just like that stupid right-wing and left-wing bullshit. I mean, it's messed up how White people have just changed everybody's names."

Peter agreed and leaped off Troy's dresser. "Well, I got some studying to do, my brother, so I'll see you tomorrow," he said as he left.

The next day before dinner, Troy, Bruce, Clay, and Doc went to Demetrius's room. Demetrius, Doc's friend, lived on Troy's floor. They sat around and talked about various inventions.

Demetrius was returning to college after a year in the "real world." He was roughly six-one, and athletic-looking. He appeared to be a weight lifter, with one of those health-nut looks. His VCR-equipped room was becoming a popular hang-out.

"You know what, man? How did White people make all of this stuff? They got TVs, satellites, space shuttles, bombs, missiles, Walkman radios, and all kinds of shit," Demetrius was wondering while sitting on his bed.

"I'on know, cuz. And I mean, it's like they pick stuff up easier than everybody else," Clay responded, taking a seat on Demetrius's dresser. "I got this White boy in my one class, and he reads all the chapters right before the test and gets A's."

"Yeah, man, it's this White girl in my class that does that, too," Doc added, standing in the middle of the room. "That shit makes me mad as hell. I study all the time and still come out with C's."

Troy was leaning up against the door looking at how light Doc was. He began to wonder if he was mixed, like many other Blacks in Marsh County.

"It's like White people wrote them books in their own special code, and they're the only ones that really know how to pick it up," Bruce said, setting in Demetrius's small sofa. "Something is strange about it, cuz. I just can't put my finger on it."

"Aw, man, White people don't have any special abilities. They got y'all sittin' around believing that dumb shit," Troy angrily refuted. "You see what happens to your mind when we come to these White schools. They lie all the time. They probably study every day, but y'all in here believing that cramming shit works. Most of 'em had this same stuff in high school, so of course they can pick it up easier."

Demetrius agreed with him. "Dig, man, 'cause they don't know anything, for real. They say that we came from apes. That's crazy if you think about it. I mean, how come the rest of the apes didn't change?"

They laughed as Demetrius continued.

"I wonder where we did come from," he pondered. "I remember I used to wake up when I was a kid and just wonder."

Everyone added to the discussion as Troy thought about a dream he had had as a kid.

"Yeah, cuz, I thought about that, too," Clay said.

"Me too," said Doc.

"Hell yeah, cuz," Bruce responded as everyone chattered on.

Troy told them his dream. "Did y'all ever have a dream where you woke up and asked, 'Why am I Black, and how come I'm in America?' I did, and that shit was crazy. It kind of felt like I was in a glass jar, looking out at the rest of the world."

No one seemed to comment. The room was suddenly quiet enough to hear a pin drop. And after the discussion had wound down, Troy left them all in the room and went to have an early dinner.

It felt strange that no one commented on his dream. Troy theorized that maybe everyone had the same dream, but no one wanted to talk about it. Maybe if they admitted that they have asked, Why am I Black and living in America? they would be confessing to the world that they needed a purpose. What is the purpose for Black people in America? Troy asked himself. He began to contemplate as he solemnly rode the elevator down to the cafeteria. I wonder what Black people really feel about being Black. He realized that they all lied to themselves, suppressing the race issue to get along with White people.

He remembered that the Whites were always in

authority over his Black relatives as a kid. The White people always wanted to send him away whenever he had done something wrong in school. The White people wanted to put him into a boarding home. And as long as he could remember, they were always on top.

Troy sat down to eat with the two freshman, Scott and Roy, who both sat with Peter. The adrenalin flowed over from his earlier animosity. He looked around the room to see that Blacks continually prayed, while Whites did not. Every day since he had been in college, it was the same. The Whites never said, "God bless you," whenever he had sneezed. At least one Black person would say it. Always.

"Look at us, man. We nuts. They got us prayin', and they don't even believe in that religious shit," Troy said out of the blue. "It's funny to see how stupid we are."

"You don't believe in God?" Roy asked him.

"Fuck no! That shit is just used to trick us."

"Ay', my brother, don't let the White man fool you into believing that God doesn't exist," Peter warned.

"Aw man, shut up. The only reason that you got religious is because you couldn't get no ass last year, and it messed up your studying. You still ain't getting no better grades and no girls. So what does it mean?" Troy exclaimed, raising his voice at the table.

Scott and Roy began to snicker. They weren't familiar with Peter's story.

"Look, Troy, all this material stuff is going to end when it's time to be judged for the afterworld. So you better start believing," Peter insisted. He remained calm despite Troy's embarrassing revelation.

"And what's gonna happen if I don't? I'm gonna

burn up in hell in a blazing fire. I mean, come on, now. If y'all listen to that shit, it don't even make no sense."

The two freshmen chuckled again as Roy commented. "But Troy, there is a God, though," he assured.

"No it ain't," Troy said. "The pope in Rome probably shits on golden toilets. And he's the closest person to God. He has all that money while people are starving all around the world, kissing his fuckin' feet.

"That's crazy as hell! He ain't no closer to God than anyone else. He ain't no damn prophet. And Peter, how come he don't give people food and stuff, if he's so holy? All I see is people giving the church money."

"Ay', man, you gotta stop talkin' like that, 'cause going to hell ain't no game," Scott said.

"I know, but I'm going to hell already. The Bible said that money is the root to all evil. I'm gonna get paid like a motherfucker and go straight to hell with all the White people," Troy joked.

"Ay', my brother, you may be going to hell, but that don't mean that it's gonna be a bunch of White people down there with you," Peter said, keeping a serious face.

"Man, I'm tired of y'all holy people forgiving the White man. Just like the White man teaches in physics, the world is based on equilibrium. If they are rich and we are poor on earth, then they are poor in hell and we are rich in heaven. So if it's a lot of White people when you go to heaven, Peter, then you know we've been had," Troy said.

The four friends continued to talk about religion as they rode the elevator after dinner. Scott, whom Troy called the professor or the historian, stepped off with him to get something straight with a hardheaded friend. The concerned freshman was afraid that Troy was heading for a disaster.

"Troy, you really don't believe there's a God, man?" Scott asked him seriously.

Troy sighed. "Naw, cuz."

Scott shook his head. "This is serious. Don't be thinking about going to hell, because you don't want to go there," he insisted. "Aw'ight, look, I don't go to church and all, but you don't have to go to church to believe in God. That Roman Catholic stuff ain't real, man. They elected that pope, and people can't do that. We all make mistakes. They have built him right up next to God. And yeah, people kiss his feet and everything, but it ain't right. They even worship the statue of Mary. You ain't supposed to do that. Their religion is wrong, man, and Jesus Christ was colored. They got him in their churches all blond-haired and blue-eyed. He was born in the hot sun out near Israel. Now how you gon' be White out there? And he had woolly hair. Read it in the Bible.

"It was said that Blacks are the real Jews, and I believe it, because we have suffered the most," Scott said. "But don't keep on goin' the way you are, Troy, 'cause hell is more than what you think it is. I mean, just imagine, we will live forever in heaven. This down here is nothin'. This is dirt and filth down here. If you think that money can buy you happiness down here, you're wrong, 'cause heaven is the only true happiness."

"Just answer me one question, then, Scott. In the

Bible, it says that the present ruler of the earth will be condemned to hell, right?" Troy waited purposely for an answer before he would continue.

"Yeah, that's right," Scott answered.

"And White people rule the earth right now, right?"

"Yeah."

"So they should be condemned to hell, and all people of color, who have suffered on earth, should be in heaven, if it's fair. That's all I'm sayin', man. White people cannot be numerous in heaven if God is fair. There is no way that White people can be forgiven for all the pain they have caused the colored world. That's all I ask, is for the Lord to be fair to us who have suffered the most," Troy argued, with tears of emotion filling his eyes.

The freshman paused, unsure of his response. "I don't know, man, maybe you're right. But like Peter said, it may be more than just a Black and White thing. I think it's a human thing."

Yet it was to no avail. Troy was not one to compromise.

"Yeah, whatever, cuz," he responded tartly. "I say we gotta' think Black first, because I know I'm human already."

MALCOLM X

TROY ATTENDED EVERY BLACK SPEAKER'S EVENT HELD ON OR around campus. Time and again the speakers were from Florida A&M, Tuskegee, Xavier, Howard, Morehouse, Lincoln, Hampton, Morgan State, Fisk, Spelman, and other African-American universities. They were not treated as minorities on campus and they didn't act as such. They could reach for the sky unhampered by White buffers. Troy realized that Black institutions would have been more suitable to quench his own thirst for truth and leadership.

He weighed the idea, gathering information about Black college students. They had become the big businesspeople. They were the students featured in *Black Enterprise, Ebony, Essence,* and *Jet* magazines. And they possessed pride and confidence. White universities, on the other hand, curbed Blacks to remain in a secondary role. With great excitement, Troy decided to transfer to a Black university at the end of the school year. He wanted to be recognized as top quality. At State University, he believed he would never reach that goal.

* * *

"Look at all these plastic people, man. You know it's a game this morning, Pete, 'cause that's the only time these White people get up so early," Troy assumed. It was Saturday morning. Game day. He and Peter moved into the cafeteria line to gather breakfast.

Peter smiled. "I know," he agreed. "I thought they didn't like Black people. But they be the main ones screaming and yelling for a bunch of big Black football players."

"Yeah, but the thing about that is, they only like 'em when they're on the field," Troy mentioned. "I remember when I was on the basketball team last year. I'd turn around and see a blanket of White behind me every game, no matter who we played."

Peter nodded. "The way they use our people is pitiful. Then they just kick them out after four years to do nothing."

"Most of the athletes are too happy to know, though. They all think they got a shot at the pros," Troy responded. "They're on top of the world right now. It's only when people are miserable, like me, that they ever see anything."

They obtained their food and picked a table to sit and eat their meal.

"Hey, my brother, have you seen Matthew lately?" Peter asked, changing the subject. Troy would have talked about race affairs all morning long.

"Naw, man. Matter of fact, I was trying to get with him so we could do them chemistry labs. I'm messing up in that class, now."

"What? Troy's messing up in a class?"

"Look, man, nobody's perfect. Matthew is a Black

hero cause he got a four-point-oh, but he can make mistakes down the road, too."

"That's true, my brother."

"You know what I've decided, Pete?" Troy asked all of a sudden.

"What?"

"I'm gon' transfer to a Black school."

Peter's eyes opened wide "Yeah. Aw man, I wish that I could do that. But I still gotta finish a couple more C.M.P. classes."

Troy barely heard him, trapped in his excitement. "Yup, man, I'm tired of talkin' about it. I'm gon' do it, now. I've heard a lot of people say it, but y'all act like y'all stuck in this school or something."

James came and joined them with his tray of food.

"Ay', Jay, Troy is transferring to a Black school," Peter told him.

"For real, homes?" James asked, shocked.

Troy, mouth filled with food, nodded his head.

"Damn, I wish I could do that," James responded. "But I think I'm stuck on State U's big name, homes. This school is the shit! It's talked about all over the country.

"Naw, man, I'm gon' graduate from here," he said, smiling. "I know it's gon' be girls galore at a Black college, but their education ain't all that."

Troy shook his head, becoming defensive. "You know what, we're all anxious to believe that shit, but the fact is, you get much more help in Black schools."

"Aw'ight, homes, and when job day comes, I bet I'll get a job before you will," James said with a smirk.

Troy only frowned. He figured he was fighting a losing battle. James was blinded by State U's glamour.

Peter snapped his fingers and dissipated the tension. "Oh yeah, Troy, I forgot to ask you. Who was the pretty girl I saw you with yesterday?" he asked, face aglow.

Troy smiled and began to chuckle. "See, man, church people nosy as hell," he commented. "But that was my girl I was telling you about."

"Oh yeah. That's right," Peter remembered.

"I vowed that I would stop searching for just light-skinned girls when so many dark-skinned, good-looking ones are around," Troy said.

James started to giggle. "Naw, homes, I'm still gon' marry me a red-bone. I'm already dark, so I want a girl that's Peter's complexion."

Troy grinned at him. "Yeah. It figures."

Troy rushed back to his dorm to call his mother about the news.

"Yes, I would like to make a collect call," he told the operator. After he gave his name and the number, the operator put him through.

"Hey, Mom, it's me . . . Yeah, I'm OK. I just wanted to tell you that I'm sending away for applications to some Black schools.

"I *know* you told me, Mom. I'll tell you all about it when I get home for the holiday. We don't want to run up the phone bill . . . I love you, too."

Troy sat up in bed, staring at his blank walls and feeling like a fool. He had been sucked into a White university simply to show the government that the school had a Black enrollment. It was not as if the administration really cared. Black students were numbers in the system. But so were most of the White students.

Troy felt embarrassed for not trusting his own people to do a good job in instruction. His mother had always suggested that a Black school would have been best. Their argument of two years ago stuck clearly in his mind. And suddenly, he wished she had won.

"Troy, I think you should go to a Black college. Your aunt Cookie went to a White school and she didn't like it at all," Charlotte had said.

"Aw, Mom, that's her experience. How you know I'm gon' feel the same way she did?"

"Troy, now look. College is more than education; it's a social experience as well. And I think you'll feel more comfortable at a Black school."

"No I won't. All they do is party and whatnot. They don't get no *real* education. Black schools don't make no sense. I don't even see why people go to 'em. I'm tellin' you now, Mom, I'm not going to no Black school. You're just wasting your breath."

Troy covered his face in shame, remembering the argument all too well. White schools could never replace the environmental comfort and the positivity of learning at a Black institution. No wonder so many Blacks from the White colleges would disappear after graduation. They had been burned out, fighting or succumbing to daily dosages of American racism.

"Damn, I'm stupid!" Troy shouted to himself. "And I'm stuck in this school for another semester!"

* * *

That Monday morning, he had an interview with Professor Jameson, the White instructor of Black literature.

"So, Mr. Potter, what do you want to do for your project?"

"I was always interested in finding out about Malcolm X. So I would like to read his autobiography and explain his character."

After receiving the OK, Troy dedicated every spare moment of his time to reading one of the most important books in Black history. It took six days to complete, more than five hundred pages' worth.

Troy read from early in the morning until late at night. He got addicted to the book and couldn't put it down. Neglecting all his other studies, he then concentrated on doing his paper.

Why was Malcolm X viewed in such a controversial manner? What was America's position on his character? Why was he not an acceptable hero like Martin Luther King Jr.? And how come Malcolm had no holiday in litigation?

Troy Potter
Black Literature
November 12, 1988
The Analysis of Malcolm X

Even in the early years of life, Malcolm Little was deemed as special. His father, being a dark-skinned religious activist, favored his lightest son. This individual was to be a fast and active learner in his racist environment. He was one to speak the bold truth, control his own destiny, and startle those who might oppose him. Malcolm discovered the meaning of his Black world in America through self-evaluation and practice. As a kid, he learned to make noise in order to get what he wanted. He was able to see all the challenges that his youthful world had to offer. From the beginning of his time, Malcolm captured his goal no matter what it was.

In school, this young individual observed with the ability of great sight and detailed memory. Outside of school as well as in the academic realm, he was a skilled learner. His dominating and extroverted personality made him an intriguing person to know. He was not your average Joe Blow.

Malcolm's passion to learn made him wise. He was destined to be the best and to work toward human perfection. Being such a man as described, he was a leader and one with the determination and dignity to be followed.

A person must understand that Malcolm was not at all gifted, and did not see himself as such, but was rather a man who put body and mind, heart and soul, and one-hundred-percent effort into everything he did. With such drive, it was easy for him to become a top student even among the Whites he attended school with. With such drive his color should have been irrelevant.

As a youth in White schools, while living with a White family, in a world where people of

White skin ruled, Malcolm tried his best to be White. He went to White parties and acted White to integrate himself. If any Black individual having color to his skin, kinks on his head, wide meat on his nose, and with full lips could have been accepted by the White majority, that person was Malcolm Little. But after years of academic excellence, class leadership, social compatibility, and total politeness to White individuals, there was no crossover.

Malcolm had been a Black student at the top of a White class. He was a poor individual from an oppressed Black family, and was a descendant of a people who were seen as utterly unintelligent. Above all odds, he was supreme.

In his view of the world, nothing was too far to reach. He truly believed that he could accomplish anything with hard work and determination. It was no surprise that Malcolm would go against all odds of the Black man's integrity to claim himself as a predestined lawyer before being crushed by the hands of racist America in a response that he, a Black boy, could never be a lawyer. He could possibly be a farmer, but not a lawyer. He could be a carpenter, but not a lawyer. He could possibly be a mechanic, but never a lawyer.

His favorite subjects were English and history. He disregarded math because of the lack of argument or proof. He displayed a great desire to explain, argue, and comprehend complex abstractions of social studies and was interested in speech and reactions. All of the above would have made him perfectly suitable for the task of being a lawyer. Malcolm's mastery of these skills would have made him a great lawyer, but he was a Black man in White America.

Malcolm had overtly experienced where he was to be placed as a Black male youth. He now projected an attitude that Whites were only out for their own race, while pretending to help Black people. Whites had planned all along that his place was to be among the Blacks and that all other progress would be halted. Now he could see how he had been tricked into believing that he could be an able Black man in White America. Tricked into believing that his White family and peers accepted and liked him as a person of human flesh, human emotions, dreams and thoughts of success and self-worth. What he found to be true was that the Whites gained from him a sense of enjoyment. The Whites gained from him a sense of pride from their faked pity and concern.

Greatness could not help Malcolm to escape the weight of the heavy Black world which was made by White American authority. Hard work was not enough for Malcolm to overcome, like some kind of Black American Hercules, this mighty weight which held them down. Determination would still fall short of what was needed for Malcolm to lift the weight of the Black earth which had been so fertilized by many failures before him. So he was humiliated and angered. Though he was angered, he was no longer confused.

Whites had killed his father, oppressed his Black community, caused his mother to go out of her mind, and then blamed it on her. White people had taken him from his home and had allowed him to show his intellect while gaining pride for himself, only to throw him back down to the hard earth that he would again have to adjust to. "Adjust" was a fitting word to describe Malcolm's life. He had to adjust to the slick Black ghetto streets of Harlem.

Malcolm was always a lover of action and always a doer instead of a watcher. He was a man of actions instead of idle plans. A man of true words as compared to practiced words.

He never saw himself as being better than the rest. However, because of his fast-lane experiences, great biological growth, and speedy understanding, it was only natural for him to look upon those who were older than he and more experienced. He wanted to attain more knowledge from those who knew the Harlem streets.

He had a subliminal bond and a submissive desire to be involved with the hipsters of the streets up north. He admired and was greatly attracted by their style and glamour. They possessed the ability to take the streets and drain a sense of importance for themselves among Black peoples. They possessed poetic dialect and were involved in the action world, which Malcolm felt such a great need to be a part of. He felt at home with the wild lifestyles that the slicksters lived, and disregarded those Blacks who felt themselves better than the majority. Malcolm had been through the White desert and came across an ocean of Black Power in the New York streets.

He took to the slick ghettos up north with the same drive that he pursued everything in his life. An average Black youth, Malcolm received an average conked hairstyle with an average black zoot suit to start his slickster days. He did not have any great name and there was no particular reason to know him. But in due time, Malcolm, "the Activist," would once again show his greatness in progression and assertion. He became a hustler, a hood, a thief, a con man, and a hit man. He became a skilled dancer, a pimp, a numbers runner, a drug dealer, and a junky. Once again, he was highly sought after.

He maintained the cunning and passionate thrust toward being a Harlemite from the trying lessons which he had learned as a kid. He had learned that "if someone was doing something better than you in a certain task, they were obviously doing something that you were not." He would do any- and everything to be on top.

Even before becoming a complete man at the age of twenty-one, his lifestyle was more complete than most people's entire lives. He had escaped death, outsmarted cops, feared more than several times for his life, took more chances than the average slickster, and had arrived as a premier Harlemite gangster, "Harlem Red." Was it the red hair inherited through near-White blood which gave him his fire? What was the part of Malcolm which enabled him to become tops of a game which so many had played and failed in? This was a game of slickster kill-or-be-killed, hoodlum rob-or-be-robbed, as well as dealer deal-more-than-the-next-guy.

Malcolm was a true character who was so entrenched in the Black ghetto world that he was unafraid to die, not willing to lose, and convinced that he could do anything and outclass anyone. So the X-man, on that long, wild, youthful road to peril and destruction, had gained his fame as one of the top gangsters of New York.

He was to be respected, feared, hunted, and finally imprisoned, luckily, instead of being killed before even becoming what society considers a man. But the imprisonment, he believed, was more a sentence for being involved with White women than for robbery and theft.

Malcolm had recognized the light in Negroes' eyes when in the presence of White girls. And he believed that every Negro's desire was to have one, as he himself had. White girls gave a brother prestige and they were honored when accompanied by one. However, he also believed that White women were corrupt and deceptive as they ran about with Black men and had White husbands at home. He had been in a predicament where his life could have been lost over the corruption of his White female cheating on her husband. Yet it was true, and the pimps had the gift to know, that the White girls could fool the strongest of men.

From the beginning of the Bible, Adam was tricked by Eve, which set the tone for women's tricky hold over men. Malcolm was well aware of this history yet he was being sentenced to jail and mocked for his involvement with two White girls who had helped set up a crime.

Now a prisoner from the hard-core streets of Black America, he was an antireligious man with a disrespect for religious followers. He had always rejected religion and considered it a cop-out and a healing for the weak-minded. He was a man who had known too much, carried too heavy a burden, and lived too hard a life to accept the passive ways of the Christian faith.

The Christian faith taught Negroes to be happy and wait for good things to come in the afterworld, like death, heaven, and rejoicing in the Lord. Those Blacks lived in a realm of hope. These Black criminals were the individuals who had tasted the world's true flavors and had gotten captured. What could religion do for them?

These men had followed a path of destruction established by the White oppressors. They were trapped like all those who tried, as the slicksters had, to get over in White America. Here lay Harlem Red, who once again received a nickname for himself as "Satan" for his greatly expressed antireligious attitudes. He had thought that Christianity was established to further enslave Blacks in America as well as other colored people around the world. He had lived a solid life that most feebleminded Christians could never even imagine. His present circumstances were just right for a Black man to accept the teachings of the Nation of Islam.

"The White man is the devil." What statement could have stirred Malcolm X more, a man filled now with bitter hatred of the White world, besides this one? This statement easily summed up the devastation that Malcolm had felt as a result of White oppression in youth, in school, in the ghetto, and while in prison. He began to think of all the unjust acts which had been inflicted on him and his family. His dad's death, his mother's craziness, his education in the White school, the ghettos of Harlem, and the total disregard of Black people in America.

His desire to find out more about the Nation of Islam and the truths of the world influenced him to read countless books from the prison library. He found that he did not understand many concepts or words and could not get any meaningful detail from his readings. He then decided that he would learn every word he possibly could in order to understand all that he read. So he began with *a*, and read the entire dictionary.

He read books on history, science, politics, and theology. And he sent letters of gratitude to the leader of the Nation of Islam, Elijah Muhammad, for his work to uplift lost Black souls in America. Reading absorbed all of his time in prison as he confined himself to the silence of his cell. He read late into the morning without lights, causing him to need glasses.

This was typical of a man who, from the start of life, had done things exceptionally well. Malcolm X was a character who had gained the most attention as a kid, a student, a hoodlum, a dancer, and even a prisoner. Now, in the next phase of his life, he would put one hundred percent of his worthy effort into the project of setting up a stronghold following of the Nation of Islam, bringing truth and dignity to his Black brothers and sisters all across America.

He became a great speaker, and never had a man spoken with such bold truths of racism across the world, infiltrating "the white devils." He had learned the story of the blue-eyed devil and his creation, as well as the purity and greatness of the ancient African kingdoms. He had learned the truth about Jesus Christ, Egypt, and the great messengers of Allah. He soon would know a great deal of things and could convey his knowledge convincingly.

Malcolm spoke of the infliction of pain and hate of the Black man and all people of color. He spoke of the reality of supposed nonviolent coexistence among Blacks and Whites. He spoke of the belief in Christianity, which he still felt was used to trap and confuse people of color. He spoke about the Black-on-Black hatred and distrust among Negroes. He spoke of the wars where "a black man was sent to kill a yellow man by a white man and for a white man." Blacks would kill for the right to be enslaved and discriminated against in America.

He had set up Muslim temples and gave speeches across the country in the name of Elijah Muhammad and the Nation of Islam, to whom he gave respect and honor. The people arrived in the truth of their own heritage from blindness. Temples were built in the name of the Nation of Islam to teach the people self-respect and dignity. Malcolm was great in his work once again.

As he spoke out on Black activism in honor of the Nation of Islam, he had received unwanted credit from the White media and "Black stooges" who opposed him. Continually he was misquoted. Time after time he received the credit from the White media which should have been contributed to the Nation of Islam.

He was labeled a hater of White people and a reverse racist from "Black stooges."

The Nation of Islam tried to uplift the spirit of brothers and sisters across the country, and Malcolm played a major part in its goal. Maybe Malcolm helped too much, spoke too diligently, taught too impressively, and was too dedicated to the upbringing of Black America. It seems that he was too great for his own good. He caused too much emotion, anger, pride, dignity, fear, and guilt among those who followed and of those who opposed him.

Malcolm, however, was still merely a man. He

was a great man, a respectable man, a challenging man, yet just a man. Because of his great political and public prowess, tension was high between him, Elijah Muhammad, and other followers within the Nation. Malcolm X had become a name to fear and one of great concern and awareness. He had gained too firm a reputation from his efforts. Being in an unescapable predicament and sensing the great pressure of his people as well as those against him, he was due to make a mistake. He was thought to be a troublemaker, had influenced Black America to be self-supportive, and slipped up when he scorned the death of a most loved American president, John F. Kennedy. This was it, and Malcolm could feel the end approaching.

He knew that his sentence of a ninety-day silence was the end, and he would not be accepted again by the Nation. He had once again been set up to fail because of his greatness, which, in simple words, was too much. Once again he was to adjust to a new task and position in life. This time he had the backing of Black America, who admired and expressed a desire to follow him. So the X-man adjusted to a different role, to set up his own house of worship to continue the uplifting of Black people. But he would have to watch his back from forces out to kill him.

Being an intelligent and wise man, he decided to go to the holy land of Mecca to find all that he could learn from the Qur'an. He went to Africa, witnessing people of all colors with humility, pride, honor, justice, truth, worship, and cohabitation. Whites, Yellows, Reds, Browns, and Blacks were in a singular worship of Allah. He learned that the White man in America had set himself up to be supreme. He arrived once again in a new truth that White men could be just and honest. They could actually feel true pity and be trusted and respected. Malcolm then traveled to other parts of Africa to experience the pleasure that the African brothers had for him, only to come home and soon be gunned down.

Malcolm X was expected to die by the hands of fate. For he was truly a great man of history who would die like all great men of history. He would die like all great men who strived for excellence and a better way, like one who is all-deserving to have his story told throughout history. He was not simply a Black American racist, but a man of truth and fire. Let the truth be known to all men that Malcolm's name should not be torn down, but lifted up. For Malcolm was a total man and a pure example of a warrior in a racist White world. Malik El Hajj Shabazz.

Troy was captivated. Malcolm X was very much like himself. He had lived a life so similar that Troy felt he was reading his own autobiography. He wasn't wrong for feeling discontent with Whites. He was born to succeed, and therefore he struggled to reach his goals despite oppression.

Malcolm X had rekindled Troy's fight, instilling newborn confidence. He felt that no man could have influenced him more than Malcolm. He had given his *all* to uplift Black people.

The joy was simply overwhelming. Troy had never felt so proud to be Black in his life. Every Black person in the world should read *The Autobiography of Malcolm X*, he thought to himself. He wanted to read more about the teachings of the Qur'an and the Nation of Islam as well. His mind had been unsealed.

Troy went on to read about Hannibal, Marcus Garvey, and the Black Panther Party. He read articles on colored peoples in world affairs. He read about every country suffering under White imperialism, and he sympathized with their constant racial strife.

He began to feel positive again that colored people could rise if they only believed in themselves. They could rise if they came together as a group and took complete control of their own destiny.

It's time for us to find ourselves and our history, Troy told himself. He was refilled with energy and ready to battle.

"Just trim down the sides and block up the top, Troy," Reggie said while getting his hair cut.

"Yeah, Rej, I haven't seen you for a *long* time. Where you been at?" Troy asked him while adjusting his equipment.

"I been studying, man. 'Cause I ain't got no more time to mess around. You know. I'm already behind," Reggie responded.

Troy nodded, eager to state what he had been

doing. "I just got finished writing a paper on Malcolm X," he mentioned.

"Oh yeah. My Mom loved Malcolm X, man. She used to talk about him all the time," Reggie told him.

"He was the man, cuz. And we killed him," Troy said, depressed.

"I know. It's like Black people are scared to follow a real Black leader. We would rather kiss White people's ass all the time. I mean, Martin Luther King was cool, but Malcolm X was the stronger man," Reggie commented.

Troy went on. "Yup, I knew it before I read the book. Black people were scared of Malcolm. But to tell you the truth, his death looks set up, to me. I think the F.B.I. and the C.I.A. had something to do with both of their assassinations. I read that the Secret Service also played a part in that John F. Kennedy and Robert Kennedy shit," Troy informed him. "They fucked over the Black Panther Party, too.

"I read about some shit called COINTELPRO. I forgot what it means, so I'll have to look it up again. But it was talkin' about turning different Black groups against each other."

"Yeah, where you read that at?" Reggie quizzed.

"I met some old-head brother in the library. The brother had some documents on it. Dude is supposed to be writing a book."

"Shit, they might try to kill cuz," Reggie said, half joking and half serious.

Troy chuckled. "Yeah, well then we'll know it's true. Like Martin Luther King once said, 'A man not willing to die for a cause is not fit to live.' "

Reggie did an about-face, needing eye-to-eye confirmation. "Get outta here! Martin Luther King said that?"

"Yeah, man. I saw a couple of his speeches on video at this seminar last week. It's this group called the Preservation of Black Male Leaders, and they say that the media is purposely denigrating Martin Luther King to that 'I have a dream' shit. And yo, the brother was much deeper than that, man. *Much* deeper."

Reggie was impressed. "Damn, Troy, you really be knowing some shit."

"I don't know nothin' yet. I'm just a baby," Troy responded humbly. "It's all kinds of information out there that we don't know nothin' about. Like they say, knowing is half the battle. So if we don't even know shit, then we really a long way from home."

Reggie nodded and smiled. "Yup, cuz, you ain't never lied."

Troy smiled back. "I never meant to."

KNOWLEDGE OF SELF

Bloomp bloomp bloomp.

"Yo, come in," Troy offered. He was stretched out across his bed, Friday night, listening to Public Enemy's urgent calls for Black revolution.

Peter walked in and immediately turned down the volume on Troy's recently purchased radio. "Where you been this week?"

Troy turned it back up a notch. "I was at the library, reading *The Autobiography of Malcolm X* and doing a term paper."

"Yeah, well that's one heavy book, my brother."

Troy became excited, expecting another conversation on Malcolm. "What, you read it?" he asked.

Peter shook his head. "Naw, I just heard about it."

"Oh. It figures."

"What do you mean, 'It figures'? Are you trying to say that I don't read? 'Cause I've read a whole lot of books; specifically the Bible. The Lord says that the Bible is the only sword I need," Peter responded with confidence.

Troy grinned and turned the music off. "What do you need a sword for?"

"What do I need a sword for?" Peter repeated. "To protect me and to fight off evil deception."

"Oh. You mean the White man."

Peter frowned. "OK, I see you startin' to talk that Malcolm X stuff."

"That's not from Malcolm X. That's the truth, my brother," Troy mocked him.

Peter chuckled and shook his head. "You're wrong, my brother, too wrong. The devil is no man. The devil is an evil spirit, and that's what I came to tell you about.

"My church is having a seminar for young Black men that I want you to go to this Sunday. We're having a special guest preacher from Washington, D.C., and I'm hoping that you can find faith in the Lord."

Troy simply smiled. He then got out of his bed and looked into his desk drawer. He took out an old notebook and flipped through the pages.

"Here it is. 'January twenty-third, nineteen eighty-eight,' " he read. " 'I was weak to the trickery of the devil, and now I have the strength I need to fight him off and not fall into temptation. The devil has a lot of trickery in this world, and you have to see through that before you can know the light of the Lord. I have just begun, but as I learn more about the Lord and his words, I can be better equipped to help my confused brothers.' "

Peter stood there, smiling, and Troy smiled back.

"So you memorized it and wrote it down, hunh, my brother?" Peter queried.

"You damn right!" his friend exclaimed. "That was the heaviest shit I've ever heard you say. That's the night that I couldn't sleep and ended up praying for guidance. Now I truly see that 'the Lord works in mysterious ways,' 'cause I met a brother that put me down with the fact that Jesus was Black, the prophets were Black, and the real Jews were Black. Or should I say, the Hebrews."

Peter continued smiling while Troy closed his book and put it back in his desk.

"So you been reading the scriptures, my brother?" Peter asked.

"Naw, not yet. But I'm down to go to church with y'all this week."

"All right, then," Peter said. "Oh yeah, are you going on that bowling trip tonight?"

"Naw, man. Tonight is my night to relax. I've been working hard, and the Lord did give us a sabbath day," Troy commented with a grin.

Peter laughed. "So what happened to your girl? You not gon' hang out with her tonight?" he asked as he walked toward the door.

"Ay', brother, didn't the Ten Commandments say, 'Thou shall not covet thy neighbor's wife'?" Troy quizzed sarcastically. Then he smiled. "Naw, man, I'm just jokin'. Me and my girl gon' have a study session in the library tomorrow."

Peter nodded. "OK. Well, I'll see you in church Sunday." He left and closed the door.

Troy leaped back onto his bed and turned his music on. Feeling sensuous, he began to wish that Karen was with him. He had been seeing her for over a month, and they had not even kissed. She was so aware of the issues and so intriguing that the thought of having sex with her had slipped his mind on several occasions. But suddenly he desired to be more intimate with her. He figured that tomorrow might as well be their day.

"So, did you have a good time at your uncle's crib last night?" Troy asked his new woman friend. They sat inside the library that Saturday morning.

"No, 'cause he and my father played chess all night. My aunt was sick, and all my cousins had gone out," Karen responded to him.

Troy pulled a few books out of her bag and spread them out across their small library table. He then sat back in his chair and smiled. Karen smiled back with no comment.

"So, what are you gonna teach me today?" Troy asked her.

She hunched her shoulders. "I'on know. You know a lot already, but my father was tellin' me about melanin studies a couple of nights ago."

He nodded. "Yeah, that's for pigmentation in the skin, eyes, and hair. We learned a little about that in biology."

"Yeah, but he said it's even deeper than that, 'cause he was talkin' about melanin in the brain, making you think faster and have hand-and-eye coordination and rhythm. He also told me that melanin gave Black people a higher spiritual connection."

"Hmm, that shit is deep. I'm gon' have to check that out," Troy responded.

"You know what, Troy? I think you curse too much."

"Yeah, you right. But what else did your pop say about it?" he said, brushing Karen's comment aside.

"Umm, he was talkin' about the Black kids that were killed in Atlanta years ago, and about White scientists doing test studies on melanin from live materials."

"Live materials? So they can try to inject themselves, or some shit? Oh, I'm sorry," Troy said, catching his curse word.

Karen gave him a sly stare before continuing. "Yeah, 'cause he was talkin' about the ozone layer deteriorating and white skin not having protection from the sun."

"Yeah, that's deep. White scientists do some crazy stuff, like in all the crazy movies they make. Remember that movie *The Island of Dr. Moreau,* and them experiments mixing animal and human genes?" Troy asked.

Karen nodded her head and smiled.

"Yeah, that movie was crazy," Troy commented. "What White man thought of some crazy stuff like that? I think they're devils, for real."

Karen shook her head in disagreement. "White people have done a lot of crazy and evil things, but we have to set our priorities straight. We can't make our entire movement against White people, so we have to go much further than Black nationalist philosophies."

"Yeah, well I'm down with the Black Panther Party and Marcus Garvey. They were about action. I mean, even Elijah Muhammad formed a nation. We gon' have to form some kind of a nation," Troy pleaded, as if Karen was in authority.

"Well, my father believes in education through an

African-centered approach. We have to learn how to think right if we're going to form a nation," Karen responded, grinning at Troy. He smiled back, believing that he had influenced her. "The African-centered approach came before Islam, but the Islamic principle of metaphysics is very productive. I will say that," she added.

"Metaphysics?" Troy responded quizzically. "I know you gon' break down what that means, right?" He had never heard the term "African-centered education" before either.

"Metaphysics is the study of the nature of things, asking how, when, and why. Basically, it's the philosophy of critical thought. You ever read *Things Fall Apart,* by Chinua Achebe?" Karen asked.

"Naw."

"Well, you need to read that, 'cause that can introduce you to the principles of African deities, folklore, and culture.

"African spirituality is based on the principles of reason and nature. The Creator, who has many names, is manifested in everything," Karen explained. "White people couldn't make that link when they went to Africa. Many people still think that holistic nature is based solely in witchcraft, but it's not. Africans have always believed in one superior being; however, they give importance to *all* that has been created.

"You also should read *The African Origin of Civilization,* by Cheikh Anta Diop; *The Destruction of Black Civilization,* by Chancellor Williams; *Stolen Legacy,* by George James; *Before the Mayflower,* by Lerone Bennett; and *They Came Before Columbus*, by Ivan Van Sertima."

"*Shit!* I mean, dag! You read all that!" Troy exclaimed, smiling again at the curse word.

"Yeah, we definitely have to work on your mouth," Karen responded seriously. "We don't have to express ourselves like that. It makes me sick to hear people using profanity up and down the street. Then parents tell their kids not to, while they're cussing up a storm."

"Aw'ight, my fault. But what does your father think about the pope?" Troy asked, moving along. He was excited about the information Karen presented him, and she wasn't even attending college yet.

"When I was little, my father told my aunt that the pope was going to be the great deceiver. He said that the pope is the Antichrist, because my aunt is Catholic. Or she was Catholic. I don't know what she believes now. But you also have to study the Coptic Christianity of Ethiopia to understand the many contradictions of Western Christianity," Karen explained.

"Man, whatever," Troy replied. It was too much information at one time. "What religion do you believe in?" he thought he'd ask.

"It doesn't matter. All of the major Western religions have African roots. It's even a book called *African Roots of the Major "Western Religions,"* by Dr. Ben, that discusses the linkage."

"So what's this book right here?" Troy asked, picking up a colorful title from the desk.

"That's this professor at Temple University. You from Philly, and you never heard of him?" Karen quizzed.

"Naw. *Afrocentricity,* by Molefi K. Asante," Troy read.

Karen smiled. "My father just got that book for me."

"So your pop really didn't want you to go to college until he got you to read all these books, hunh?"

"Yup. He said it's too much miseducation going on at the college level and down through elementary school. He said it's like poison to the Black mind."

"You talk about your father a lot, I notice."

" 'Cause," Karen said, "after my mom died and we moved here from Chicago, I was the only one who listened to him."

Troy was shocked that she had gotten so personal without any warning.

"You never told me that your mom died. I just figured she didn't live with y'all or something," he responded.

"Yeah, 'cause she died when I was four. My father had to raise all six of us by himself."

"Dag, your pop is a hell of a man. But I still wouldn't have kept you out of college your first year," Troy said. "What school do you want to go to anyway?"

"Harriet Tubman. They have the strongest African-centered program, and it's an independent school."

"Yeah, well, I'll see you in the hallways," Troy responded with a smile.

Karen raised her brows. "What are you talkin' about?"

"I'm transferring there too, after next semester. My Mom already sent me the application."

"Dag, I feel good to hear that," Karen told him.

"Yeah, so we'll be with each other," Troy assured her. He reached out and softly rubbed her hand, thinking of evening intimacy.

After talking for hours, it was nearly five o'clock before they realized it, and Karen was hungry. She took Troy to a Jamaican restaurant on the northwest side of town. It was a warm and colorful place that served only vegetarian foods and featured Caribbean art and music. Karen then told Troy she ate only one meal a day.

"Dag. How can you do that?" he asked her as he looked over the menu.

"You really only need one meal a day. Everything else is addiction. That's why I was happy when you told me that you don't smoke. But we gotta work on that drinking now."

"It ain't like I drink every day. As a matter of fact, the last time I even touched a bottle was when I was home with my boys. We were celebrating me going back to college."

Karen just shook her head as the waitress appeared with an order pad and a pen.

"Can I take your order?"

Troy took a quick peek at her beautifully rounded backside. She watched him as well.

"Yes. I would like to have the vegetarian chili and rice, if you don't mind," Karen said with an attitude. The waitress seemed to air her backside to Troy purposely. He tried not to laugh, but he had a smirk on his face.

"It's your turn to order, Troy," Karen said. She gave him a clear message to stop looking.

"Oh, aw'ight," he responded, smiling helplessly. "I'll have the, umm . . ." He stopped and looked over the menu, not knowing what most of the food was. "Well, just give me what she got."

"OK, two chili and rice. Would you like anything to drink with that?" the waitress asked Karen.

"Water, and can we have some plantain chips?"

"Sure. And you? What would you like?" she asked Troy.

He took a quick look at her breasts and then at Karen, knowing that he was caught. "Ah, well, umm," he stammered. He couldn't get his words out, still trying to reduce his smile. "Just give me whatever she gets."

Karen looked even prettier to him as she pretended to look away, as if she was not bothered by the flirting.

Troy stared at her until she looked back at him.

"What are you looking at?" she asked playfully.

He smiled and threw his hands over his face. "You know what, Karen, you make me feel like a kid and shit. Oh, I'm sorry," he said, with a grin. Another curse word.

"Yeah, well, you act like a kid, too, just like my hardheaded brother. Just swore you knew where you was going. Didn't you?" she asked, grinning back.

"Look, I thought you said to catch the 34B."

"Well, if you wouldn't have been all in a rush, you would have heard me. But no, 'It's cold out here, Karen,' " she mocked with a laugh.

"OK, so I guess you gon' keep rubbing it in, hunh? But why did you get on the wrong bus with me, then?" he quizzed.

"I'on know. I guess 'cause you got me."

"I got you? What are you talkin' about?"

Karen looked into his eyes seductively. Then she dropped them to her plate as it arrived. She waited for the waitress to leave before repeating herself. "You got me, Troy."

She was beautiful: small eyes, curly hair, and perfect brown skin. Troy smiled and giggled and felt sexy and could feel his nature rising, all at the same time. Definitely, tonight was their night.

They rode the bus back to campus speechless. Troy thought Karen might announce that she was going home as she usually did. Previously, it didn't matter much to him because he always had such a good time with her. But not tonight. Tonight was *the* night.

He signed her in and they went to the room. Troy was feeling sensuous already. Still, neither said much as he opened the door to a neatly made room. The pleasant strawberry fragrance from the incense that he lit before going to meet Karen filled their noses.

Troy hung their coats in his closet and set the mood. He turned on his radio, turned off the lights, and began to dance with her.

"You silly," Karen told him.

"I know."

They danced in the middle of his small dorm. He began to kiss her and she kissed him back. She began to hold him tighter. Troy then licked inside her ear and kissed her again, reaching smoothly around to the back of her skirt. But then Karen stopped him.

"No, Troy."

He stopped himself. "I'm sorry. I just feel real sexual," he admitted.

They stood silently, holding each other in the dark while the slow music played.

Troy looked down and into her placid face. "What are you thinking about?"

Karen broke away softly, turning the light back on and turning the music off. "Come here," she said, reaching her hands out to his. He did as she said, loving how she seemed to take control. "I like you, I think, more than I ever liked a boy in my life, but you have to learn when and when not to do things."

"Aw'ight," Troy responded hurriedly. He felt slightly disappointed. But Karen continued to hold his hands as she went on.

"How do you feel right now?" she asked him.

"I feel like I wanna make love to you," he insisted.

"But it ain't time yet, Troy."

He felt an urge to break away. But her subtle hand-holding method was effective in keeping his attention.

"Troy? What do you want to do with your life?" she asked him.

"I wanna live like anybody else," he responded. He thought it was a ridiculous question. "What chew ask me that for?" he queried with a smirk.

"Well, I kind of thought you wanted to be a soldier for Black people," Karen said. She was serious, not smiling, and still, she held his hands.

"Yeah, well I do."

"Well you gotta respect the Black woman, then."

Troy felt like Karen had hit him with a brick. He was guilt-ridden.

"You understand me now?" she asked, staring into his eyes.

"Yeah," he told her. He felt as if he had just received a beating. His heart was racing, and he felt as if he had no control over his emotions. Karen had stripped him of his male aggression. Troy was used to sleeping with whomever he wanted to and whenever he wanted, but not with her. It was frustrating to accept, but he knew in his heart that she was right.

Karen gave him time to think about it before she continued. "I just want you to know that this is not about sex. I am a virgin, and you will be the first, but only when I say so.

"This is about discipline. You are gonna have to have sexual discipline and respect for Black women in order to have purpose for Black people. There's too many Black men talkin' 'bout 'Fight the power' while they still run around and treat Black women like dirt."

Troy was stunned, yet Karen maintained her grip upon his hands, calming him. She then wrapped them around her and placed her head against his shoulder. "I've known you for a while, Troy," she said to him.

"What do you mean by that?" he asked. He thought she was going to tell him something like, "It was meant for us to be together."

"You was going to all the speak-out functions that I was going to. And I guess you never noticed me before. But I always noticed you. I don't stop and talk to any boy that says, 'Hey, what's your name?' " Karen told him through her smile. "I knew you before you met me. And I knew what kind of mind you had from the things that you would say. So now I got you. And you just need a little training."

Troy smiled back, surrendering. "Yeah, aw'ight." He felt himself finally loosening up. Karen told him that her father trusted all of his children to make their own decisions once they reached eighteen. So she spent the night, and Troy was afraid to touch her; but he felt that once she allowed him to, it would be wonderful.

"Yo, what's up, Troy?" James asked. "You goin' to church this morning, homes?"

Troy was wearing a trench coat, slacks, shirt, and a tie at breakfast that Sunday morning inside the main cafeteria. Walton Hall didn't serve food on the weekends.

"Yeah, man. I'm going to the young Black men's seminar with Peter and them down on Charleston Street," Troy told him.

"Oh yeah? Well, yo, homes, I got this twenty-three-year-old last night and shit," James said, grinning. "That's why I'm up so early. I had to drive her home for work."

"Yeah," Troy responded unenthusiastically. He thought about the first night in his life where he had spent the night with a date without taking her clothes off.

"So I heard you was wit' your girl last night."

"Yeah," Troy answered. He hoped James wouldn't probe into his business. But he knew that he would.

"So you finally got it last night, homes?"

"Nope. She said she didn't want to yet," Troy whined, getting it over with.

James giggled. "Don't look all down, man. It's plenty of girls that told me that. That's just how it goes sometimes," he explained, still grinning.

"Yeah, I guess so," Troy mumbled. "I gotta' get over to this church, cuz, I'm already late. I'll talk to you later," he said as he left his tray on the table.

When Troy arrived at the African Baptist Church, he found that several State U students had become members. He looked around and did not see Peter, Roy, or Scott. Then it occurred to him that there were only women in the congregation.

"Excuse me, are you looking for the men's seminar?" a sister whispered into the aisle as Troy stood there, confused.

"Yeah," he answered.

She pointed him toward a basement door. "It's down the stairs."

"Thanks."

Troy descended the stairs and joined close to thirty Black men. Only eight were his age, six of whom were college students. He was surprised that there were not more "young Black men" there. Nevertheless, he took a seat next to Peter and listened.

"You a little late, ain't you, my brother?" Peter asked with a smirk.

"Yeah, well, I didn't get much sleep last night."

Peter smiled, suspecting the wrong thing. Then again, it was Troy's rep that had Peter thinking what he was thinking.

"I would like to say to all you men here today that I'm proud to be here. And the Lord brought me here safely even though the weatherman said it was supposed to snow. But you see, the snow can't stop the Lord's work," the guest preacher announced.

"Ay-men, brother!" went the response.

"We are going to talk like men and about men. Can I hear somebody say 'amen'?"

"Ay-men!"

The preacher smiled and went on. "I came here today to tell you that *Black men* need to come together and get our house in order. We gotta live truth instead of just talkin' about it."

The short, dark, and round guest preacher possessed a deep and powerful voice, more powerful than Mike X had. The preacher roared when he spoke.

"I don't think y'all hear me. *I said, can I get an 'amen?'* "

"Ay-men!"

"We got too many preachers that speak the words on Sunday and dance with the devil on Monday."

"Ay-men!"

Troy held in his laughter.

"We have to let our younger brothers see some true examples of some real men of the word. 'Cause see, we got too many out here that don't read and study the word, but dey say, 'Oh, the Lord is in my heart.' Somebody say *'amen!'* "

"Ay-men!"

"You need to get the Lord in your mind, body, and soul and stop playing possum with him. 'Cause the Lord knows who's sleeping and who's awake. And he knows who's naughty and who's nice. But the Lord is much greater than some Santa Claus. I don't think y'all hear me. *I want somebody to say 'amen!' "*

"Ay-men!"

The guest preacher spoke about what Black men had to do and how the streets had turned them sour. He talked about "sleeping with ten sisters and thinking the Lord wouldn't know." Troy enjoyed his speech and keyed in when he started to talk about Jesus.

"Now see, we got a difference between the Muslim brothers and the Christian brothers when we start to talk about Jesus. 'Cause some of the Muslim brothers seem to think that Jesus was a wimpy man," he said. He then looked around at the church walls. "I'm glad I don't see no *white pictures* of a *Black Jesus!"* he roared with a smile. "We gotta let the truth be known that *Jesus was Black, like us!* And if you read the scriptures, using your mind, you'll know that Jesus was Black, like us. The Muslim brothers know it, so how come some of us Christian brothers don't know? I say you gotta know the word before you can teach the word! *Can somebody say 'amen'?"*

"Amen, brother! Tell it like it is!" an older man shouted from across the third row. Troy looked at Peter and smiled. Peter nodded his head in confirmation. The guest preacher then got a volunteer to be Jesus. He told the man to take his shirt off. He then told him to bend over, put his hands behind his back, and act as if he was carrying a cross.

"After they had whipped Jesus and ripped the skin off of his back, they poured vinegar over his head and into his sores and put a crown of thorns as long as your fingers on his head. They then beat the thorns into his head and made him carry his cross. And Jesus, a *Black man,* did all this to save the souls of all men."

The guest preacher told the volunteer to extend his hands. "Then they took his wrists, and they drove the nails into them because the weight of his body would rip through his hands.

"So they took and nailed him to the cross, breaking the bones and veins in his wrist. And then they placed his feet together and drove a long nail through both of his feet, breaking more bones. After all of that, the cross that he hung on had a rough surface with splinters on it.

"Now, let's talk about wimpy," he said intensely. "I don't think y'all hear me out there. *I say, can I get an 'amen?'* "

The preacher got another *"amen,"* and Troy was touched, feeling the pain of what Jesus must have gone through. He had never imagined such a graphic explanation of the Bible. Television did not do the tale any justice. And all the white photos of Jesus all around the world were false and deceptive. So when the preacher asked for those men who had not yet been "saved," Troy could not help but go up and get baptized with oil. He accepted it with his heart, filled with emotion, but in his mind he wanted to know more, so the preacher took his phone number.

Honestly, Troy was more moved by the oratorical spirit of the preacher and not so much by the Christian doctrine. He had already known that Christianity was not the only religion. There was more to be learned about religious history, more to be read and understood. And concerning Jesus, Karen told him, "Jesus never died on the cross, and Jesus never called himself 'the Christ.' Those are things that *man* said and created."

"So did you learn anything today, my brother?" Peter asked Troy. All four college friends headed back to the dorms after being fed at the church.

"Yeah, I learned a lot. But what did you learn?" Troy challenged.

Peter smiled. "OK, my brother. I know you said that Jesus was Black. So are you gonna start goin' to church with us now?"

"Naw, 'cause the Black church got a whole lot of learning to do," Troy said. "Did you see all that pork and food they was eatin? All them big, fat women in the church? My girl says that's addiction. She eats one meal a day."

Scott nooded in agreement. "Yeah, that's why I didn't eat much in there. My pop told me that I should never eat pork."

"I guess ain't nothin' out here right to you, hunh, Troy?" Roy asked.

"I believe that the last days are right around the corner, man. And we ain't got no more time for deception. So I'm gon' call you on anything that ain't right," Troy told him.

"Well, what about you and your girl last night, Mr. Potter? I saw you sign her in, like, ten o'clock at night," Scott quizzed.

"Believe it or not, we didn't do nothin'," Troy revealed.

Peter frowned at him. "Yeah, right. So how come you say you were so tired this morning?"

They crossed Madison Avenue, heading west.

"Because I don't ever get any sleep in small beds if somebody else is in it. So I would have been tired if we had done something or not. I need a lot of space to go to sleep," Troy snapped back.

Peter gave no rebuttal as they reached the dorm and rode the elevator.

"So, Troy, how you gettin' home this week for Thanksgiving? Peter's getting a ride with me when my pop comes up to get us," Scott said before Troy got off at the fourth floor. Scott, Roy, and Peter all lived on the eighth.

"Oh, cuz, can I get a ride with you?" Troy pleaded, holding the elevator door open.

"Yeah, man, we got room. I'll call you tomorrow."

Troy got back to his room and remembered that he was supposed to meet Karen's father right before he went home for the holiday. But Scott and Peter were leaving one day early. Troy called Karen up and told her that it would be better, economically, to get a free ride home instead of paying $86 dollars for a round-trip bus ticket. She agreed and made arrangements to have him over after the holiday. Karen had already told her father about Troy. He was anxious to meet the young scholar.

On the long, five-hour journey from Marsh County to Philadelphia, the four Black men talked about race, gender, politics, and economics. Scott's father talked about his days in the army and his travels around the world. Then Troy asked him what he thought about Malcolm X.

"To tell the truth, I thought Malcolm started compromising his strong racial views when he got caught up into that international arena," Scott's father said.

"That's the only thing that I didn't like," Troy agreed. "And now people talkin' 'bout Malcolm was into that 'brotherhood of man' stuff. But my problem is: how can we trust White people to be our brothers? They are some of the most misinformed people in the world. And it's hard for them to give up the privileges that they have in being White to become our brothers."

"Yeah, you're right. They got crackers down South that swear they're superior to Blacks. And most of them crackers ain't got sense the first," Scott's father responded.

"What do you think about African-centered education?" Troy quizzed.

"I think that's the only way to do it. But I wouldn't call it African-centered, I'd call it 'truth curriculum.' A lot of people, even Blacks, will not accept anything from Africa. The first thing they'll say is, 'I ain't no damn African.' So we gotta get them to listen first."

"Yeah, but that is the truth. Africa is where all life, language, and civilization began. So if they can't accept that, then it ain't no hope for 'em."

"Every man who has faith in the Lord has hope, my brother," Peter interjected to Troy.

"Peter, if you got people having faith in lies and forced religion like Catholicism, then it's going to be a whole lot of people deceived, my brother," Troy argued with mockery.

They dropped him off in downtown Philadelphia. Troy really wanted them to see his neighborhood, but they would have been heading in the wrong direction. Scott's father still would have driven him home, yet Troy did not want to be a bother. It was one of those confusing back-and-forth deals that Troy wished Scott's father had won. He ended up waiting nearly an hour for a SEPTA (Southeastern Pennsylvania Transportation Authority) bus.

Charlotte was away at work when her son came home. The house was empty, except for Grandmom Bessie, who was sleeping. Normally she had at least four grandchildren to watch over. Fortunately, Cookie had taken everyone to the movies and had a sleepover.

Troy dashed over to Scooter's house, where he could always find his same friends, doing the same things and talking about the same dreams while they let the days go by.

"What's up, my nigga?" Raheem shouted as soon as Troy stumbled down the steps. "Yo, cuz, you right on time for a hit. This is our Thanksgiving Day bash," he said, holding up a forty-ounce bottle of Olde English 800.

"Y'all brothers down here gettin' drunk, hunh?" Troy asked them.

"Naw, man, not drunk. We just gettin' nice," Blue answered.

"Yeah, cuz, I only took a couple swigs, 'cause these niggas is down here trippin'," Scooter said.

"Stop fuckin' lying, man. You always trying to play

Mr. Nice Guy whenever Troy comes home and shit. Now you was down here gettin' zooted like the rest of us," Raheem said from the couch.

"I know, 'cause he do be jockin' Troy all the time," Blue agreed.

"Man, I think they sleepin' together," Raheem added.

"Yeah, aw'ight. Y'all niggas is drunk, not me," Scooter said.

"Yeah, well this drunk nigga gon' get some sex tonight, from a new fly girl. 'Cause I done spent, like, two hundred dollars on this chick, and I definitely feel that's enough for some drawers," Raheem said.

Troy sat on the couch beside him, thinking that there was no way out for his friends.

"Yo, Troy, my Puerto Rican chumpee got an abortion, cuz," Blue told him.

"For real?" Troy responded blandly. He had figured as much. Blue wasn't ready for kids.

"Yeah, man, 'cause that chick started actin' crazy. She was talkin' 'bout she need money all the time. And yo, that shit got on my nerves. So I gave her Spanish-speakin' ass, like three hundred dollars and said, 'Here, go have an abortion, 'cause I'm not gon' be dealin' with you no more.' "

"Dag, cuz, you told her that?"

"You damn right! This is my life and my money," Blue snapped, shaking the forty-ounce bottle in his right hand.

Troy shook his head, depressed. "Man, what am I gonna do with y'all brothers?"

"What? Ay', man, don't come back here talkin' that

black shit, cuz. I'm really gettin' tired of hearing that shit," Scooter said to him.

"Oh, now Scooter gon' try to have a fight with his boyfriend," Raheem said, giggling.

"Naw, man, I'm sayin', that's the only thing that Troy talks about," Scooter explained.

"Well, it's something that we all gotta get into," Troy insisted.

Blue stared at his college friend drunkenly. "No it ain't. All I gotta do is stay Black and die, cuz. Fuck niggas!"

Raheem looked at Troy and laughed. "You wastin' your time, Troy. You might need to find some new friends, cuz. These niggas ain't going nowhere."

"Raheem, who the fuck are you to talk, man? You 'bout ta get locked the hell up soon!" Scooter shouted at him.

"I can't leave y'all, man. I love y'all brothers. That's why I always come back," Troy said seriously.

Blue laughed at him. "You sound like a damn White man, cuz. 'You old niggers are the best thing I ever had.' "

"Aw, cuz, shut up. You the only one in here Black enough to be a nigger," Scooter said, cracking up himself.

"Yo, man, we can still all make it out. Malcolm X did it," Troy alluded.

"Uht-oh, he's a Malcolm X fan now," Raheem said before taking another drink from his bottle. "What chew know about Malcolm X, boy? You don't know a *damn* thing about that man. So shut ya wise ass up."

Blue and Scooter laughed.

Troy refused to let it faze him. "I was thinkin', y'all. If we could all start up our own business or something, we could get rollin'," he persisted.

Scooter sighed as if he were bored to death. "You just don't get it, do you, Troy? If that Black shit was all that, then there wouldn't even be no ghetto."

"Naw, man, it's a ghetto because it was set up like that," Troy told him.

"We all know that, so what you plan to do? What chew gon' try ta change it?" Scooter challenged.

"Yeah, but it ain't the effort of one man. It's a holistic thing."

Raheem interrupted again. "Uht-oh, now he's talkin' 'bout Africa."

Troy looked at him. "How you know what I was talkin' about?" he asked, wanting Raheem to say what he knew.

"What chew think you the only one that can read, nigga? I read about ancestor worship, medicine, science, and African spirituality, cuz. That shit ain't nothin' new. It might be to these niggas but not to me," he answered, shaking his bottle at Blue and Scooter.

"He don't know shit. My grandmother from Trinidad was tellin' me about that when I was little. But fuck it, 'cause we in America now," Blue said.

"Yeah, but that don't mean that we can't think like Africans," Troy reasoned with him.

"OK, then, Troy. How the hell are we gonna get money for that shit, if we gon' *think* like Africans? The last time I heard, Africans were poor as shit, unless something changed recently," Scooter commented.

"We gotta nationalize our products like they do in socialism," Troy answered.

Blue choked on his drink. "Oh, and then everybody supposed to give up their shit? Naw, fuck dat, 'cause my shit is mines. I'm not givin' no nigga my money. O-o-o-h n-o-o. Fuck dat," he wailed, grabbing his left pocket, filled with greenbacks.

Raheem silenced Blue with a raised hand. "Hold up, cuz. Go head, Troy, 'cause you got some good-ass ideas goin' on," he said.

"First of all, Black people need to be reading more. Then we will all come to the same conclusions," Troy reasoned.

"So what chew trying to say, we all think alike?" Scooter asked.

"Basically. We all have common sense, but we've been misinformed. So if we all get the right information, we can come to the right conclusions.

"See, there's a group of White men who are running the world and controlling the information. That's done through the schools, the churches, the television, radios, and in the newspapers. The Bible is even messed up," Troy answered.

"So who the fuck told you all this?" Scooter asked, astonished.

"The boy been readin', dummy, somethin' that you never do," Raheem snapped. "But the shit still don't matter, cuz. We too fucked up, now. You ain't got a shot in hell to reeducate over thirty million niggas in America, let alone the rest of the confused niggas around the world. And who the fuck said that the White man is gonna let you?"

Raheem starting putting his coat on. "Well, it's been nice chattin' wit' y'all niggas, but I'm 'bout to go get me some drawers."

Troy followed him out, grabbing his own coat. "So you know more than you tell, cuz," he said to Raheem.

They walked outside into the chilly November air.

Raheem faced him. "Look, man, I went through the shit you goin' through right now, like, two years ago. I couldn't take the shit, and that's why I dropped out of school," he revealed. "I felt like all the White teachers were tellin' me the wrong shit. Then I was like, 'Fuck workin' for a White man.' So that left me where I'm at today, livin' in an underground economy."

"But if we make networks, we can get away from the underground economy," Troy told him.

"What networks, cuz? Networks to punk-ass niggas that kiss the White man's ass! They all spending the same money, Troy!" Raheem responded passionately. "White people got shares in all their shit. That's why Africa is so fucked-up now. They should have an underground economy where Europeans don't know that they're exchanging goods, 'cause you know what happens once White people get in shit," he explained.

"Well, what about if you get locked up?" Troy cautioned.

"For what, Troy, drug possession? Fuck it, man. I ain't got no record yet, plus I'm 'bout to start workin' with my uncle anyway! I'm 'bout to get outta this drug shit, cuz!"

"Yeah, that sounds good, but I don't know if you really gon' do that. You can tell me anything."

Raheem calmed down and shook his head. "Yo, it's like dis, Troy. Education and African studies is cool and all, but niggas need money, man. That's what this whole shit is about, the love of material things. And if niggas can't pay for food and shelter, you can talk all the Black Power and African-centered-education shit that you want. And I'm gon' tell you something else, *Black man!* It's gon' come a day when White people gon' try to set up a system of one currency. And the shit is gon' be computerized. Then niggas ain't gon' be able to buy nothin'. And see, the Bible talks about the numbers of the devil in your right hand or on your forehead. And it may not be six-six-six, but it will have some type of numerical code. So while you talkin' all that shit about education, you better start tellin' niggas to form their own economy. *Underground!*"

WAITING IN AGONY

AFTER RETURNING TO SCHOOL FOR FINALS, TROY WAS TOTALLY unfocused. He had been sitting at his desk for three hours attempting to force himself to study.

"That's it!" he angrily announced to himself. "I'm tired of studying."

He closed his book, stood up, kicked off his shoes, and leaped into his small, unmade bed. He plugged a pair of borrowed earphones into his radio, which rested on top of his headboard cabinet, and pumped up Public Enemy.

Brrrloop brrrloop.

He was still able to hear the telephone ring. Bouncing from his bed excited, he was expecting Karen. "Hello."

"Yo, what's up, Troy? It's Rej. Come sign me in, cuz."

"Aw'ight, I'll be down."

Grabbing his keys and forcing on his Nikes, Troy dashed out of his room, closed his door and sprinted down the stairs to the sign-in table. Reggie Mason was standing next to the dorm monitor waiting to be signed in. After showing identification cards, they leaped onto a departing elevator to the fourth floor.

"So what's been up, man?" Reggie asked.

"Nothin' much. You know, basic studying," Troy answered. "I thought you was my girl, though, Rej. She's supposed to call me to go to the movies. I'on really feel like going to the movies, but you know how it is."

"Dig. Babes will have you doing anything, even when you don't feel like it most of the time," Reggie commented. He took off his coat once they had arrived at Troy's room. "Where do you want me to put this?"

Troy looked around. "Just throw it in that chair," he said, pointing to the sofa. "So how do you want it cut, the same way as last time?" he asked.

Reggie stooped down and looked into the large mirror over the dresser. "Yeah, Troy, just block it up again and put that same part on the side," he answered. He took a seat in Troy's desk chair.

Troy wrapped a towel around Reggie's neck and clipped it into place with a safety pin. He then went to work with his clippers.

"Yeah, so Rej, I seen you with that White girl the other day. Are you into that?" Troy probed.

Reggie shook his head urgently. "Oh no, cuz, we was just studying. I can't talk to White girls. I'on even know what to say to them juhns."

Troy nodded with a grin. "I had a few of 'em from being on the basketball team last year. But this year, I ain't even thought about it."

"I never had a White girl before," Reggie said. "As a

matter of fact, I haven't had anything out of our race. All I've had is Black women, cuz."

"Yeah, I can dig it," Troy told him. "When I go to Tubman next year, it's gon' be honeys galore, from every city. But my girl gon' be goin' there with me. So I'm cool." He grinned from ear to ear.

Reggie pondered as Troy worked on the block shape of his haircut. "You goin' to Harriet Tubman University, Troy?" he asked.

Troy reflected. "Yeah. I didn't tell you that?"

"Naw, man, you didn't tell me. Why you goin' there, though?"

"Because I'm tired of being with all these White people up here," Troy snapped. "I'm losing my concentration up here, man. I wanna be a student instead of a minority on campus, you know. And who knows, I might even be a student president at Tubman."

Troy finished shaping the top of Reggie's hair and got his scissors out to cut off the loose ends. "Plus, Tubman has one of the strongest Afrocentric curriculums in the country," he added.

"Yo, man, it's a White world," Reggie said. "And this shit ain't Africa."

Troy was disappointed. "Let me tell you something, cuz. African people started civilization, so the most important education that you can get is from knowing your roots and African achievement. African descendants were the first to know all things."

"Yeah, well we don't know shit now," Reggie responded humorously.

"Aw'ight, I agree. A lot of us don't know shit. But unfortunately, Rej, if we stay in these White schools, most of us will only learn how to remain slaves, whether we have a high-paying job or not. And if you notice, Rej, all of the people who come to give lectures in our programs are always from the Black colleges.

"They say that up to forty percent of all African-American graduates are from Black colleges. And there are damn near three or four times as many Black students in these White schools. Nevertheless, Black schools graduate almost half of our educated workforce," Troy said, starting to preach the race thing again.

He felt a surge of relief after letting Reggie in on some statistical information he had read in *Black Collegian* magazine.

"Damn, cuz. That's a sharp-ass haircut," Reggie commented, looking in the mirror. "Anyway, that's probably true, man. But I'on know. Since I've been in this mug for three semesters already, I might as well hang in here and finish," he insisted. He reached into his pocket and pulled out a roll of green. "You got change for a twenty, Troy?"

Troy dug inside his desk drawer and pulled out his roll.

"Damn, cuz, you rackin' up, hunh?!" Reggie exclaimed. "My man Troy got a fat knot!"

They grinned as Troy peeled through his twenties and took out a ten and four ones.

"How much do you make in a week?" Reggie asked him.

"Like, forty to sixty dollars, depending on how many people want a haircut. I can't make nothin' if nobody wants a cut," Troy answered. He got out his broom to clean up the hair.

"Dig," Reggie agreed. "But brothers always need haircuts to look pretty for these black sweethearts out here, you know."

They chuckled again as Reggie grabbed his coat.

"Yeah, man, my girl is like that," Troy said. "She was like, 'Since you're a barber, I know you keep a haircut.' "

Reggie laughed while preparing himself to go. "My man, Troy. You be trippin', cuz."

Brrrloop brrrloop.

They both looked to the phone.

"Yup, Troy, that's probably your girl now," Reggie commented.

"It should be. She was supposed to call an hour ago," Troy said, picking up the phone. "Hello . . . What's up, girl? You was supposed to call me an hour ago." He looked at Reggie while listening to her explain.

"Yeah, yeah, excuses, excuses," he said. He and Reggie smiled at each other as he continued to listen. "So that means you ain't gon' be here in time for the movie?"

Reggie took another peek at his sharp haircut in the smaller mirror over Troy's sink. "Yo, cuz, this a suave-ass cut," he repeated. He then opened the door and walked into the hallway.

"Oh, Rej, you gon' sign yourself out?" Troy asked, taking his mouth from the phone.

"Yeah," Reggie answered.

"Aw'ight, then, man, I'll check you out later," Troy

said as Reggie left and closed his door. "So, umm, Karen," he continued, returning to the phone, "you just gon' spend the night now or something? . . . What time you gon' get here?"

He leaned against the wall next to his dresser and rolled his tongue around the inside of his mouth. After two minutes of listening to the hassles of Karen's long day, he finally got another chance to speak.

"Yeah, aw'ight, then. Bring 'em. So you gon' be down here, like, ten o'clock? . . . Bet. Call me when you get here."

He hung up the phone and put away his barber equipment. He then turned on Public Enemy, *It Takes a Nation of Millions to Hold Us Back.*

Usually, on Friday nights, Troy would do homework, locking himself in his room until hustling a party. Or he would call one of his lady friends over for late-night sex. But Karen was special to him. He had been with her the longest, and she had literally forced him to respect Black women sexually.

Bloomp bloomp bloomp.

"Yo, Troy, can I get a haircut, man?!"

"Ay', Doc, stop bugging me!" Troy hollered through his door.

"Ay', Troy, I'm for real, man. I need a haircut."

"I don't feel like cutting no more. Come back tomorrow."

"Come on, Troy . . . Well, yo, just let me use your edgers right quick."

Doc sounded confident that his barber friend

would open up the door and let him in. However, Troy decided to ignore him.

BLOOM!

"Aw'ight, then, you punk. I'll remember this shit!" Doc yelled after kicking the door. He stormed up the hallway feeling angry and defeated.

Troy was curious. He decided to go see how bad Doc needed a cut. He didn't have far to walk as he stumbled across a floor mat and tripped into Demetrius's room, around the hall.

Doc howled. "You punk! That's what you get."

"Ay', Troy, you should have heard Doc in here cussin' you out, man," Demetrius said. "He's mad as hell about that big wolf on his head. I mean, just look at it, Troy. It looks like Yellowstone Park. He looks like one of Buckwheat's boys and shit."

Troy and Demetrius chuckled. Doc bounced onto Demetrius's bed to watch a videotape. His dark curly hair was all over his head.

"What movie is that?" Troy asked.

"Shut up, man," Doc snapped. "You ain't gon' let me use your clipper, right? Now see if I ever give you anything again."

"I mean, Doc, I let you use my clippers all the time. You don't even come to me for a haircut no more."

" 'Cause you might fuck my hair up. You ain't got no license.

"You know what I mean, Meat. He might be mad 'cause he got a F on his test or something, and take it out on me," Doc explained.

Troy sucked his teeth while they laughed at him.

"How many people have you seen me mess up? Seriously, cuz, all I give is fresh cuts."

Demetrius attempted to side with Troy. "Dig, D. Troy do give some nice-ass cuts."

"So how come you don't let him cut your hair?"

"I'on know, man. He might fuck my hair up, too."

Doc fell out across the bed with laughter. Demetrius chuckled at the comment himself. All the comedy forced Troy to join in and smile.

"See, Troy, Meat don't trust you to cut his head either," Doc said. "I gotta get something to drink." He was still giggling as he headed toward the door. When he got close enough, Troy gave him an elbow to the chest.

"Oh Troy, all that, man?" Doc asked seriously.

Troy threw his hands up in a boxing stance. "Yeah, boy, you don't want none. So go 'head."

Doc took heed and retreated as Troy smiled in victory.

"Yo, Troy, I heard you going to Tubman University," Demetrius said.

"Yeah, man, I gots to get away from these White people."

Demetrius frowned, confused. "Get away from White people? You can't get away from White people," he responded with a smirk. "I mean, once you get out of school, they gon' be right there waiting for you, unless you go back to Africa or Haiti or some shit, where it's, like, limited White people. I mean, that's just the real world, man. You better wake up and smell the coffee. You just gon' make yourself miserable."

Troy shook his head in disbelief as Doc returned to the room.

"I'm telling you, Troy, if you going to a Black college to get away from White people, you just fooling yourself," Demetrius added. "This is their country. They took this shit from the Indians, and they ain't trying to give it up to no niggas. That's just plain factual."

Doc looked Troy over and smiled. "He ain't goin' there to be with Black people. He really goin' for the girls."

"Dig, that must be it, 'cause you can't get away from White people if you plan on making a lot of money in this country," Demetrius said. "And you wanna be a doctor, Troy? Now, come on, man, you know you gon' have to deal with them."

Troy sat on Demetrius's dresser and prepared himself, mentally, for battle. "Yo, cuz, we gotta learn to change the rules of the game. It's enough blacks with money to help us. We just gotta put pressure on them and do what we say we gon' do."

Demetrius threw his hands up in the air as if he was exhausted with the conversation. "Look, man, if you think these Black businessmen gon' come to your rescue, forget about it. Niggas only be thinking about themselves," he insisted.

"Yeah, you right. That's why we gotta stop being niggas and start being humans. African humans," Troy snapped. "I can see right now that that selfishness manifests itself right here on this college campus. We gon' have to look out for our fellow African descendants sooner or later."

Doc found amusement in Troy's statement and began to snicker. "Ay', Meat, he called us African descendants and shit."

Troy shook his head and turned to leave the room. "Brothers gon' have to work it out, man."

"Yeah, aw'ight, nigga!" Demetrius shouted into the hallway. "You better stop listening to that Public Enemy shit. I mean, they cool and all, but don't let that shit go to your head!"

Troy rumbled to his room still hearing the mocking laughter of his college friends. He entered his room feeling betrayed and hateful and didn't notice that it was a quarter after ten. Karen was downstairs waiting for him in the lobby, and after lying across his bed to gather his thoughts, Troy finally realized that it was late.

"Damn! It's ten-twenty!" he yelled right as the telephone rang. "Hello," he answered, grabbing it off of the wall.

"Boy, I've been down here for thirty minutes, trying to call you. Where have you been?" Karen declared.

"I was down the hall and lost track of the time. But if you trying to rank me, you can stay down there even longer."

They laughed as Troy hung up the phone and went to sign her in. At the sign-in table, at least five couples were waiting in line already. Karen sat with her bag on a couch behind the desk. Troy went over and sat next to her without saying a word. He eagerly watched the line move.

"Lot of people, ain't it, Troy?" Karen asked him.

"Naw, not really. I just don't feel like standin' in no lines."

She smiled. "Tell me something new."

After Troy didn't respond, Karen felt concerned.

"What's wrong? Did you have a bad day or something?"

"Yup," he pouted.

Karen chuckled, disclosing her chinky eyes and her beautiful smile. Having seen her smile at least a hundred times before, Troy still got a chill down his spine, loving how pretty she was. He felt proud of himself for having her.

"Yup, all my buddies need education," he alluded.

"Oh, is that it? You've been preaching again, hunh?" Karen asked, grinning at him. "You always gotta have people see things your way. Come on, they're all gone now."

She stood with her bag and headed for the table.

"Do you think I'm wrong?" Troy asked her, moving up to the desk and getting out his I.D.

"No, but you have to understand that some things take time to happen," Karen explained. "Just because you've become conscious doesn't mean everyone else has."

"Yeah, but it's gon' have to happen sooner or later."

Unfortunately, an old White woman, whom Troy didn't like too much, was the nighttime monitor. She irritated him every time he went to sign someone in.

"Come on now, dear, get out your I.D. I don't have all day, and other people are waiting," the woman said to Karen, who was searching through her pocket-book. "Do you have an I.D. card with you?" the woman persisted.

Troy gritted his teeth, giving the woman an evil eye.

"Come on, come on," the woman repeated impatiently.

"She's getting the shit out, OK! Damn!" Troy shouted, no longer able to suppress his anger.

Karen finally pulled out her I.D.

"You don't have to display an attitude and use profanity young man," the old woman said.

Troy was unleashed. "*What?* Well look, you ain't gotta be rushing her!" he screamed through the glass window.

White couples behind them looked on with astonishment, as if it was unheard of to argue with the dormitory monitor. To make things worse, a White resident accidentally bumped into Karen as he got off the elevator.

Troy shoved him to the side. "Ay', yo, cuz, you better watch where the hell you walkin'! You 'bout to get punched in your damn jaw!"

"Jesus Christ, man! What did I do?"

Troy attempted to launch a mob of fists, but Karen quickly grabbed him onto the elevator. And like throwing kerosene on a house fire, a White girl smiled at him.

"What the fuck are you smiling at?" Troy shouted in disdain. "I'm tired of you fake-ass White people! Gon' smile at me for no reason!"

No one dared to speak a word on the elevator as Karen covered her face and looked to the floor. Fortunately, Troy only lived on the fourth floor.

"Yo! Public Enemy!" Doc hollered down the hall. Karen asked Troy what Doc was referring to as soon as they arrived at his room.

"Don't worry about that. He's just jokin' around," Troy told her.

She walked inside and stood at the door after closing it.

Troy turned and wondered what she was doing as he kicked off his shoes. "What the hell? Are you modeling now, or are you gonna take your coat off?"

Karen simply stared. "You know, Troy, you can't go around flaring off like that. That was extremely embarrassing." She then unbuttoned her coat. "And I thought you said you was gon' stop cursing."

"Shit, I'm fuckin' trying, Karen! But I can't help it when I get mad!"

"OK, that's it!" Karen snapped. She tugged her coat back on and reached for the doorknob.

Troy rushed over to her. "OK, OK, OK. It's my fault and I need to learn to control my mouth and my actions, but I love you and you can't leave me or I'll kill myself," he said, grinning and grabbing her hands. He placed them around his waist and held her at the door. "I need you more than anything in the world. You can't leave. Without you, I would have fallen to pieces months ago."

"But you don't listen to me, Troy, and I'm sick and tired of trying to tell you things."

"I know, I know," he said, just holding her there.

After a few minutes, he finally got her to hang her coat inside the closet. Karen wore a red, yellow, and green plaid skirt, a green turtleneck, and green stockings.

"Well, don't you look colorful and green today," Troy teased.

"If you don't like it, I can go back home," Karen responded with a smile. She kicked off her black shoes and pounced onto the sofa next to Troy's desk.

"So where's the books?" he asked her.

"They're in my bag," Karen told him. "You thought I was gon' forget them again? I said I would bring 'em this time." She got up and fell across his bed, stretching out like a cat.

"Dag, this is a big book," Troy said, taking one from her bag. "I wish I could scan it and have all the information in my mind already."

Karen playfully rolled her eyes at him. "You silly, you know that?"

"So why you love me, then?" Troy quizzed, thinking he had caught her off guard.

At first Karen just laughed, but then she answered him. "Because you remind me of my father," she responded, turning the tables and catching him off guard.

"Hmm, that's a new one. No girl ever told me that before."

Karen grinned seductively. "If I can have it my way, no other girl will ever have you either."

Troy was excited on the inside but remained calm on the outside. Karen's boldness was a major reason for him liking her so much. All he could do was smile, reflecting his comfort and trust in her as he cuddled up beside her on the bed. Karen covered them both with his heavy quilt blanket.

"Karen?"

"Hunh," she husked, sounding tired.

"I got two weeks till finals, and then a semester to go before I'm outta here," Troy told her. "I came to this White school like a fool, and it changed my entire life."

He stared up at the ceiling as he continued. "Had I known I would have come across all this racism here, I would have gone straight to Harriet Tubman. Then again, maybe all of this was for a greater purpose."

The room got quieter, it seemed, with each word he spoke; and Troy began to tell his story from day one, freshman year, to a wise and beautiful companion whom he had grown to love.

SOLUTIONS

Troy's chatter to Karen, reminiscing on all he had learned and how much he had changed in only a year of college, put him in a deep sleep. His peaceful rest was abruptly ended in the middle of the night.

Bloomp bloomp bloomp bloomp bloomp.

"Open up! It's the campus police!"

Bloomp bloomp bloomp.

"Hey, kid, you're 'bout to be heading downtown if you're not out here in two seconds!"

The sudden disturbance awoke Troy. Karen followed suit.

"Aw, Karen, I don't believe this. That old White lady must of called the cops on me."

Troy struggled from his bed to open the door. Outside in the hallway stood the Black security guard and four White police officers from Marsh County. The officers all wore black leather jackets, black hats, black nightsticks, black leather boots, and shining silver-and-gold badges. The security guard wore only a dark blue uniform with sewn-on cloth labels for identification.

"You got some kind of a problem, son?" the first

White officer asked. He stared into Troy's face to see if he could provoke him. He was heavyset and tall, reminding Troy of the riot control police in Philadelphia.

Troy was familiar with being questioned by officers throughout his childhood and he remained perfectly calm.

"What are you looking at, kid? Do you want me to bust your head open?" the officer challenged.

Troy looked to the Black security guard. "Did I do something wrong?"

"Well, the front desk monitor said that one of the kids had an attitude problem," the security guard answered meekly. It was apparent he no longer had any authority in the situation.

"Look, I oughta run you down to the precinct. Now, when the lady tells you to do something, you do it, and with no back talk," the first White officer demanded. The three others just stared, waiting.

Troy remained poised until the heat cooled off.

"Next time you do just what the lady says," the Black guard suggested.

Troy looked at him with a sly smile.

"Yeah, well I tell you what, he better do what she says," a second, thinner officer interjected. They then walked to the elevator down the hall, and Troy returned to his room.

"You believe that, Karen? They called all them cops up here for one student. They really trying to keep us in check up here," he said.

"Yup, the cops are always beating people up in this city, especially if you're Black," Karen told him. She dropped her head back into the pillow.

"What time is it?" Troy asked before looking. "Dag, it's only two o'clock, Karen. I thought I was sleeping for days."

"I was just happy that you finally shut up and went to sleep."

"What, I bored you?"

"No, you had an important story to tell, but I was just too tired to be listening, that's all."

"Yeah, well now you know how it happened to me."

Karen smiled and closed her eyes for some much needed sleep.

After signing Karen out that Saturday morning, Troy maintained a high level of racial annoyance and hostility. Anything could trigger an outburst if he was provoked. White students never failed in making him flip. Nevertheless, he had to remain focused to complete one more semester at State U.

He headed toward the main cafeteria for breakfast. To enter the cafeteria, student employees would check identification cards for a meal plan. Most of the students would simply run the card through the electronic device. Few looked at the pictures; it was tedious and very time-consuming.

Most of the student employees were White. However, a Black student, whom Troy had known since freshman year, was on duty.

"Hey, what's up, Troy?" he asked.

"Nothin' much, George."

Troy gave up his card on the go, expecting to get it right back. George flipped it over to check his photo and slowed him up.

"Ay', George, what chew do that for, man?"

"I have to check I.D.'s. It's my job."

Troy gave George an evil eye. "Aw, man, you've seen me come in on other weekends. I don't see dem White people checkin' for the picture," he argued. He was causing another stir as White students looked on from behind. But George withheld a response as Troy went in to get his food.

He spotted Matthew sitting by himself. "Yo, Mat. I can't seem to catch up with you at all, cuz," he commented, sitting down to join him.

"I've been studying at the library," Matthew quickly responded.

"Cool, man. But I need help studying chemistry."

Matthew nodded while forcing down a mouthful. "Aw'ight. But I want you to know that I got other finals to study for. And I always study a week in advance," he informed Troy.

"Well, just get with me when you study chemistry," Troy said, pressed about the lab exam. "Don't they put all the sections together for the final?"

"Of course, man," Matthew snapped.

Troy decided to ignore it. "Ay', Mat, you know George?" he asked.

"Yeah."

"Well, that goofy dude think I'm trying to get over with my meal plan."

"What did he do?"

"I was in a hurry, right, like I always am, and he's gon' turn my card over to look at the picture."

Matthew chuckled. "That's his job, man."

"So what? It ain't like he don't know me. He acts

like he's gonna get whipped if he don't check I.D.'s or something."

Matthew thought Troy's complaint was trivial. "Yo, man, you be gettin' into that race stuff too much," he alluded.

Troy sighed. "Yeah, maybe I oughta cool down about that until I can get outta here. But hell, I've calmed down a lot already," Troy said. "This White environment is making me run around in circles."

Matthew leaned over the table to whisper to him. "When I was young, this White boy called my mom a black bitch, and I kicked his ass," he said, chuckling to himself. He then leaned back to speak aloud. "Yeah, but I'm cool with White people now."

Troy wanted to say something about the whispering. It annoyed the hell out of him! Yet he needed Matthew's help for the final and he didn't want to hurt his feelings, so he kept it to himself.

Troy studied all day after breakfast and then after dinner. He was taking his finals seriously. His application to Harriet Tubman University had already been sent off and he could not wait until his final term was completed.

Bloomp bloomp bloomp.

"Yo, Troy! Walk to the video shop with me, man."

"Who is it?" Troy shouted from his desk.

"It's Demetrius."

"Aw'ight, hold up."

He got up and grabbed his coat and hat from the closet for the bitter cold. He opened the door and Demetrius was all ready to go. "Dag, cuz. It musta gotten colder, hunh, Meat?"

"Yeah, man, it's freezin' out dere. I don't see how them White people can do it," Demetrius said, walking toward the elevator.

When they got downstairs to the lobby, Clay was waiting for them. "Oh, Mr. Transfer is going with us," he said with a smile.

"Like Public Enemy said, 'Freedom is a road seldom traveled by the multitude,' " Troy responded with a smile. They walked outside to begin their cold evening journey.

"Watch, Troy gon' go up there with all the girls and probably end up failing," Clay predicted.

"My girl is goin' there with me. And she's the only woman I need."

Clay frowned with doubt. "You say that now, but it's a lot more pretty girls up there. I mean, we got nothin' compared to Tubman."

Demetrius nodded. "I know, man. You could have, like, five girls up there and they probably won't even know each other."

Troy sucked his teeth. "All y'all thinking about is the girls. I'm thinking about gettin' more out of college. It's gon' be Black people from all over the country there."

They ran across Charleston Street in their rush to the video store while still conversing on the way.

"I'm tellin' you, Troy. Go on down there and have fun, and watch I get a job over you. I'd rather get C's at State U. than get A's at a Black college, 'cause they don't get no respect," Clay said.

Demetrius looked at him as if he were a lunatic. "Man, you going crazy now. I'd get straight A's at

Shit State and come out the man! Fuck what you sayin'!"

Troy laughed helplessly. "I can't even believe he said that. That just shows how brainwashed he is. That's why I can't wait to get outta' this school," he mentioned.

They finally arrived at the video store and began looking through different titles. Most of the Black films were placed on the shelves toward the back of the shop. Troy was still in a race-conscious mood. Yet he remained calm about it.

"Ay', Troy, look how they got the Black movies all the way in the back," Demetrius said, instigating.

Clay chuckled and nudged Demetrius in his ribs. "Come on, man, don't get him started."

Troy just shook his head, tired of it all.

"Look at all these dumb movies they put Blacks in. And we always be in the ghetto and shit," Demetrius tacked on. He and Clay shared a laugh. Still, Troy was unprovoked.

As they searched the shelves, Troy noticed the many titles where women of color were seduced by White men. He was overwhelmed by their numbers. It was something worth speaking on.

"Ay', man, you ever notice how White guys always get a jungle girl in their movies? A Black guy never gets a White girl," he shared with Clay, who was closer to him. However, he spoke loudly enough for the surrounding customers to hear.

Demetrius and Clay started to snicker as Troy continued:

"They always get the island woman, the Asian woman, the African woman. That's pitiful, man. And we gotta kiss ass or be a fuckin' star to get with their White women."

"Dig, man," Demetrius agreed. "The only movie where a black dude got a White girl is *Mandingo*. And they roasted his ass."

"That's probably how they started porno movies, from rapin' slave women," Troy suggested.

Clay and Demetrius laughed again.

"Ay', Troy, cuz, cool out, man," Clay told him.

"Aw man, shut up. You scared of White people," Troy rebutted. He turned and stared at a middle-aged White man, who turned his head to avoid a confrontation. "Tell y'all the truth, I'm 'bout to just Rambo some White people," he warned aloud.

"That's it, cuz. You gonna get us rushed in here," Clay whispered. He was serious, too, but Troy didn't care.

"Yeah, whatever," he snapped. "I know White people think we loud and violent, but what we ever do to them? They messed the whole world up, but now they the nice ones," Troy shared with everyone who cared to listen.

None of the video store members dared to respond. The young man appeared to be losing his sanity.

Clay and Demetrius quickly trotted away from him.

"Troy's goin' crazy," Clay uttered.

Demetrius agreed. "I know, man. He's a brick-ass nigga."

They giggled as Troy wandered over to the front

counter. He looked down and read it, right in front of the counter as people walked in. Black customers walked right past it and didn't say anything. Troy read it five times, making sure he wasn't imagining. Clay and Demetrius then stepped up to the counter to rent the movies they had chosen. They were still laughing, considering Troy crazy, and yet they missed it. But the sticker was right there in front of them.

"Yo, Demetrius, read that out loud," he said, pointing to the sticker at the front desk.

" 'If your children are unattended, they will be captured and sold as slaves.' " Demetrius was shocked. Clay read it too, before they left.

"Now, y'all still think I'm overexaggerating about this race shit?" Troy asked them both. "White people think that shit is funny. But any Black person who laughs at that needs help."

"Dig, man. That shit is out!" Demetrius exclaimed. "Why didn't you say something about it, or tear it down or something?"

Troy hunched his shoulders. "What difference does it make? If other Black people walk right past it and don't say nothin', then they would just call me crazy for sayin' somethin', like y'all do."

"Man, they couldn't put no sign up in Philly like that. Black people in our city would tear that store down. Wouldn't they, Troy?" Clay asked.

Troy was hesitant. "I don't know anymore, man. Black people are just a big disappointment to me. That's why I gotta get out of this environment. I can't emphasize it enough."

Troy went on to tell his college friends something else. "Four White cops tried to intimidate me last night for some dumb shit," he revealed.

"What did you do?" Clay asked him, smiling.

"That's typical of a nigga to ask," Troy snapped. "What did I do, right? What about asking me what happened, instead of assuming that I did something already? Anyway, I told that White lady off at the front desk for disrespecting my girl."

Clay said nothing. He simply grinned, heading back to the dorms.

"Yo, man, you just gotta learn to be cool," Demetrius said to Troy.

"Yeah, well that's easier said than done when you're a warrior. This school is driving me crazy. I gotta get the fuck out of here!"

Back inside his room, Troy thought about the present state of Black consciousness. His deep thoughts inhibited him from concentrating on his studies. As he wrangled to free his mind of unnecessary mental stress, his friend Peter walked in on him.

"What's up, my brother?"

Bruce and Scott walked in behind him.

"Yo, y'all better knock next time," Troy commented playfully. He was more than happy to have pleasant company.

"Aw, shut up, mayn," Bruce responded, smiling.

Troy stood up from his desk chair in obvious excitment. "Ay' Pete, I was just thinking about something, man. Imagine if Black people didn't have their own magazines and Black TV shows. And imagine if we didn't have all-Black neighborhoods. Who would care about us? We would be totally ignored completely as a people. So we need some type of unit to bring us together politically, economically, religiously, and culturally. We need, like, a Holistic Foundation or something."

"That's what Martin Luther King was talkin' about," Peter responded. "But we should just drop this racial thing, altogether."

"What, are you crazy? If we do that, we'll end up being the dumbest people on the face of the earth. As a matter of fact, we already are!" Troy shouted, shaking his head in disgust. "In this integrated city, for example, Blacks don't know shit, but the White people do. That's how they fool you in integration. Like, a lot of them Whites who hang out with Black people. They know where they're headed, but what about us?"

"Well what about your girl?" Scott asked, challenging.

"She's from Chicago," Troy told him. "The Nation of Islam is out there with a whole lot of Blacks on the South Side. But even their city was fooled when Martin Luther King went there. They had a bunch of Black stooges talkin' about it wasn't no racism in Chitown. And they told King to go back down south.

"Chicago does have a whole lot of Black businesses," Scott mentioned.

Bruce changed the subject, bored with the race talks already. "Ay,' cuz, you wanna go to the mall with me tomorrow?" he asked.

"Yeah, aw'ight. As long as Peter knows that I'm right. Integration ain't gonna help us," Troy declared.

"The United States of America is racist. And you better never forget that."

Next morning Troy and Bruce waited on Madison Avenue to catch a bus to the suburban mall. Bruce had forgotten how to get there and Troy had never been, so they asked bystanders what bus to catch. Troy was so hateful of Whites that he preferred to ask Blacks only.

"Excuse me, do you know how to get to Northside Mall?" he asked a young mother.

"No, I never been out there," she told him. She smiled, giving him her full attention and desiring a more social conversation.

"Don't you live here?" Troy asked snappishly.

"Yeah, but I don't know how to get out there," the young mother repeated. She switched her blanket-covered child from her left arm to her right to give herself a better view

Bruce began to chuckle as he viewed the disgusted look on Troy's face.

Troy rudely walked away and asked another young mother, "Excuse me, do you know how to get to Northside Mall?"

"Unt-unh."

He then went and asked an older man. "Excuse me, do you know how to get to Northside Mall?"

The short, gray-haired man rubbed his thick beard and shook his head. "No, not really. I drove out there a couple times, but I don't know what bus to catch out there."

An old, homely White man stopped and listened. "Hey, son, the 54C will take you right there," he said.

Bruce snickered. "He don't know what he's talking about. He looks homeless and shit," he whispered.

Troy asked a younger brother standing near Mellon Bank. "Yo, cuz, what bus do I catch to get out to Northside Mall?"

"I'on know, man."

Two friendly White women overheard.

"You're heading to Northside Mall?" the first asked.

"Yeah," Troy answered, not really wanting to.

"The 54C will take him right there," the second added.

"Yeah, that's it. The 54C," the first agreed with a nod.

Troy withheld a "Thank you." He walked back toward Bruce, who had wandered out near the curb to spit. "You see how nice White people are in this city, Bruce? In Philly, they probably would have let us get lost. White people love it when you don't know nothin'," Troy said aloud. Both White women turned from him in embarrassment.

Bruce laughed. "You crazy as hell, cuz."

Bystanders began to turn and witness Troy mouthing off.

Bruce said, "You gonna get us in a rumble if you keep this up. But I'm down to bust up some White people."

Troy chuckled, sensing nearby Whites becoming frigid.

"I bet that they ain't into Malcolm X in this city," he assumed aloud. "I bet they love Martin Luther King, though, and don't even know the man. They just know his media image."

Troy noticed an older Black woman frowning in

discomfort. Yet he could care less. He had lost respect for everyone, White and Black, for not feeling as he felt or believing as he believed.

A plump and cheerful White student walked past and eyed him. "Hi, Troy. Do you remember me? I'm in your physics class," she said with a huge smile.

Troy turned his back to her. "See that, man. I don't really talk to her. She actin' like we're the best of friends or some shit. She must think a Black boy is supposed to leap at a chance to screw her big ass."

Bruce burst out laughing as the bus finally pulled up.

A Muslim had shown a Louis Farrakhan speech about the movie *The Color Purple,* based on an Alice Walker novel and directed by Steven Spielberg. Black students in attendance sat astounded by the information presented concerning the racial psychology of America. A day later, Troy sat with Peter, Scott, and Roy for another race discussion inside the cafeteria.

"Hey, Troy, did you hear that Farrakhan speech last night?" Roy asked. He was teary-eyed and upset for some reason.

"Yeah. Did you see it, Peter?" Troy quizzed.

"Naw, I had some studying to do," Peter answered.

"I didn't like what he said about White people. All White people aren't like that," Roy alluded.

"Was that the only thing you got out of the speech?" Troy asked sternly.

"Well, that's one of the things that I didn't agree with."

"Did he say anything that you did agree with?"

"Well, a lot of the things he said were true, but a lot of Black people are just not making an effort."

"How the hell do you know, man? You grew up in the suburbs with White people!" Troy shouted at him.

"I had to go through trials, too. It's not like I wasn't hit by White society," Roy rebutted. "I had to fight a lot of kids for calling me a nigger. I mean, what is it that gets in their way? If you work hard, you succeed."

Troy nodded. "I thought that same way before I got on the basketball team. But now I realize that I was used."

"You did make the basketball team, though," Peter interjected with a smile. "And you did quit."

Troy bit his bottom lip to remain calm. "Everybody talks about making the team," he commented, getting aggravated. "I sat the bench, man. Do you know what that means? That means that I might as well have been in the stands watchin' my damn self. *So fuck this* team *shit until we can play, man!*"

"I see where you're coming from, Troy. But everyone must learn to work as hard as we do. And we can't ever quit," Roy insisted.

"It just ain't that easy, though. I'm struggling now, and I study all the time," Peter intervened again.

"Man, I know what you're thinkin'. You're thinkin' that Black people don't have what it takes to make it," Troy accused the freshman Roy. "You're thinkin' they're too lazy or something." He ignored Peter's comment. As far as Troy was concerned, Peter was blowing hot air, talking about studying all the time.

"I'm not saying that at all," Roy snapped. "What I'm saying is, we can do it if we put more effort and time into it. All they have to do is work hard, and they succeed. That's very simple. I can't see why they can't do it."

"Hey, Roy, both of your parents went to college and settled down in a White neighborhood, right?" Troy asked with a sense of urgency.

"Yeah, so?"

"So they had educations, right?"

"Yeah, and . . . ?"

"So you were born with an advantage already. And you'll never be able to understand the people who start from scratch," Troy told him.

Tears began to swell up in Roy's eyes again. His sensitivity reminded Troy of Matthew. But he didn't want Roy to become spoiled like Matthew. So he pressed on. "What are you getting all upset about?" he asked him.

"I just can't understand what it is that you're talking about. I've had it hard too, but I kept my head high and did what I had to do."

Troy began to settle down. He reached over and shook Roy's hand. "You got a good heart, man. You're heading in the right direction. But do you have any concrete plans?" he probed.

"Well, I'm planning to set up my own business and help as many people as I can. I'm not just going to work for some White man all my life," Roy answered. "I figure that I can work about ten years, and then I'll start my own business and hire Black people."

"How many do you figure you can hire, maybe ten, twenty people?"

"Well, you can't hire everybody."

Scott nodded his head and spoke up to end his silence. "I thought about that too. All that will do is cause jealousy from the people you can't help."

"Yeah, and then they try to rip everything up and make it bad for everybody. Like at the parties and stuff," Peter added.

"So what is the answer to our problem, then, Troy?" Roy pressed.

"I don't know yet. But my boy was talkin' about havin' an underground economy," Troy answered. "I'm starting to think that some type of socialism would be beneficial myself."

"The way I see it, you can't help people who don't want to help themselves," Peter said.

"That's exactly the way that I see it," Roy agreed.

"Are you tellin' me that Black people don't want to get help and would rather live in a ghetto, sellin' drugs?" Troy questioned.

"No, but what else is the reason?" Roy asked. "If they need help, all they have to do is go get it."

"What if they come to you for help? Would you help them out?" Troy asked, challenging Roy again.

"What, you think that I wouldn't?"

"I'm not worried about if you would or wouldn't, I'm worried about if you could," Troy reasoned.

Peter and Scott laughed, confused. Roy chuckled himself. Troy, however, maintained a serious face.

"Now what do you mean by that?" Peter asked him.

"Look, Pete, you have to live through somethin' before you can understand it," Troy answered. "Now, both of you have already had a head start on me, and all of the people I hang out with back home would be considered straight-up hoods to y'all. But I came from there and I know how it is. Or at least I *did* know."

"Well, what's so hard to understand about it?" Roy queried.

"Look, Roy, if you grew up with X, Y, and Z, then you don't know how to explain how to get it. But if you grew up with just X and Y, you can most likely explain how to get Z, if you succeed yourself," Troy philosophized. "Do you see what I'm saying? I'm talkin' about building."

"Yeah, that makes sense. But I didn't have X, Y, and Z either. So tell me what you mean," Roy pleaded.

"You do have it! That's why you can't understand me now! Your parents gave it to you!" Troy shouted.

"Hey, you all, we're closing up!" a staff member yelled. They were the last four students left inside the cafeteria. As they packed up and walked out, Roy tried to get the last word in.

"I'm trying to understand what it is you're talking about, Troy," he said.

Troy smiled. "Ay', man, keep searchin'. I'm just trying to make you into a soldier. You gonna be important soon. And we need all the people we can get."

Two days later, with finals approaching, Troy remained unfocused. He was tired of studying so he decided to venture to Bruce's room to chat.

"Ay, what's up, mayn? You ain't studying?" Bruce asked, opening his door to let Troy in. "I thought you'd be studying every day now."

Troy grimaced. "Cuz, what I don't know now, I ain't gonna know. This is one of my don't-give-a-fuck-about-homework nights."

Bruce cracked a laugh. "Yeah, mayn, 'cause you been too worried about that race shit. It's ripping you apart," he said. "You sittin' around in your room every day worried about what White people got and what we ain't got. I mean, it's their world, cuz. What do you want us to do?"

"It's not their world, Bruce, and I want us to *think,*" Troy answered. He sat on Bruce's bed and thought a second. "All I wanted to do at first was go to college and get a nice job. But now I understand that I'm on a mission."

"Yeah, well you bein' all mad at the world won't change anything," Bruce told him. He got up and shot his small basketball into the toy hoop attached to his mirror. "The way I see it is this: the White people killed for this country and they ain't tryin' to give it up, especially not to us. No matter what you do, it's gonna be White people in your way. So you might end up being an old, grouchy man for the rest of your life," he predicted, lying out across his bed.

"Yeah, man, I've heard that a million times, and I'll never accept it," Troy told him. He got up and shot a hoop himself. "I just gotta get out of this environment. When I get on Harriet Tubman's campus, I'll have the atmosphere that I need to think and grow. Beause like y'all keep tellin' me, it ain't no sense in hating White people. That ain't gonna change nothin'. Plus, I've had some excellent White teachers. I need to think about that. But see, ignorant White people are set up as a distraction to us. And all Black people are set up as a distraction to them, to stop us all from realizing that we're being deceived by a few rich White men who rule the world."

"You keep talkin' 'bout that shit, cuz. How do you know about dat?" Bruce quizzed.

Troy sat back on the bed. "Because it makes sense. There's always a big boss who's runnin' the show. That's how European society is. You just gotta know the history of the aristocracies and fascist oligarchy."

Bruce giggled. "Shit, cuz. Now you droppin' shit that I don't know shit about. Fascist oligarchy, hunh?"

"Yup," Troy answered with a smile. "That's a system where a society is ruled by a few who use the state against the people to stay in power."

"Like a con man, paying off the police, hunh?"

"Yeah, only these con men are rich enough to pay off countries and leaders. That's how big this shit is."

"Yeah, cuz, I thought you and Matthew was supposed to study for a test," Bruce said, changing the subject. He never seemed to remain on one issue long, and Troy was developing a reputation for being a race preacher.

"Man, Mat ain't trying to help me out," Troy said, frowning. "He been hidin' from people ever since he got that four-point-oh. He used to help me all the time. That damn chemistry lab test is on Monday."

Bruce shook his head. "See, mayn, in this world, White people got everybody goin' for self. That's the real reason why we can't get nothin' done."

"Yeah, 'cause when me and Mat had about the same grades, everything was cool. But now since he got that four-point-oh, everybody wants to smother him," Troy added.

"Can you blame him, though, cuz?" Bruce asked.

"Naw, man. I guess you just got to survive the best way you can, hunh, Bruce? But then again, it should be the responsibility of successful blacks to help their people, no matter what. The world is hard as shit for all of us."

Bruce nodded his agreement. "That's it."

"Now I think of all the times that I said, 'Fuck the next nigga' in my life,' " Troy commented. "I guess what we need is full cooperation."

Bruce grinned at him. "I don't know if you ever gon' figure this out, cuz. But if you do, when you talk about Black cooperation, it may never happen."

Troy sighed. "Yeah, cuz. I know."

ONLY THE STRONG SURVIVE

IT WAS THE LAST WEEKEND BEFORE FINALS, FRIDAY NIGHT. TROY tried once more to lock himself in his room to study for his upcoming exams. They would complete the first semester of his sophomore year at State U. He continued to dwell, however, on the possibilities of a more adventurous lifestyle. Yet he could not stop thinking about a cure for the racial plague that White men had caused in the world.

Bloomp bloomp bloomp.

"Yo, Troy, man, it's me."

"Come on in, professor," Troy yelled through the door.

"I need a haircut," Scott said on entrance.

"Cool, cuz. Hop in the chair," Troy told him. He stopped studying at his desk and set everything up to cut Scott's hair. He could use the break. "You want your regular cut?"

"Yeah, just block it up again," Scott answered.

"So what you gon' do tonight, Scott?"

"I was gon' study for finals."

"That's what I was trying to do," Troy told him.

"What you gon' teach me today, scholar?" Scott asked.

"You the professor. I'm just searchin'," Troy responded with a smile.

"Well, scholars are the best people to teach, 'cause you've already drained me of all that I know."

"Man, you know how people are, though. They never wanna hear the truth. The world is full of big white lies, and they'll just call me crazy," Troy said.

"Well, keep searchin', scholar, 'cause I figure you'll know a whole bunch of shit, eventually," Scott assured him.

Troy completed Scott's haircut and showed him the finished job from a small hand mirror. It had taken only twenty minutes.

Scott was pleased. "You gettin' better every time," he said cheerfully.

"Each time I cut, I learn something new," Troy told him.

"So why can't we be like the Japanese?" Scott asked Troy, suddenly. He sat on Troy's bed and gave his full attention as Troy pushed his chair back under the desk and sat on his dresser.

"Man, the Japanese have always been closer to the White people, to me. That's why the Chinese and Koreans don't like 'em," Troy answered. "Japan has this arrogant attitude that they should control all of the Orient, just like the WASPs (White Anglo-Saxon Protestants) feel they're superior to other White people. But I do give Japan credit, though. Them and Ethiopia were the only nations of color that held off

White imperialism prior to World War Two. But what you ask me that for?" Troy queried.

"Because the Japanese look like they're beating the White man in his own game," Scott answered.

"Yeah, well, that's bullshit. Germany is still on top and Great Britain ain't that far behind," Troy snapped. "Rich-ass White businessmen rebuilt Japan. And then United States got Japan to demilitarize.

"Now, I don't give a fuck what Japan has done technologically; if they ain't got no military against the White man, they ain't got shit. I even read that a lot of the American carmakers and investors have shares in Japanese companies."

Scott nodded. "I heard that too."

"Yeah, 'cause after a while, Japan got to the point where they thought they could be as powerful as the European nations," Troy went on. "Japan even fucked Russia up at one time," he said. He then stopped and thought to himself. "Dag, cuz. I gotta control my mouth. I really do curse a lot." He shook his head and smiled.

"You told me your girl was talking about that," Scott alluded. "But then Japan bombed Pearl Harbor," he continued.

"They say that they could've gotten to California if they would have flown on course," Troy informed him.

Scott was puzzled. "Are you tellin' me we could have been invaded?"

"Yup. And the White people thought about who it was and had a race thing where they wanted to show the colored Japanese that they were still White and superior by dropping the A-bomb and locking Japanese-Americans in concentration camps," Troy responded. "But I think Pearl Harbor was set up. They had radar or somethin' that they could have warned people with."

"So you think everything is set up?" Scott asked, smiling again.

"Just about, man," Troy charged. "See, you have to understand that White people are like mad scientists. They experiment and plan things in advance. 'Cause when you think about them wars and about the armies needing supplies and food, you come to the conclusion that somebody was getting paid."

"I never thought of it like that," Scott said.

"Yeah, man. The United States was supplying weapons and food during World War One and World War Two. European nations owed the United States *billions* of dollars. World War Two also got the United States out of a depression," Troy said. "But the thing that got me was that the United States ended up in debt after all of it was over. So I did some research to find out that Europe had established the Bank of England in nineteen sixty-four, that wasn't controlled by the state. This bank could basically do what it wanted. They could even loan countries war money.

"Now, how 'bout that, cuz? They've established the World Bank and the International Monetary Fund. And see, these banks can set up their own laws for world currency, accounts, and loans."

"Well, isn't Japan the most technological country in the world now?" Scott asked. "*They* should be makin' a lot of money."

Troy shook his head. "Japan uses a lot of their government's money and loans to perfect technology, but the United States supplies most of the information. Ain't that somethin'? It's like the United States is setting the whole thing up. But then they make it out in the news like Japan is all that America is, just using them as her international enemy."

"Like Russia, hunh?" Scott quizzed.

"Yup, now you got it. 'Cause I never been able to figure out why the U.S. keeps talkin' about Russia. Then these so-called superpowers run around the world makin' money off of Third World countries in these fake wars."

"Yeah."

"Yeah, man," Troy said. "Most of the wars in South America, Africa, the Caribbean, the Middle East, and a whole lot of other places are funded. 'Cause you figure, if these countries are so backward, where do they get their weapons and stuff from? The U.S. and Russia. Then the people fight over some so-called democracy while their land is being raped of its resources and their government goes further into debt."

Scott shook his head in disbelief. "Wow," he said. "This all makes perfect sense, if you think about it."

"You damn right it makes sense. Theories say that it's a few rich White men setting up the whole thing with this good guy/bad guy stuff and using religion as the middleman."

"Yo, you should write a book one day," Scott suggested.

"Naw, not yet, 'cause I don't know enough yet. But

I'll definitely think about it, if I ever learn to write well."

"Dag, man, I know brothers back home right now doing nothing," Scott responded. "And here you are up in college finding out all kinds of stuff."

"But don't give up on 'em, man, 'cause everybody is good for something, even if it's just being your company," Troy told him. "My buddy Raheem said that Black people need money, though."

"We do," Scott quickly agreed.

"Yeah, because we're trapped inside of this capitalistic system," Troy said. "Booker T. Washington said that we have to make our labor profitable. We also gotta set up a Black economy. Raheem hooked me on that too."

Scott nodded. "Yeah, well he's right. Everybody needs necessities."

Troy sighed. "Man . . . I just feel like droppin' out of school to be an entrepreneur sometimes," he revealed out of the blue. He stretched out on the bottom half of his bed while Scott sat at the top half. "I get bored in college now. But I feel it's my duty to learn somethin' for African people while I'm in here."

"Yeah, why you call us African peoples, man?" Scott asked, grinning. It was something he had wanted to ask Troy for a while.

"Well, life started with one people and divided into many. So if you want the source of mankind, it's us, and we have the genes to produce all other colors," he answered. "Africans are the common denominator of man and it's important that we begin to recognize who we are, no matter if we are in Africa, America,

Jamaica, Brazil, Israel, Asia, Europe, or on Mars. And every Black man and woman is just as important as the next." Scott chuckled and nodded his head in affirmation. Troy then snuck a peek at his clock. "Yo, man, that's it. Study break is over," he announced.

"All right then, man," Scott said, getting up to leave.

"Aw'ight, Scott, I'll catch you on the rebound."

Troy found himself in the school library Saturday morning, taking out a couple of books. He was studied out. He had planned to read a few books over the rest of the weekend, instead of studying more chemistry. He still could not find Matthew, and he couldn't seem to put two and two together with his lab notes. Again, Troy needed at least a high B to pull his grade out of the hole. On the way back to his dorm he ran into his old roommate.

"Hey, Troy, how are ya?" Simon said, reaching out for a handshake. He looked down at his old roommate and smiled. "You're getting tall as me, guy."

Troy shook his hand and smiled back. "They say that some people keep growing."

"So what's been going on?"

"I've just been studying and reading shit, man," Troy said. "But I found out a lot about Jews, Simon. I found out a whole lot of bad things, too. But I can't say 'em, 'cause you'll probably call me an anti-Semite."

Simon frowned. "Naw, man. Like I told you last year, I really don't care about all that."

"That's good. Because a lot of Jews are just not being truthful, man."

"I see you're still into that racial stuff," Simon commented.

"Yeah, but I'm not a racist."

"What makes you think that?" Simon quizzed. He was bewildered, wondering what Troy's disposition was.

Troy grinned as he answered. "I would have to have some type of power to discriminate against another person of color to be racist," he suggested. "So what can I do, scare a White person and be called a racist? All I can do is talk. And most of the time, when Black people are called racists, it's because we're talking about something that's true, and White people don't wanna hear it.

"Blacks don't have any power to be racists. But Jews do. In Israel. Or is it Palestine? Or what was it before that, Simon?"

Simon couldn't believe his ears. "You know what, Troy, you won't get far in life with this polar attitude that you have," he warned. He was angry and ready to move on. But Troy was pressed to get in the last word.

"It's funny that, you mention that Simon, 'cause it seems to me that no matter what kind of attitude African people have, you White people still try to control us."

Simon shook his head and walked away, leaving Troy feeling a pinch of guilt. Simon had been a good roommate to him and a good man.

Test day had finally arrived and chemistry was first. Troy had counted on Matthew to help him, yet he had no such luck.

He entered the auditorium hallway along with hundreds of White students and a few specks of color. He looked around for Matthew and spotted him easily. Matthew stood like a giant over everyone. He had always been tall but he had never stood out as much as he did on test day.

He spotted Troy moving toward him, pushing White students from his path. They did not bond when they shook hands; they nodded and remained impersonal toward each other.

The instructor opened the door and the students hurried in. Troy walked in slowly, watching for Matthew. He knew he needed his friend's help, yet he figured he would try his luck with guessing first.

Students were nervous and jumpy, selecting seats near one another. Troy suspected that many would cheat. He sat down on an end chair by himself, next to a group of five eager White girls. He zipped down his coat, took it off, and placed it over his right arm.

Matthew walked in calmly, oozing confidence, and took a seat in the middle of the auditorium. Troy watched him while still needing his help and fighting a losing battle with his conscience about not asking for any. He got up swiftly from his seat and circled around the back of Matthew like a swooping vulture. His New York friend didn't comment at first. Then he quickly turned and smiled.

"Yo, troop, what are you sitting behind me for?"

"So I can cheat," Troy frankly answered.

Matthew's nervous smile faded. "Yo, man, this is the finals. You gotta go for self now," he said. "As a matter of fact, I'll sit right next to you so nobody can cheat off of me."

Troy suspected from the time he saw Matthew hiding behind the White students that he didn't want to help. The tests would alternate, and if Matthew sat next to him they would end up with different tests. Nevertheless, only the order of questions would be different.

Matthew forced conversation on Troy in an attempt to be friendly. But Troy barely responded. His academic future was on the line. He could suddenly taste the tension of failure stirring inside his mouth and nauseating his stomach. The restless, butterflylike energy began to increase as the instructor's assistants passed out four-different-colored exams. Troy received a lime-colored exam while Matthew received an orange.

Troy answered all of the questions he knew, a mere twelve out of thirty. He was dying for help, stopping short of begging. He gave a second look and guessed ten more. With eight questions remaining he started to aggressively peek at Matthew's test, which was unfortunately covered.

Matthew was left-handed and sitting to Troy's right. He curled his hand around his pencil, blocking Troy's view.

At home, a friend would never sell out a friend. If he did, he would suffer the consequences of the group. New York streets were probably no different. Yet State U held no such neighborhood bonding. College effectively served as a weeding institution.

"Ay', Mat, what's the answer to this?" Troy whispered forcefully. He watched the assistants carefully. By then, many of the White students were cheating in their small groups, just as Troy had suspected. "Ay', Mat, what's this, man?" he urgently repeated.

The first time, he thought maybe Matthew didn't hear him. But it quickly became evident that he didn't want to respond. Troy then slid his test paper in Matthew's immediate eyesight. He even circled the question so his friend could easily recognize it.

"Please help me, cuz. *Please!* What's the answer to some of these questions?"

Matthew whispered back. "Wait, man. I gotta finish mine first." But he was taking his sweet time, which Troy was running out of.

"Naw, man, the time is almost up, cuz. Help me now," he begged with desperate tears swelling up inside his eyes and his heart pounding frantically.

"We got different tests anyway. I probably don't have the same questions as you," Matthew responded. He didn't even look to see the questions.

Troy gave up. Matthew was not interested in helping him. He was making excuses.

Troy no longer cared. He *couldn't* allow himself to fail. He *had* to score. He asked the White students cheating all around him. White girls were cheating in back of him. A group of White guys were cheating in front of him, beside him, and all around him.

Troy nervously decided to ask the White guys sitting to his left. He wrote down their suggested answers as Matthew slyly listened in on him but didn't say anything.

Their answers were all wrong.

"Ay', Mat, I know you didn't want to cheat, but what were the answers that I asked you for on the test?" Troy queried. He was hoping he had gotten the right answers from the White students.

"I don't know," Matthew lied. "We had different tests."

Troy snatched his friend's question sheet, realizing what he had known all along. Matthew knew it too, as he tried, unsuccessfully, to buffer his ridiculous lies.

Troy then looked over to the White students still sitting to his left. They were whispering and laughing and pointing at him. They never whispered well. Troy heard their comments loud and clear.

"Hey, Jeff?" one asked his friend.

"Yeah," Jeff answered, peeking in Troy's direction to his right.

"I gave him about ten wrong answers."

Troy looked at Matthew's answers, all different from the ones he had received from the White students. Possibly they were the right ones. He then gave Matthew's question sheet back and walked out into the auditorium hallway disgusted.

He was handed an answer sheet from the assistants. Matthew approached and stood beside him. Troy walked the other way, avoiding him while checking his answers. He scored only fourteen out of thirty correctly. He then headed back to his dorm in a state of shock, feeling betrayed. He wasn't exactly angry at Matthew for not wanting to cheat, however. He knew that the test was fair and square. He was not prepared. And he had failed.

Troy's room had been empty all semester long, but now it *felt* empty. He had failed for the first time in his life. The intense agony was overwhelming. An internal war was raging, which he had no control over. He felt like going after Matthew. He felt like attacking the White students. He felt like yelling. He felt like breaking something, stealing something, getting drunk, taking drugs, committing crimes, making babies, and killing someone to release his pain.

A burst of energy tempted him to run to Matthew's isolated dorm room and do battle. But it wouldn't change his failure. It was not a successful solution.

Vibrations in Troy's throat and chest challenged him to laugh at the humor of the situation. Yet there was no humor in failure. Instead, he cried like a toddler. Not since the age of six had he cried. He had gotten stung by five bumblebees at the playground. He had invaded their hive and they gave him what they thought he deserved. Now, he had been stung again.

Slippery tears dropped helplessly from his smooth brown face and rolled down to his neck. No muscle in his arm was willing to contribute to stopping them or wiping them away. He was simply exhausted from all of the unnecessary strife.

"I don't believe this," he said to himself as he lay across his bed and stared up at a blank ceiling. He laughed through a cracked voice filled with too much emotion. His heart seemed to burn through his chest as new tears rolled down his face.

"Ain't this a *bitch*!" he yelled to himself. "It's just one setback, though. I ain't finished yet. They not gon' break me this easy. I've come too far to quit."

He began to smile as he nodded his head with new spirit. "I gotta keep my focus. That's all. I ain't done yet. People need me. And I gotta set an example."

When he had finished wiping his eyes and his neck, he sensed a new strength and outlook. It seemed that he had just gone through a trial of sorts. Failure could to lead to resurrection. He believed that, maybe, he was being tested to see how strong his willpower was. He was determined not to fail again.

He rose from his bed with newborn inspiration, and the telephone rang.

"Hello," he answered on the first ring.

"So, how you do on your test?" a familiar voice asked.

Troy smiled, feeling like he could see her through the phone. "I failed, Karen," he answered, upbeat, as if he were excited about it.

"Well, you don't sound like the Troy that I know. You wasn't mad at all?" she asked him.

"Of course I was mad, Karen. But I recuperated. And it was like I realized that I'm still livin', still learnin', and I'm still a scholar. I don't have to pass the White man's test. Education is to be utilized for the self and for the people. And I know it may sound crazy to you, but I feel invincible now."

Troy smiled again and walked over to the window, stretching the phone cord. Outside it was beginning to snow. At the downtown office where she worked, Karen smiled herself, understanding more than what Troy could. She had already been taught to remain strong and focused.

"So, are you ready to try again?" she quizzed him.

"You damn right," Troy told her. And he was serious.

"Well, my father is dying to meet you," Karen alluded.

"I'm dying to meet him too. I got a lot of questions I want to ask him."

Karen was immediately excited. "Oh, well, he gon' love you, then. My father has a lot to teach, but few are willing to listen."

Troy nodded and felt calm. Karen seemed to control his emotions again, soothing him with her voice, her strength, and her self-assurance. He felt confident knowing that he would learn more to succeed and that she would support him. The battle was not over. It had just begun, and it would be continuous. He had learned that the struggle for Black Americans lasted a lifetime. And he was still a soldier, ready for combat.

Those who possess patient self-control shall become virtuous.

Those who possess confidence shall achieve great things.

Those who think and question shall attain wisdom.

And those who stand strong in faith shall be invincible.